Vermin . . .

The All of Us race was unaccustomed to dealing with other sentient species. One of the primary reasons for this was, simply, their size; by almost any standards, the H'rulka were giants.

An adult H'rulka consisted of a floatation gas bag measuring anywhere from two to three hundred meters across, with brain, locomotion and feeding organs, sensory apparatus and manipulators clustered at the bottom. Most other sentient species with which they'd had direct experience possessed roughly the same size and mass ratio to a H'rulka as an ant compared to a human.

When the H'rulka thought of other life forms as "vermin," the thought was less insult than it was a statement of fact, at least as they perceived it. Within the complex biosphere of the H'rulka homeworld, there were parasites living on each All of Us colony that were some meters across. H'rulka simply found it difficult to imagine creatures as intelligent that were almost literally beneath their notice in terms of scale.

"Commence acceleration," Ordered Ascent directed. "We will move into the region of heavy radio transmission, and destroy targets of opportunity as they present themselves."

The H'rulka warship, more than twenty kilometers across, began falling toward Sol, the inner system, and Earth.

By Ian Douglas

Star Carrier
EARTH STRIKE
CENTER OF GRAVITY

And the Galactic Marines Series

The Inheritance Trilogy
STAR STRIKE
GALACTIC CORPS
SEMPER HUMAN

The Legacy Trilogy
STAR CORPS
BATTLESPACE
STAR MARINES

The Heritage Trilogy
SEMPER MARS
LUNA MARINE
EUROPA STRIKE

CENTER OF GRAVITY

STAR CARRIER

BOOK TWO

IAN DOUGLAS

HARPER Voyager
An Imprint of HarperCollins*Publishers*

This is a work of fiction. Names, characters, places, and incidents are products of the author's imagination or are used fictitiously and are not to be construed as real. Any resemblance to actual events, locales, organizations, or persons, living or dead, is entirely coincidental.

HARPER Voyager
An Imprint of Harper Collins*Publishers*
10 East 53rd Street
New York, New York 10022-5299

Cover art by Gregory Bridges
ISBN 978-0-06-184026-5
www.harpervoyagerbooks.com

First Harper Voyager paperback printing: March 2011

Harper Voyager and) is a trademark of HCP LLC.

Printed in the U.S.A.

10 9 8 7 6 5 4 3 2 1

To Brea,
my guiding star

CENTER OF GRAVITY

Prologue

12 December 2404

Emergence, Arcturus System
36.7 light years from Earth
0310 hours, TFT

The recon probe emerged from its Alcubierre bubble of tightly warped space, bleeding off excess velocity in a burst of high-energy photons. An artificial gravitational singularity the size of a small dust particle and as massive as a star flicked on and off a few meters beyond the craft's bulbous nose, dragging it forward with an acceleration of nearly five thousand standard gravities. At that rate, the craft would be crowding the speed of light within another one hundred minutes.

Only slightly larger than a VG–10 Krait smart missile, the ISVR–120 probe was too small to carry sentient organics; its pilot was a Gödel 2500 artificial intelligence packed into the solid-state circuitry that filled the pod's core and so, technically, could be said to take up no space at all. Certainly it needed none of the bulky life-support equipment necessary for organic life.

The AI was called Alan, named after Alan Turing, one of the giants in the development of the first computers four and a half centuries earlier.

Within seconds of the probe craft's emergence from the warp bubble, Alan had scanned the system ahead, a volume of space dominated by a single bloated and brilliant orange star. The Confederation Naval Standard Ephemeris entry on the star resided within Alan's surface memory.

STAR: Alpha Boötis

COORDINATES: RA: 14^h 15^m 39.7^s Dec: +19° 10′ 56″ D 11.24p

ALTERNATE NAMES: Arcturus, Alramech, Abramech, 16 Boötes

TYPE: K1.5IIIFe–0.5

MASS: 3.5 Sol; **RADIUS:** 25.7 Sol; **LUMINOSITY:** 210 Sol (Optical 113 Sol)

SURFACE TEMPERATURE: ~4300°K

AGE: 9.7 billion years

APPARENT MAGNITUDE (SOL): –0.04; **ABSOLUTE MAGNITUDE:** –0.29

DISTANCE FROM SOL: 36.7 LY

PLANETARY SYSTEM: 6 planets, including 1 Jovian and 5 sub-Jovian gas giants, plus 47 dwarf planets and 65 known satellites, plus numerous planetoids and cometary bodies.

One gas giant satellite, Jasper, is of interest with somewhat earthlike conditions due to gravitational/tidal effects. . . .

Arcturus, depending on how one measured such things, was the third or fourth brightest star in the night skies of Earth, a bright orange point at the base of the kite-shape of the constellation Boötis. From Alan's emergence point some eighteen astronomical units out, Arcturus was a dazzling gold-orange beacon 113 times brighter than Sol would have been at the same distance. At infrared wavelengths, Arcturus was even brighter, flooding ambient space with sullen heat.

Alan's primary objective lay almost directly beyond the star from his emergence point. His final approach would be masked by the star's glare . . . if everything went right.

By the time Alan had traveled a third of the distance toward Arcturus—some 900 million kilometers—he was moving at a hair better than 99 percent of the speed of light. Velocity transformed his view of the surrounding universe, compressing it into a circle of light dead ahead—most of it infrared light from Arcturus, blue-shifted into optical wavelengths. The AI's sensory correction program, however, was able to untangle the flood of speed-distorted light into its separate components and correct for the distortion. His velocity also distorted time, by seven to one at this velocity. Each passing minute for Alan was seven in the universe outside; it created the illusion that he was hurtling deeper into the Arcturus system much faster than he actually was.

Some two hundred minutes objective after entering the Arcturus system, Alan passed the star, skimming the giant's photosphere. The probe's electromagnetic shielding deflected the worst of ionizing radiation but had little effect on radiant heat. Briefly, the probe's hull struggled with temperatures approaching 900 degrees Celsius. Nanotechnic currents within the hull laminates helped distribute the heat, radiating much of it harmlessly astern.

And then the star—its monstrous, turbulent, and roiling girth nearly twenty-six times larger than Sol's—fell away behind, red-shifting abruptly to a near-invisibility, illuminated at optical wavelengths solely by red-shifted X-rays.

Alan's objective now lay directly ahead, 20 astronomical units out.

Long-range detectors were already picking up ships, enemy ships, though at this distance those images were more than two and a half hours old. As expected, most of the enemy targets were grouped closely around a Jupiter-sized gas giant, listed in the database as Alchameth, and its Earth-sized moon, Jasper. Orbiting the moon was Arcturus Station, a terraforming base established by the Confederation three years ago to begin the process of turning Jasper into a human-habitable world.

But fourteen months ago, the Turusch had come. A Confederation naval task force stationed here had been all but wiped out, the orbital station had been captured. So far as could be gathered, nearly six thousand technicians, planetologists, xenologists, terraform specialists, and first-down colonists on the station—men, women, and children—had been butchered.

The probe's sensors were picking up the faint reflected gleams of Arcturus Station two hundred kilometers above Jasper, and two Beta-class Turusch battleships hanging close alongside, each a small asteroid, crater-pocked and immense. Numerous smaller vessels swarmed in the giants' shadows—Juliet- and Kilo-class cruisers.

If more distant Turusch warships were positioned far enough from Alchameth that they could have observed the emergence flash of the probe on the far side of Arcturus, there was no sign . . . though he was picking information out of light that had left Arcturus Station less than an hour after his entry into the system. A warning might well be on its way to those docked warships from sentries more than a light hour away.

Long minutes crawled past. The probe was hurtling toward the enemy vessels out of the glare of the local star, invisible . . . but before long the Turusch sensors would detect the distortions in space caused by the probe's enormous AGM, its artificial gravitational mass. For a time, Alan considered the possibility that they simply weren't looking in his direction, that he was not going to be noticed at all . . . and then the smaller warships alongside Arcturus Station began accelerating. Moments later, a cloud of missiles streaked in his direction. Alan began shifting the singularity drive randomly in different directions, causing the speeding probe to jink unpredictably. The time lag between his position and theirs gave him an advantage, time to calculate incoming trajectories and arrange *not* to be at their endpoints when the missiles detonated.

Alan's recon pod was unarmed.

He increased acceleration, tacking additional nines onto his current percent *c*. Anti-ship missiles closed with him, and for a few moments Alan engaged in a deadly game of tag, jinking hard this way and that to confuse enemy missiles and defense systems. A nuclear fireball flared to port, dazzling and intense, the hard radiation sleeting across his screens.

Alan survived.

The gas giant Alchameth showed a disk, now, swelling rapidly as Alan's sensors continued correcting for the speed distortion, becoming a vast, ringed and banded gas giant almost directly ahead. Alan focused on Jasper, visible now, high and to one side. A final course correction put him squarely on target. At 99.99% *c*, he flashed through the final 10 million kilometers in just 4.8 seconds subjective, passing Arcturus Station at a distance of just 315 kilometers.

He was prepared for the passage, with certain sensor collection heads extruded through the nano-liquid outer hull of the probe, trained on the enemy-held base, on the surface of the planet-sized moon, and on a large volume of surrounding space.

There was something else there . . . something just emerging now, not from behind Alchameth, but from within the gas giant's seething, turbulent atmosphere, something unseen until this moment. Something *huge* . . .

High-energy beams lanced toward him as he passed, one grazing his screens and melting a portion of his hull.

And then he was past, speeding outbound at just less than the speed of light itself, as enemy ships and missiles scrambled to pursue.

But they needed to accelerate first, and would never be able to catch him.

Alan was injured, however; the grazing near-miss had burned out critical sensors, parts of his lateral maneuvering projectors, and his energy screen itself. That last was serious, because it meant that incoming radiation would fry his circuitry within the next few subjective hours.

Somehow, though, he needed to get the accumulated data from his near-passage of the station back to Earth.

And he was going to need to commit the AI equivalent of suicide to do so. . . .

Chapter One

21 December 2404

TC/USNA CVS America
Approaching SupraQuito Fleet Base
Earth Synchorbit, Sol System
1235 hours, TFT

The star carrier approached the gossamer structure with a delicate grace that belied the vessel's titanic mass. Her hemispherical forward shield, pitted and scarred by innumerable impacts with dust motes and radiation, bore her name in sandblasted letters ten meters high: *America.*

Mushroom-shaped, the ship was 1,150 meters long. The forward cap, 500 meters across and 150 deep, served as both radiation shielding and as holding tank for 27 billion liters of water, reaction mass for the ship's maneuvering thrusters. The slender kilometer-long spine was taken up primarily by quantum-field power plants, maneuvering thrusters, and stores; twin counter-rotating hab rings tucked in just behind the shield cap carried the ship's crew of nearly five thousand. Around her, escorting vessels paced themselves to their ponderous consort's deceleration, minnows in the shadow of a whale.

Thirty-six thousand kilometers ahead, Earth gleamed at half phase—with dawn breaking across eastern North America, while the Atlantic, Europe, and Africa lay in full light between swirls and shreds of brilliant white cloud. At this distance, the planet spread across just 20 degrees of arc pole to pole, appearing delicate and impossibly fragile.

More fragile still, though, was the web of orbital structures just ahead in *America*'s path. SupraQuito hung suspended on the slender tether of its elevator cable in synch-orbit, directly above Earth's equator some 35,783 kilometers above the top of the mountain to which it was anchored. The structure—or interconnected series of structures, actually—was an enormous collection of hab modules, shipyards, orbital factories, environmental facilities, power plants and collectors, agro spheres, and docking facilities suspended between the elevator dropping to Earth, and the support tether leading up to the anchor some thirty thousand kilometers farther out.

From here, SupraQuito—including the tangle of structures that housed the Earth Confederation government—was visible, barely, as a thread-slender gleam of reflected sunlight, with constellations of tiny stars showing in the shadows. Some day, a thousand years hence, perhaps, SupraQuito would join with the other two space elevators, at Singapore and at Tanganyika, and become a true, inhabited ring encircling the Earth. At the moment, the entire massive structure appeared gossamer and delicate, far too insubstantial to trap the oncoming bulk of the Star Carrier *America*.

America herself was at the helm. The powerful AI residing within the carrier's electronic network possessed far more memory and processing power—by several orders of magnitude—than did a merely human brain. Exact comparisons between the relative brainpower of man and machine were meaningless, however, and probably impossible to calculate in any case. *America*'s mind, if that was the proper term, was wholly focused on the ship, its systems, its functioning, its navigation and control. At the moment, she was judging the remaining distance between her prow and Docking Tube One at the SupraQuito Military Fleet Base now just a few hundred kilometers ahead, and her own rate of deceleration. With a closing velocity of 8.64 kilometers per second, she needed to increase the gravitational mass currently being projected dead astern by 37 percent in three . . . two . . . one . . . *now.*

America kept up a running dialogue with her counterpart at Fleet Base Approach Control, with every aspect of her vector checked hundreds of times each passing second. The docking facility was not stationary, of course. Its *omega*, its angular velocity, kept it precisely above its attachment point in the Andes Mountains of Ecuador. At synchronous orbit, this worked out to 3.0476 kilometers per second.

For ten long seconds, *America* decelerated. With the ship enmeshed within the gravitational field of the projected singularity aft, the deceleration was unfelt by the vessel's passengers and crew. For them, the slowly rotating hab rings provided spin gravity. *America* slowed . . . slowed . . .

A final, precisely timed nudge from singularities to starboard gave her the necessary 3.0476 kps lateral velocity.

And with perfect choreography the massive carrier dropped into the sweet spot just five kilometers off the docking port, all singularities winking out before they could warp the delicate structure of the base. Grappling tethers, extended along the carrier's length, reached toward the dock. *America* would be warped into her berthing space—an ancient seafaring term that had nothing to do with her space-bending Alcubierre faster-than-light drives. The tethers connected with grappling points along the berthing area and began to contract. A small fleet of powerful little tugs emerged from the base, taking up station and nudging the carrier toward the dock. Slowly, very slowly, the quarter-million-ton carrier was hauled into port.

While *America*'s AI was far more powerful in most respects than human intelligence, the ship possessed nothing like human emotion. She heard the cheers from personnel on her bridge and in her CIC, from lounge decks and ready rooms and flight decks where members of her crew had gathered to watch the docking. Most of them, evidently, were delighted to be *home*, though the carrier had only an academic understanding of what that might mean. *America* had been on extended patrol for the past six weeks, watching for evidence of further incursions by the enemy Turusch. Her admiral had been ordered home to attend a ritual that *America* did not understand at all, even in theory.

The tether cables continued to contract and the dockyard tugs continued to nudge, drawing the ship closer and closer to her berth. Braces gently swung out to arrest that movement with a jar barely felt by the humans on board. Magnetic clamps snapped home, and the debarkation tube extended from the berthing module to *America*'s quarterdeck, located in zero-G at her central spine, immediately abaft the shield cap and just forward of the still rotating hab modules.

"All hands, this is the Captain." The voice was that of Captain Randolph Buchanan, *America*'s commanding officer. "Welcome home!"

But for the Star Carrier *America*, this certainly was not home.

This was a temporary waypoint, a momentary interruption of her duties, of her electronic life.

For *America*, home was always . . . *out there.*

Admiral's Quarters, TC/USNA CVS America
SupraQuito Fleet Base
Earth Synchorbit, Sol System
1405 hours, TFT

"Why in a quantum-warped hell do I have to *go* to this thing?" Rear Admiral Alexander Koenig glared at his own image projected on the wall screen in his quarters.

"Your adoring public, of course," a voice replied in his head. "They want to see you, shake your hand, and give you the worship due a conquering hero."

"Bullshit," Koenig growled. "I think it's just more politics, and the sooner I'm back on *America*'s flag deck the better, so far as I'm concerned."

"Harsh words from the man who saved Earth."

He winced a bit at that. He'd saved Earth, yes, in what was now being called the Defense of Earth, a rare and hard-won naval victory just two months ago. But there'd been losses . . . terrible losses. And one of them . . .

"Let me see you, Karyn," he said.

The room's electronics projected a holographic image into the suite's sunken living area, a smiling woman Koenig's age in the black-and-gray dress uniform of a Confederation Navy rear admiral. She looked . . . perfect, exactly as he remembered her.

Exactly as she'd been before the high-velocity Turusch impactor had slashed through the military synchorbital base above Mars known as Phobia, wrecking Mars Fleet CIC, the fleet dockyard, and killing thousands of civilian, Marine, and Navy personnel . . . including Karyn Mendelson.

He'd recovered her PA, her personal assistant. Copies had resided within his own communications implants, and in his office on board the Star Carrier *America*, and elsewhere. When she'd been alive, it had been able to project an AI simulacrum, an avatar, of Karyn indistinguishable from the living person over any communications or virtual net links. PAs could project the owner's image to field the flood of routine requests and calls received every day. Such avatars were smart enough to hold conversations and even make routine decisions for the original.

They weren't the same, though, weren't as responsive or as smart, and most important, they weren't flesh and blood.

God, he missed her.

The image in front of him looked a little sad. "You really should see the psych department," she told him. "You're hanging on to the . . . memories, using them to keep yourself from having to grieve."

"Since when did you get reprogrammed as a psytech?" he asked the image. He tried to keep the words light and bantering, and knew he'd failed.

"Karyn Mendelson had considerable psych experience," the image told him. "She commanded the fleet at Arcturus Station last year, remember, before she was assigned to Admiral Harrison's command staff."

"I know, damn it, I know. I just . . . I just don't want to lose you." *Again. . . .*

"Alex, you *have* lost me. Lost *her*, rather. A PA simulacrum cannot substitute for a real human."

"Maybe not," he replied, stubbornly sullen. "And maybe you're how I can . . . get used to the idea that she's gone."

"A psytherapy session would be better, Alex."

"Look, I don't want to talk about it now, okay? I'm supposed to be at this damned reception tonight. The Eudaimonium Arcology."

"Yes, Alex."

And that, he thought glumly, perfectly summed up the difference between a PA avatar and the real person—ignoring the fact that you couldn't *touch* an avatar. The real Karyn would never have let things rest there, would have kept arguing with him if she thought he was doing something stupid. Her PA's holographic projection, directed by certain software protocols, simply agreed with whatever he told it to do.

It didn't help that the AI program, likely, was right. The Navy relied heavily on advanced psychiatric medicine these days, including the use of elaborate virtual psytherapeutic replays of traumatic events, to treat the casualties of modern warfare. He'd been through virtual simulations himself more than once. Nothing to it. . . .

He just didn't want to forget her.

A comm signal chimed in his head. "Admiral?" It was his senior aide, Lieutenant Commander Nahan Cleary.

"Yes, Mr. Cleary."

"It's time to go ashore if you want to get there in plenty of time."

"I'll be right there." He checked his inner time readout. Just past nineteen, Fleet Time, which was GMT for Earth. SupraQuito was in the same planetary time zone as the Eudaimonium Arcology, a five-hour difference; it was now 1409 EST.

Lieutenant Commander Cleary was stretching somewhat the need for urgency. Admirals did *not* ride the space elevator with the general public, which would have meant a two-hour trip down the express to Quito, and another hour in the subsurface gravtube to New New York. The admiral's barge on board the *America* would get him to the Eudaimonium

Arc in less than an hour. The invitation was for seventeen, local time, so he still had almost two hours before he absolutely had to leave. Cleary, however, like all good aides, tended to fuss worse than a nagging PA, and didn't like to entertain even the possibility that his admiral would be late.

He wished he could blow off the invitation entirely, though. He was busy working on a set of tactical evaluations with Fleet HQ, and he didn't have time for this nonsense.

But for military personnel an invitation from the president of the Confederation Senate himself was an order, not a suggestion, and Fleet Admiral Rodriguez would be there as well.

Better to go and get the damned thing over with.

Another chime sounded, and this time Karyn's image appeared, his personal assistant serving now as his secretary.

"What is it, Karyn?" he asked.

"An incoming fleet communication, Alex," she said. "You're really going to want to see this."

"Put it through."

A window opened in his mind, and he felt the flow of the encrypted data feed. Keys within his implanted circuitry opened the message, and he found himself looking down on another world.

"ONI/DeSpaComCent to all units with Crystal Tower clearance and above," an emotionless voice, probably an AI, said. "We have an incoming transmission from an ISVR-120 dispatched to the Arcturus system six weeks ago. Data is raw, with only preliminary analyses by this department. . . ."

Within his mental window, Koenig could see the planet and its moon. A cascade of printed data scrolled down one side of his awareness, but he didn't need to read it to recognize the gas giant Alchameth and its largest satellite, Jasper. A bright blue targeting reticule marked a silvery pinpoint—Arcturus Station in orbit over a cloud-swathed moon. A dozen smaller reticules, each bright red, marked Turusch ships in orbit around Jasper.

His experienced inner eye took in the Turusch ships, each with its id tag giving type, mass, and readiness. Two Beta-class battlewagons, plus at least ten cruisers, light cruisers, and destroyers. That was a fair-sized battle fleet, and suggested that the Turusch were waiting for a possible Confederation counterattack into the system.

Not that that was going to happen anytime soon. Confederation Fleet Command had been reluctant to re-engage the enemy. The Defense of Earth might technically have been a victory, but it had been a damned close-run thing.

The gas giant, simmering in the sea of radiation from giant Arcturus just 20 AU distant, showed the bright yellow, orange, red, and brown striations of atmosphere belts, whipped around the massive planet by violent high-altitude winds.

The scene moved jerkily, frame by frame, and the images were grainy and difficult to resolve. They would have been pulled from a seemingly uniform starbow of light by sensory correction software on the probe, and, as the voice had warned, hadn't yet been massaged by the ONI analysts on Luna. But as the probe moved past planet and moon, the moon dropped from view outside of the camera angle and the probe's optics began zooming in on Alchameth.

Another blue reticule appeared, highlighting something above the banded cloud tops. Koenig resisted the impulse to squint, patiently waiting as the images—drastically slowed by the relativistic time difference between the probe and the outside world—zoomed in frame by frame.

There was *something* there. . . .

Sunlight glinted, a silver-orange glitter above orange clouds. A spacecraft? The probe's optical sensors zoomed in closer. It looked like a flattened balloon, but it must have been immense to be visible at this range, many kilometers across. And it was rising above the highest cloud layers, now, so it must be a ship . . . or possibly an aircraft.

A side window opened, showing schematics of a H'rulka ship, something encountered by humans only once so far.

Turusch and H'rulka ships together at Arcturus, just 37 light years from Sol.

The afternoon, suddenly, had become a *lot* more interesting.

VFA–44 Dragonfire Squadron
Approaching Columbia Arcology
United States, Earth
1655 hours, EST

Lieutenant Trevor Gray descended above the ocean, dropping toward the ruin of Old New York.

Linked in with the AI computer of his SG–92 Starhawk, his cerebral implants were receiving optical feeds from sensors grown temporarily all over the craft's fuselage. From his point of view, his fighter was invisible—in fact, he *was* the fighter, hurtling through the early evening sky off the eastern seaboard of the United States. The winter sun had set twenty-five minutes before; the sky was still a crisp and brilliant blue, the twilight illuminating the dark rolling waves below.

Around him, in the crystalline sky, eleven other Starhawks traveled with him in close formation, each jet-black ship now morphed into atmospheric flight mode—broad delta shapes with down-curving wingtips carving through thin air at a sedate four times the speed of sound. They'd departed from the military spaceport at Oceana just five minutes earlier, swinging far out over the ocean to avoid disturbing coastal communities with their sonic boom. The Manhat Ruins now lay only a few kilometers ahead.

"Look smart," the squadron leader said over the unit's tactical channel. "They want a nice show down there. Cut back to fifteen hundred kph and descend to twelve hundred. Tighten it up, people."

Commander Marissa Allyn was the CO of VFA–44, the "Dragonfires," and flying the lead Starhawk, hull number 101. Until recently, she'd been the CAG of *America*'s Space Wing, though she'd never been confirmed and, just days ago, a new CAG had been brought on board. *America*'s fighter wing was still reorganizing, still licking its wounds after the terrible casualties suffered during the Defense of Earth.

In three groups of four flying wingtip to wingtip, the Starhawks dropped closer to the blur of blue-gray water beneath their keels.

"And . . . descending to eight hundred meters," Allyn continued.

To port, Gray was aware of a smear of movement, the coastline of the old state of New Jersey, a stretch of ground until recently given over to swampland and mangrove but now swept clean, barren and forbidding. Still descending, they rocketed past the sweeping, broken curve of the Verrazano Narrows Dam, one of the megastructures raised in the twenty-first century in what had proven to be an expensive but unsuccessful bid to save the city ahead.

Still slowing, still descending, the squadron passed over what was left of New York City.

Forests of steel superstructure marking the largest building, the crumbling façade of the TriBeCa Tower, all rose above dirty, surging water. Vine-shrouded structures slowly eroding into the sea. Where once there had been a square-grid network of city streets, there were now narrow canals, canyons filled with water and the dark pockets of the coming night.

New York City had first been submerged three centuries before, when Hurricane Cynthia had smashed a half-kilometer gap through the Verrazano Narrows Dam and the sea—now twelve meters higher than the southern tip of Manhattan—had poured in. The vibrant metropolis had been smashed, then drowned; the shattered buildings still standing had rapidly crumbled into decayed ruins or been overgrown by green masses of porcelain-berry, kudzu, and other creeping vines, giving them the look of sheer-sided green islands rising with a curiously geometric orderliness from the sea.

Even so, the Ruins of Manhattan had been . . . home.

Gray had been a Prim, one of some thousands of people living in the Ruins outside the all-encompassing embrace of modern technology. For him, until five years ago, home had been the shattered shell of the old TriBeCa Tower Arcology, a torn and battered mountain passing now to port.

The scene, spread out around and below him now, however, illuminated by the pale glow of twilight, seemed alien now. The place was changed, shockingly so. During the Defense of Earth two months earlier, a Turusch high-velocity impactor had generated a tidal wave that had smashed north through the Narrows. Hundreds of the remaining buildings sticking up out of the water had been toppled, and a vast forest of tangled debris was now strewn across Morningside Heights, Yonkers, and the swamps of Harlem. Most of the building-islands, once covered by lush vegetation, were naked now, stripped of all life by the passing wave two months before.

Thousands of people—Prims and squatties, like Gray in his former life—had lived within the ruins, comprising a modern-day hunter-gatherer society largely ignored by the *civilized* folk inland.

Gray wondered how many had survived the tidal wave . . . how many of the people he'd once called family and friends survived.

And the civilized communities here had suffered as well. The tidal wave had swept across Morningside Heights, bringing down the kilometer-high tower of the Columbia Arcology. An instant after crossing the shoreline between the Manhat Ruins and Morningside Heights, Gray saw the mountain of rubble that was all that was left of Columbia.

Angela. . . .

She hadn't been there when the tower had fallen. At least, he didn't think so.

But he hadn't heard, not for sure.

He forced his thoughts from that pain, focusing instead on his flying. At just above the speed of sound, the twelve spacecraft thundered across the Hudson River and past the Palisades Eudaimonium precisely on schedule.

The eudaimonium—the name came from the ancient Greek philosophical concept of perfect and complete happiness—was part of the Greater New New York complex north of Manhattan. Protected from the impactor tidal wave two months before by the towering walls of the Palisades overlooking the Hudson, it was the heart of the New City, a cluster of arcology towers, arches and skyways, domes, slabs, and floater habs housing 5 million people. Tonight, the local population had increased by at least a third. As the Starhawks roared past, Gray could see the lights and thronging crowds below, an ocean of people celebrating what had been rather grandiloquently billed as the "Yule of the Millennium." The central Eudaimon Plaza appeared to be packed with celebrants; lasers arced across the sky amid the flicker and pop of fireworks. Tens of thousands of decorative lights created the impression of a galaxy picked out in reds, greens, and golds.

"Landing lights, people!" Allyn commanded, and the squadron lit up, twelve dazzling stars streaking across the darkening sky at five hundred meters. The sonic boom of the squadron's passing must have rattled walls and transplas windows ten kilometers away.

The squadron over-flight had been timed to rattle those windows at seventeen precisely, kicking off the festivities at the arcology complex. Confederation Senate President Regis DuPont was down there, somewhere, as were the presidents of the North American Union, America del Sur, and Europe; a dozen Confederation senators; a host of VIPs from the military, from the Union capital at Columbus, Ohio; and even a handful of governors from extrasolar colony worlds—from Chiron, from Thoth, and even from Bifrost.

The party tonight was a *very* big affair.

Mission accomplished, the squadron banked and decelerated, making for the Giuliani Spaceport northwest of the city. A flotilla of civilian pubtran fliers was waiting for them there; the Dragonfires, too, had also been invited, though they'd be arriving at the party a few minutes late.

As he peeled off for final approach, morphing his Starhawk into landing configuration, Gray could only think about the person he'd left behind . . .

. . . About Angela.

ONI Special Research Division
Crisium, Luna
1201 hours, TFT

"What the hell do we know about the H'rulka?" Dr. Kane demanded.

"Not enough," Wilkerson replied. "Not enough by about fifteen hundred parsecs."

"Maybe your pets can shed some more light on the subject."

"They are not," Wilkerson replied evenly, "my *pets*."

Until two months before, Dr. Phillip Wilkerson had been the head of the neuropsytherapy department on board the Confederation Star Carrier *America*. After the return from Eta Boötis, however, he'd been summarily transferred to the Office of Naval Intelligence—specifically to the xenosophontological research department, headquartered beneath the Mare Crisium on Earth's moon. He'd brought with him eighteen Turusch POWs, and almost two thousand more had arrived shortly after—survivors of one of the big enemy asteroid-battleships disabled in the Defense of Earth.

The Turusch community now comprised a de facto alien colony occupying a former warehouse excavation two kilometers beneath the main Crisium dome, sealed off by airlocks and pumped full of a high-pressure atmosphere composed of CO_2, sulfur dioxide, carbonyl sulfide, water vapor, sulfuric acid droplets, and a mist of sulfur. The mist constantly cycled between its liquid and solid phases at temperatures close to the boiling point of water. The Turusch home planet was hypothesized to be, as Wilkerson himself had once suggested, a less extreme version of the planet Venus, with a thinner atmosphere bathed in heavy ultraviolet radiation from its parent star. For almost two months, Wilkerson had been working with the colony, leading a small army of xenosophontologists, linguists, and ETC AIs, trying to learn how the Turusch thought.

The task, he'd long ago decided, would not be complete anytime in this century.

Dr. Howard Kane was one of his project specialists, on loan from the ONI's XS department. An unpleasant man with an acidly sarcastic attitude, he seemed to specialize in finding exactly the wrong thing to say to his colleagues. Wilkerson so far had managed to keep him from communicating directly with the Turusch. That task was difficult enough without bringing ego and attitude into the mix.

"This Crustal Tower message," Kane said, "says a H'rulka ship has been spotted at Arcturus Station. "But as far as I can see, we don't know jack about them."

"The Turusch have mentioned the H'rulka during a number of sessions," a third voice put in. "They state that the two species share key philosophical concepts."

The invisible speaker was a specialist AI variously called Noam or, sometimes, "Chom," after the twentieth-century linguist, cognitive scientist, and philosopher Avram Noam Chomsky.

"There was nothing else in Alan's recording?" Wilkerson asked.

"No. The AI known as 'Alan' effectively ceased to exist upon partition."

Wilkerson nodded understanding. An artificial intelligence like Noam, or like the smaller and more mission-specific AI on the Arcturus recon probe, required a certain size, a certain complexity of internal circuitry and processing power in order to maintain the electronic version of consciousness. Details were still sketchy, but the ISVR–120 interstellar probe apparently had elected to split itself into four separate parts. The probe hardware was designed to allow such a division in order to guarantee that its memory made it back home . . . but the circuitry carrying those memories simply wasn't adequate to maintain something as complex as a Gödel 2500 artificial intelligence.

The AI Alan Turing had in effect committed suicide in order to get its information back to Sol.

Kane dragged down a virtual window, which glowed in the air in front of him and Wilkerson. The data file with what little was known about the H'rulka scrolled down the screen. "Floaters!" Kane said, reading. "The presumption is that they're intelligent gas bags that evolved in the upper atmosphere of a gas giant."

"Interesting, if true," Wilkerson said, reading. "I'd like to know how they managed to develop a technology capable of building starships without access to metals, fire, smelting, solid raw materials, or solid ground."

"What is it they're supposed to share with the Tushies, Chom?" Kane asked.

"It is difficult to express," Noam replied, "as are most Turusch concepts. It appears, however, to be a philosophy based on the concept of *depth*."

"Yeah, yeah. They order things higher to lower, instead of the way we do it."

"It's no different than when we say something is second class," Wilkerson said, "and mean it's not as important or as high-up as first class."

"It's still bass-ackward," Kane said.

"The three conscious minds of a Turusch are considered by the Turusch to range from 'high' to 'here' to 'low,'" Noam pointed out, "with 'high' being the most primitive, most basic state of intelligence, and 'low' the most advanced and complex. For the Turusch, something called the *Abyss* represents depth, scope, danger, and tremendous power. We think the Turusch evolved to live on high plateaus or mountaintops on their world, with lower elevations representing sources of wealth or power—maybe a food source—as well as deadly windstorms. *Abyssal whirlwinds*, they call them."

"So, if the H'rulka *are* Jovian-type floaters," Wilkerson mused, "they might relate to the idea of the Abyss as the depths of a gas giant atmosphere. Hot, stormy, high energy, and definitely dangerous. A point of cognitive contact or understanding between them and the Turusch."

"Sounds far-fetched to me," Kane said. "Besides, intelligence *couldn't* develop in a gas giant atmosphere. Absolutely impossible."

"I've learned in this business to mistrust the phrase 'absolutely impossible,' Doctor," Wilkerson said. "Why do you think that?"

"Because the vertical circulation of atmospheric cells in a gas giant atmosphere would drag any life form in the relatively benign higher levels down into the depths in short order," Kane replied. "They would be destroyed by crushing pressures and searing high temperatures. There'd be no way to preserve culture . . . or develop it, for that matter. No way to preserve historical records . . . art . . . music . . . learning. And, as you just said, they wouldn't get far without being able to smelt metals or build a technology from the ground up." He smirked. "No ground."

"But we do have lots of examples of Jovian life," Wilkerson said.

"None of it intelligent," Kane replied. "It can't survive long enough."

"Maybe." Wilkerson moved his hand, and the columns of writing on the virtual window were replaced by the image received by the ONI a few hours before . . . a transmission from a burned-out interstellar probe that had dropped into the outskirts of the Sol System and beamed its treasure trove of data in-system that morning.

An alert with raw-data footage had been passed on to a number of government offices and military commands a few hours ago; the fact that the H'rulka were at Arcturus was *big* news. It meant, potentially, disaster. . . .

"Whether they're gas bags from a Jovian atmosphere, or something more substantial," Wilkerson observed, "they mean trouble. We've only met them once, but that was enough."

The ongoing exchange of hostilities known as the First Interstellar War had been proceeding off and on for the past thirty-six years. It had begun in 2368 at the Battle of Beta Pictoris, with a single Terran ship surviving out of a squadron of eight. In the years since, defeat had followed defeat as the Turusch and their mysterious Sh'daar masters had taken world upon human-colonized world, as the area controlled by the Terran Confederation had steadily dwindled.

Most of those defeats were suffered by Earth's navies at the hands the Turusch va Sh'daar, a species that appeared to be the equivalent of the Sh'daar empire's military arm. Once, however, a dozen years ago, a Confederation fleet approaching a gas giant within the unexplored system of 9 Ceti, some 67 light years from Sol, had been wiped out by a single enormous vessel rising from the giant's cloud layers. A single message pod had been launched toward the nearby human colony of Anan, just seventeen light years away, at 37 Ceti.

The Agletsch, the spidery sentients who'd been Humankind's first contact with other minds among the stars, had looked at images from that pod and identified the lone attacking ship as *H'rulka*. The name was an Agletsch word meaning, roughly, "floaters." They'd claimed that the aliens were huge living balloons that had evolved within the upper atmosphere of a distant gas giant like Sol's Jupiter. The term *H'rulka va Sh'daar* suggested that the H'rulka, like the Turusch and like the Agletsch, were part of the galaxy-spanning empire of the Sh'daar.

No one knew what the H'rulka called themselves, what they looked like, or anything at all about them. Many human researchers, like Kane, were convinced that even the information about a gas giant homeworld was either mistaken or deliberate misinformation.

What *was* known was that a few weeks after the fleet at 9 Ceti was lost, all contact with Anan was lost as well.

If the H'rulka were at Arcturus, apparently working with the Turusch, it suggested that the Sh'daar had just upped the ante, bringing up some big-gun support for their Turusch allies.

"We could start talking to our Turusch about whether they've worked with the H'rulka before," Wilkerson suggested. "It might give us some insight into how they fit in with the Sh'daar hierarchy."

Three millennia earlier, Sun Tse had pointed out that a man who knew both himself and his enemy would be victorious in all of his battles. That might have worked for the ancient Chinese, but complete knowledge simply wasn't possible—certainly not of beings as completely *alien* as the Sh'daar, the H'rulka, or the Turusch.

"Do you think that's important?" Kane asked.

Wilkerson shrugged. "At this point, *every* datum is important. We're not even sure why they're attacking us."

"I thought it was because the Sh'daar wanted to limit our technological growth."

"So the Agletsch told us. But how accurate is that? And

if it is, *why*? We call the Sh'daar polity an empire . . . but is it? Do the Sh'daar really control all of their client species, tell them what to do, who to trade with, who to attack? Or are the Turusch, and now the H'rulka, attacking us on their own? *We don't know*."

"The term *empire* serves well enough," Kane said. "We may not need to know the details."

"Maybe not . . . but we won't know what we need to know until we winkle it out, translate it, and analyze it."

"Well, let's see what the slugs have to say," Kane agreed. "You don't sound very enthusiastic."

"Enthusiastic? No. Those big gastropods give me the creeps. I keep wanting to reach for the salt shaker . . . a very *large* salt shaker. . . ."

Chapter Two

21 December 2404

Palisades Eudaimonium
New York State, Earth
1725 hours, EST

The spaceport's pubtran flier touched down lightly on the landing platform, a broad concourse suspended several hundred meters above the ground in front of the Grand Concourse. Trevor Gray stepped out of the flier and stopped, momentarily transfixed by the spectacle below, a dazzling constellation of lights stretching from horizon to horizon. Near at hand, concentric circles of lights, illuminated buildings, glowing red and green holiday decorations and animations, and the shifting displays of adwalls all combined to create a bewildering tangle of moving light. In the distance, toward the southeast, lay an ominous swath of darkness punctuated by the light—Columbia, Manhattan, and on the horizon, the ocean.

Someone thumped his shoulder hard from behind.

"Move it, Prim," Lieutenant Jen Collins snapped. "You're blocking progress."

Gray turned sharply, fists clenched, but then stepped aside as the others filed out of the flier. Lieutenant Commander Allyn was coming off the flier last, and was watching him. "Uniform, Lieutenant," she reminded him. "This is a formal affair."

"Ah, you should have let the Prim wear his jackies," Collins said with a bitter laugh.

"Yeah," Lieutenant Kirkpatrick added, grinning. "The dumb-ass doesn't know any better. It'll be fun watching him try to mix with *our* kind."

"Hey, back off," Lieutenant Ben Donovan said. "We're all a bit nervous tonight."

Gray looked down at his uniform, which was currently configured for flight utility—the plain and unadorned dark gray skinsuit worn by pilots jacked into their fighters—"jackies," in flight-line slang. Angrily, he slapped the set-patch on his left shoulder, calling up a menu within his inner display. Mindclicking on *Full Dress, Formal* engaged the nanotechnic interface. With a somewhat tingling sensation, his clothing rearranged itself, tightening, unfolding, and taking on texture and color.

Confederation Navy formal full dress was a glossy black skinsuit, throat to soles, with an intricate layer of bright gold knotwork sheathing the left third of his body—arm, side, and outer leg, extending all the way from shoulder to ankle. His rank tabs glowed to either side of his throat, and a panel over his left breast displayed a fluorescent animation of awards and decorations. He'd only been in for five years, so the cycling award display was a short one: Confederation Military Service, the Battles of Everdawn and of Arcturus Station, and the newly awarded Legion of the Defense of Earth, with cluster for distinguished service.

"That looks better!" Donovan said, grinning.

"I feel like a damned adwall," Gray replied, referring to the ubiquitous multistory display panels serving as animated or live-action advertising displays on the walls of arcologies and city buildings.

"But a squared-away, Navy adwall," Donovan said. He slapped Gray on his gold-entwined arm. "C'mon! Let's check out the party!"

The Grand Concourse was an immense, domed-over plaza of light, crowds, and color. At the near end, the boulevard wrapped around a depression, a terraced bowl well over two hundred meters across, with standing, sitting, and reclining room for some thousands of people at once. A touch and a thought could grow a chair from the floor, soften to a sunken lounger, or extrude tables complete with a seemingly endless variety of food and drink. Everywhere there was light; the Yule celebrations marked the holy seasons of at least three major religious groups, all of them festivals of light, and the air was filled with twisting, cascading, and shimmering veils of liquid radiance and starbow hues.

"Best behaviors, Dragonfires," Allyn's voice whispered in their heads. "Corders, secmons, and deets on at all times, and we *will* know if you switch them off."

Several of the pilots nearby grumbled at that. Corders were recording sensors grown within the weave of military uniforms. If anyone got into trouble tonight, there'd be a full audiovisual record of the incident for the court-martial afterward. Secmons were security monitors, non-AI software routines designed to warn personnel about possible security breaches. Deets were detoxifiers. There were quite a few sense-altering drugs, scents, and beverages on display, but the micrometabolic processors nano-grown within each pilot's brain would sample chemicals in the bloodstream, monitor sensory input, and harmlessly filter out the offending chemical before he or she developed more than a light buzz.

For the Navy, *professionalism* and *decorum* were the watchwords. *Always.*

As Gray descended into the crowded concourse bowl, he felt momentarily disoriented. Walls were grown as easily as chairs or appetizers, and could be called into being to create small and cozy alcoves or private spaces, creating a labyrinthine effect, and as walls and rooms came and went, it became difficult to navigate. Some walls appeared to be solid, carved stone; others were screens apparently of wickerwork or painted panels, or of woven vines or other vegetation. The air seemed to grow hazier, the deeper into the bowl he traveled. At the moment, the air glowed with a deep red light, though an ultraviolet component was making the black of his uniform fluoresce with a deep, electric shimmer of ultramarine. Overhead, constellations of lights gleamed brightly, mostly in red and green, for some reason.

There seemed to be no particular theme, save that of *people.*

The crowd within that one hall must have numbered five thousand—roughly the same as the crew on board *America.* He saw a few other military uniforms, most of them the richly patterned black and gold of senior naval officers, or the ancient red, white, and blue of Marine full dress. They stood out within the far, far larger number of civilians, who wore a bewildering array of costumes, from brilliant, swirling plumage, much of it glowing under the UV light, to swirling patterns of iridescent skin nano to complete nudity.

The men seemed to be more conservatively dressed, he noticed—formal skinsuits or robes, though there were a few bright-colored ones aglow in light or with pulsing animations writhing about their bodies. The women, though, all were spectacular in their multihued displays. One strikingly attractive woman in front of him was wearing a startling, meter-high headdress that appeared to be a spray of suspended fiber-optic threads, the light shimmering in a halo effect around her—and nothing else. She saw him looking at her, raised her glass in a mock toast, and winked.

The woman she was talking with appeared to be wearing nothing but white light, as though her skin has become brilliantly luminous, with stars set in her hair and hovering about her head.

"Someone is pinging you," his personal assistant told him.

"Who?"

"I'm sorry. Her id is blocked."

" 'Her'? A woman? Where is she?"

An inner tug gave him a direction. *That* way. "Range: eighty-seven meters," his PA said.

Odd. Personal ids—the term was pronounced as a word, rhyming with "lid"—were normally open to all within the electronic world of personal assistants and implanted communications and information hardware. The ping might mean she was interested in him, or it might mean she was just curious, tagging his personal information. That she was not revealing her own personal data, though, meant she wanted to remain anonymous, at least for now.

Who would be looking for him here? If it was Allyn or another shipmate, their military ids would have registered with his PA immediately, a kind of personal IFF. A civilian, then . . . but he didn't know anyone at this gathering.

Nor, really, did he care to. The only time in his life when he'd actually sought out civilians in the civilized parts of New York had been when he'd taken Angela to the Columbia Arcology in a desperate attempt to save her when she'd had a stroke. The inhabitants of the Periphery—the fallen-away outer fringes of the old United States, which included the Manhat Ruins—weren't considered to be full citizens, and normally they didn't have access to modern medical services. All but the most severe cardiovascular emergencies were easily treated in a modern medical center like the one in Columbia; in a Prim community in the Periphery, a stroke could kill you or leave you helplessly paralyzed.

He'd gotten Angela to the med center while she was still alive . . . and they'd repaired her. The cost, however, had been *him*, a ten-year term with the Confederation military.

Of course, the treatment had also cost him Angela. They'd done something to her brain while saving her . . . something that had shut down her affection for him. Or, maybe that had been an effect of the stroke. That's what they'd told him, anyway, that that sort of thing often happened when old neural pathways were burned out, new paths channeled in. Whichever it had been, his once-wife had chosen to leave him rather than going back to the canals and vine-covered islands of the Ruins.

Hell, he couldn't even blame her for that. She'd downloaded the skill sets allowing her to become a compositor, a career classification completely unknown to him. She'd moved north to New New York City's Haworth District, he'd heard, and was living with an extended family there.

At least she hadn't been in Columbia when the impactor wave had brought the arcology tower down. Or at least, so he hoped. He hadn't heard from her since he'd left for the Naval Training Center five years earlier. He'd been told she'd moved to Haworth and that she didn't want to see him . . . but he didn't *know*.

"Shall I reply?" his PA asked.

"Negative," he said. He couldn't imagine this crowd having anything *pleasant* to say to him.

He'd tried to get out of coming tonight. Lieutenant Commander Allyn had told him yesterday, in the squadron ready room on board *America*, that he'd been volunteered for the fly-by show, with attendance at the Yule Festival afterward.

"Why me?" he'd asked. "I've got nothing to do with Earthies anymore."

"Oh, I don't know," the Dragonfires' skipper had replied. "Maybe because you had something to do with saving all of their asses?"

That again. "Fuck that, sir," he said, using the Navy's preferred gender-neutral honorific, though *ma'am* would have done as well. "I was doing my job."

"And maybe your job includes being a visible symbol of the Confederation Navy," she'd told him. "Don't give me grief, Gray. You're on the flight roster, like it or not."

And here he was.

In a nearby temporary alcove, Donovan was holding a young woman very closely indeed. She was wearing a sheath of golden, rippling light, and appeared to have extended the field to include Ben in her embrace. Gray looked away, embarrassed, and found himself looking into another alcove, this one with two men and a woman on a round sofa bed, engaged in some extremely passionate foreplay.

Angry, he turned his head again and strode forward, determined to find something to eat. He felt *so* damned out of place here. . . .

Within the Periphery, the necessities of survival tended to draw people into close, monogamous couples. Elsewhere, at least through much of North America, family groupings tended to be larger and extended, polyamorous, and impermanent. Throughout much of the background culture of the Confederation, the half-barbaric denizens of the Periphery were seen as amusingly quaint, or worse: as narrow-minded or even sexually perverted. They were commonly called "Prims," which was short for "primitives," of course, but the epithet held the double meaning of someone who was self-righteously prudish or closed sexually. "Monogies" was another derogative term for Prims who preferred a monogamous lifestyle; why would *anyone* want to restrict their life and their love to a single person?

Gray was neither prudish nor self-righteous. He knew other communities did things differently when it came to sex and marriage, and had no problem with the fact. Extended social group marriages and sexcircles simply weren't for *him*. The thought of casually coupling with a woman he didn't know—and couldn't trust—left him vaguely uneasy.

A table extruded from the floor beneath an enormous transparency overlooking the Hudson was covered by dishes of various kinds, all of them pretty, few of them things he actually recognized. *America* had a decent mess deck and good food-processing software, but nothing as fancy as this. Some of the items actually looked as though they'd started out as vegetation growing in the ground or an aerophonics module rather than a collection of CHON turned appetizing by a molecular assembler.

He tried something green and crunchy with an orange paste spread across the top. Interesting . . .

"You are being pinged again by the same person," his PA told him. His internal direction sense said, *That way*, toward an outside veranda. "Range: thirty-one meters and approaching."

"Let her," Gray said.

He kept eating.

H'rulka Warship 434
Saturn Space, Sol System
1242 hours, TFT

The H'rulka didn't name their starships. A name suggested an individual personality, and the concept of the individual was one only barely grasped by H'rulka psychology. The H'rulka were, in fact, colony organisms; a very rough terrestrial analogue would have been the Portuguese Man of War . . . though the H'rulka were not marine creatures, and each was composed of several hundred types of communal polyps, rather than just four. Even their name for themselves—which came across in a hydrogen atmosphere as a shrill, high-pitched thunder generated by gas bags beneath the primary flotation sac—meant something like "All of Us," and could refer either to a single colony, in the first person, or to the race as a whole.

Individual H'rulka colonies took on temporary names, however, as dictated by their responsibilities within the community. Ordered Ascent was the commander of Warship 434, itself until recently a part of a larger vessel, Warship 432. The species didn't have a government as humans would have understood the term, and even the captain of a starship was more of a principal decision maker than a leader.

Ordered Ascent was linked in with 434's external sensors, and was studying the planet just ahead. The alien solar system comprised a single star and four planets, plus the usual scattering of rubble and debris. The planet some eighty thousand *shu* ahead was almost achingly familiar in size and mass and gently banded color, a near twin to the homeworld so many *shishu* away, right down to the sweeping rings of minute, reflective particles circling it.

"It looks like home," the aggregate being called Swift Pouncer whispered over the private radio link. H'rulka possessed two entirely separate means of speech, two separate languages—one by means of vibrations in the atmosphere, the other by means of biologically generated radio bursts. Their natural radio transceivers, located just beneath the doughnut-shaped cluster of polyps forming their brains, allowed them to interface directly with their machines.

"Similar," Ordered Ascent replied. "It appears to be inhabited."

"We are receiving speech from one of the debris-chunks orbiting the world," Swift Pouncer replied. "It may be a vermin-nest. And . . . we are receiving speech from numerous sources much closer to the local star."

Ordered Ascent tuned in to the broadband scanners and saw the other signals.

Those members of Ordered Ascent capable of rational thought chided themselves. No matter how long they served within the far-flung fleets of the Sh'daar, it was difficult to remember that vermin-nests frequently occurred, not within the atmospheres of true planets, but on the inhospitable solid surfaces of debris.

It was an unsettling thought. For just a moment, Ordered Ascent allowed themselves to pull back from the instrumentation feeds, to find steadiness and reassurance in the sight of the Collective Globe.

The interior of the H'rulka warship was immense by human standards, but cramped to the point of stark claustrophobia for the species called All of Us. The area that served as the equivalent of the bridge on a human starship was well over two kilometers across, a vast spherical space filled by twelve free-floating H'rulka colonies in a dodecahedral array. Connected by radio to their ship, they used radio commands to direct and maneuver the huge vessel, fire the weapons, and observe their surroundings.

They lived in the high-pressure atmosphere of gas giants, breathing hydrogen and metabolizing methane, ammonia, and drifting organic tidbits analogous to the plankton of Terran oceans. Until one of the Sh'daar's client species had shown them how to use solid materials to build spacecraft that defied both gravity and hard vacuum, they'd never known the interior of *anything*, never known what it was like to be enclosed, to be *trapped inside*. The interior of Warship 434 was large enough—just—to avoid triggering a serious claustrophobic-panic reflex in All of Us aggregates. Sometimes, they needed to see other aggregates adrift in the sky simply in order to feel safe.

Feeling steadier, Ordered Ascent relinked with the ship and their fellow H'rulka. "Can we be sure that this is the system to which the alien probe fled?" they asked.

"Yes, with a probability of eighty-six percent plus," one of the others replied. "The shard that we followed almost certainly came here."

Warship 432 had pursued the probe that had passed through System 783,451. The probe abruptly had split onto four pieces, four shards each independently powered, each traveling in a different direction.

The H'rulka ship had split into four sections as well in response. Warship 434 had followed one fragment, a difficult feat in the weirdly distorted continuum of faster-than-light travel, but possible given the power of certain Sh'daar instrumentation. The selected shard had dropped out of faster-than-light drive after some periods of travel, changed heading, and accelerated once more. The new path had brought it, and the pursuing All of Us, *here*.

"The system is known to the Sh'daar," Pouncer reported. "They list it as System 784,857."

Data streamed down the radio link through Directed Ascent's consciousness. The inhabitants of this system were indeed native to the system debris.

Vermin . . .

The All of Us race was unaccustomed to dealing with other sentient species. One of the primary reasons for this was, simply, their size; by almost any standards, the H'rulka were giants.

An adult H'rulka consisted of a floatation gas bag measuring anywhere from two to three hundred meters across, with brain, locomotion and feeding organs, sensory apparatus and manipulators clustered at the bottom. Most other sentient species with which they'd had direct experience possessed roughly the same size and mass ratio to a H'rulka as an ant compared to a human.

When the H'rulka thought of other life forms as "vermin," the thought was less insult than it was a statement of fact, at least as they perceived it. Within the complex biosphere of the H'rulka homeworld, there were parasites living on each All of Us colony that were some meters across. H'rulka simply found it difficult to imagine creatures as intelligent that were almost literally beneath their notice in terms of scale.

"Commence acceleration," Ordered Ascent directed. "We will move into the region of heavy radio transmission, and destroy targets of opportunity as they present themselves."

The H'rulka warship, more than twenty kilometers across, began falling toward Sol, the inner system, and Earth.

Palisades Eudaimonium
New York State, Earth
1750 hours, EST

Admiral Koenig looked out over the sea of people filling the Grand Concourse of the eudaimonium and wondered, again, just what he was supposed to be doing here.

He'd been the center of attention for a number of politicians and Confederation military leaders ever since arriving here an hour before, but there seemed to be no particular point to it, other than allowing wealthy or important civilians to get a sense of their own importance by being close to the Man Who Saved Earth.

What unmitigated bullshit.

He was standing on a railed platform high above the bowl-shaped main floor filling much of the Grand Concourse, along with a number of senators and high-ranking military officers, members of the Confederation Senate and of the Joint Chiefs of Staff.

John Quintanilla, a senior political liaison between the Senate and the military, stood next to him. "Well, Admiral?" Quintanilla asked. "Are you ready?"

"No," Koenig told him. "But I don't suppose that's going to change things, is it?"

Quintanilla grinned. "Not in the least!"

The man seemed . . . animated. Koenig rarely got to see this side of Quintanilla. Usually, the liaison was, if not an enemy, exactly, at least in the way . . . obstructionistic, fussy, and difficult. Political liaisons were a necessity, Koenig supposed, a means for the civilian government to exercise their control over a potentially dangerous military, but he didn't like it. For member-states of the Confederation with long traditions of having a military subject to government oversight—in particular the United States of North America—that tradition and a sense of duty alone was enough to guarantee the military's loyalty to the government. Other members of the Confederation, though—the European Union, los Estados de las Americas del Sur, the Empire of Brazil, the North India Federation, and many of the extra-solar colonies—had long histories of having their militaries dictating in one way or another to their governments, hence the need for direct oversight of military operations.

Koenig had thrown Quintanilla off of his flag bridge once, an act that could have inflicted serious harm on Koenig's career. *Success*, however, covered a multitude of sins. The incident had been quietly smoothed over and forgotten.

"The president's about to start his speech," Quintanilla told him. "You stand . . . here." Quintanilla guided Koenig to a holographic transmission disk set into the floor. The disk was inactive, its light off.

"Ladies and gentlemen," a voice boomed from somewhere overhead. "The President of the Confederation Senate!"

Accompanied by the powerful, martial beat of *Ad Astra*, the Confederation's anthem, a glowing figure materialized in the air above the crowded bowl, an older man in a stylish formal robe, ten stories tall and eerily translucent.

"We are here," the looming figure boomed in somber tones and without preamble, "to honor the Man Who Saved Earth. . . ."

The president's speech went on for a long time.

Under the terms of the original Constitution of the United States, government had been divided three ways between a two-house legislative congress, a president, and a supreme court, each applying checks and balances against the others in order, it was hoped, to limit government and avoid tyranny. That system, ultimately, had failed with a succession of weak presidents and corrupt legislators. The devastation wreaked by the Wormwood asteroid strike 272 years before had shattered much of the old United States and very nearly ended the fragile experiment in democracy begun in 1776.

The Earth Confederation had been an attempt to create a single-world government and end the possibility that any single nation-state would ever again threaten another nation—or the entire human species—with extinction. The attempt had been only partly successful. The Chinese Hegemony, which had launched the asteroid strike in the first place, back at the end of the Second Sino-Western War, was still not a full member, and the Islamic Theocracy was barely tolerated, permitted to exist only under the terms of the earlier White Covenant at gunpoint.

The system creaked and tottered. There were no checks and balances now, and corruption was as much of a problem as it had ever been. A Confederation Senate oversaw both the legislative and executive processes of government, with numerous directorates handling individual areas of interest—lawmaking, the military, the economy, and others. The president of the Senate was largely a figurehead, elected by the Senate body once every ten years.

The current president of the Confederation Senate, now towering above the crowds filling the eudaimonium's Grand Concourse, was a former representative of the European Union named Dolph Schneider.

" . . . for it is in times like these, times of crisis, that History herself steps forward and presents us with the man or the woman of the hour, the person who can and will confront the crisis and unite the people in their struggle against . . ."

Koenig listened with only half an ear, more aware of the inflection and meter of the speech than of the words themselves. He cared nothing for politics, and dismissed most political speeches as hand waving designed to justify decisions already made. But the outward *form* of democracy, of political debate and accountability, had to be preserved.

". . . and it gives me *great* pleasure, *great* satisfaction, to introduce Rear Admiral Alexander Koenig, the Man Who Saved Earth!"

The disk beneath Koenig's boots winked on, and the immense figure of the president hovering above the Concourse was replaced by his own.

Koenig had been briefed shortly after his arrival at the event. He came smartly to attention and said nothing. A shadowy figure hovering in the surrounding crowd nearby detached itself and walked toward him, stepping onto the disk and entering the holographic field.

Admiral of the Fleet John C. Carruthers was the senior naval officer of the Confederation Joint Chiefs of Staff, and the highest-ranking military man within the Senate Military Directorate . . . meaning the highest-ranking without being a senator.

"Admiral Koenig," Carruthers said, facing him directly, "for service above and beyond the call of duty in the defense of Earth, it is my pleasure to bestow upon you this, the Star of Earth." An aide at his side offered Carruthers a box. Reaching inside, he removed the decoration, a gold medal hanging from a deep-blue ribbon agleam with stars. He placed the ribbon over Koenig's head.

Koenig executed a crisp salute. "Thank you, Fleet Admiral."

Carruthers returned the salute. "Thank *you*, Admiral, from a grateful planet, a grateful Confederation." And he shook Koenig's hand.

Somehow, Koenig kept a straight face. *Bullshit*, he thought.

As Carruthers stepped back, Koenig looked out over the audience. They'd told him several million people would be watching from various parts of the Palisades Eudaimonium, and with as many as two billion watching from around Earth and near-Earth space. The ceremony would be rebroadcast across the entire Confederation once courier ships could carry it across the light years.

"This medal," he said, tapping the device lightly, "rightfully belongs to the men and women of Carrier Battlegroup *America*, not me. . . ."

And the light beneath his feet winked out.

His image, however, remained huge within the cavernous Concourse, continuing to speak, to gesture.

". . . and I am especially grateful to President Schneider and the august assembly of the Confederation Senate, whose support . . ."

Platitudes. Empty words. *Damn* them!

"Well done, Admiral," Quintanilla said, stepping up to his side. A burst of wild cheering rose from the concourse floor, thousands of voices yelling, many chanting his name. "Your public adores you!"

"It adores my electronic puppet," Koenig said, bitter.

"Now, I told you we'd have a PA step in for your speech. Military men rarely have the stomach for good speech making. Or the time, come to that."

"I meant it." He tapped the medal again. "This belongs to my people. They saved the planet. They earned it."

Quintanilla shrugged. "Do what you want with it, Admiral. It's just a trinket. But the public needs heroes, people whom it can look up to, whom it can admire. And you, like it or not, are that man."

"Bullshit," Koenig said.

The cheering continued from the floor below.

It was going to be a long damned party.

Chapter Three

21 December 2404

Palisades Eudaimonium
New York State, Earth
1804 hours, EST

Lieutenant Trevor Gray cheered and applauded with the rest of the crowd, but he wasn't applauding the body of the speech. No, the Old Man had slipped out just one line at the very beginning, something about the medal belonging to the *America* battlegroup, before the faintest of flickers ran through the holographic image hovering overhead, and it began sounding like some empty-headed acceptance speech at the Virtual Reality Entertainment Awards night. "I'd like to thank the Senate . . . I'd like to thank the president of the Senate . . ."

Nah, *that* wasn't the Old Man. Not his style at all. Every man and woman in the Fleet knew Admiral Koenig had exactly zero time and zero tolerance for glad-handing or for sycophantic public relations. That was an electronic agent up there, a personal assistant programmed to look and sound like Koenig reciting the holy party line.

The image continued speaking, but Gray had already tuned it out. He reached for another appetizer, a Ukrainian tidbit consisting of a sausage covered in chocolate.

"Trevor? . . ."

Something jumped and twisted inside him. Dropping the sausage, he turned.

Angela. . . .

"You!"

She was wearing a conservative evening dress for this crowd, a flowing white something aglow with light that changed colors as she moved.

"Hello, Trevor. It's been a long time."

He nodded, numb. In the background, Admiral Koenig's image rambled on about duty and honor.

"What are you doing here?"

She gave him a thin smile. "I *live* here, remember? Or in Haworth, anyway. Just ten, twelve kilometers north of here. I think just about everybody in New New York came down to see the Yule ceremony tonight. Are you . . . are you stationed on Earth now?"

He shook his head, a curt, sharp negative. "I'm a fighter pilot assigned to the Star Carrier *America*. They brought me down for the flyby earlier."

"Were *you* flying one of those things?"

"I was flying an SG–92 Starhawk, yeah."

"They told me you were joining the service. I didn't know you were a *pilot*."

Yeah, you didn't ask what had happened to me, did you? he thought. The last time he'd seen her had been just before he'd been forced into military service in order to pay her hospital bill. He'd tried to look her up on several occasions after, while he'd still been in a training squadron at Oceana, but his e-calls had always been blocked.

"Are you still with Frank?"

"Fred."

"Whatever."

"I'm part of an extended family up in Haworth, yes."

"Are you happy?"

"Yes."

"Then that's okay, then." *Damn*, this felt awkward.

"How about you?"

"Me what?"

"Are you happy?"

He wondered how to reply. His life turned upside down, the woman he'd loved horribly changed and taken from him.

He was forced to live and work with people who laughed at his old life and called him "Prim" and "squattie" and "mon-ogie," forced to leave the place that had been home since his birth. . . . Was he happy?

"Sure, I'm happy. A laugh a minute, that's my life."

She looked at him uncertainly, as if trying to decide if he was being sarcastic or bitter. He looked down at the palms of his hands, where slender gold, silver, and copper threads were woven in an uneven mesh imbedded in the skin, exactly like her implants. He'd had to get his when they inducted him into the Confederation Navy; all personnel had to have them in order to control everything from meal dispensers to the locks on their personal quarters to the cockpit instrumentation in an SG–92.

But Angela had gotten hers as a part of the treatment after her stroke, class-three implants within the sulci of her brain. They'd also regrown sections of her organic nervous system. And it had changed her, changed her attitude, her feelings toward him.

Of course, he still loved her, though she'd lost all affection for him.

"So," he said, wondering what to talk about. "You just happened to be here? You weren't looking for me?"

"No, Trev. I was just . . . here. Small world, huh?"

A little too small. Gray found himself wishing he were back on the *America*. Life on board ship was *so* much simpler.

But then, she *had* been pinging him. His PA confirmed that it had been her electronic signal seeking him out of the crowd. Maybe she was still interested in him after all.

"I've got to go," he said sharply. He turned and walked away, leaving her standing there by the food table.

High Guard Destroyer Qianfang Fangyu
Saturn Space, Sol System
1325 hours, TFT

"What the holy fuck is *that*?"

Jordan Reeves floated in the main control room of the

High Guard destroyer, staring into the holographic display showing the long-range scan of the intruder.

Captain Liu Jintao glanced at the liaison officer with distaste, and then passed his hand across the display controls, increasing the magnification factor by another ten.

"I would say," Liu replied in his slow and halting English, "that it is a problem."

The target was some 20 million kilometers out from Saturn—and at just about the same distance from Titan at this point in the giant moon's orbit. That actually placed the intruder well within the outskirts of Saturn's far-flung system of moons, within the retrograde Norse group, in fact.

And that made the intruder of *supreme* interest to the High Guard.

Within the display, the intruder appeared as a gleaming point of light, attended by a flickering sidebar of data giving mass and diameter, velocity and heading. The ship—it had just dropped out of the space-twisting bubble of Alcubierre Drive so it *had* to be a ship—was huge, two kilometers across and massing tens of billions of tons. At optical wavelengths, the object appeared . . . odd, a flattened sphere with a shifting surface that defied analysis.

"It's highly reflective," Liu said.

"It's *black*."

"Because it is reflecting the black of surrounding space. This data suggests that it is almost perfectly reflective . . . like a mirror, or a pool of liquid mercury."

"So who are they, and what are they doing in the Norse group?"

The Norse group was the outer cloud of Saturnian moons, some dozens of bodies circling the planet retrograde and at high inclination. Phoebe, at 216 kilometers, was the biggest of these; the rest, named for figures from Norse mythology, were rubble, little more than drifting mountains. Ymir was just 18 kilometers wide.

"Is he trying to rendezvous with any of those rocks?" Reeves asked.

"Not yet," Liu replied. "The nearest to the intruder's position is S/2004 S 12 . . . at just over one hundred thousand kilometers. And the intruder is traveling prograde."

The Norse group moons were retrograde, circling Saturn east to west. The intruder was currently flying against the flow, as it were, meaning it was not attempting to match course and velocity with any of those hurtling mountains.

Yet.

Over two and a half centuries before, the Second Sino-Western War had been fought both on Earth and in space. Toward the very end of the conflict, a Chinese ship, the *Xiang Yang Hong*, had used nuclear warheads to nudge three two-kilometer asteroids into trajectories that would have landed them in the Atlantic Ocean, one right after the other; the resultant tidal waves would have devastated both the eastern seaboard of the United States and much of the European Union, as well as much of Africa and South America. Had the attempt succeeded, there was little doubt but that the Chinese Hegemony would have emerged, not merely victorious, but as the single most powerful nation on the planet.

Beijing had claimed that Sun Xueju, the *Xiang Yang Hong*'s captain, had gone rogue, that he'd been operating independently of Beijing's orders when he'd attempted what amounted to a global terror attack. The attempt had come uncomfortably close to success; a U.S.-European task force had destroyed the *Xiang Yang Hong* and two of the incoming asteroids . . . but the last, dubbed "Wormwood" by the media, had slammed into the sea between West Africa and Brazil, and half a billion people had died.

The Chinese Hegemony had been shamed by Sun's act, and had been paying for that event ever since, blocked from joining the Earth Confederation, savaged by trade and commerce laws imposed by foreign governments, regarded as second-class representatives of Humankind . . .

. . . not to mention being forced, Liu thought bitterly, to accept foreign political observers on board Hegemony military vessels.

The Earth Confederation had started off three centuries before as little more than a loose trade alliance, but immediately after the Second Chinese War it had become the planet's *de facto* government. Under the Confederation's guidance, the High Guard—originally an automated deep-space system designed to track asteroids that might one day pose a threat to Earth—had been expanded into a small, multinational navy.

The High Guard was similar to the seagoing coast guards of earlier eras, but patrolled the outer solar system in search of asteroids that might threaten a populated world . . . or renegade ships like the *Xiang Yang Hong* attempting to change the orbit of an asteroid in order to create a planet killer. The High Guard paid special attention to possible sources of planet killers—the Kuiper Belt, the main asteroid belt, and the tiny, outermost moons of Jupiter and Saturn.

"We should warn SupraQuito," Reeves said.

"We sent off an alert twelve seconds after the intruder appeared on our displays," Liu told him. "The time lag at this distance is seventy-six minutes. The question is, what do *we* do about that . . . craft?" He pulled down another display, checking the ship's library. "The only vessel ever encountered even remotely similar to this one was in 2392, at 9 Ceti. The Turusch call them . . ." He hesitated at the awkward, difficult name. "Heh-rul-kah."

"An enemy?"

"A single ship wiped out a small Confederation battlefleet."

"That thing is two kilometers wide," Reeves said, shaking his head. "Too big for us. I suggest we follow it, perhaps try to get a closer look . . . but take no action."

"I fear you are right," Liu said. He was reluctant to agree with the liaison officer, but the *Qianfang Fangyu* measured just 512 meters from mushroom prow to plasma drive venturis, and massed 9,300 tons. Unlike many of the Guard's older, Marshall-class destroyers, she still had a primary ranged weapon—a spinal-mount mass driver—but that would be of little use in combat against something as massive as a H'rulka vessel 20 million kilometers away.

"Captain!" his radar officer called in *Guānhuà* over his internal link. "The intruder is accelerating rapidly!"

Liu could see that for himself, as numbers on the display

sidebar rapidly changed. The massive vessel was rapidly moving out of Saturn space.

It was moving sunward, toward the inner system.

"Helm!" Liu snapped. "Engage gravitics, five hundred gravities. Pursue the intruder!"

It would be like a mouse pursuing an ox. A *dangerous* ox. Liu wasn't exactly sure what the *Qianfang Fangyu* could do if it actually caught the intruder, but they needed to pace it.

And to see to it that Earth was warned as quickly as possible.

But his oath as a High Guard officer—and his determination to see the ancient Middle Kingdom cleansed once and for all of the shame of the Wormwood Strike—made that pursuit imperative, no matter what the outcome.

The *Qianfang Fangyu* broke free from Titan orbit, accelerating toward a sun made tiny by distance.

Palisades Eudaimonium
New York State, Earth
1925 hours, EST

Admiral Koenig looked at Carruthers with surprise. "They're doing *what*?"

"I know," Carruthers said. "But the Senate majority feels that we don't have a viable alternative."

"But we do. Operation Crown Arrow."

Carruthers gave a grim smile. "Not all of them see it that way. Especially if it turns out that these H'rulka are involved. They don't wish to leave Earth open to attack. Not again."

They were standing in a small temporary alcove within the concourse bowl. Carruthers and several of his aides, along with Rand Buchanan, Koenig's flag captain, had retreated to the relative privacy and soundproof isolation of the alcove as the party outside continued to throb into high gear. Carruthers had asked Koenig to join them there. He'd ordered a martini from the local assembler, and was sipping it in an attempt to rid himself of the bitter taste of his electronic doppelganger's speech earlier.

"But a special AI designed to negotiate with the Turusch? We've had Turusch POWs on Luna for two months now, and communicating with them is still a problem. What makes the Senate think we can pull off something like that?"

"I suppose," Carruthers said slowly, "that they see it as an alternative to extermination."

"The Sh'daar Ultimatum," Koenig said, looking at his drink, "as delivered by their Agletsch toadies, made it pretty clear what the enemy wants of us. An absolute freeze on all technological development, especially GRIN technologies . . . and a limit to our expansion to other, new systems. Too high a price."

"The Sh'daar Ultimatum was . . . what?" Carruthers said. "Thirty-seven years ago? And we've been steadily losing the war ever since it started. The Peace Faction is beginning to think that the price of admission may not be too high after all."

"The Senate," one of Carruthers' aides put in, "is afraid." Her name, Koenig could see from her id, was Diane Gregory, and she was a Navy captain. "The enemy got entirely too close to Earth last October," she continued, "and the Peace Faction feels that it is only a matter of time before they succeed in an all-out attack on Earth's technical infrastructure."

No one was sure why the mysterious Sh'daar—the presumed overlords of an interstellar empire in toward the galactic core—had insisted that Humankind give up its love affair with a steadily and rapidly increasing technology. The presumption, of course, was that there were weapons just around the technological corner that might pose a threat even to the unseen masters of the galaxy, that the Sh'daar, through their subject races, were putting a cap on the technologies of emerging species in order to preserve their place at the top of the interstellar hierarchy.

But like so very much else about the Sh'daar, that was just a guess. So far as was known, no human had ever seen a Sh'daar; some human xenosophontologists had even suggested that they were a fiction, a kind of philosophical rallying point for diverse species like the Turusch, the Agletsch, the Nungiirtok, and the H'rulka.

But that, too, was just a theory . . . and not, in Koenig's estimation, even a particularly likely one.

And not even the super-weapon idea managed to explain the Sh'daar concern with human science, specifically with genetics, robotics, information systems, and nanotechnology—the so-called GRIN technologies. GRIN had been the driving forces of human technical progress for four centuries, now, so much so that in many ways they defined human culture, technology, and economic growth. That was why it had been unthinkable, at least to the Confederation leaders of thirty-seven years ago, that Humankind surrender its fascination with those particular technologies.

It was difficult to imagine a weapon system relying on *all four* technologies that might pose a threat to godlike aliens inhabiting some remote corner of the galaxy. Nanotechnology? Absolutely. Robotics? Possibly, but not very likely. Genetics? Again, possibly . . . though what kind of biological weapon could threaten a species that itself must long ago have mastered the most intimate secrets of biology? Information, computer, and communications technologies? Certainly a necessity, at least for controlling such a hypothetical super-weapon.

But . . . why those four? Why not another "G"—gravitics? Projected singularities made possible both inertia-free acceleration and the space-bending Alcubierre Drive, which reduced a 4.3-year voyage to Alpha Centauri at the speed of light to something just less than two and a half days. Being able to make micro black holes to order might well lead to some interesting weapons systems one day.

Or how about adding an "E" for energy? Artificial black holes within a starship's quantum-tap power plant extracted seemingly unlimited amounts of raw energy from the vacuum fluctuation of the zero-point field. If it could be harnessed, that kind of energy release could almost certainly be developed somehow into a truly nasty super-weapon.

No, there was something specific about GRIN technologies that the Sh'daar didn't like, that they *feared*. But what?

Koenig had always opted for the super-weapon theory. Think-tank study groups, he knew, had been working on that angle ever since the Sh'daar Ultimatum had been delivered, but with no solid leads so far. The notion that advanced technologies a century or two hence might enable humans to snuff out a star or transform the nature of reality itself would remain sheer fantasy until some idea could be developed showing where GRIN was taking the human species. The exact nature of the innovative leaps, the inventions, the unexpected technological advances of even the next fifty years simply could not be anticipated.

There was no way, even with the most powerful virtual simulations, to predict what was going to be discovered, and when.

"So . . . tell me about this virtual diplomat," Koenig said.

"They're calling it 'Tallyrand,'" Carruthers told him. "They're supposed to be programming him now at a facility on Luna."

"Tallyrand?"

"A historical diplomat. Eighteenth- and nineteenth-century . . . France."

"They called him the 'Prince of Diplomats,'" Gregory said. "Charles Maurice de Talleyrand-Périgord is widely regarded as the most versatile and influential diplomat in Earth's history."

"You seem to be up on your history, Commander."

She grinned. "The admiral has had me over on Luna as an observer at the software labs where they're writing him. So, yeah. I downloaded a lot on the original Tallyrand, at any rate."

"I suppose they're being hopeful with that name," Carruthers said.

"They can be as hopeful as they like," Koenig said. "How do they expect this . . . this virtual diplomat to communicate with the Sh'daar?"

"It will be an advanced AI residing within a starship," Carruthers said with a shrug, "probably something like an ISVR–120 or a 124. No organic crew, just the software. The idea would be to send it into Agletsch space, out in the direction of Canopus, where we think their stellar polity is centered. And the Agletsch would pass it on to the Sh'daar."

Koenig chuckled at that. "Good luck to them, then. Considering that computer technology is part of what the Sh'daar want to restrict, I'd say that Tallyrand would be a great way *not* to impress them. Or, maybe a better way to say it . . . it would impress them, but in exactly the wrong way!"

The others laughed.

"But how can they even consider caving in to the Sh'daar?" Buchanan asked. "Hell, nanotech alone is wrapped up one way or another in just about everything we do, in medical science, in assemblers, in retrievers, in nanufactories. . . ."

"Even more so for information systems and computers," Koenig said. "We've been inextricably entangled with our computers for four centuries now. Giving up computers would be to give up being human!"

"Not entirely, sir," another of Carruthers' aides said. His id identified him as Commander Jesus Vasquez. "There are people out there today who don't rely on computer technology."

"Squatties," Gregory said, making a face. "Prims."

"Exactly. In any case, the Sh'daar seem to just want us to stop *further* technological development."

"This far and no further, eh?" Carruthers said.

Koenig shook his head. "And I would argue, Commander, that *that* means giving up an essential part of our humanity as well. We're always going to be tinkering. We find a way to make a hotter fire . . . and that in turn leads to discovering copper and tin when they ooze out of the rocks around the campfire. We play with those, find we can mix them, and we discover bronze. Meanwhile, someone builds an even hotter fire and learns how to smelt iron. Technological innovation started with knocking chips off the edge of a piece of flint, and it hasn't stopped since."

"But progress can't keep going on forever, can it?" Gregory asked. "There has to be a point where there's nothing more to be discovered. No more inventions, no more improvements to be made."

"Can't it? I wonder. Have you ever heard of the technological singularity?"

"No, sir. What's that?"

"Old idea, late twentieth century. Back then, science and technology were improving at a steadily increasing rate, at an exponentially increasing rate." Koenig moved his hand as though following a line on a graph, going up gradually, then more steeply, then straight up. "At some point, it was theorized, technological advancement would be accelerating so quickly that life, that humanity itself, would become completely unrecognizable within a very short span of time. It was called the technological singularity . . . or sometimes the Vinge Singularity."

Carruthers got the faintly glassy, distant look of someone pulling data down from the local Net. "Ah," he said. "Vernor Vinge, right?"

"That's the guy. Of course, we haven't hit the singularity *yet* . . . at least not to that extent. Someone from five hundred years ago would still be able to relate to the world we know today. Nanassemblers might seem like magic, sure, but with a little training and some minor surgery to give them the necessary implants, they'd get along in our society just fine. Life hasn't changed fundamentally, not to the extent some theorists envisioned."

"I'm beginning to think some sort of new super-weapon is going to be our only hope," Carruthers said. "But we're going to need to develop it damned fast, because if the Sh'daar Empire doesn't take us down pretty soon, I'm beginning to think the politicians will."

"So what is the current status of Crown Arrow?" Koenig asked with blunt directness.

"On hold in committee in the Military Directorate," Carruthers told him. "The vote has been delayed again, indefinitely, this time. I was told two days ago that we don't want to provoke the Sh'daar into hasty action."

"What, they don't want us to make them mad?" Koenig asked. He laughed. "I'd say they've been royally pissed at us for thirty-seven years!"

"Maybe. And maybe an empire of some billions of worlds is so big they move slowly."

"And maybe we need to buy ourselves time, which is what Crown Arrow was supposed to do in the first place!"

Operation Crown Arrow was a strategic concept originally presented by Koenig to the Senate Military Directorate ten months earlier, shortly after the previous year's twin defeats at Arcturus Station and Everdawn. The ONI had tentatively identified a major Turusch staging base at Alphekka, a star that, from Earth, was the brightest star in the constellation Corona Borealis, the "Northern Crown." Koenig's plan called for a large-scale carrier strike against the enemy base there, seventy-two light years from Earth. By taking the war deep into enemy-held space, the Sh'daar's timetable might be thrown off, and forces now being gathered for an assault against Sol and its inner colonies might be drawn off.

The Joint Chiefs of Staff had given the oplan their unqualified support, but for the past ten months, the Military Directorate had dithered, passing it through various committees and subcommittees, requesting clarifications and revisions, running it through virtual simulations to determine likely military, political, and economic outcomes, and always failing to bring it to a final vote.

Carruthers palmed a contact on the table next to them, and the assembler inside produced another drink, which seemed to rise up out of the table as though extruded from the hard black surface itself. He picked up the glass, studied it for a moment, and then downed it in a single gulp.

"I hear you, Admiral," Carruthers said after a moment. "Believe me, we all do. We have allies in the Senate who are doing their best, but . . ." He shrugged and set the glass back on the table. After a moment, it seemed to dissolve back into the tabletop from which it had been nanufactured. "We're going to have to be patient," he said, finally.

"Just so long as the Sh'daar and their allies are patient as well," Koenig said. "I do know one thing, though."

"What's that?"

"We humans are a technic species. Our technology, the pace of our technological advance, is a part of us, a part of everything we do. If we surrender our ability to make our own technological decisions to the Sh'daar . . ."

"We can't do that, damn it," Buchanan put in.

"No," Koenig agreed. "For us, that would be racial suicide. *Extinction. . . .*"

"Slow extinction if we surrender to the Sh'daar Empire," Carruthers said, "and quick extinction if we keep fighting them, and lose. It seems our species has damned few alternatives open to it."

"*Very* few," Koenig said.

Outside the light and noise of the eudaimonium, the night seemed very dark indeed.

Chapter Four

21 December 2404

High Guard Destroyer Qianfang Fangyu
Entering Earth Space, Sol System
1440 hours, TFT

The intruder had left the High Guard destroyer trailing far behind. *Qianfang Fangyu*'s top acceleration was five hundred gravities, and after seventy-five minutes, the vessel was traveling sunward at 22,500 kilometers per second, and had covered about one third of an astronomical unit, less than 4 percent of the current distance between Saturn and Earth. The intruder—the H'rulka ship, if that's what it was—had rapidly begun accelerating at an estimated ten thousand gravities, swiftly outdistancing the High Guard ship, which was lagging farther and farther behind. By now, if the H'rulka vessel had held to that incredible acceleration, it would be traveling at just under the speed of light, and would have already covered nearly six AUs.

It would now be within thirty minutes of Earth.

The *Qianfang Fangyu* had had continued broadcasting warnings at radio and at optical wavelengths throughout the past seventy-five minutes, however.

The messages should be arriving in Earth-space any moment now. . . .

Palisades Eudaimonium
New York State, Earth
1941 hours, EST

"Trevor, you can't just run away from me. We need to *talk*!"

He'd found a private alcove halfway up the stepped interior of the bowl. She'd found him, though, trailing the id broadcast by his implant.

He looked up. "About what?"

"About us? About what happened. . . ."

"I don't see where talking is going to change anything. Unless you want to come back with me?"

She shook her head.

"I didn't think so. Look . . . they explained it to me. You had a stroke, the stroke changed some of the neural pathways in your brain. You don't love me anymore. I . . . I understand that. I don't like it, but I understand."

"They said you saved my life, Trev," she told him. "By getting me to the medical center. And by agreeing to join the military, so they'd treat me. I never thanked you."

He shrugged. "Nothing to thank." In fact, he'd not realized at the time that he *had* agreed. The events of that horrible night five years ago were still blurred in his mind. He did remember the terribly icy fear, and knew he would have agreed to anything, *anything* to get treatment for Angela.

Later, Navy psytherapists had offered to clear up those memories . . . or to remove them. He'd refused on both counts.

He did find it interesting, though, that modern nanomedical science could fix a broken brain, but had very few ideas when it came to fixing a broken heart.

"I've missed you, Trev."

He didn't answer.

"Trev? Goddammit, don't be like this!"

"And how am I supposed to be, Angela?" he demanded. "We had a good life together—"

"As squatties! Grubbing about in the Manhat Ruins like . . . like animals!"

"I don't recall any complaint about it on your part at the time! So maybe life wasn't so good. We had each other. We had our life together. *I* thought we were happy." When she didn't say anything to that, he pushed ahead. "You turned it all upside down, wouldn't talk to me, wouldn't even agree to see me! One meeting, *one meeting* with a counselor . . . and all you give me is an ultimatum. No discussion. No compromise. An ultimatum. You won't live with me anymore."

"Trevor . . ."

"By that time, I was already signed up for the service. They'd already tested me, found out I would make a good pilot, scheduled me for flight training. So it wasn't like I was able to go back to the Ruins anyway."

"Trev, if we'd gone back to live in the Ruins again, we'd both be dead now. You know that, don't you? That impactor surge wiped out all of the Old City."

He kept his face impassive, but . . . gods. What she'd just said hit home like an impactor in its own right. No. No, he'd *not* thought about that.

He wondered how he'd missed that small fact. For a long time, he'd thought Angela was dead . . . before realizing that when the impactor had sent that tidal wave smashing north through the Narrows, she was already living with her new family in Haworth, beyond the wave's reach. For a time, he'd not even been sure where Haworth was; it might have been a part of Morningside Heights, all of which had been washed away.

He'd never stopped to think at the time that if things had worked out the way he'd wanted, he and Angela would have been on Manhattan when the wave struck. They *might* have survived—part of the TriBeCa Tower where they'd lived was still standing even yet—but there would have been no guarantees.

"Look, it's no good talking about what might have happened," he told her. "We're here, and we're who we are now. And to tell the truth, I don't know you anymore. You're not the girl I fell in love with any longer."

"I've grown, Trevor. And I've *healed*."

"Yeah, they cured you of me, didn't they?"

"That's not fair!"

"Well, well," another voice said, interrupting Gray's retort. "What have we here? A couple of sweet monogie pervs?"

Gray blinked and looked to his left. Collins was there, smirking at them, with Kirkpatrick looming behind her. "Go to hell, Collins," he told her. "This is private."

"That's right. *Private*. Just one partner at a time, and you mate for all eternity." She made a face. "Disgusting."

"Do I know you?" Angela asked. She would be checking Collins' military id through her own implants. "Lieutenant . . . Collins?"

"No, honey. We've not met. I've heard a lot about you, though, from your monogie lover here!"

"Damned squattie," Kirkpatrick muttered. "Thinks he's good as real Navy. . . ."

"You're obviously drunk, Kirkpatrick," Gray said mildly. "How the hell did you manage to bypass your deet?"

"None've . . . your fuckin' squattie business, squat-face," Kirkpatrick managed to say. Was it alcohol, Gray wondered, or a recreational drug? Either way, he rather hoped that the man's corder was picking this up. It meant nonjudicial punishment at the very least, a court-martial at worst . . . and that simply couldn't happen to a more wonderful guy. . . .

Collins seemed to be her usual coldly mocking and cruel self. She was too smart to get herself wasted like that. Unfortunately.

"I don't recall inviting either of you into this alcove," Gray told them. "You want to make fun of me, fine, but have the decency to leave this person out of it."

"That's great!" Kirkpatrick said. "A . . . a *monogie* talkin' 'bout *decent*!"

"Come on, Kirkpatrick," Collins said. "We know when we're not wanted!"

"Damned monogies . . ."

"How much *did* you have?" Collins asked him as she led the unsteady Kirkpatrick away.

"Friends," Gray said thoughtfully as they moved out of earshot. "Got to find myself some."

"Those were . . . friends?"

"No. They're in my squadron, but friends? No."

Learning his place within the culture in which he'd suddenly found himself, learning to *fit in*, had taken up a lot of Gray's attention and energy over these past five years.

Life in the Periphery, scrabbling for survival within the half-flooded ruins scattered around the margins of the North American Union, tended to be hard and it tended to be short. It had also been forced to adapt. Two-adult-person family units loosely allied with other two-adult units had proven to be the most successful when it came to the necessities of hunter-gatherer lifestyles. With larger communities pooling food and other scarce resources, there were always shortages—and shortages either led to brutal and usually fatal fights to determine who went without, or else everyone in the group suffered when the little that was available was shared with all. Smaller units tended to be more flexible . . . and they isolated groups exposed to the Blood Death virus or other pathogens.

For the full citizens of the Union and the larger Confederation, larger, extended families had been the norm for centuries. With nanoassemblers literally building food and other necessities from dirt and garbage, there was more than enough to go around. Children were best raised in crèche-schools where they learned to socialize with others as they received their electronic educational downloads. And the Blood Death and other diseases were, for the most part, nonexistent, or at the least well controlled by modern nanomedical science.

For the citizens of the Union, the Prims of the Periphery were old-fashioned, stubborn, ignorant, and dirty—much like the inhabitants of Appalachia who still lacked electricity or indoor plumbing back in the twentieth century. There was even a memory of that in one of the names civilized New Yorkers had for the Manhattan Ruins: "Newyorkentucky." For the inhabitants of the Periphery, full citizens of the Union were selfish, self-centered, and shallow, far too preoccupied with social fads and electronic toys, superficial at best, decadent and perverted at worst. *Spoiled*, in other words.

The divide between the two had become far wider and deeper over the past couple of centuries, to the point that there seemed to be no way of bridging the gap.

Somewhat to his surprise, Gray *did* have friends in the Dragonfires. Ben Donovan was one. And Commander Allyn wasn't a *friend*, exactly—you weren't friends with your commanding officer—but at least she seemed to be on his side. Most of that, though, he was pretty sure, had to do with his combat skills. He'd held up his end of things during the Defense of Earth, and they thought of him as a fellow Starhawk pilot, not as a Prim or as an outsider.

The problems were people like Kirkpatrick—bigoted and conceited—and Collins, who still seemed to blame him for the unpardonable sin of *surviving* two months ago when her partner, Howie Spaas, had been killed.

"I still want to talk, Trev," Angela was saying. "I don't want us to be . . . enemies."

He gave her a cold look. "The enemies are out there," he told her. "The Turusch. The Sh'daar. You're just . . . someone I used to know."

"Trevor—"

"Attention, everyone," a new voice said, booming from somewhere in the auroral radiance shifting overhead and cutting across the crowd noise and conversations of the eudaimonium. "We apologize for the interruption, but all military personnel will return to their duty stations now. Special shuttles are being deployed to the Giuliani Spaceport for those who came down the Quito Elevator."

As the message went out over the concourse speakers, another message was winking inside Gray's head: *recall*.

"Trevor? What is it?"

"I've got to get back to my ship," he told her. "Something's happening."

"Happening? What?" She looked around wildly, as guests at the party wearing military uniforms began gathering into groups and moving off.

And when she turned to look at Gray again, he was already gone.

H'rulka Warship 434
Cis-Lunar Space, Sol System
1446 hours, TFT

The H'rulka vessel decelerated hard, approaching the sources of the heaviest radio traffic in the alien star system designated as System 784,857. Ahead—though they didn't think of them as planets—were two large planetary bodies, a double planet, in fact. The smaller one was typical sub-planetary rubble, airless and cratered; the other possessed a trace of poisonous atmosphere and vast regions of liquid di-hydrogen oxide. This last was important. The H'rulka lived at an altitude within their homeworld's atmosphere where that compound was liquid, which suggested the possibility of life despite near-vacuum conditions and the deadly presence of free oxygen.

Thousands of points of radiant energy clustered around the double worldlet marked hives of the creatures—bases, cities, and industrial facilities, some in orbit around the planet, some deep within its atmosphere . . . or, though it was hard to imagine such a thing, on the surface itself.

And ships. So many ships . . . all as tiny and as insubstantial as the worlds among which they traveled.

This, then, was the star system to which the fragmented intruder probe had traveled. It was impossible to tell, of course, precisely where the probe fragment had gone in this teeming sea of energy and space-borne craft. The heavy concentration of energy-radiating points on and near the sub-planet directly ahead, however, the one with the poisonous atmosphere and liquid surface, appeared to be the heart of this system's activity.

Ordered Ascent called up Warship 434's encounter records, and swiftly found a match there with some of the alien ship energy patterns ahead. The H'rulka had drifted into this species just once before, some ten-twelfths of a *gnyii*, one rotation of the homeworld about its sun, ago. Evidently, they called themselves *humanity*, a burst of low-frequency sound without meaning. The Sh'daar masters called them *Nah-voh-grah-nu-greh Trafhyedrefschladreh*, a complex collection of sonic phonemes that meant something like "20,415-carbon-oxygen-water." Humanity was very nearly the twelve to the fourth intelligent species encountered so far by the Masters that was carbon-based, breathed oxygen, and used liquid dihydrogen oxide as a solvent and transport medium.

Repulsive vermin. No floater sac, no feeder nets or filter sieves, no manipulators—unless the two jointed appendages sprouting from near the top of the creature were used for that purpose. Only two tiny photoreceptors, instead of broad photoreceptor patches of integument. Surface crawlers. Poison breathers. The images in the H'rulka records had been made of creatures captured in that one encounter, but none of the specimens had survived long enough for their captors to learn how or what they metabolized, how they got around, how they reproduced, or how they managed to *viiidyig* without having a colony component designed for it.

And somehow the disgusting creatures had managed to build starships and enter the Great Void. Ordered Ascent never ceased to be amazed at the inventiveness of the natural order.

"Some of the vermin ships have taken notice of us," High Drifting reported. "They are accelerating away from the larger of the two sub-planets ahead. We will soon be under attack."

Ordered Ascent considered this. They'd pursued the probe they'd detected in System 783,451 in order to determine where it had come from. When the fleeing probe had divided into four independent sections, the H'rulka ship had split as well.

It was imperative that Warship 434 return to an Imperial base and report. The vermin occupying Star System 784,857 were not as technologically advanced as the H'rulka, obviously, but they *were* close enough in terms of ship and weapons technology to be of concern. The Sh'daar needed to be informed.

"Set navigational coordinates for System 644,998," Ordered Ascent directed. It hesitated, then added, "and prepare for Divergence."

This last was an uncomfortable order to give, and more uncomfortable to obey. The H'rulka, long ago in their pretechnological Eden, had evolved as herd-dwellers, drifting in vast islands in the skies of their homeworld. Just as they felt claustrophobic when they were enclosed, they felt a terrifying isolation when separate colonies were cut off from one another.

But the H'rulka of Warship 434 were well trained and disciplined. Across the cavernous interior of the control area, each of twelve massive gas bags drifted outward toward a wall, where a section of the curved surface flowed and ran suddenly like liquid dihydrogen oxide, then dilated open. Ordered Ascent moved through the nearest of these openings, entering a far smaller, more claustrophobic space forming around it.

"Weapons ready for combat," Swift Pouncer reported.

"Warship 434 ready for Divergence," Wide Net, the navigation officer, added.

"Accelerate now. . . ."

And the H'rulka ship began twisting space.

VFA–44 Dragonfire Squadron
Giuliani Spaceport
New York State, Earth
2018 hours, EST

Trevor Gray jumped out of the pubtran and onto the spaceport's tarmac. The Starhawks of VFA–44 were lined up ahead beneath the field lighting, sleek and mirrored jet-black, each, at the moment, a rounded ovoid of light-drinking nanosurface perhaps seven meters long and three tall and wide. As the squadron pilots approached, the central section of ten of the ships yawned open to receive them.

"Where the hell are Collins and Kirkpatrick?" Commander Allyn demanded as she stepped off the 'tran.

The other pilots, already starting to jog toward their waiting spacecraft, pulled up short. "They were with Prim at the party," Lieutenant Walsh said, using Gray's hated squadron handle.

"Gray?"

"I don't know, sir," Gray replied. "I did see them earlier, but . . ." He ended with a shrug.

"Shit." She looked around, as if searching for another transport from the eudaimonium. "They'll just have to make it when they make it, then. Let's strap 'em on, ladies!"

Gray reached his waiting Starhawk, grabbed the upper lip of the opening, which shaped and hardened itself to his grasp, and dove into the black interior feetfirst. His skinsuit was already reshaping itself for flight ops; his helmet was waiting for him inside.

He wondered if he should tell Allyn what he'd seen at the party. Kirkpatrick had definitely gotten into something he shouldn't have, and had been flying-impaired. There was no way he was going to be able to operate a fighter; though if Collins could get his deet engaged, he had a chance. Missing an emergency recall, though, was serious.

He found himself grinning as he pulled the helmet over his head and let it seal itself to the unfolding collar of his skinsuit.

His palms came down on the fighter's control contact plates, one to his left, one to the right. At a thought, the body of the fighter faded to invisibility, and he could see the tarmac, the other fighters, the sky-glow of the eudaimonium a few kilometers to the south as clearly as if he'd been standing out in the open. Another thought switched on the fighter's power plant and engaged the diamagnetic outer hull fields. The opening flowed shut like water, sealing him in. The Starhawk's hull began growing longer and thinner.

Starhawks and other military fighters utilized what was known in the trade as VEG, variable external geometry. The various elemental components of the hull—carbon, iron, iridium, and dozens of others—were arranged within a nanotechnic engineering matrix that allowed them to reshape themselves within the ship's informational morphic field. Standard flight configuration was a needle-slim shard twenty meters long, with a swelling amidships large enough to accommodate—just barely—the pilot and the primary ship systems: power, drives, life support, and weapons. As he brought the ship to flight-ready status, it lifted itself above the tarmac in a silent hover, almost as though straining against the gravitational bonds tethering it to the planet.

"Dragon Three, ready for boost," Donovan's voice reported.

"Seven, flight ready," Lieutenant Walsh said.

The others began chiming in, one after another. "Dragon Nine, ready to lift," Gray said, as around him the other fighters drifted up from the ground, levitating a few meters into the night sky. Only two, Dragonfires Five and Eleven, remained lifeless on the tarmac.

Perhaps, Gray thought, he *should* say something to the skipper. But one societal quirk of the Navy was identical to one found in the squatters living in the Manhat Ruins. You didn't carry tales about others, even if you hated them. Being marked as an informer, a *tattler*, could be as socially crippling as being a Prim.

So long as withholding the information didn't compromise the squadron or a mission, he would keep what he knew about Kirkpatrick to himself.

"Situational update is coming on-line," Allyn told them.

Gray saw the data coming through . . . a ship of alien design, almost certainly one belonging to a Sh'daar subject race, was approaching cis-lunar space. He looked at the stats and gave a low whistle. The thing was *huge*.

"VFA–44," a voice came in over the com link, "this is New York Met ATC. You are cleared for emergency launch, vector one-zero-eight plus four-one degrees at ten gravities, over."

"New York Met ATC," Allyn replied. "We copy clear for emergency launch, vector one-zero-eight plus four-one degrees at ten gravities. Thank you."

"Roger and Godspeed, VFA–44."

"Stand by to boost, close formation," Allyn said. "Nav on auto."

Together, the ten fighters swung their needle prows up to a forty-one-degree angle off the tarmac, then swung to face the southern horizon. Gray could see the string of faint stars marking the SupraQuito strand up in synchorbit almost directly ahead.

"Ten gravities, in four," Allyn continued, ". . . three . . . two . . . one . . . *boost*!"

As one, the ten fighters hurtled skyward at one thousand meters per second per second. Gray had a brief, blurred impression of the massed lights of the eudaimonium falling away below and behind as the fighters shrieked through fast-thinning atmosphere. He thought of Angela . . . and decided it was good knowing she was alive.

He wondered if he would ever see her again . . . wondered if he *wanted* to.

The Starhawks had been in their atmospheric configuration for their flight in over the ocean earlier that evening, their manta-wings stretched wide to assist with banks, turns, and lift. There was no need for such finesse on the way up, however. To reach space they required only raw, savage power and high Gs. The needle configuration gave the greatest streamlining and, as the fighters climbed above the forty-thousand-meter line, they were able to feed more and more power to the flickering singularities off their bows, increasing their accelerations to just over five hundred Gs, increasing their velocities by half a million meters per second per second.

As they rose above the tenuous, uppermost wisps of Earth's atmosphere and the stars became colder, harder, and more brilliant, flight control transferred from New York Metropolitan to SupraQuito. At the halfway point, eighteen thousand kilometers out and just two minutes later, they switched their singularities around to aft and began slowing.

"So why are we going back to the barn, Skipper?" Lieutenant Terrance Jacosta asked. "This download says the enemy is just half a million kilometers out!"

"Because we're flying just a little light on snakes right now, numb-nuts," Allyn replied. "Get your head out of party mode and get with the program!"

"Oh, yeah. Right."

They'd not needed missile or impactor round load-outs for a fly-by above a friendly city, so the only weapons capability the squadron had at the moment were their StellarDyne Blue Lightning PBP–2 particle beam projectors, since those weapons pulled charged particles directly from the zero-point field. The weapons of choice for long-range work, however, were VG–10 Krait smart missiles. Starhawks generally carried a warload of thirty-two Kraits, or snakes, plus fifty thousand rounds apiece for their kinetic-kill Gatling cannons.

Gray looked at the schematic of the intruder. Sending a squadron up against *that* thing with nothing but beam weapons would be suicide the easy way. At least with Kraits, usually carried in load-outs with variable-yield warheads of five to fifteen kilotons, you could stand off at long range and pound the bastard until something gave. With the PBP, you had to be close, and you had to be surgically precise. With something *that* big, you might get better results giving the alien the finger.

In close formation, then, the ten fighters neared the SupraQuito dock facility. Gray could see *America* in her berth, connected to the main base structure by a transit tube and a web-work of mooring lines. Still slowing, now, to a few tens of meters per second, they passed the carrier and the dock beneath their keels—though concepts such as *up* and *down*, of course, had no meaning in microgravity. Clearing the structure by seven hundred meters, they continued decelerating, balancing their drive singularities to bring them to a dead halt relative to the *America*, just half a kilometer off her stern.

"VFA–44," a voice said, "you are cleared for trap in Landing Bay Two."

"Dragon One," Allyn's voice replied. "Copy. Okay, people. Switch to AI approach. Land by reverse numbers."

Cutting their drives and flipping end-for-end, they opened aft venturis and fired their plasma-maneuvering thrusters, using jets of super-heated water as reaction mass. Unlike uniform gravitational acceleration, the thrusters had a kick.

Gray was plastered against the embrace of his seat at three Gs as he began gaining speed once more, this time directly toward the aft end of the *America*.

In normal space operations, they would be using their gravitic drives and coming in from much farther out, at much higher speeds. Trapping on board a carrier snugged up to the dock was child's play by comparison, or it would have been if a missed cue or a lapse in concentration hadn't risked punching through the gossamer strands and struts of the synchorbital base.

The hab modules on board the carrier were turning, providing spin gravity for the crew. Each approach had to be precisely on the money; Dragonfire Twelve—Lieutenant Jacosta—made the first approach, accelerating slightly as he slid into the deep shadow beneath the carrier's belly, then at the last moment fired his lateral thrusters to give him a side vector of seven meters per second, matching the movement of the landing bay as it swung in ahead and from the right. Dragonfire Eleven—Kirkpatrick—was missing from the formation. Tucker was next, in Dragon Ten.

The landing bay was rotating at 2.11 turns per minute, so every twenty-eight seconds, the opening swung around once more and another incoming fighter was there to meet it.

And now it was Gray's turn. Traveling at one hundred meters per second, he passed into the shadow beneath the carrier, watching the massive blisters, domes, and sponsons housing the ship's quantum taps and drive projectors smoothly passing seemingly just above his head. It took almost ten seconds for him to traverse the length of *America*'s spine. His AI used his thrusters to adjust his speed with superhuman precision, dropping into the sweet-spot moving pocket and nudging him to port for that critical side-vector of seven meters per second. For an instant, the gaping maw of the moving docking bay appeared to freeze motionless as the fighter swept in across the line of deck acquisition lights. At the last moment, he entered the tangleweb field that slowed his forward momentum sharply, bringing him to a halt.

Magnetic grapples clamped hold of his ship and rapidly

moved it forward, clearing the docking bay for the next incoming fighter, just under thirty seconds behind him. As the fighter dropped through a liquid-nano seal and into the pressurized bay immediately beneath the flight deck, he thought-opened the Starhawk's side and pulled off his helmet with a heartfelt sigh of relief.

He was home, and where he belonged . . . even if for only a few minutes.

Chapter Five

21 December 2404

High-G Orbital Shuttle Burt Rutan
Approaching SupraQuito Fleet Base
Earth Synchorbit, Sol System
1532 hours, TFT

Captain Randolph Buchanan and several of his aides had gone down the Quito space elevator that afternoon to reach the eudaimonium. Normally, he would have taken the captain's gig down to Giuliani, but an engineering downgrudge report had taken his gig off of flight-ready status, and he'd relied on civilian transport instead.

That had left him at something of a disadvantage when the fleet recall had come through. He could have gone back to the ship with Admiral Koenig, but there'd not been time to find him or the admiral's barge in the chaos down there.

Instead, the *Burt Rutan* had been summarily commandeered by no less a luminary than Admiral of the Fleet John C. Carruthers, and Buchanan and several other high-ranking officers and aides had climbed aboard a mobile passenger module at the eudaimonium docking area for the short flight north to the spaceport.

The *Rutan* was a cargo transport, designed to boost heavy loads up to synchorbit for the ongoing construction of the bases and facilities tethered high above Quito, and she was not designed with passenger comfort in mind. The passenger module slipped into the big shuttle's cargo deck and locked home. It was claustrophobic on board, with few amenities, but with a boost of five hundred gravities, it would take less time to reach synchorbit than it had for the flight from the eudaimonium to Giuliani.

Buchanan leaned back in the embrace of the hab seat as the vast, light-dusted blackness of Earth's night side, aglow with cities, dropped away aft. He was linked through his implant to Commander Sam Jones, *America*'s executive officer. Admiral Koenig was riding the link from the Admiral's barge, which was trailing by a hundred kilometers, following the *Rutan* in to the docking facility. Koenig was listening in, but not interfering. Captain Barry Wizewski, *America*'s brand-new CAG, was also on board the civilian shuttle, linked in with the communications net connecting the *Rutan* with the carrier's CIC.

"Damn it, Sam, I want full readiness for space five minutes after I step onto the quarterdeck," Buchanan growled.

"We're working on it, sir," Jones replied, "but things are kind of chaotic on board right now. We have *civilians* on board . . ."

He spoke the word with evident distaste. In fact, there would be several hundred civilian contractors on the ship, part of the small army of inspection teams and drive magicians who came aboard each time the carrier entered its berth.

"They can come along with us, Number One. We won't be going far."

"We also have about a thousand ship's personnel coming in from liberty. A lot of them won't make it for an hour or two."

"Then we'll boost without them," Buchanan said. He glanced at the comm icon representing Koenig. "What's the status on the fighter wings?"

"VFA–44 is coming on board now, sir. We're ten for twelve there. VFA–31 is on deep patrol but has been recalled. They should get the recall order in another two hours. VFA–49 is on Ready Five. The others are scrambling. We went to GQ about seven minutes ago."

America carried six fighter and fighter-attack squadrons in all.

"Whiz?" Buchanan said, addressing *America*'s CAG. "I'd like to get the Peaks out there, too. What do you think?"

"I'm giving the orders now, Captain."

VQ–7, the Sneaky Peaks, was *America*'s reconnaissance squadron, flying under the flamboyant Commander James Henry Peak. Flying CP–240 Shadowstars, they would have the best chance of getting close to the intruder spacecraft without being noticed.

"How long before the Dragonfires are rearmed and set for launch?"

"Twenty minutes, sir."

Buchanan nodded. Twenty minutes was damned fast. The ready crews would be busting ass to turn those fighters around.

"Do you have anything to add, Admiral?" he asked.

"I suggest that we get *all* squadrons spaceborne ASAP, and keep them out there," Koenig said from his barge. "Priority to the fighters, of course, but get the EW and SAR squadrons off the carrier as quickly as you can. *America* will be a target, especially while she's in dock."

"Aye, aye, sir." That made sense. If *America* was crippled or destroyed while still in dock, at least her fighters would be spaceborne and on an attack vector.

"Number One," Buchanan continued, "get my ship out of dock if you have to cut the lines with a pocket knife and haul her out on your shoulder." He glanced at the *Rutan*'s bulkhead display. The shuttle was approaching the carrier now, approaching over the curve of her shield cap. He could see a fighter coming in from astern, heading for a trap on the hangar deck. The *Rutan* wouldn't be going in that way. They would dock in zero-G, the quarterdeck docking bay, just forward of the rotating hab modules. "We're about five minutes from docking, so stop gabbing with me and get on it!"

"Aye, aye, Captain."

When it came to wielding a star carrier, three men, in a sense, shared the command responsibilities. Buchanan himself commanded the *America*. Captain Wizewski, as CAG, was responsible for the 102 spacecraft of CVW–14, the Carrier Air Wing, currently deployed aboard. And Admiral Koenig was in overall command of *America*'s Carrier Battlegroup, CBG–18, which included not only the carrier herself, but the nine other ships currently attached to the CBG. His orders, and his strategic and tactical thinking, had to take in all ten vessels *and* the deployment of *America*'s fighters.

He was grateful that Koenig hadn't interfered as he'd given orders to Jones. Too many group COs did that . . . and it undercut a captain's authority on his own bridge. Koenig, he knew, was probably champing at the bit to get the *America* under way more than was Buchanan, but he'd spoken only when directly asked if he had any recommendations.

The admiral was one of the good ones, the sort of CO for whom the entire CBG would go to hell and back. He checked the update on the intruder. It was accelerating now . . . possibly maneuvering to head out-system, though it was too soon to tell. Taking on *that* puppy would be akin to a stroll in hell, yeah.

Impatiently, Buchanan remained still and silent as the *Rutan* maneuvered toward the quarterdeck docking bay. The bulkheads of the *Rutan*'s passenger hab were projecting an all-around view of the exterior now, creating the illusion that they had gone translucent. Directly to port, the underside of the carrier's shield cap rose like an immense, gray-black cliff; to starboard, the vessel's hab modules continued their steady and stately rotation, making one complete swing around *America*'s central spine 2.11 times each minute, or once in twenty-eight seconds.

Ahead, a rectangular hatchway had opened in the side of the carrier's spine, illuminated by bright white lights set into the deck. From this angle, the quarterdeck accessway connecting the ship with the base docking facility seemed to drop in from directly overhead and slightly aft of the open bay.

And then the *Rutan*, on AI pilot, glided silently through the opening and into the Star Carrier *America*.

H'rulka Warship 434
Cis-Lunar Space, Sol System
1534 hours, TFT

"We are not going to strike the vermin?" Swift Pouncer asked over the ship's internal communications network. Speaking only in radio, without the added color and modifying overtones of its sonic speech, the words were empty of all emotion.

But Ordered Ascent knew what the others must be feeling.

"We have the technological advantage," Ordered Ascent replied, knowing that all of the other All of Us were listening closely. "But that advantage is not great enough to allow us to fight an entire star system. Too many of us would fall into the Abyss. It is far more important that the Masters know of these aliens, and that they have been sending probes through System 783,451, than it is for us to destroy their ships. The destruction will happen later, be sure of that."

"A number of vermin ships are closing with us," High Drifting reported. "We estimate that they will launch weapons within fifteen *vu*."

"The vermin defend their nest," Swift Pouncer added.

Ordered Ascent watched the unfolding tactical situation through its electronic feed from Warship 434's tactical mind. No fewer than fourteen enemy ships were currently with range of 434's weapons. It was tempting to destroy those fourteen before dropping into the emptiness between the stars.

The All of Us had served the Masters for some twelves of thousands of *gnyii* now, ever since the Starborn had first shown the H'rulka how to extract metals from the winds of their world, how to bend gravity to their will, and how, at last, to build ships that would take them to the treasure troves of metals and other elements in orbit beyond the homeworld's atmosphere. The H'rulka had gone from being essentially atechnic to a star-faring species themselves within the space of twelve-cubed *gnyii*, the twitch of a minor tentacle, so far as the Masters were concerned.

Ordered Ascent wondered, and not for the first time, why

the Masters insisted on suppressing technological advancement throughout the entourage of species they'd brought into the embrace of their feeder nets. The H'rulka had come so far; their combat advantage over these vermin would have been that of the windstorm to the foodfloater, had they been permitted to keep developing their technology.

No matter. The advantage was sufficient.

Ordered Ascent checked other data feeds. Ship 434 was ready to diverge, if necessary, and would be ready to enter metaspace within mere *vu*.

Any damage done to the enemy was to the good. So long as combat didn't weaken Warship 434 or threaten her mission, there was no reason not to swat the vermin before they were even close enough to engage.

"Swift Pouncer," Ordered Ascent said, "destroy those that we can reach."

"With the pleasure of gentle winds, Ordered Ascent."

And Warship 434 reached out into the darkness. . . .

TC/USNA DD Symmons
Cis-Lunar Space, Sol System
1536 hours, TFT

Captain Harry Vanderkamp, commanding the *Symmons*, watched the tactical display unfolding around him as the ship plunged toward the interloper. The alien ship was accelerating fast, pulling at least seven hundred gravities, and would slip beyond range soon.

Symmons was a member of CBG–18, a fleet destroyer 576 meters long, massing just under thirty thousand tons, and armed with a variety of weapons, including thirty-six launch tubes for VG–24 Mamba smart missiles, variable-yield ship killers ranging between twenty and forty-five kilotons apiece. The H'rulka vessel was 327,000 kilometers ahead now, out of range for most guided weapons, but still within reach of the Mambas.

The problem, though, was that *Symmons* did not yet have clearance to fire. The ship ahead had clearly been identified as H'rulka, an enemy combatant . . . but it had been twelve years since the single known encounter between them and Confederation vessels, and Vanderkamp knew he would need clearance from Fleet HQ. There might be diplomatic issues of which he was unaware, or an attempt under way to communicate with the alien.

Symmons had burned repeated laser and radio messages to Fleet Base, only a few light seconds away, but so far with no response.

His gut instinct was to fire. That H'rulka monster might be a recon probe in advance of a larger force.

The enemy ship was accelerating harder now. In seconds, it would be out of range completely. Hell, it might already be too late. . . .

"Sir!" Vanderkamp's tactical officer cried over the bridge link. "*Kaufman* has been hit!"

"Show me!"

The tactical display switched to a view from one of the other destroyer's external cameras, looking forward up the spine toward the underside of the ship's massive shield cap. The shield, backlit by a hard blue glare, was deforming, *crumpling* with shocking suddenness, as though it were collapsing into . . .

"*Milton* is hit!" A second battlegroup destroyer was folding around her own shield cap. "Target is now breaking up."

"Breaking up? Breaking up how?"

"It's just . . . just dividing sir. Twelve sections, moving apart from—"

"Incoming mass!" his exec shouted. "Singularity effect! Impact in seven . . . in six . . ."

Vanderkamp saw it, a pinpoint source of X-rays and hard gamma on the forward scanner display, a tiny, brilliant star sweeping directly toward *Symmons'* prow.

There was no time for thought or measured decision, no time for anything but immediate reaction.

"VG–24 weapon system, all tubes, *fire*!" he yelled, overriding the exec's countdown. They were under attack, and that decisively ended any need for weapons-free orders from base. "Maneuvering, hard right! Shields up full! Brace for—"

And the H'rulka weapon struck the *Symmons.*

It hit slightly off center on the destroyer's bullet-shaped forward shield cap, causing the starboard side to pucker and collapse in a fiercely radiating instant. Water stored inside the tank burst through the rupture, freezing instantly in a cloud of frozen mist that burst into space like a miniature galaxy. The port side of the cap twisted around, collapsing into the oncoming gravitic weapon effect. Vanderkamp felt a single hard, brain-numbing jolt . . . and then the five-hundred meter spine of the ship whipped around the object, orbiting it with savage velocity as the entire 29,000-ton-plus mass of the *Symmons* tried to cram itself into a fast-moving volume of twisted space half a centimeter across. Pieces of the ship flew off in all directions as the spine continued to snap around the tiny volume of warped space; the strain severed the ship's spine one hundred meters from her aft venturis, and the broken segment tumbled wildly away into darkness. Abruptly, the remaining hull shattered, the complex plastic-ceralum composite fragmenting into a cloud of sparkling shards, continuing to circle the fierce-glowing core of the weapon until it formed a broad, flattened pinwheel spiraling in toward that tiny but voracious central maw.

The disk of sparkling fragments and ice crystals collapsed inward, dwindling . . . dwindling . . . dwindling . . .

And then the *Symmons* was gone.

Seven of her Mamba missiles had cleared their launch tubes before the weapon struck.

TC/USNA CVS America
SupraQuito Fleet Base
Earth Synchorbit, Sol System
1540 hours, TFT

Last on, first off was the custom for boarding and debarking by seniority. Buchanan swam out of the *Rutan*'s cargo deck hab module and into the boarding tube, followed by other, lower-ranking officers. Rather than wait for *America*'s forward boat-deck docking bay to repressurize, it was simpler to hand-over-hand along the translucent plastic tube and emerge moments later on the carrier's quarterdeck.

By age-old tradition, a vessel's quarterdeck was her point of entry, often reserved for officers, guests, and passengers . . . though on a carrier like *America* it served as an entryway for the ship's enlisted personnel as well. The boat deck offered stowage for a number of the ship's service and utility boats, including the captain's gig—the sleek, delta-winged AC–23 Sparrow that by rights should have taken him planetside and back. The quarterdeck was directly aft.

"*America*, arriving," the voice of the AIOD called from overhead as he pulled himself headfirst into the large quarterdeck space, announcing to all personnel that the ship's commanding officer had just come on board. Following ancient seafaring tradition, Buchanan rotated in space to face a large USNA flag painted on the quarterdeck's aft bulkhead and saluted it, then turned to receive the salute of the OOD.

"Welcome aboard, Captain," Commander Benton Sinclair said, saluting. Sinclair was the ship's senior TO, her tactical officer, but was stationed at the quarterdeck for this watch as officer of the deck.

"Thank you, Commander," Buchanan replied. "You are relieved as OOD. I want you in CIC *now*."

"I am relieved of the deck. Aye, aye, Captain."

The ship's bridge, along with the adjacent combat information center, were both aft from the quarterdeck, just past the moving down-and-out deck scoops leading to the elevators connecting with the various rotating hab modules. Both the bridge and the CIC were housed inside a heavily armored, fin-shaped sponson abaft of the hab module access, and were in zero gravity.

"Captain on the bridge!" the exec announced as Buchanan swam in through the hatchway. Using the handholds anchored to the deck, he pulled himself to the doughnut, the captain's station overlooking the various bridge stations around the deck's perimeter, and swung himself in. The station embraced him, drawing him in, making critical electronic contacts.

He sensed the ship around him. In a way, he became the

ship, over a kilometer long, humming with power, with communication, with life. He sensed the admiral's barge slipping into its boarding sheath forward, sensed the gossamer structure of the base docking facility alongside and ahead.

And he sensed the battle unfolding just half a million kilometers away. God in heaven, how had they gotten so *close*?

Long-range battlespace scans showed four Confederation vessels . . . no, five, now, *five* ships destroyed, three of them members of CBG–18. The enemy ship was accelerating now at seven hundred gravities . . . and, as he watched, it appeared to be breaking up.

"Tactical," Buchanan said. He felt Commander Sinclair slipping into his console and linking in. "Is it . . . is the enemy ship destroyed?"

"Negative, Captain," Sinclair replied a moment later. "It appears to have separated into twelve distinct sections. Courses are diverging . . . and accelerating."

Missile trails pursued several of the alien ship sections. It appeared that *Symmons* had managed to get off a partial volley before slamming into the alien's gravitic weaponry.

"CBG–18, arriving," the AI of the deck announced.

Good, Koenig was aboard. Buchanan allowed *America*'s status updates to wash through his awareness. Her quantum tap generators were coming on-line, power levels rising. The last of VFA–44's Starhawks were on board and on the hangar deck being rearmed. Dockyard tugs were already taking up their positions along *America*'s hull, ready to push her clear of the facility. Weapons coming on-line. . . .

"Seal off docking tubes," he ordered. "Prepare to get under way."

"Docking tubes sealed off, Captain." That was the voice of Master Chief Carter, the boatswain of the deck, in charge of the gangways and boarding tubes connecting the ship with the dock. A number of ship's personnel were still inside the main tube, or at the debarkation bay at the dock, as the tube began retracting. The last men and women to make it on board were scrambling for their stations.

"Ship's power on-line, at eighty percent," the engineering AI reported.

"Very well. Cast off umbilicals."

Connectors for power, water, and raw materials separated from *America*'s hull receptors, reeling back into the dock.

"Dockyard umbilicals clear, Captain," Carter reported.

By this time, it was obvious that the H'rulka ship was intent on fleeing solar space, that *America* and the synch-orbital naval base were not in immediate danger. Buchanan did not understand the alien's tactical reasoning; the bastard could have approached the base closely enough to utterly destroy the base and perhaps a hundred warships docked there. That they had not done so suggested other mission imperatives—a strategic withdrawal, perhaps, to get reconnaissance data back home, but it ran counter to Buchanan's own instincts.

It suggested a certain conservative approach to their tactical thinking, which might be useful.

"The ship is ready in all respects for space, Captain," Commander Jones reported.

"Very well. Cast off all mooring lines."

"Mooring lines retracting, Captain," Carter reported.

"Ship clear and free to maneuver," the helm officer added.

"Take us out, Helm. Best safe vector."

"Aye, aye, sir. Tugs engaged. Stand by for lateral acceleration."

"Attention, all hands," the voice of the ship's AI called over both link and audio comms. "Brace for real acceleration."

Buchanan felt a slight bump through the embrace of the doughnut as the tugs nudged *America* sideways and away from the dock. For several seconds, he felt weight, a distinct feeling of down in *that* direction, to his right. For the sake of clear communications, the navy took care to distinguish acceleration—meaning *gravitational* acceleration—from *real* acceleration, which was imposed by maneuvering thrusters or dockyard tugs. The former might involve accelerations of hundreds of gravities, but were free-fall and therefore unfelt. The tugs were shoving *America*'s ponderous mass clear of the docking facility with an acceleration of only a couple of meters per second per second, but that translated as two-tenths of a gravity, and a perceived weight, for Buchanan, of nearly eighteen kilograms—disorienting, and potentially dangerous for members of the ship's crew who still weren't strapped in. Out in the rotating hab modules, where spin gravity created the illusion of a constant half G, it was worse, as "down" began to shift unpleasantly back and forth with the hab modules' rotation.

He drummed his fingers restlessly on a contact plate. Best safe vector meant *slow*, and without benefit of gravitics. A mistake here could wreck a substantial portion of Fleet Base. By the time the carrier warped clear of the dock, the enemy ship—no, *ships*, he corrected himself—would be long gone.

He'd half expected Koenig to reverse the orders to take *America* out of dock. If the enemy left the solar system, there was no need to continue. On the other hand, Koenig might be preparing for a further enemy incursion . . . or for a sudden change in course by the fleeing H'rulka vessels. The safe bet was to get all warships clear and maneuvering freely and to keep them there until it was certain the enemy threat had passed.

There'd been no additional orders from the Admiral in CIC, and so Buchanan had continued to follow the last set of orders he'd received. *Take her out.*

On the tactical display, some of the missiles fired by the *Symmons* an instant before her immolation were slowly closing on one of the H'rulka ship sections. . . .

H'rulka Warship 434
Sol System
1544 hours, TFT

With divergence, the situation had become considerably more desperate.

Ordered Ascent drifted in the center of a claustrophobically enclosed space less than three times the diameter of its own gas bag, with scarcely enough room for its own manipulators and feeder nets to drift without scraping the compartment's interior walls. Images projected by the ship across the ship-pod's interior surfaces created the comforting illusion of vast, panoramic vistas of cloud canyons, vertical cloudwalls, and atmospheric abysses, but the touch of a tentacle against the invisible solid wall shattered the comforting sense of openness, and could bring on the sharp madness of claustrophobia.

Each of the other vessels—434 had retained its number, but the others, upon divergence, had received new identifiers—was accelerating now on a slightly different heading, somewhat more vulnerable now to enemy weapons, and certainly more dangerous for the crew emotionally.

The tactic essentially reproduced a natural response among H'rulka colonies that had evolved half a million *gnyii* among the cloudscapes of the homeworld. Certain pack hunters that had shared those skies with the All of Us preyed on adult colonies by attaching themselves to underbodies and slicing at them with razor-edged whip-tentacle limbs evolved to surgically sharp efficiency for the task. H'rulka survived by jettisoning their immense gas bags as the predators approached, allowing themselves to plummet into the Abyss; each colony-group separated naturally into twelve sub-colonies—*divergence*.

Each sub-colony unfolded a new, much smaller gas bag, heating hydrogen through furiously pumping metabolic bellows to arrest the fall before the group dropped into the lethal temperatures and pressures of the Abyssal Deep, a descent of only a couple of thousand kilometers, and often less. In essence, the adult colony had reverted to a juvenile form, and much of the original colony's intelligence and memory were lost. H'rulka civilization, in fact, had begun perhaps 12^5 *gnyii* ago with the collection of communal records maintained as a kind of living, constantly recited encyclopedia broadcast endlessly over certain radio frequencies. Those records were a direct response to the effects of the predators on the cloud communities at large, and had led, ultimately, to the discoveries of science, of polylogue mathematics, and, eventually, technology.

But divergence was still exceptionally traumatic for All of Us colonies, and some of the terror associated with the breakup and the precipitous fall continued to haunt them even when the divergence was strictly technological, a means of ensuring that one, at least, of the H'rulka colonies would make it back to base.

Enemy weapons were pursuing several of the retreating pods. None were in close proximity to Warship 434, but Rapid Cloud in 440 and Swift Pouncer in 442 both were being closely pursued by what appeared to be intelligent, self-steering missiles. The devices were primitive technologically, compared with All of Us singularity projectors, but would possess nuclear warheads that might seriously damage even an intact H'rulka warship.

Only a few *vu* more, and they would be able to slip into the safety of bent space.

A trio of dazzlingly white flashes ignited close alongside Swift Pouncer, and another just behind Rapid Cloud. Ordered Ascent felt the electromagnetic pulse, felt the telemetry warning of systems failure . . .

But then critical velocity was reached, and the retreating colony-pods began dropping into bent space.

Chapter Six

21 December 2404

CIC, TC/USNA CVS America
Earth Synchorbit, Sol System
1532 hours, TFT

Admiral Koenig sat in his workstation in *America*'s Combat Information Center, the large, circular compartment that served as the command nerve center for the entire carrier battlegroup. The surrounding bulkheads were currently set to show the view from the carrier's external optical sensors, the input from dozens of cameras merged by computer into a seamless whole that edited out the sheer cliff of the shield cap forward, and the kilometer-long length of the spine aft. At the moment, they showed the docking facility receding slowly to port, and the much vaster sweep of the entire SupraQuito base beyond, partially blocking the slender, brilliant crescent forward that was Earth.

Dozens of other ships filled the sky. Half of CBG–18 had been docked at the base, the other half on patrol as far out as the orbit of Luna. Koenig had given orders for all of the battlegroup's ships to get clear of the port as quickly as possible, and to deploy in the general direction of the intruder.

The precaution, it seemed, had been needless. The intruder was now accelerating rapidly out-system, pursued by a number of Confederation vessels. Moments before, it had lashed out at seven of the closest vessels and destroyed them, including the destroyers *Kaufman* and *Symmons*, and the frigate *Milton*, all members of CBG–18. *Symmons* had gotten off a spread of Mambas, however, and those were slowly closing on the enemy, which had just, unaccountably, divided into twelve smaller vessels.

The enemy was now about one light minute distant, and moving so quickly—close to sixty thousand kilometers per second—that it was likely that, by now, those ships had already either gone into metaspace or been struck by *Symmons*' salvo.

The intruder's behavior was puzzling, to say the least. H'rulka military technology was, at a guess, a century or two ahead of Earth-human mil-tech. At the Battle of 9 Ceti twelve years ago, a single H'rulka warship had wiped out a small battlefleet of fourteen Confederation vessels, including the light Star Carrier *Illustrious*. Their primary ship weapon appeared to be a means of creating small gravitational singularities, artificial black holes launched at high velocity and with unerring precision, something that was completely beyond current human technology. Their drive systems were better, too; their huge ships could accelerate faster than any human warship, as fast or faster than many human missiles, and their equivalent of Alcubierre Drive allowed them to drop out of metaspace much deeper within a target star system than could human vessels.

With those advantages, why had the intruder gotten as close to Earth as Earth's moon, less than two light seconds away . . . and then turned tail and run? The obvious answer—that they'd decided to return valuable data to their home base or fleet rather than risk a general engagement—was only a small part of the story. They *could* have wiped the Confederation fleet out of the sky, wrecked Earth's space elevators, and left the planet almost completely helpless.

And that was just *one ship*.

Or, arguably, twelve. Koenig wasn't yet sure what to make of that twelve-in-one surprise trick.

The tugs were drawing back from *America*'s flank. In another minute, the ship scene outside began to swing counter-clockwise as the carrier pivoted . . . and then the dockyard slid past and fell away astern. *America* was under way at last.

"Admiral?" Captain Wizewski called over the CIC net. "Permission to begin launching fighters."

Koenig checked the readout on squadron flight status. The last of VQ–7's Shadowstars had dropped from their hab module launch bay moments before *America* had been nudged clear of the dock. And VFA–49 was on Ready Five, ready for launch in five minutes.

"Let's hold that, CAG," Koenig decided. "Give the Peaks some space to run their metrics. I want to know if that intruder is alone, or if there are lurkers."

"Aye, aye, sir."

Starships, even monsters like the fleeing H'rulka craft, were insignificantly tiny against the backdrop of an entire star system. Even in the Sol System, heavily traveled and scattered with bases, outposts, and comm relays, at ranges of more than a few kilometers the largest ships were essentially invisible if they weren't powered up and under way. Those H'rulka vessels were sharply visible at a range of one light minute, now, because their drive singularities were creating the three-dimensional equivalents of wakes as they plowed through empty space.

If they weren't moving, if their power plants were off and their life support was drawing battery power only, if their IR emissions were damped, if they weren't being directly painted by radar or lidar, no one would know they were there. Koenig was concerned that the chase now being played out between the orbits of Earth and Mars was a diversion, a show arranged to convince the Confederation fleet that the threat was gone, perhaps even to draw defending ships away from Earth herself.

America's reconnaissance squadron had especially sensitive instrumentation that would detect all but the most stealthy of stay-behind lurkers.

And the squadron now ready for launch off *America*'s forward rails was VF–41, the Star Tigers, a squadron still flying the older SG–55 War Eagles. They didn't have anything close to the acceleration necessary to catch the receding H'rulka ships, and their drive singularities would screw the local metric of space, making it impossible for the Sneaky Peaks to pick up powered-down lurkers.

If there wasn't an *immediate* need to get *America*'s complement of fighters off her decks, it would be better to let the recon squadron do what they did best . . . scouting ahead, looking, listening, sensing with every electronic trick at their disposal for the presence of hidden enemy craft.

"Captain Buchanan?" Koenig said.

"Yes, Admiral?"

"I want—"

A close-spaced trio of nuclear fireballs pulsed against the darkness ahead.

"Direct hit on one of the enemy ships!" Commander Sinclair called. In the next instant, a fourth fireball appeared, expanding, slowly fading from its initial glare of incandescence.

"Ten of the H'rulka craft have just gone FTL," Commander Katryn Craig, the CIC's operations officer, reported. "Two appear to have lost their drives."

Several people in the CIC cheered.

"Belay that," Koenig snapped. "We don't have them yet! CAG, put the Star Tigers over there. I want a closer look at those ships."

"Aye, aye, sir."

Both H'rulka vessels were continuing to travel out-system on divergent paths with the same velocity they'd had when their drives were cut—about sixty thousand kilometers per second.

"Commander Craig?"

"Sir."

"We need a VBSS team over there. What assets do we have in the area?"

"SBS–21 is at SupraQuito, Admiral. And the *Tarawa* is there too."

"Let's give this one to the SEALS. Patch a call through."

"Aye, sir."

"Captain Buchanan."

"Sir."

"Take us closer to those disabled ships. We're going to put some fighters in that area."

"Yes, Admiral."

America swung slowly to one side, accelerating. The cluster of habs and facilities at Synchorbit fell rapidly astern, followed a moment later by Earth's moon.

Ahead, the four nuclear fireballs from *Symmons*' barrage continued to expand and fade.

ONI Special Research Division
Crisium, Luna
1612 hours, TFT

"We are trying," Dr. Wilkerson said slowly, "to understand you."

He heard the rasping buzz of the Turusch language as the AI translated his words and put them out through the NTE robot.

From his point of view, he was hovering above the deck in one of the rooms off to the side of the main Turusch colony cavern, occupying a white sphere hanging from the ceiling. In front of him was the pair of alien Turusch brought back from Eta Boötis two months before—the two known jointly as Deepest Delver of the Fourth Hierarchy. Each looked like an immense terrestrial slug, more or less, but with the forward quarter of the body covered by a jointed carapace, and the belly covered by leaf-shaped, overlapping scales. Slender tentacles, always in whiplash motion, sprouted from seemingly random parts of the unarmored bodies.

The two, Wilkerson knew, in some way not yet fully understood by human xenosophontologists, were in fact one. They seemed to think of themselves as a single individual—as Deepest Delver. Two separate brains—and yet neuropattern scans had shown that their brains appeared to fall into synch with each other when they spoke, using a buzzing sound generated by four tympani located in recessions on either side of their armored heads.

He heard the Turusch reply in a humming buzz. On the translation window open inside Wilkerson's mind, he read three lines of dialogue.

Deepest Delver 1: "I occupy my world."

Deepest Delver 2: "You occupy your world."

Joint: "There is no understanding."

A dead end. Again. Wilkerson sighed with pent-up frustration, and not a little exhaustion. He'd been at this questioning for over three hours now.

This three-part trilogue was a defining characteristic of the Turusch. When they spoke, the speech of one overlapped the speech of its twin. The two sets of sound together generated resonating, harmonic frequencies that produced the third line, carrying a third, higher-level meaning.

Wilkerson stared through his robotic avatar for several moments. What kind of brain could think on multiple levels at once like that? It was possible, probable, even, that the Turusch in absolute terms were far more intelligent than humans; certainly they were far quicker in their thought. But they were so completely alien that humans might never be able to understand them well.

There is no understanding. . . .

"Dr. Wilkerson? *Dr. Wilkerson!*"

He blinked. A communications request light had been blinking at the periphery of his awareness for some minutes now. The voice was that of Caryl Daystrom, one of the other ONI researchers at the facility.

"Yes, Caryl," he said.

"I'm sorry to interrupt, Doctor, but there's an important message for you. Priority Alpha."

He sighed. "I'm coming out," he told her. Opening the channel to the Turusch pair, he said, "We will continue this later. There *must* be a way for us to truly understand one another."

Deepest Delver 1: "We will share speech again."

Deepest Delver 2: "I, too, desire understanding."

Joint: "Your thought is shallow."

He made a mental note to check in with the R & D lab. "Your thought is shallow" was a frequent complaint made by the Turusch to human interrogators. Used to thinking and speaking with one another on three levels simultaneously, they appeared to be frustrated in conversations with humans, who could carry on only one line of dialogue at a time. So far as they were concerned, that was the greatest impediment to full and intelligible communications.

To that end, the ONI research and development team was working on AI software that might be able to duplicate Turusch speech patterns. Take two AIs paired together, have them speak separate lines together with the resonant frequencies generating a third level of meaning . . . simple.

Except for the fact that you really needed to think like a Turusch pair to use their mode of communication, and that was something that might well forever be beyond the reach of human minds, or even of the minds of AIs programmed by humans.

He broke his connection with the Noter, as non-terrestrial environmental robots were known in the human research community, and found himself back at his workstation. The Turusch, with their hot and poisonous atmosphere, the intense ultraviolet, the steaming mist of sulfuric acid and sulfur droplets—all were gone. Caryl Daystrom was there, had come to him in person rather than calling him over the link.

"An Alpha message?" he asked her.

"A-comm, from Admiral Koenig, on the carrier *America*," she replied. "I thought it *might* be urgent."

She was being humorously sarcastic. An Alpha-flagged message was by definition urgent.

"Thank you," he told her as she turned and left. He palmed a contact on his desk, opening an avatar comm channel. The room's electronics projected the image of Admiral Koenig into the space where Caryl had stood a moment before. It appeared to be wearing Confederation naval blacks, with the gold filigree of a flag officer down the left side.

It was, of course, an avatar only, an electronic image generated by a message AI, and not live.

"Dr. Wilkerson," the image said, "I don't know if you've been looking out your window lately, but we've got visitors out here."

A data display plane opened next to the Admiral's AI-generated electronic double, showing empty, star-scattered space behind a roughly spherical, deep black object, grainy with the high magnification used to capture the image. As he watched, the object appeared to unfold itself, then split suddenly into twelve separate sections, like segments of an orange.

"We think it's H'rulka," Koenig's voice went on, "and we think it followed a recon probe we'd deployed to Arcturus for a look-see. It destroyed seven of our warships, then began boosting out-system with an obscene acceleration."

On the display, the image shifted to show one of the ship sections, evidently several moments later, to judge by the running time stamp in the lower left corner. It had started out looking like one segment of an orange, but it rapidly collapsed in upon itself, forming a flattened sphere. Three dazzlingly bright and utterly silent flashes engulfed the tiny, distant object, blotting out for several seconds everything on the display.

"We managed to stop two of the things," Koenig continued. "Whether the crews are alive or not, we don't know . . . but we're about to try to open those hulks up and see what's inside. I'd like you to shuttle out to *America* ASAP, for first contact. I've put in a request, through ONI channels."

The display pane winked out. The admiral's projected image continued to stand there, smiling.

"How many H'rulka are on board that ship, Admiral?" he asked.

"Unknown," was the reply. Koenig himself, of course, was some light seconds away, or further. The avatar AI, programmed with key aspects of Koenig's knowledge—at least what he knew about this situation at the time when the A-comm had been transmitted—was answering for him. "So far as we know, no human has ever met one. The ship, though, is huge—over twenty kilometers across for the first, single vessel. The smaller ones each were about ten kilometers across, more or less. They can apparently morph to a far greater degree than can our fighters."

"I'll be out there as quickly as I can manage it," Wilkerson said.

"Thank you, Doctor. It'll be good to see you again."

"One question?"

"Certainly. If I can answer it." The AI would be sharply limited by the narrowness of its personal database.

"Okay. Why me?"

"It occurred to me that your Turusch friends there might be able to enlighten us about the H'rulka." Koenig's image told him. "In any case, I thought you'd want in on this, Doctor. If any of them survived over there, it means a whole new alien mindset to play with!"

"Thank you."

"See you aboard soon." The image winked off.

And Wilkerson began thinking about how he could phrase a question that would get a meaningful reply from the Turusch before he left.

Black Recon One
Approaching H'rulka Ship
Sol System
2243 hours, TFT

Chief Robert Garrison lay within the close embrace of the VBSS boarding pod and counted off the remaining seconds to the target. This op, he decided, was going to be damned hairy.

But, then, that was what SEALS were for.

The original Navy SEALs had been born during the mid–twentieth century, their name an acronym of the elements within which they moved and fought: Sea, Air, and Land. In the late twenty-first century they added Space to the list, and officially became the SEALS, though a single Navy special warfare operator continued to call himself a SEAL, in the singular. Attached now to the Confederation Armed Forces, the USNA SEALS retained the elite warrior traditions, training, and sense of duty of their predecessors.

But their technological underpinnings had come a long way from submarines, rubber boats, and rebreathers. The VBT–80 boarding pod within which he and five other SEALS were closely enclosed was a gleaming black cigar twenty meters long and five wide, with an outer shell almost completely composed of programmed disassemblers. Launched from a Navy assault craft, in this case the light gunboat *Ramage*, the pod slid toward the objective at ten kilometers per second, its surface selectively absorbing or scattering any incoming radiation that might have revealed the pod's presence.

The objective loomed ahead, enormous and sheathed in as deep a light-drinking black as the VBSS pod. The alien continued to drift out-system at some 62,000 kilometers per second, ignoring all attempts to contact it. Numerous ships had matched velocities and approached it during the past tense hours; the alien had shown no response whatsoever.

The thing appeared to be dead.

"Whadaya think, Chief?" Gunner's Mate First Class Archie Lamb asked. "Is he playing possum?"

"We'll know in a minute, Arch. You all set back there?"

"Ready to kick alien ass, Chief."

"Assuming we can figure out which part of their anatomy that might be. Okay . . . ninety seconds. Final load-out check."

The naval commandos checked out one another's gear, looking for anything loose or potentially noisy. The alien, ten kilometers across, blotted out the stars of half of the sky.

VBSS stood for Visit, Board, Search, and Seizure, a military term from the late twentieth century utilized by Marine and Navy personnel faced with boarding a potentially hostile vessel at sea. The problems associated with this sort of operation had become far more complex and deadly when the venue had changed from sea to space, to an unforgiving environment where a breached hull could replace atmosphere explosively with hard vacuum, killing anyone not protected by an environmental suit. If the members of the H'rulka crew of that thing were still alive, their capture might provide an intelligence treasure trove for ONI and Confederation Intelligence.

He watched the alien vessel closely as they made the final approach. It hadn't fired on any of the other Confederation craft that had matched vectors and moved in close, but that was no guarantee for the SEALS boarding team. There might be point-defense weapons or even automated close-in defenses. Worse, the ability of this craft to remold itself into a new hull configuration after separating from the larger vessel suggested nanotechnology, and a fairly advanced understanding of the science at that. An outer hull nano-disassembler layer would make what they were about to try impossible . . . and fatal.

He checked his internal com link. Some thousands of members of the Confederation military brass and a fair percentage of the government would be literally looking through his eyes right now, and those of his men. All of those links were passive—meaning they could watch but not speak—save one. Admiral Koenig, the CO of CBG–18, could speak to him, though he'd promised not to microman-age. Garrison appreciated that. This job was tough enough without backseat piloting by gold-braid REMFs.

Koenig, in turn, was linked in with some XS-types, xe-nosophontologists working for Naval Intelligence, and he'd been told that a particularly sophisticated translation AI was live on the open Net.

Good. Garrison would take any help in that department that he could. He was keenly aware that no human—none who'd lived to tell about it, at any rate—had ever seen a H'rulka. The best guess as to their appearance, based on accounts by the Agletsch, was that they must be animated balloons or dirigibles, organic gas bags evolved to live in the atmosphere of a gas giant.

But that, he knew, was only theory. He and his men were about to learn the truth.

CIC, TC/USNA CVS America
Earth Synchorbit, Sol System
2243 hours, TFT

Admiral Koenig watched through the Navy SEALS' eyes.

This was a particularly sophisticated neural-graft hookup. Navy SpecOps personnel, the field operators, at any rate, had been given a number of special enhancements. Their nano-chelated cerebral implants allowed multiple observers to look over their shoulders, in effect, while they were engaged in a mission, and gave them useful tools for cracking computer security codes or engaging enemy software systems.

Breaking alien computer languages, though, was not a consideration on this mission. Whatever the H'rulka used for computer software would be utterly alien, completely unrelated to anything ever designed and used by humans.

But the technology allowed Koenig to ride along inside Chief Garrison's head, in effect, as though the SEALS were an NTE robot. He couldn't hear the man's thoughts, of course, unless they were deliberately sub-vocalized and captured through nanosensors grown alongside his larynx. If Koenig spoke aloud, Garrison would hear him through his audio circuitry.

Not that Koenig would intrude on the man's thoughts now.

The hull of the alien was less than one hundred meters ahead now, a vast, death-black cliff blotting out the stars as the VBSS probe slowed sharply to avoid a lethal impact. Koenig searched that cliff face for signs of damage from the three nuclear blasts that had engulfed it, but saw none. The surface appeared smooth, not pitted or worn or burned at all, with numerous ribs or folds running across it in a seemingly random pattern.

Sixty meters. A through-hull docking collar began deploying on the cigar-shaped pod's nose.

"Here we go, ladies," the voice of Chief Garrison said over Koenig's link. "Forty meters. Brace for impact."

Seconds later, the docking collar struck alien metal. The contact surface of the collar was composed of a thick layer of nanoreassemblers, molecule-sized machines that began latching on to the individual molecules of the alien metal surface, analyzing them, breaking them apart into their component atoms, and then putting them back together in an orderly and carefully calculated way.

The vacuum seals between the flight and hangar decks of a star carrier worked on the same principle. Solid metal could be reconfigured into an artificial allotrope with markedly different properties . . . in this case turning solid composite metal into a viscous liquid that maintained the atmospheric seal, but allowed the cigar-shaped probe to slide into and through the hull, rather than breaking or burning open a hole. The black liquid, looking much like molten tar, closed around the boarding capsule's hull and swallowed it, closing up behind it as it moved forward.

A radio transceiver would have been deposited on the outer surface of the hull as the pod entered, and a connecting thread of fiber-optic cable, fantastically strong but no thicker than a human hair, played out behind it. That cable would be the means by which the SEALS could stay in touch with people outside, ensuring a secure two-way audio connection and one-way visuals.

Despite this, for several long moments, all Koenig could see over his link was darkness, overlaid by the glowing schematics and windows of Garrison's in-head display. If it hadn't been for the IHD, Koenig would have assumed that the communications cable had been broken. There was very little room inside one of those boarding pods, with the men stretched out full-length inside tubes barely large enough to hold their heavily armored forms. Those tubes were not lit, and the men inside had only the sensor feeds from the pod's external optics with which to see out of their prison.

"Preliminary analyses of the hull metal suggests a sub-nano matrix," the voice of one of the other SEALS said. "They use liquid-doorway technology, same as us."

"Thick hull," Garrison's voice said, though whether he was addressing his men, Koenig, or the universe at large was impossible to say. "This damned thing is mostly solid. Sonic readings show we're almost through, though. . . ."

And then the boarding pod's nose emerged from the hull metal and into the alien craft's interior. Koenig had a blurred and confused impression of light, and it took a moment for the light to coalesce and resolve into something intelligible, if not exactly comprehensible. From Koenig's point of view, he appeared to be looking out across a dizzyingly vast gulf of sky and cloud. Gravitic readings showed that the pod had passed into an artificial gravity field of some sort, that it was emerging into a vast interior space from below and to one side. The interior walls were projecting a skyscape—an intensely deep, rich blue above, with cloud walls like the faces of multihued cliffs rising on all sides, with the illusory floor of the mammoth chamber growing darker and darker as though representing a bottomless well descending deep into the cloud layers.

The cloud-cliffs showed impossibly fine and detailed structure, the fractally complex surfaces carved by wind and movement into entire landscapes of color—reds, browns, yellows, golds, silvers—in intricate patterns of mountain and valley, ridgeline and furrow. Directly overhead, a tiny but brilliant sun gleamed white within an encircling ring of light—diffraction, Koenig guessed, through ice crystals in the upper atmosphere.

"Atmospheric readout coming through," one of the SEALS reported. Koenig saw a window open in his mind, giving a breakdown of the ship's interior atmosphere. The temperature, surprisingly, was twelve degrees Celsius, warmer, somehow, than Koenig had expected. The gas mix was mostly hydrogen—no surprise there—and helium, with methane, ammonia, water vapor, and other compounds in trace amounts. As expected, a typical gas-giant atmosphere, quite similar, in fact, to that of Saturn.

The sheer scale of the scene was so alien that Garrison didn't notice the aliens at first. When Lamb called his attention to them, however, he saw them clearly enough . . . a vast field of pale mushroom shapes in front of one of the cloud walls. It appeared to be a herd, some hundreds of individuals, adrift on alien winds. He studied them for a long moment before deciding that these, too, were a part of the background display. An illusion . . .

A shadow moved across the cloudscape.

Garrison looked up, and Koenig saw through his eyes the alien . . . if that was what it actually was. It was hard to make sense of what he was seeing—an immense island of pale and plastic-looking surfaces, a ring of growth encircling the base, like an upside-down forest of vines and branches.

And it was descending—descending *rapidly*, directly toward the SEALS. . . .

Chapter Seven

21 December 2404

Black Recon One
H'rulka Ship, Sol System
2248 hours, TFT

Chief Garrison had only a second or two to make a decision—to pull back into the alien vessel's bulkhead or push the pod forward and into the interior. The H'rulka, an enormous ivory-colored balloon, was dropping toward the point at which the boarding pod was emerging. It would take time to unship the pod's stern docking collar, too much time . . .

He gave the mental command to squeeze the pod forward and into the open.

A fringe covered tentacle as thick as a sequoia and twice as high swept past the pod, shaking it with the shock wave of its passage. The boarding pod darted forward, narrowly missed by the tentacle, which brushed across the portion of the bulkhead from which the pod had just emerged.

Garrison's first thought was that the giant alien had been trying to crush the pod, but once the SEALS were in the open, the monster took no notice of them at all. Instead, it appeared to be concerned about a patch of tarry black interrupting the cloudscape projected on the bulkhead. When the pod's docking collar had melted its way out of the ship's bulkhead, it appeared to have interfered with the cloud-display illusion, leaving a blank space perhaps twenty meters across. The alien—a mushroom-shaped gas bag fully 280 meters across at the top, with a forest of tentacles and fuzzy-looking appendages hanging from a narrow circle below—appeared agitated, and seemed to be feeling the damaged section with questing appendages.

The pod had deposited a second radio transceiver there, connected by the fiber-optic thread with the one outside. Garrison held his breath, wondering if the creature was going to scrape the transceiver away, cutting off all communications with the outside world . . . but the device was flat and slightly inset within the black wall. His telemetry coming through his IHD showed that they were still in touch with the Star Carrier *America* outside.

The pod shuddered, then started to fall.

"We're not going to be able to hold altitude, Chief," EN1 Roykowski said. "These pods aren't designed for this sort of thing."

The local gravity field, he noted, was 890 centimeters per second squared . . . about nine-tenths of a G. Good. There'd been some concern going in that they might find the aliens' artificial gravity, if they had such a thing, set to something appropriate for Jupiter—two or three Gs, say. That would have made getting around difficult.

Even in near-Earth gravity, though, the VBSS pod wouldn't serve as an aircraft. Designed to get a boarding team onto an enemy vessel, it possessed a small gravitic drive, but delicate maneuvering—hovering, for example—just wasn't possible. It could move forward with a fair acceleration, but was not designed as a lifting body, and its dorsal grav thrusters were for changing attitude, not resisting a steady .9-G pull. Archie Lamb was keeping the pod airborne at low speed, but the craft was starting to fall.

What, Garrison wondered, were the options? The pod was intended to deposit its payload of combat boarders on the interior decks of an enemy ship . . . but this thing didn't *have* internal decks other than the featureless and gently curving spherical wall of this kilometer-wide inner chamber. He studied the alien for a moment longer. Although attaching emotion or rational meaning to something that alien was problematical, to say the least, it truly appeared to be anxious about the bulkhead surface area damaged by the pod's entry, and didn't even seem to be aware of the pod itself. He thought about it. A human might be aware of it when a portion of a large flatscreen monitor a few centimeters across went dead . . . but he probably would not notice an ant crawling across the sofa he was sitting on, not unless he was looking for it.

As he watched, the black area of the inner surface lit once more, a seamless part of the surrounding vista of cloud-cliffs and sky. The alien, like some unimaginably vast medusoid jelly in Earth's seas, began rising again, rotating slowly in the clear, crystalline air.

Garrison was using the pod's optical sensors, zooming in on the alien. The surface of the thing seemed smooth from a distance, but under high magnification, much of it appeared rough, even convoluted.

In his mind, using the in-head display he was sharing with the others, he indicated a portion of the enormous being's anatomy. "*There,*" he said. "Take us *there.*"

The pod accelerated toward the H'rulka giant.

CIC, TC/USNA CVS America
Sol System
2302 hours, TFT

"This is incredible," Dr. Wilkerson said. "Absolutely amazing!"

Koenig smiled. Wilkerson had patched into Koenig's link with the SEALS on board the alien ship, and he seemed to be drunk with excitement. "Are you talking about the alien, Doctor? Or the way Chief Garrison is carrying out his mission?"

"Oh, your SEALS are obviously remarkable individuals," Wilkerson said. "But I was referring to that . . . that life form. That is a H'rulka?"

"We think it must be," Koenig told him. "It seems to fit

what the Agletsch told us about them twelve years ago. Hot-hydrogen floaters, very large . . . though I didn't expect them to be *this* large!"

"How big is it?"

Koenig glanced at the telemetry being transmitted from the SEALS. "Just over 280 meters across the top. The gas bag is two hundred meters high . . . and the tentacles hang about a hundred meters below that."

"I don't think I'll ever get over just how inventive life is. Do you know . . . there was actually a time, back before we'd made contact with other species, when we assumed that anything we met out among the stars would be more or less like us?"

"I guess the Agletsch were a bit of a shock, then."

"I guess they were."

Garrison was taking the pod directly toward the H'rulka's underbelly. The other H'rulka in the image, the huge swarm of them far off, appeared to be part of the background projection. That, Koenig reasoned, might be a clue to the aliens' psychology. The illusion of wide-open, cloud-walled spaces must be there to remind the ship's crew of home. They might well be claustrophobic if they couldn't see clouds and open sky . . . which would be a serious disadvantage for any star-faring race.

And if that drifting herd of gas bags visible in the far distance was any indication, individual H'rulka might get nervous or depressed if they couldn't see other members of their own species. There apparently was only one real H'rulka on this ship . . . or in this chamber, at any rate.

It occurred to Koenig that this ten-kilometer-long vessel might be the H'rulka equivalent of a single-seat fighter.

"Damn," Wilkerson said. "What the hell are those SEALS trying to do?"

The VBT–80 was close enough to the H'rulka now that the thing's body blotted out the entire view forward—a red-brown-yellow-black forest of feathery tentacles and things like trailing vines hanging down around the upward-drifting balloon. The pod brushed across a number of tentacles, which had the appearance of an enormous and complex tangle of tree roots, but the touch didn't seem to elicit a reaction from the titanic being. The pod was angling over now, flying level instead of up. It emerged above the twisting mass of tentacles, and seemed to be moving toward a kind of ledge or organic platform running around the creature just above the base of the gas bag.

"I think Chief Garrison has found a place to land," Koenig said.

"Base, Black One," Garrison's voice said. "Any ideas for talking with this thing?"

"Can you patch me through to him?" Wilkerson asked Koenig.

"You're on."

"Yes, actually," Wilkerson told the SEALS. "I understand you have a PRC–2020 SMRS?"

"The Prick–2020, yeah."

"Uh . . . yes. If you can get that onto the creature, we might have a chance."

"Listen," Garrison said, "we're getting a lot of background radio noise in here. Some of it seems to be coming from our big friend, the rest from the surrounding bulkheads."

"Modulated radio signals, yes. We think that is the H'rulka speaking."

"Yeah? Who's he talking to?"

"His ship."

The VBT–80 pod grounded on the ivory-white platform, a frilly, pasty white horizontal surface extending out from the swell of the gas bag by a good ten or fifteen meters, and apparently running all away around the body of the thing. The tentacle mass rose slightly above the layer of the platform from underneath, looking a little like a wall of dense jungle vegetation, but moving with a slow, writhing agitation.

"End of the line!" Garrison called. The walls of the boarding pod split wide, and six Navy SEALS spilled out onto the fleshy platform. Each man was wearing highly specialized combat armor, form hugging, with myoplas musculature that responded to his movements and amplified his strength.

Their surfaces were coated with nanoflage that absorbed and re-emitted light of appropriate wavelengths, creating . . . not invisibility, quite, but a hazy blur that rendered each man indistinct against his surroundings.

Three of them carried laser rifles, three packed man-portable plasma weapons. Garrison hauled a large backpack out of the open pod, which he dragged toward the vertical surface of the gas bag close by.

"Now I know how a fuckin' flea feels," one of the SEALS said.

Koenig was seeing the SEALS' surroundings through the eyes of Chief Garrison, and so could only see what the chief was looking at. The glimpses he got of the interior of the sphere were of spectacular vistas of cloud and sky, of an incredible beauty awesome in both its intricate detail and its scale. Unfortunately, the chief was more focused on the job at hand, and had no time for sightseeing. Setting the satchel against the gas bag wall, he opened the pack and exposed the control panel for the PRC–2020. His glove was inset with a mesh of gold and copper threads matching the implant in his palm; he brought that down on the contact pad and opened the primary channels.

"We have data flow," Wilkerson said. "Good signal. . . ."

The unit included a powerful linguistic computer coupled with a broadband receiver and spectrum analyzer. The Agletsch, according to the records, had said that the H'rulka used radio for communications both with others and with their own kind. The Turusch colony on Luna that Wilkerson had been working with had confirmed this. The H'rulka talked with one another by radio . . . and evidently communicated with their machines in the same way. The PRC–2020 would analyze the radio environment inside the H'rulka ship and transmit its findings to the XS teams outside by means of the fiber-optic relays the SEALS had embedded in the alien ship's hull.

"Shit," one of the SEALS said. "What the fuck is *that*?"

Koenig's point of view whipped around to the left. There was . . . *something* on the wall of jungle a few meters away.

Black Recon One
H'rulka Ship
Sol System
2307 hours, TFT

Garrison's eyes opened wide. What *was* that thing?

Superficially, it resembled a terrestrial octopus, but possessed only three arms. It was a bright, glossy blue in color, and something like a single round eye with a three-branched pupil was staring at Garrison from the center. Like an octopus, it had lines of suckers down each slender tentacle, but it didn't seem to be using them to hold on. It was hanging, gibbon-like, from two looping, vine-like tentacles stretched above it,

A second blue creature swung up beside the first . . . followed by a third. Those cyclopean stares were unnerving.

"Hold your fire," Garrison's voice said. "I think they're harmless. . . ."

But how did you know whether something this alien was harmless or not? Koenig noticed that several of the larger suckers close to the base of the creatures' arms were, in fact, openings ringed by bony plates, and pulsing as if in time to breathing or heartbeat. If those were mouths, they could do considerable damage . . . though probably not to SEALS armor. As he watched, one of the creatures wrapped all three arms around a tentacle the size of a man's thigh, its central body everting somehow so that the eye remained visible, staring at the humans a few meters away. Garrison had the impression that it was *feeding* on the H'rulka's tentacle.

Or . . . was he seeing something else, and simply not understanding it? For a scary moment, he wondered if the blue three-armed octopi were the real H'rulka, the huge floater simply the alien forest in which the octopi lived.

But . . . no. He'd seen the jellyfish-like floater reacting to the damage to the ship's inner hull with apparent intelligence . . . and these blue things didn't have much room in those bodies for brains. It was far more likely, he thought, that . . . just as humans were infested with skin mites, chiggers, and other parasites so small they were literally beneath the notice of their hosts, so, too, there might be entire alien ecosystems living in and on the bodies of these enormous beings, tiny by comparison . . . but in this case as large as a small dog.

"Chief!" Lamb yelled. *"Watch out!"*

The pale flesh underfoot had been trembling slightly all along, Garrison had noticed, but now it gave a convulsive jerk as a meter-wide slit opened up in the organic ground just a short distance away, and something flashed out into the open. Garrison had a blurred impression of something like an enormous segmented worm, pale yellow and brown and covered in chitinous armor. Each segment had three curved spines, like legs, spaced equidistant around the body, giving it the look of an enormous centipede with extra legs running down the back. The head was a nightmare of tentacles spreading out around a gaping mouth full of sharp, bony plates.

The thing exploded from the slit, towering above the startled SEALS for a moment, the upper end of its body swaying back and forth as though it was undecided. The thing was at least three meters long, and not all of its body had emerged as yet. Lamb raised his plasma weapon, but Garrison slapped his armored pauldron with a gloved hand. "Don't shoot!" he yelled. "No one shoot! No one *move*! I don't think—"

With blinding speed, the swaying monstrosity whipped around and slashed at one of the blue octopi nearby, its own tentacles closing around the alien parasite and dragging it off the H'rulka giant's looped tentacles. Garrison saw a ripple pass down the length of the thing's body as it swallowed . . . and then it rippled across the platform and out over the mass of tentacles curling up just beyond. As the barbed and hooked tail of the thing emerged and vanished over the side, Garrison estimated that the creature was something more than ten meters long.

The three-armed octopi, the ones that hadn't been eaten, had vanished. The severed tips of two slender blue tentacles remained curled about a larger tentacle, showing where the one had been hanging when it was devoured.

"What the hell was *that*?" Lamb demanded. "Pest control?"

"Something like it," Garrison said. He was remembering an old, humorous poem he'd heard somewhere.

Big bugs have little bugs upon their backs to bite 'em.

And little bugs have lesser bugs, and so ad infinitum.

Curious, he thoughtclicked for a quick search of *America*'s e-Net. The lines had been written by Jonathan Swift.

"Admiral Koenig?" he said.

"Go ahead, Black One."

"Is everything flowing okay?"

"We have solid telemetry," Dr. Wilkerson's voice said. "What we're going to be able to do with it, I don't know."

"Permission to exfiltrate, sir," Garrison said. "It just occurred to me that this critter might have other symbiotic defenses in place . . . something with a taste for Navy SEALS."

"Use your best judgment, son," Koenig's voice came back. "If the prick is secure and nothing's trying to eat it, I'd say there's no reason for you to stay there."

"Aye, aye, sir." Garrison turned to the other SEALS. "Gentlemen, I think it's time for us to get the hell out of Dodge."

H'rulka Warship 442
Sol System
2330 hours, TFT

Swift Pouncer wondered if it was going mad. It was beginning to hear voices.

The nuclear detonations had left Ship 442 adrift, with no hope of rescue. The faster-than-light drive was out, communications were out, weapons were out, even the ability to see outside was gone, and the rest of the H'rulka ship-group would by now have dropped into metaspace and be out of reach. Swift Pouncer felt trapped within the too-small confines of its ship. Some 12^3 *vu* ago, a tiny portion of the ship's interior display had failed, and Swift Pouncer had nearly discorporated with shock and fear. The thought that the reassuring vista of cloud, sky, and other All of Us adrift in the distance might fail, that Swift Pouncer would find itself in a close, tight, and utterly lightless and claustrophobic enclosure was terrifying.

So when it began hearing voices—or, at least, unintelligible noises—on its primary communications wavelengths, it could only imagine that the awareness of its confinement had begun causing it to hallucinate.

There was *always* a hiss and buzz of radio static in the background, of course. The homeworld, as did most real planets, continually broadcast radio noise which was . . . simply *there*, without meaning, and part of Swift Pouncer's illusory surroundings were recordings of that comforting crackling hiss.

This, however, was different: sharply voiced and modulated spikes of radio noise that had the pacing and timbre of speech . . . but which it couldn't understand.

Swift Pouncer considered the possibility that the vermin outside were attempting to communicate at radio wavelengths, but discarded the thought. Warship 442's communications suite was disabled, the external antennae burned away by nuclear explosions, and radio waves simply could not penetrate the ship's hull structure otherwise.

Odd. If someone outside of Warship 442 had been trying to communicate, the message would have come through the ship's comm suite, broadcast to Swift Pouncer's organic receivers from the hull of the ship. These . . . noises, however, appeared to be originating from Swift Pouncer's body itself, almost as though one of the colony components of the H'rulka floater were trying to speak to the others.

Which, of course, was flatly impossible. Only a few of the individual colony organisms that made up an adult H'rulka were self-aware, and those possessed very little individual sentience and had no way of communicating with the rest of the body on anything more than a purely biochemical level. Intelligence, for the H'rulka, was an emergent phenomenon arising from the cooperation of several different brains.

Madness! . . . Confinement is destroying my sanity!. . .

And then the seemingly random noises dropped several distinct and comprehensible words into Swift Pouncer's awareness, and, somehow, that was worse.

Speech . . .

Understand . . .

You . . .

But the words were in a language Swift Pouncer recognized. They weren't the speech of fellow H'rulka, and with no audio component, the words were flat and completely without an emotional dimension, but they sounded like a computer-generated language that Swift Pouncer thought of as something that might be translated as "Agletsch Trade Pidgin."

The Agletsch—the Masters called them *Nu-Grah-Grah-Es Trafhyedrefschladreh*, or "1,449-carbon-oxygen-water"—were a vermin species widespread among the stars, best known, perhaps, for their far-reaching information trade network. The All of Us had first met the Agletsch shortly after the Starborn had given them the freedom of space and other worlds. The aliens had presented All of Us with a simplified and artificial language that allowed communications with the Masters, with the Agletsch themselves, and with other species with which the Agletsch were in contact.

Where H'rulka radio speech carried information in the timing of distinct pulses, however, the Masters/Agletsch language conveyed meaning through modulation of pitch, tone, and frequency. These strange signals appeared to be like that, like *audio* speech, in other words. They carried meaning in the same way as the spoken words that normally served as a kind of modifying, secondary language superimposed over the usual radio speech.

It was utterly strange, and wildly confusing.

It was, in fact, *alien*, and must be some form of communications being transmitted from the aliens outside. Just how they'd managed to accomplish that, through the solid walls of Warship 442, was beside the point just now.

Swift Pouncer wondered if it wanted to communicate with such beings . . . with *vermin*.

If it wanted to avoid death, or the far worse prospect of claustrophobically induced madness, however, there were few alternatives.

Swift Pouncer sent out a questing call.

CIC, TC/USNA CVS America
Sol System
2342 hours, TFT

"Admiral?" his aide's voice said. "Admiral . . . I'm sorry to interrupt . . ."

Koenig pulled back from the IHD connection, blinking. "What the hell?"

"Admiral," Lieutenant Commander Nahan Cleary said. "I'm sorry, but you have an Alpha-priority message. It's Mr. Quintanilla, sir."

Koenig was very close to telling Cleary exactly what Quintanilla could do . . . but bit off the sharp retort. Biting off Cleary's head would be less than constructive, and an Alpha-priority message was important. Koenig didn't think that even an officious little prig like Quintanilla would ever dare misuse the urgency protocols.

In any case, his usefulness in the operation was at an end. Garrison and his SEALS had reboarded the pod, given it a nudge from its drives, and sent it toppling over the edge of the fleshy parapet. It fell rapidly through the dense hydrogen atmosphere toward the lower curve of the alien ship's internal spherical chamber.

Turning the open comm channel with the pod over to Wilkerson, he nodded.

"Okay. I'll take it here."

A new channel opened, and Quintanilla's image appeared hovering in the CIC immediately in front of Koenig's workstation. It was, Koenig knew, an avatar. The disabled alien spacecraft had been traveling at just over sixty thousand kilometers per second for eight hours and twenty minutes; in that time it had covered twelve astronomical units, a distance so vast that any signal from Earth transmitted to the

America would take ninety-six minutes to reach her, with another hour and a half plus required for the reply.

It had been all *America* and her escorts could do to catch up with the fast-moving hulk. A number of tugs were now being deployed to begin decelerating the crippled alien vessel, but Koenig didn't want to give that order until some sort of communications had been established with the craft's crew.

"Good evening, Admiral Koenig," the image said. "Special orders are being uploaded to your personal e-comm net."

"I see. And why the avatar escort?"

"I anticipate a certain amount of . . . resistance to these orders. I am here to answer questions you may have, and to ensure your full compliance."

Koenig's jaw clenched with a momentary, sharp anger. "I am not in the habit of disobeying lawful orders, Mr. Quintanilla."

"Oh, these orders are lawful. There is no doubt of that."

"I assume this is something from the Senate Military Directorate?"

"Higher than that, Admiral. This comes from the desk of Confederation Senate President Regis DuPont himself."

Koenig mindclicked on his personal security code, and the orders opened within a window in his mind.

OFFICE OF THE PRESIDENT OF THE SENATE OF THE EARTH CONFEDERATION

GENEVA, EUROPEAN FEDERATION

2250 HR 21 DEC 2404

FROM: PRESIDENT REGIS DUPONT

TO: ADMIRAL ALEXANDER KOENIG, COMMANDER CBG–18

VIA: COMM UPLINK 7894, GENEVA

SECLAS: BLUE DIADEM/PRIORITY ALPHA/URGENT

SUBJ: RETURN ORDER

ATTACHMENT 1: 847823 SPECIAL ASSIGNMENT/SENATE SPECIAL ORDER

1. YOU ARE REQUIRED AND DIRECTED TO DECELERATE TC/USNA CVS *AMERICA* AND RETURN AT BEST SPEED TO THE SUPRAQUITO NAVAL DOCK FACILITY, SYNCHORBIT, EARTH.

2. UPON YOUR RETURN TO SUPRAQUITO, YOU WILL BE IMMEDIATELY RELIEVED OF YOUR COMMAND PENDING ASSIGNMENT TO NEW DUTIES, AS SET FORTH IN ATTACHMENT 1. CAPTAIN RANDOLPH BUCHANAN WILL ASSUME COMMAND DUTIES OF CBG–18.

3. YOU WILL TAKE AVAILABLE MILITARY TRANSPORT TO BERN SPACEPORT, WHERE TRANSPORTATION HAS BEEN ARRANGED FOR THE TRIP TO THE CONFEDERATION GOVERNMENT COMPLEX.

4. YOUR PRESENCE AT GENEVA WILL BE PHYSICAL, YOUR UNIFORM FULL DRESS.

5. YOUR PRESENCE IS REQUIRED FOR A CLOSED SESSION OF THE SENATE POLITICAL AFFAIRS COMMISSION, SCHEDULED FOR 1400 TFT, 22 DEC 2304.

[SIGNED]

HENRI GERARD

BY ORDER OF

Regis DuPont, Senate President

"ConGov?" Koenig said with distaste. "What the hell do they want with me?"

"Well, I can't tell you very much," Quintanilla's image told him. "But a full Senate hearing has been called, and they very much wish to speak with you."

A hearing! Was he being accused of mishandling the

battlegroup? If so, the message would have come from the Senate Military Directorate, not from the Senate as a whole.

He opened the attachment, which consisted of short several lines indicating that once relieved of command, he would be under the direct orders of the Senate, pending the outcome of the meeting in Geneva.

There was so much Koenig wanted to say in that instant . . . and no point in berating a low-level message AI. He cut off the transmission without comment, and wondered what the hell they were trying to do to him back home.

Chapter Eight

22 December 2404

Ad Astra Confederation Government Complex
Geneva, European Union
0920 hours, TFT

Admiral Koenig stepped out of the private grav capsule he'd boarded at Bern Spaceport, walked through the airlock, and emerged in front of the shuttle access onto the Place d'Lumiere in front of the ConGov pyramid. He squinted against the glare. It was like stepping into bright daylight once more, after his journey by tube beneath Lake Geneva, though in fact the Confederation capitol was covered over by the span of a twenty-kilometer geodesic dome. The climate beneath the dome was comfortably warm despite the bitter winter conditions outside, with an interior space high enough to allow clouds to form within. The morning sunlight was green-tinted as it filtered down through the plaspanels high overhead.

The Ad Astra Confederation Government Complex itself was an immense green glass pyramid located almost exactly at the center of the city, just behind the broad Plaza of Light and its labyrinth of parkland, fountains, and statuary. Popolopoulis's *Ascent of Man* gleamed golden in the light at the center of the plaza, towering nearly forty-five meters above the citizens on the marble paths at its feet . . . taller than the corroded green body of the crumbling Statue of Liberty back in the United States of North America.

"Pretty impressive, isn't it?" Quintanilla said at Koenig's side. "The sight always chokes me up."

"It's . . . impressive," Koenig replied.

It was, Koenig thought as his handlers led him toward the government building, quite a show.

And it *was* just a show, a grand advertisement on an epic scale, designed to awe and, perhaps, to intimidate. The Terran Confederation liked to advertise itself as the representative government for Earth and all of her colonies, but that was a fiction, pure and simple. Both the Chinese Hegemony and the Islamic Theocracy had off-world colonies of their own, but so far had not applied for admission. The South Indian States had a non-voting membership, and the Union of Central Africa was being courted by both the Confederation and by the Islamics, but was as yet undecided.

One of the deepest fears within the Confederation's halls of government was the dread that the Islamics or the Chinese might make a separate peace with the Sh'daar Empire, might even join the Sh'daar as allies against the Confederation. Of course, that seemed quite unlikely now in light of the enemy's attack on Everdawn, the Chinese colony of Yong Yuan Dan, a year ago, or with the more recent conquest of the independent Islamic outpost at Eta Boötis IV. The Sh'daar and their Turusch, H'rulka, Nungiirtok, and other servant races appeared unwilling—or, perhaps, unable—to distinguish among the myriad political flavors of Humankind.

As they walked through the Ad Astra statue's shadow, Koenig studied his companions with some distaste. There were five of them: John Quintanilla and four others who had the look of armed security bodyguards. He thought of them as his handlers; they'd met him at the Bern Spaceport, separated him rather rudely from his aides, and shepherded him closely past customs and into the underground vault where a private grav shuttle had been waiting. They seemed especially anxious to keep him from talking with anyone. At the spaceport, Koenig had seen Captain Diane Gregory, Admiral Carruthers' aide, standing in a crowd behind a security barrier. They'd made eye contact and she'd mouthed something at him—he *thought* it was "We need to talk." But he couldn't pick up her id, and his own electronic senses were being blocked, at the moment. He wondered if his handlers were responsible for that as well, or if he'd simply been in one of the spaceport security areas at the time.

He had the feeling that there were certain electronic constraints on him, on his freedom to communicate.

As they crossed the plaza, Koenig decided to test those limits. He assumed that it was Admiral Carruthers who wanted to talk to him, not his aide, and normal military channels should have made a connection to the JCS simplicity itself . . . but his signal was clearly being blocked. There were no signs of official electronic jamming . . . but his implant was not connecting with the local Net, and his personal AI, Karyn's avatar, could only report that there didn't appear to be a local Net with which she could connect.

Which was impossible, of course. Geneva was *not* a Periphery wasteland or primitive reserve.

"So why are you jamming me, Quintanilla?" he asked in a conversational tone.

"Ah . . . well . . ." Quintanilla looked uneasy.

"You do realize that it's illegal to jam without my awareness, don't you? Freedom of Electronic Access is a fundamental Charter Right."

"Of course, of course it is. But . . . this is an unusual situation. The Commission requested that you be, um, temporarily shielded from external influences until we can have this meeting."

Stranger and stranger.

"Am I under arrest?"

"Of *course* not, Admiral!"

"Have I been charged with something? Is this a formal inquest?"

"Absolutely not! Just . . . be patient for a little longer. Believe me, everything is fine!"

When someone representing the government said that, Koenig felt like diving for cover.

"I would appreciate knowing, then, why I am being held incommunicado."

"Admiral, there are certain . . . political realities we're

having to deal with here. Be patient, and everything will be explained."

Political realities?

The Earth Confederation—officially the Terran Confederation of States—was hanging on by its fingernails, he knew that much. The war of the past thirty-some years had put a tremendous strain on the Geneva government, principally because many of the member states didn't agree with the war. Geneva had been unable to persuade China or South India to join the Confederation, and they'd deliberately blocked the Theocracy from full membership. And, lately, there'd been rumblings within established member states. Russia was threatening to secede from the Confederation because of Arctic Ocean trade issues, and America del Sur was discussing the possibility of a public referendum on secession over religious rights. If either Russia or South America pulled out, the Confederation might well fall.

What Koenig didn't understand was what he had to do with these "political realities," as Quintanilla had called them. Koenig, like the other North American members of the Confederation military, was an officer of the USNA Navy with a joint commission with the Terran Confederation, just as the CVS *America* was a USNA vessel in Confederation service. If the Confederation government fell, Koenig, the *America*, and her crew would all find themselves back in USNA service. Their orders simply would be coming from the USNA Confederal Union capital in Columbus, District of Columbia, instead of from Geneva.

Like many in the Confederation military, Koenig had mixed feelings about the arrangement. His *first* loyalty, he felt, was to the Confederal USNA. Normally, the USNA's best interests dovetailed well with those of the TC, but that might easily change if a break-up occurred.

The thought of a Confederation civil war was not a pleasant one, especially in the face of the continued campaign against Humankind's interstellar polity.

Quintanilla and his security escort led him through the security screening at the front of ConGov pyramid, then down an elevator into the nuke-shielded lower levels that, reportedly, extended far out beneath the placid waters of Lake Geneva. High Guard headquarters were based in Geneva as well, while the Confederation Military Directorate and the headquarters of the Confederation Star Navy were located in a separate facility to the south, deep beneath the granite of Mont Blanc.

Koenig kept wondering why the Senate, instead of the Senate Military Directorate, wanted to see him.

The meeting was being held in one of the Senate conference chambers, an auditorium carved out of solid bedrock some one hundred meters below the surface of the lake. He went through four security checkpoints, including backscatter X-ray, DNA checks, and retinal scans, before he could enter the innermost sanctum. They took security *seriously* here.

A long mahogany table at the front of the auditorium was for the meeting's principal participants. Many of the auditorium seats were already occupied, however, by expensively dressed people—senators and their personal staffs.

The meeting was called to order by Senator Eunice Noyer. President DuPont was conspicuous by his absence.

Koenig didn't know anything about Noyer, and reached for her public id. His personal electronics, however, were still being blocked.

Interesting.

"Admiral Koenig?" Noyer said, standing at the head of the table. "We appreciate your coming on such short notice."

"I got here when I could," he told her. He didn't add that Quintanilla's message avatar had seemed most upset at his delay in setting course for Earth. Koenig had been determined, however, to make certain the SEALS team had emerged from the crippled H'rulka vessel and been recovered safely by the gunboat *Ramage*.

He was *not* going to abandon his people on the whim of some conclave of bureaucratic assholes back home. He'd delayed until the SEALS were back, then waited for Dr. Wilkerson and his staff to transfer to the railgun cruiser *Kinkaid*. Reportedly, Wilkerson's staff had managed to make contact with the lone H'rulka aboard that huge ship, though no real information had been exchanged yet. The fleet tugs with the CBG, though, had begun gently decelerating the H'rulka ship. It would take some weeks yet to reverse the vessel's heading and bring it back to the fleet base at Mars.

But *America* had required long hours to reverse course even at maximum combat accelerations, and she'd had to hump hard to make it back to Earth Geosynch in time.

"We're glad you made it, Admiral," Noyer told him. "We have . . . an offer to make, one which we do hope you will accept."

An offer? Not a reprimand, then. Koenig was more curious than ever.

"It must be fairly important," he said, "to require illegally sequestering me from free access."

His words caused an uncomfortable stir around the table, and many of the senators up in the auditorium seats began whispering back and forth.

"Not 'illegal,'" Noyer said. "If you'll recall, you were relieved of your command of CBG–18 and assigned *special* duties at the behest of this commission. Those special duties include certain security requirements which, I assure you, are temporary only."

Koenig wondered if any of that would hold up in a court of law. The attachment to his orders had placed him under the direct command of the Confederation Senate, but said nothing about him signing away his Right of Access . . . or any other rights, for that matter.

He decided to say nothing and see what the commission had to say.

"Naturally, Admiral, anything said inside this chamber is to be considered Ultra-class secret, and is not to be discussed with anyone else. Do you agree?"

He hesitated, then nodded. "I do, Madam Senator."

"Very well." She paused as if reading an internal display. "The truth sensors in your seat suggest no evasiveness or intent to deceive. The data will be appropriately logged."

Truth sensors? Again, ordinary citizens had to agree to be scanned for that to be legal. Military personnel by definition gave up many of their civic and public rights, but it still seemed like a highly questionable breach of legal ethics.

"Admiral Koenig, I'll get right to the point. This commission would like to discuss with you the possibility of *you* being selected as our next President of the Senate."

Koenig opened his mouth, then shut it again. He was stunned, literally unable to respond right away. President of the Confederation Senate? *Him?*

"I see the news caught you by surprise," Noyer said, grinning. "That's good, actually. There have been a *lot* of rumors circulating about the possibility, especially since the presentation at the Yule ceremony last night in New York. One reason for the heightened security is to avoid public debate on the matter . . . and to avoid a certain, ah, *poisoning* of your own attitude by that debate.

"Madam Senator . . . I'm not sure what to say. . . ."

"Tell us you'll consider it, Admiral."

"It is, in a way, quite a natural evolution," Frank Lovell said. Lovell was another senator—representing the California District of the USNA. "The Man Who Saved Earth becomes the man who *leads* Earth!"

"Is that why President DuPont isn't here?" Koenig asked.

"It was thought best that he recuse himself from these hearings," Noyer said. "But, for the record, he *is* in agreement. His tenure as Senate president ends in nine months. At that time, we would like you to take over from him."

"Madam Senator . . . I'm not a senator."

"Not yet." She nodded toward another woman at the conference table. "Senator Lloyd, of thc USNA's District of Pennsylvania, has agreed to step down. A special election will be held for her district, and with your current popularity with the public, especially in your home state, we expect that you will easily be elected. If not . . ." She shrugged. "There are other parliamentary procedures that will bring you on board. All we really need is your agreement."

A memory forcefully and unpleasantly intruded itself—the sight and sound of that towering avatar of himself delivering a speech to the crowds at the eudaimonium the night before, speaking words, speaking *platitudes* that had little to do with his own beliefs or feelings.

The Senate president was not entirely a figurehead; he or she had the deciding vote in deadlocked sessions, and could veto legislation . . . though a simple majority vote was all that was required to overturn a veto. But the office was more window dressing than anything else, a human face for the public's awareness of the putative world government. As president, he would have little more say in government policy decisions or affairs than he'd had with his electronic double's speech last night.

"I am afraid, Madam Senator," he said slowly, "that accepting would mean a considerable conflict of interest on my part."

Noyer scowled at him, Lovell looked away, obviously uncomfortable, and other senators at the table began again whispering among themselves. "What conflict of interest?" Noyer demanded.

"Operation Crown Arrow, of course," he said. "I do *not* agree with the policies of the Peace Faction, Madam Senator, and am convinced that Crown Arrow is the only viable alternative to complete capitulation." He smiled at her. "I assume you, and most of the others at this table, *are* with the Peace Faction?"

"Some of us are," she admitted. "But I'll ask you to remember that the Confederation Senate does not utilize political parties, but seeks instead to find consensus among different possible solutions to political problems. I resent your assumption, Admiral, that this is a *factional* debate."

Even, Koenig thought, if it was indeed just that.

Party politics—or the ancient division of political groups into factions with labels such as "conservative" or "liberal" were widely seen as corrupt—the *old* way of doing things, and one that had not, after all, worked very well. The two-party system of the old United States had collapsed centuries ago in scandal and corruption. Multi-party governments—some with as many as a hundred different competing political parties seeking to achieve short-lived balances and alliances—had failed when they became so complex that they could get nothing done. Political parties, as such, had been abandoned in favor of a general governing body seeking consensus.

But humans being humans, labels were still necessary. The Peace Faction, though not an established party, nonetheless was a convenient label for those members of the Senate determined to find common ground with the Sh'daar and bring an end to the three-and-a-half-decade-long Human-Sh'daar interstellar war.

"As a military man," Noyer said, "I imagine you would have an objection to finding a peaceful settlement. The political realities of the situation, however, are quite different . . . as I'm sure you will learn in time."

"As a military man," Koenig replied, "I probably want peace more than you do . . . more, certainly, than you can possibly imagine. It is military personnel, I will point out, who suffer considerable discomfort and hardship and who all too often *die* in order to protect the civilian population at home."

"If that's true, Admiral, then you should be the first to embrace the Peace Faction's agenda. An end to war . . . a war that many of us believe cannot be won. A war that could easily end in the utter extermination of the human species."

"The price, Madam Senator, is too high."

"Too high, for the survival of Humankind? I think not!"

"The Sh'daar Ultimatum," Koenig said, "requires in effect the surrender of our technological growth to the Sh'daar or their agents. Surrendering our technological growth means the sacrifice of our economy. The entire history, the essence of our evolution and growth is the history of our technological advancement, from bone clubs and chipped-flint hand axes to starships and AIs, from fire to quantum power taps. Give up our inventiveness, Madam Senator, and we give up who we are, give up our own human nature."

She gave a tight smile. "You make persuasive speeches, Admiral. I'm surprised you are not already a member of this body. As it happens, I fear that this Operation Crown Arrow of yours is going to be voted down. The members of the select Senate Military Directorate are, as might be expected, in favor of the idea . . . but in light of yesterday's attack by the—what are they called? The H'rulka, yes—the majority of the senators in this body feel it necessary, vital, in fact, to keep the Confederation Fleet here in the Sol System, in order to protect Earth."

"Really? And how do the Senators from Astrild feel about this? Or Dhakhan? Or Inti? Or Amaterasu? Or Chiron?"

"As I said, this body builds *consensus* among—"

"There are more senators from nations on Earth," Koenig said, "than there are from all of the colony worlds put together, am I right? Each colony world, regardless of population, elects one senator to represent them here? I'd be most interested in how many of those two hundred and some extrasolar senators joined your consensus to essentially ignore the extrasolar colonies in order to defend Sol. That's the idea, isn't it, Senator? To let the Turusch and the Nungiirtok and the Gadareg pick off the extrasolar colonies one by one, until nothing is left to us but our own solar system?"

"Admiral Koenig, that is *enough*!" Noyer said, her voice rising to a shout. "It is not your place to lecture this body in this manner!"

"Let him speak, Eunice!" a lone voice cried from somewhere up in the auditorium.

"Si!" another vice added. *"Me gustaria oir!"*

Other voices joined in, coming too fast and too thick for the room's translation system to handle all of the voices in a dozen different languages.

"Order on the chamber floor!" Noyer shouted. "Order, or we will have the chamber cleared!"

The voices died down, though an undercurrent of murmured conversation continued.

"Admiral," Noyer said after a moment, "you obviously have no idea of the delicate balance involved in providing for the security of the people!"

"An excellent reason for me *not* to stand as Senate president, Madam Senator. It occurs to me that losing the colonial senators would consolidate the position of the Peace Faction by quite a large degree."

"You are out of line, sir," Senator Lloyd shouted.

"I am? I apologize. As Senator Noyer said, I don't know what I'm doing.

"I do know *this*, however, speaking as a Confederation Star Navy admiral and as a star carrier battlegroup commander: appeasement *never* works. It just makes the bastards greedy for more. If you just wait for them to come, they *will* come, and they will *keep* coming until they've ground down the fleet to nothing, and they can walk in and take whatever they want."

"Your remarks are out of order," Noyer told him.

"No, Madam Senator, they are not. Please! You need to hear this! Hold to a defense-only strategy and a larger, more technically advanced opponent will overrun you, sooner or later! The only way to avoid disaster is to take the fight to the enemy!"

"This hearing," Noyer said, "is adjourned. Thank you for coming, Admiral. I am truly sorry that our . . . *philosophies* did not better agree."

"Madam Senator!" a voice called from the audience. "Point of order!"

"What?"

"You must *move* to adjourn!"

"Very well. Move to adjourn. Do I have a second?"

"Madam Senator," Koenig said.

"You are not a member of this commission, Admiral. You cannot second."

"I have one more statement before you close."

She hesitated, as though weighing the advisability of letting Koenig say anything more. This hearing, evidently, had gone badly for Noyer, and she would be trying to salvage from it what she could.

"Very well. What is it?"

"Only this: 'Those who would give up essential liberty, to purchase a little temporary safety, deserve neither liberty nor safety.' "

"The sentiments of some military leader?"

"No, Madam Senator. A statement attributed to a member of the very first congress of the original United States: Benjamin Franklin."

"I've never heard of him."

"Then, to quote another philosopher . . . you are condemned to repeat the mistakes of the past."

"Second the move to adjourn, Senator Noyer," Lloyd said.

"Moved and seconded. This hearing is adjourned."

An hour later, Koenig sat alone at a sidewalk cafe several blocks from the ConGov pyramid, drinking coffee with Admiral Carruthers and Captain Gregory. Koenig's own aides had been sent back to Bern and the waiting admiral's barge. He would be returning to the *America* that afternoon, but he wanted to talk with Carruthers first.

"I can't talk about what happened in there," Koenig told them. "They slapped me with a secmon."

The security monitor would warn him if he violated certain programmed security rules or agreements . . . and report him if he broke them.

"They're being a bit heavy-handed with the security issues, aren't they?"

"Let's just say that what happened this morning might be construed as an embarrassment."

Carruthers laughed. "You could put it that way."

"You were there?"

"No. But friends were. Friends who weren't forced to carry a secmon. *Damn*, but that's insulting!"

Koenig shrugged. "They're trying to protect their asses. So far as I can tell, that's *the* number-one entry in any politician's job description."

"I'd hoped to talk with you before the meeting," Carruthers told him.

"I thought as much, when I saw Captain Gregory here, at the spaceport."

"Security was *very* tight," she admitted.

"Senator Andrews was very impressed with your argument."

"Andrews?"

"The honorable senator from Osiris," Gregory said. "That's 70 Ophiuchi A II."

"Osiris is concerned that they're next on the Sh'daar hit

list," Admiral Carruthers added, "and with some justification, evidently."

"Ah. Was he the one who called out?"

Carruthers smiled. "Nope. That was Senator Kristofferson, of Cerridwen. Believe me when I say, Admiral, that we have a *lot* of support in the Senate for Crown Arrow."

"You wouldn't know it from the tone in there this morning."

"A stacked deck, Admiral. Even so, a fair number of hawks were able to attend as members of the audience. The meeting was supposed to be a closed session, but some of them got wind of it ahead of time and forced the issue under the transparency initiatives."

Transparency, Koenig knew, had been a major issue in political machinations for centuries. Someone always wanted to pull off important votes without opponents to the issue being present; and those opponents were always trying to make the processes of government more candid, more open to the public.

Except, of course, when it was better the public not know. Koenig despaired of the games governments played.

Koenig felt a sharp pang at his temple. He raised his hand and rubbed the spot. "I've just received a warning that I really shouldn't be discussing this stuff, Admiral."

"I understand. They should be able to do something about that on board ship."

"I was just thinking that, sir."

"You can tell us this much," Carruthers said. "What are you supposed to do now?"

"I go back on board *America* and resume command of CBG–18," Koenig told them. "I got the idea, though, that Madam Senator Noyer was *not* happy with my performance. She may want to beach me."

"That won't happen," Carruthers told him. "The hero of the Defense of Earth, on the beach? Uh-uh. The Military Directorate has direct jurisdiction in any case, and right now they're solidly on your side. If the Peace Faction tries something behind closed doors, they'll force an open vote, and Noyer and her people can't risk that yet."

"Okay. I retain command of the battlegroup. We still can't afford a defense-only war."

"No," Carruthers said. "We can't. But with the right people on the Military Directorate oversight board, I think we can manage . . . a compromise."

"A compromise? What compromise?"

"This time I'm going to pretend *I* have a secmon. Go back to your carrier and stand by. I may have new orders for you in a couple of days."

Koenig sighed. "You're the boss, Admiral."

"When it comes to the Navy," Carruthers said, smiling, "Yes. Yes, I am." He raised his coffee cup toward Koenig. *"Salud."*

Chapter Nine

27 December 2404

Admiral's Office, TC/USNA CVS America
Earth Synchorbit, Sol System
1015 hours, TFT

It wasn't "a couple of days," in fact, but almost a full week before Koenig received his new orders. Captain Gregory delivered them in person to Koenig in his office on board the *America*.

"So," he said as she walked into the compartment. "What's the verdict? Am I on the beach?"

His office was in the outer layer of the carrier's rotating hab modules, and so enjoyed the relative comfort of a half G of spin gravity. He gestured over a control interface to grow her a chair, and she sank back into it.

"Thank you, sir. No . . . not the beach. Not this time."

Koenig's heart quickened a bit. "Crown Arrow is on, then?"

Gregory made a face. "It is . . . though you may not like what some of the politicos did to it. Here . . . you should see the orders for yourself."

She palmed a contact surface on his desk, transferring the orders. He put his own palm on a contact, and opened them in his mind.

JOINT CHIEFS OF STAFF

TERRAN CONFEDERATION MILITARY COMMAND

0930 HR 27 DEC 2404

FROM: ADMIRAL OF THE FLEET JOHN C. CARRUTHERS

TO: ADMIRAL ALEXANDER KOENIG, COMMANDER CBG–18

VIA: COMM UPLINK 7892, GENEVA

SECLAS: GREEN DIADEM/PRIORITY BRAVO

ATTACHMENT: JCS DIR75756: OPPLAN CROWN ARROW, REVISION 2.6

SUBJ: CBG DEPLOYMENT

1. YOU ARE DIRECTED TO ASSEMBLE CBG–18 AT FLEET RENDEZVOUS PERCIVAL ON OR BEFORE 5 JAN 2405, OR AS SOON AS PROVISIONING AND RESUPPLY FOR AN EXTENDED VOYAGE OF AT LEAST SEVEN MONTHS IS COMPLETE.

2. YOU WILL AWAIT FURTHER ORDERS AT FR PERCIVAL. ADDITIONAL FLOTILLAS WILL JOIN YOU AT THE RENDEZVOUS POINT.

3. THE REINFORCED BATTLEGROUP WILL BE REDESIGNATED TASK GROUP TERRA.

4. ON OR BEFORE 9 JAN 2405, TASK GROUP TERRA WILL INITIATE DEEP-SPACE OPERATIONS AGAINST ENEMY BASES AND VESSELS IN ACCORDANCE WITH THE PROVISIONS OF OPERATIONS PLAN CROWN ARROW, AS OUTLINED IN JCS DIR75756 [ATTACHED].

[SIGNED]

JOHN C. CARRUTHERS, ADMIRAL OF THE FLEET

BY ORDER OF

The Confederation Joint Chiefs of Staff

Best we could do, Alex.—J.C.

The personal note appended to the end of the orders startled Koenig. He opened the attachment, and scrolled down through the oplan.

It was not, he decided, as bad as it could have been. Koenig's original operations plan, as he'd presented it to the JCS, called for a strike force composed of at *least* 5 star carriers and their attendant battlegroups . . . which would have meant a supporting fleet of 20 to 25 cruisers and heavy cruisers; 10 of the faster and more nimble battlecruisers; 5 railgun cruisers or battleships; and at least 50 destroyers, frigates, and escorts. Add to that one Marine Starforce Unit, which would amount to another two light carriers, landing ships of various calibers, and some twelve thousand Marines, and the entire fleet would have numbered over 112 vessels.

Although that had been Koenig's suggested fleet strength, he'd known that the chances of having those ships given to him were remote in the extreme. The total—112 warships—was very roughly one quarter of the Confederation's total Navy strength, and roughly half what was normally stationed just within the Sol System. The Senate, he knew, would never allow the Sol System's defenses to be stripped to that degree.

And, in fact, that had obviously been the case. The JCS and the Military Directorate had scaled back Koenig's dreamsheet considerably. The task group would be built around just *one* carrier battlegroup: *America*'s, reinforced by some 10 additional ships. MSU–17 would join the fleet at Point Percival, adding two light carriers to the force—*Nassau* and *Vera Cruz*—plus 10 support vessels. It appeared that the task group would include no more than 35 warships altogether.

Thirty-five ships to carry the war to the enemy.

He looked up at Captain Gregory. "Why the worried face, Captain? This looks pretty good."

"Admiral Carruthers thought you would be . . . disappointed."

"Hell, the important thing is that they've given us the go-ahead! I was afraid they would insist that we sit here on our asses playing defense."

She nodded. "Admiral Carruthers said the same thing. He wasn't sure you'd see it the same way."

"Thirty ships . . . or a hundred and thirty. We're going to be wildly outnumbered no matter how many ships we pull together. I would like to have more fighters along than just *America*'s five squadrons, but we'll make do with what's available. We'll have two strike squadrons with the Marine carriers . . . and we *might* be able to bring in another naval squadron or two from Oceana. It'll make *America*'s hangar deck a bit crowded." He looked up at Gregory. "I assume you have orders to take my response back to Admiral Carruthers?"

"Yes, sir. He . . . doesn't trust the comnet channels."

Koenig frowned at that, then shook his head. "I don't blame him." It was a hell of a thing to be hiding from your own government. Koenig's service with the USNA Star Navy before he'd been asked to volunteer for confederal service had thoroughly indoctrinated him with the idea that the military was subservient to the civilian command authority. And, in theory at least, it was the same for the Confederation Navy.

But Geneva had shown a distressing tendency to micromanage the military to the point where flexibility and decisiveness—both key elements of modern war planning—were lost. The JCS had managed to win a bit of freedom of action for Task Group Terra, but that freedom could be lost at any time. If Eunice Noyer and her clique picked up some aspect of Crown Arrow's planning they didn't like . . . or if they saw a way to yank the figurative rug out from under their opponents in the Military Directorate, they were fully capable of rewriting the rules and changing everything.

The rendezvous point—Fleet Rendezvous Percival—was, he saw, at Pluto, and Koenig was willing to bet that Carruthers had chosen that spot because it was comfortably distant from senatorial oversight. Out of sight, out of mind, as the old saying had it; the obstructive elements of the government would be less likely to cause trouble if the strike force was less immediately visible than it would be in Synchorbit.

It still griped Koenig like hell to have to play games like this with the planetary government.

One entire bulkhead of Koenig's office was given over to a wallscreen of the view from cameras mounted on the outer hab module, showing, in effect, what they would have seen had that bulkhead been transparent. The steady rotation of the module created the impression that the stars were sweeping past, from deck to overhead, making a complete circuit every twenty-eight seconds. Four times each minute, the structure of the Synchorbit naval facility drifted past, and with it the hab modules of the local Confederation government facility.

The Confederation government seemed to overshadow the ships based here, always watching, always listening. They were lucky that so far the Senate had failed to assign a liaison, a political officer like Quintanilla, to stick with Koenig like a shadow, sitting in on all of his meetings.

Gregory seemed to read his thoughts. "There are times, Admiral, when a military officer *must* have the freedom to do what he thinks best. We subordinate the military to the civilian government because the alternative is to have a military dictatorship . . . but if the government does more than set policy for the military to follow . . ."

"I *know*, Captain," Koenig said, a bit more sharply than he'd intended.

"I'm sorry, Admiral. I only—"

"The less said, the better," he told her. He did not want her making what amounted to treasonous statements. Everything said in his office was overheard by various AIs, and if there ever *was* a trial for disloyalty, those recordings could be used as evidence.

He looked at her closely. She was young for a captain's rank—her id gave a birth date of 2363, making her forty-one. Thanks to anagathics or to genetic modification—possibly both—she looked considerably younger . . . not that her quite pleasant physical appearance had anything to do with the matter. The point was that with anti-aging techniques as they now stood, Diane Gregory could expect to have an active and productive military career, if she chose to, lasting at *least* another two centuries.

"Excuse me, Captain Gregory," he said. "I wasn't trying to bite your head off. I just don't want anything on record that might jeopardize your career."

She smiled. "I doubt that I'll be in the service forever, Admiral."

As human medical technology—genetics and medical nano, especially—continued to advance as they had over the past four centuries, it was possible that her career would be extended across a thousand years or more.

If the Sh'daar didn't step in and impose their restrictive views on GRIN technologies on a compliant Humankind.

And, Koenig was forced to admit, assuming the military hierarchy didn't collapse under the mass of some millions of thousand-year-old senior admirals, all of them unwilling to retire or start a new career. Death, an old saying had it, was just nature's way of clearing out the deadwood to allow new ideas room to breathe.

"Just so you have the options you choose," he told her. "The government is often in the business of narrowing a person's options, cutting back on free choice."

"Now who's being seditious, sir?"

"Not me, Captain." Koenig was already calling up a stellar display on the 3-D projector in front of his workstation. "Let's go over Crown Arrow as it now stands. Are you recording?"

"Yes, sir."

A fistful of stars, indicated by colored points of light, winked on above the projector. The field of view zoomed in on one orange-yellow star in particular, expanding until only that star and its planetary system were visible.

"Arcturus?" Gregory asked.

He nodded. "Our first stop."

"I thought the objective of Crown Arrow was Alphekka."

"Tactics, Captain. The appearance of that H'rulka vessel in the Sol System the other day means the enemy spotted our ISVR–120 probe. My guess is that they began reinforcing Arcturus as soon as they realized we were interested in it.

"Second-guessing an enemy that is *alien*, who literally doesn't think the way you do, is always a risky proposition. Still, they took Arcturus Station away from us a year ago. I don't care how alien they are, they must be giving at least some thought to the possibility that we're going to launch a counterattack . . . either at Eta Boötis, which we lost two months ago . . . or at Arcturus, which is parked right next door . . . three light years. Smart money says they're reinforcing *both* systems. If we show up at one, they can bring reinforcements in from the other."

"Three light years," Gregory said. "Two days' travel time?"

"About forty-one hours, actually, if their Alcubierre Effect has the same efficiency as ours. The Turusch, the Agletsch, and the Nungiirtok all have FTL drive technology that seems to be about as good as ours. The H'rulka—we've only encountered them twice, now. Given the accelerations they demonstrated here the other day—over ten thousand gravities!—they likely can manage much better metaspace transit times. Fortunately, they're also not very common. Just the one ship at Arcturus, picked up by our probe, and we think that was the same ship that entered the Sol System last week. We saw none at Eta Boötis.

"So . . . we hit Arcturus, a quick in-and-out raid." As he spoke, colored symbols representing the ships of a task force passed Arcturus and closed on other symbols, representing the Jovian gas giant Alchameth; its largest moon, Jasper; and the tiny attendant gleams of Arcturus Station and a number of Turusch ships.

"We stay in-system no more than eighty hours, time for an enemy ship to get from Arcturus to Eta Boötis, and for reinforcements to return. The raid should, if it goes as planned, cause the enemy to delay further strikes against Sol, and to attempt to locate our task force."

The 3-D image pulled back, showing again a cloud of local stars—Arcturus and Eta Boötis close beside each other, drawing together as the scale of the image increased. Another star appeared in the display, again orange in color, and located about 4.2 light years farther out from Earth than the others.

A green line connected Arcturus with the new star.

"Just over three days, Arcturus to Alphekka," Koenig said. "We have reason to believe that there is a major enemy staging area there. We hit that, causing as much damage as we can manage. That should bring in the enemy forces from Arcturus and from Eta Boötis, and buy Earth some additional time."

"And then, Admiral? Where after Alphekka?"

"That will depend at least in part on the enemy response. I suspect we'll have captured the attention of the Sh'daar themselves, as well as other Sh'daar allies.

"But what I *hope* is that Alphekka will be only the beginning. . . ."

Naval Aviation Training Command
USNANS Oceana, Virginia
United States, Earth
0815 hours, EST

Lieutenant Shay Ryan stood at attention in front of Captain Pollard's desk. She'd been expecting a dressing-down after the incident at Port Richmond, but hadn't expected things to get quite this serious.

"You never, I repeat, *never* get into a brawl with your brother officers," Pollard told her. "Enlisted personnel do that sort of thing with appalling regularity. Officers do *not.* What the hell were you thinking of, anyway?"

"No excuse, sir," she replied. Six years in the Navy had taught her the best, the *only* reply to this kind of question.

"No, Lieutenant. None of that 'no excuse' shit. I really want to know what made you take leave of your senses enough that you assaulted three other naval flight officers with the table in a bar."

"Well . . . it kind of seemed like the right thing to do at the time."

"You broke Lieutenant Baskin's right arm. He'll be off duty for a week until the nanomeds regrow that bone. Why did you do it?"

Ryan was staring past Pollard's left shoulder, looking out through the transplas window that filled the bulkhead at his back. A full gale was blowing outside; it was early morning, but the sky was a dirty blue black, with low-flying clouds racing in from the northeast. Snow mixed with sleet was blowing horizontally past the window, and the force of the winds sent tremors through the deck.

Once, centuries before, NAS Oceana had been a naval air station located just inshore from the city of Virginia Beach. The gradual rise in the world's ocean levels, however, had drowned Virginia Beach by the end of the twenty-first century, and flooded the air station's runways with each higher-than-normal tide or storm surge. Rather than move inland, the Navy had rebuilt on the same site.

The world ocean had continued to rise, and in another century the base site had been under a depth of twenty-five meters and more than eighty kilometers offshore, as an enormous bite of tidewater Virginia and North Carolina had vanished beneath the sea. A cluster of domes rising above mean sea level on massive pylons marked the naval air station now. The base had ridden out the tsunami from the Wormwood asteroid strike with no damage, and suffered only a minor battering when the Turusch kinetic-kill impactor had struck in the Atlantic two months ago. The structure was designed to yield, slightly, under high winds and heavy waves, but the effect could be disconcerting if you weren't familiar with it.

The dome *creaked* as the wind clawed at it.

"I *said*, Lieutenant . . ."

"Sorry, sir! I was thinking. I suppose . . . I guess I've just been having some trouble fitting in. Sir."

Pollard sighed, leaning back in his seat. "Lieutenant . . . for better or for worse, you are an officer of the USNA Stellar Navy. Your training here is intended to make you ready for deployment with the Confederation Navy. You understand that?"

"Yes, sir."

"As director of the RAG squadrons at NAS Oceana, it is my duty to make certain that you do fit in . . . because you and your brother officers will be representing the United States in your new billets."

"I understand that, sir."

"I suppose Baskin, Pettigrew, and Johanson were, ah, having issues with your family background?"

"Something like that, sir."

The bastards had been on her case since she'd been assigned to the RAG, the replacement air group stationed at Oceana. Ryan was a Prim, born and raised in a Periphery region outside of the so-called still civilized USNA. Washington, D.C., once the capital of the old United States of America, had for several centuries now been a tidal estuary, with vine-smothered, once white monuments rising from the swamp that had reclaimed the low-lying ground as far north as the Georgetown Heights. Buildings in the areas of Eckington, Gateway, and DuPont Park, many half-submerged now, offered shelter for some thousands of local squatties, the Prims, who lacked Net access, modern health care, civil security, and the basic rights of citizens.

Ryan's family eventually had managed to move out of the swamp and up to the Bethesda Enclave, fifteen kilometers north of the former national capital, on ground far enough above sea level that flooding wasn't a problem; but the community—living in the slums in the shadow of the kilometer-high Institute of Health tower and the even higher Chevy Chase Arcology—was made up of people who were citizens in name only. Most were refugees from the Washington Swamps; most could not afford modern cerebral implants, which barred them from basic civilized necessities, like banking and electronic communications. The most successful bootstrapped their way up the social ladder by taking service jobs, by working in the Alexandria Reclamation Projects, or by joining the military.

Shay Ryan had chosen the last option, knowing it meant a useful education download and free hardware implants that would grant her full citizenship when she got out. When they tested her at the recruiting center at Rockville, they'd discovered in her a higher-than-normal aptitude for three-dimensional thinking, and at the recommendation of her proctors, she had been shunted into officer's training and, eventually, flight training.

Four years later, she was a newly minted USNA Navy lieutenant fresh from the flight-training center at the Sea Tower at Pensacola, and assigned to the Oceana RAG with the opportunity for assignment to a Confederation unit.

It would have been great if things had been as easy as that . . . but it seemed that her background had a way of following her. The USNA naval service and—even more so—the Terran Confederation Star Navy—were the most aristocratic of the various military services. Enlisted personnel might wear animated tattoos that writhed across their backs, or get into fights at local drinkeries, but that *never* happened to officers. Even a newbie lieutenant was expected to be "an officer and a gentleman or -woman," and any behavior construed as bringing disgrace to the uniform was unacceptable.

"It was the tattoo that started it, wasn't it?" Pollard asked.

She shrugged. "I don't know, sir. They *were* teasing me about what they called my 'tramp stamp.' "

She'd gotten the animation not long after she'd moved to Bethesda—paying for it out of her income as a member of a cleaning crew in the IST basement levels. Several million dermopixels nanogrown within the skin covering her back had, in effect, turned her into a 2-D display screen. Any of a number of tattoos could be loaded into her hardware, but the only one she'd been able to afford was a pair of delicate fairies—one male, one female, with brilliant rainbow-hued gossamer wings—that fluttered, danced, and embraced randomly, back and forth across the space between her hips and shoulders. She'd obeyed regulations and kept the tatto switched off during duty hours, but at Raphael's the other night, Ryan had been in civvies and it had seemed to be the place to let down her skinsuit's back and put her winged friends on display.

Animated tattoos as an art form had waxed and waned in popularity for centuries now—sometimes as affectations of the rich, sometimes as poor man's body art. Currently, they were rather fashionable in the upscale civilian world, and it had seemed like a mark of distinction, of *success*, and a great way to celebrate her escape from the mangrove swamps and estuaries of Washington.

She'd honestly not been aware that male-female fairy pairs were considered perverse in most circles—an animated advertisement for monogamous marriage. When Baskin had made that comment about her married parents, she'd picked up the table and hit him with it.

She hadn't *really* been trying to kill Baskin, and Pettigrew and Johanson had just caught some of the shrapnel. But the Shore Patrol had written her up for assault, and she'd ended up here in front of Captain Pollard.

Pollard sighed. "If I were you, Lieutenant, I'd lose the fairies. They won't do your naval career any good. As for what to do with you, however . . ."

He swiveled in his chair, looking out the transplas at the sleet-laden gale outside. "You've already put in for Confed duty, haven't you?"

"Yes, sir." Ryan felt a stab of fear at that. Military service with the Confederation was considered more prestigious than service with a mere national star navy. You had more chances for advancement, more opportunities for high-end hardware implants, and a better shot at good jobs when you decided to get out. Pollard, she thought, must be considering punishment that would deny her a chance at transferring to the Connies.

"I have in here," he said, turning back in his chair and sharply tapping on his desk, "a request for two squadrons to be transferred to the CVS *America*. I'm sending up the Night Demons and the Merry Reapers, but the Demons are one short. I'm thinking that if we transfer you to star duty, get you out of Oceana and the, ah, reputation you've made for yourself here, it might give you a fresh start with new people. It's Confederation service . . . but I do need to inform you, before you decide, that CBG–18 is about to be deployed on deep-star ops. *Very* deep. The deployment will last at least seven months, and quite possibly longer."

Her heart quickened. She'd heard scuttlebutt about a new deep-star mission, a multi-carrier task force heading deep into Sh'daar space to hit enemy supply dumps and reinforcement centers, to knock the enemy off balance and forestall future strikes against Earth.

"Yes, sir?"

"Are you interested?"

Was he kidding? A chance to get off this rock and out among the stars? "Yes, *sir*."

"Some of *America*'s squadrons were badly chewed up in the fight two months ago. One squadron, I believe, was down to two ships left out of twelve—that's eighty-four percent casualties. It's not going to be a picnic out there."

Ryan drew a deep breath. Her father had died shortly after the move to Bethesda. Her mother was still alive, and Ryan sent her a big chunk of her paycheck each month to help her and her sister get by. But the tiny apartment in Bethesda wasn't home, not really. In a way, she'd found a new home when she'd joined the service, and even assholes like Baskin and Pettigrew couldn't entirely take away that sweet sense of belonging.

And the chance to leave Earth . . .

"I would like to volunteer, sir."

Pollard nodded. "Very well. I'll have personnel draw up your orders. Get your kit together, because you'll be up-boosting tonight."

"Thank you, sir!"

He shook his head. "Don't thank me, Lieutenant. You don't hear that much about it planetside nowadays, but there's a *war* going on out there, a bloody, brutal, and deadly knife fight that chews up our best aviators and spits out the remains. You might not survive your first month of deployment."

"I'll manage, sir."

"Indeed?"

"I'm a survivor, sir."

He shrugged. "If you say so, Lieutenant. Just, for God's sake, lose the goddamned fairies, okay?"

Chapter Ten

3 January 2405

The Overlook
Earth Synchorbit, Sol System
2323 hours, EST

The Overlook was a moderately fancy civilian restaurant in a large, rotating hab module adjoining the naval docks and government node buildings at SupraQuito. It took its name from its elevated position above a broad, open plaza, part of the Greenhab office complex. Transparent bulkheads—revolving a full three-sixty every ten minutes—provided an unparalleled view of stars, the delicate traceries of the Synchorbit construction, and, of course, Earth in the distance.

It was close to midnight local time, so at the moment, Earth showed as a black sphere edged on one side by all of the sunsets in the world. North and South America's outlines were clear, however, picked out in a dusting of lights from the various megalopoli. Earth and stars drifted across the background in stately procession. Closer at hand, the dockyard and naval base slid past the transparencies slowly enough that observers could easily make out the details of the enormous *America*, in port a few kilometers away along with several other ships of the battlegroup.

Trevor Gray, Ben Donovan, and Katerine Tucker had come to the Overlook this evening for a final onshore fling. The scuttlebutt was that *America* would be departing from

Synchorbit in two more days, and since the three of them had the duty for the next three, this would be their last chance for time onshore. The rumored destination was off Pluto, but everyone knew that that would be a stopover, where the fleet would wait for reinforcements. The real jump into the Unknown would come sometime after that.

If the rumors were true, it would be a long time before their next opportunity for a fancy meal in a fancy restaurant.

"Expensive," Tucker said, eyes closed and one hand on a palm contact on the table in front of her as she examined the menu. Tucker was one of the few in the squadron, like Ben Donovan, who didn't seem to mind the fact of Gray being a Prim. She was a gentle, easygoing sort . . . but when she strapped on a Starhawk she was solid nitrogen ice. She often flew as Gray's wing.

"Hey, it's not like we're going to have anything to spend money on," Donovan said. "I hear the lobster here is good."

"I don't eat bugs," Tucker said, making a face.

"I wonder if they have rat," Gray said. "Back in the Manhattan Ruins, giant rats were a delicacy."

"How big were they?" Donovan asked, one eyebrow arching high.

"Oh, about yea big." Gray held his hands a half meter apart. "The big ones, anyway."

"I think I'd rather try the bugs," Tucker said.

"Man, there's just no pleasing some people!" Gray laughed.

"Do people really hunt rats with spears and stuff in the Ruins?" Donovan asked. "That always struck me as kind of a tall tale."

Gray shrugged. "Some did. We also traded with the people inland, though. The government didn't like that, of course. They couldn't tax it. It wasn't a *bad* life. . . ."

"Huh," Donovan said, looking up. "Speaking of bugs . . ."

Gray turned in his seat. The Overlook was pricey because it actually had a human waitstaff, including a maître d' in a formal black skinsuit and shoulder shortcloak with gold braid and heavy silver trim. At this kind of place, you ordered your meals through an e-link at the table, but actual *people* prepared it and brought it to your table. They'd been seated in a booth not far from the entrance to the main dining area, where the maître d' appeared to be having a confrontation of some sort with two would-be diners . . . a pair of Agletsch.

"What's going on?" Tucker asked.

"I can't hear," Gray said, "but it looks like the staff is turning the Aggies away."

"Why would they want to eat in a human restaurant anyway?" Donovan asked.

"Their biochemistries are supposed to be pretty much like ours," Gray said. He'd studied available information on all of the known nonhuman sentient species. "Same carbon chemistry . . . dextro-sugars, levo-amino acids. They can eat what we eat, and get nourishment from it."

"It still doesn't seem *right,* them coming in here," Tucker said.

The Agletsch were becoming quite animated. Popularly called "bugs" or "spiders," the Agletsch were actually very little like either. Each had an ovoid and unsegmented body a meter plus across, supported by sixteen spindly limbs. The rear legs were considerably shorter than those in the front—little more than stubs ending in sucker tips—while the foreleg-manipulators were long enough to cock the body at a forty-five degree angle off the floor, supporting the head end a good meter and a half off the ground. The rotund body was covered by a leathery skin rather than by chitin. Most of it was a soft, velvety red brown in color with yellow and blue reticulations; the legs and the flat face, with its four oddly stalked eyes, were dark gray mottled with black. Silver glinted in the restaurant's lighting; the complex metallic curlicues painted in strips along the leathery hide might have been writing, or simply decorative tattoos.

Gray heard an inner tone over his link. "Shit," he said. "They just sounded the security alarm."

"Who did?"

"The head waiter, I assume. Hang on. I want to see what's going on."

"Trevor—"

"I'll be right back."

Gray slipped out of the booth and walked toward the front of the restaurant. That alarm bothered him. It was being Netcast on a channel that most civilians would not pick up, but which would bring police or military personnel running. Normally, Gray would have stayed in the background with his friends and left the matter to the Authorities, but damn it, he'd been on the receiving end of shit from the Authorities often enough in his life that he wanted to step in. The maître d' looked like the stuffy, officious type, and he was ordering the two little aliens around with just a bit too much in the way of sneering and peremptory drama.

"This is no place for the likes of you!" the man was saying. "You have no right to be here! What were you thinking, coming into this establishment like this? . . ."

"We want no trouble," one of the Agletsch was saying. "We will go. . . ."

The aliens were wearing translators, of course, and the voice was coming from one of these. As Gray had just noted to the others, the Agletsch were similar to humans in many ways, though their outward forms were disquieting to anyone with a phobia of spiders or insects. They spoke by belching air from their upper stomachs through their mouths, which were located underneath their bodies, in their lower abdomens.

The actual Agletsch homeworld was unknown, though it was assumed it lay somewhere deep within Sh'daar space, out in the direction of Canopus, where they'd first been encountered, the very first technic nonhuman species Humankind had met after they'd begun spreading out among the stars. The Agletsch didn't seem to go in for colonizing other worlds, but they did have numerous trade outposts, with *information* as their primary unit of exchange. When the Sh'daar had issued their ultimatum, some dozens of those outposts inside Confederation space had been cut off from the rest. Some tens of thousands of Agletsch, it was believed, still lived inside human space—perhaps a quarter of them on the three Earth Synchorbits.

There were enough Agletsch living now within the solar

system that they were a reasonably familiar sight to humans, far more so than those species with which Humankind was currently at war . . . or the atechnic species discovered on various worlds but which had never developed technology of their own. Despite this, the Agletsch were not entirely trusted. They were remembered as the ones who'd presented Humankind with the Sh'daar Ultimatum almost forty years before, and there was always the unspoken assumption that they must somehow be in league with the enemy.

"What's going on here?" Gray asked, coming up behind the maître d'.

The man turned and took in Gray's dress Navy uniform. "Ah, sir. Nothing of importance. These . . . ah . . . *gentlemen* were just leaving."

Gray looked at the two aliens. "Is this guy giving you a hard time?"

He wasn't certain how his colloquial English would be translated for them, but he didn't get a failure-to-translate signal back from the aliens' speech software. Each wore a human-made translator—a small, flat, silver badge—adhering to the skin beneath the four weirdly stalked eyes.

"You are with the starship *America*, yes-no?" one of the Agletsch asked Gray. The voice sounded human, rather than electronic, but was oddly flat and empty of emotion.

A warning pulse throbbed inside Gray's head. All Confederation naval personnel had been repeatedly warned against getting friendly with *any* nonhuman intelligence, and especially with the Agletsch. Gray and the others were carrying secmons tonight, of course, as well as corders and deets. It was part of the understood agreement with all military personnel; if you wanted to go ashore, you carried them along, in your head or woven into your clothing.

And Gray's security monitor was warning him not to tell the aliens anything that might be considered classified information.

On the other hand, Gray was wearing his dress Navy uniform, and his id included the information that he was stationed on the *America*. The Agletsch had communications and information system technology as sophisticated as anything humans possessed. He'd felt them twig his own id as he walked up. It couldn't hurt to confirm what they already knew.

"America," he said, overriding the alarm in his head with a thought. "Yes."

"And we are *America* as well!" one of the aliens said. "Your guides. Your . . . escorts? Into unknown, yes-no?"

Both aliens, Gray noted, had ids of their own; a pair of green lights in a window that had just opened in his mind indicated they each had publicly accessible information records, probably running along with their translator software. He thoughtclicked one, then the other, and data scrolled down the window. The two were Dra'ethde and Gru'mulkisch; they were currently attached to the Confederation Department of Extraterrestrial Relations, had security clearances issued by the ONI at Level Five-green, the same as Gray and other pilots, and they'd only just that afternoon been assigned to *America*'s personnel roster.

Gray turned to the maître d'. "These two *ladies* are my shipmates, sir," he said. Both of them had their males with them, of course . . . tadpole-sized appendages hanging from their faces just below their eyestalks. Like terrestrial angler fish in Earth's deep oceans, the Agletsch had solved the problem of finding mates by having males quite different morphologically from the females, tiny external parasites that fed off the female like permanently attached leeches.

"But they're . . . *alien*, sir." The man said the word as though it tasted unpleasant.

"No more to us than we are to them."

"They would offend the other guests, the human guests! They . . . they *smell*! And have you ever seen them *eat*?"

In fact, Gray was only just aware of the odor of the two beings, a sweet, smoky aroma similar to burning sage, or possibly marijuana. It was not strong, and not at all unpleasant.

"I don't find the smell offensive. And no, I've never seen one eat. Have you?"

"We are not here to *eat*," the one identified as Dra'ethde said.

"Oh, no," the other one added. "In our culture, feeding is an intensely private thing, something to be done alone or with the closest and most intimate of one's *klathet'chid*, yes-no?"

"So all this"—Gray waved an arm to take in the restaurant half full of people eating in public—"must seem pretty rude to you two."

Gru'mulkisch made a complicated gesture with all four eyes and its top two left limbs. "It is not our practice to *look*," she said. "But we were told it is customary for those about to embark on board one of your ships to engage in numbing certain parts of their central nervous systems with certain drugs. This is a ritual that we of the Agletsch share with humans."

"We'd hoped to find . . . the word is shipmates, yes-no? Yes, shipmates, and share the drug ritual with them."

Gru'mulkisch's eyestalks had extended from the patch of the ovoid body that Gray was thinking of as the "face" and were deeply and seriously focused on him. The stalks were wet and a deep, dark mottled gray in color; the eyes were much like the eyes of an octopus: deep golden yellow, with a black pupil shaped like the letter *Y*. Two of the stalks were stretched far out to either side, the other two stretching just as far top to bottom, each reaching a good thirty centimeters from its attachment point. The four-eyed expression was so fetchingly comical that it was all Gray could do not to laugh out loud.

"The Authorities will be here in a moment," the maître d' said, frowning. "I suggest that you tell your . . . your friends to leave."

Gray shot a quick e-call to Tucker and Donovan and told them what was happening. "I think I just lost my appetite," Donovan said.

"Let's go someplace else," Gray suggested. "There's a bar a few levels down."

"We're with you," Donovan replied.

Both Tucker and Donovan joined the tableau at the front seconds later.

"And what," Gray asked the headwaiter, "if we choose to

eat with our friends here?" He glanced at Tucker and Donovan, and shot them an in-head query. "You two sure you're okay with this?"

"Of course, Trev," Tucker said out loud. She made a face. "This joint is too rich for my blood anyway."

"We'll just take our custom elsewhere," Gray told the maître d'. He felt Donovan sending out a general text message and grinned.

"But sir, the Overlook is *honored* to serve our young heroes of the Confederation military! . . ."

"Seems to me that these two are doing more for the war effort than you are, friend," Gray said. "So far from home, coming on board a Confederation star carrier to serve as guides and liaisons . . ."

"That's right," Donovan added. "And I think we'll be telling the rest of our shipmates what we think of your service here." As he spoke, several other naval personnel in the restaurant began standing up, leaving their tables, and moving toward the front. Some Gray recognized from the *America*—either ship's crew or from other squadrons. There were a couple of enlisted people off of the *Kinkaid* . . . and one from the heavy monitor *Warden*. Donovan's near-broadcast text message wasn't emptying the place, by any means, but a good quarter of the clientele were military, some in uniform, many in civvies. Those who'd already been served were paying their bills . . . but many others had already canceled their orders and were on their way out.

"Don't worry, sir," Gray said, still grinning. "I imagine you'll have enough civilian customers that you won't miss the fleet at all!" Turning, he gestured to the Agletsch, then followed them out, Donovan and Tucker close behind him.

"Thanks, guys," Gray told them. "Sorry to cut our dinner short."

"Hey, we stick together," Donovan said.

"Besides, it really *was* too expensive," Tucker added. "The bastards are fleet-gougers."

There were always places like that springing up around the perimeter of any military base—restaurants, bars, simsensies and ViRs, e-sexies and old-fashioned whorehouses, uniform nanoprogrammers, tattoo clinics and tobbo shops—ranging from the respectable down to the thoroughly seedy, and existing almost solely on the income provided by thousands of young men and women on their off-duty hours.

And a certain percentage of these businesses took outrageous advantage of service people—the fleet-gougers, the liberty traps, and the shit-city hustlers.

But for Gray, the Overlook's treatment of the two aliens was more telling.

"Let's go find someplace *decent* to cat," he said.

Osiris
70 Ophiuchi A
2358 hours, TFT

"Incoming!"

Marine captain Thomas Quinton dove headfirst into a shell hole as the hivel impactor struck the colony's defensive shields. The ground bucked beneath his scarred battle armor, rattling his teeth and driving the breath from his chest.

The warning had been shouted by his battlesuit's AI; there was no way to hear an incoming round before it struck, since high-velocity impactors typically traveled at forty or fifty times the speed of sound. His suit's radar could give him a second or so of warning if it picked the round up fifteen to twenty kilometers away.

Rising carefully, he looked back toward the colony. Laser fire, impactors, and plasma bolts continued to slam into the gravfield dome, which was shimmering and flickering like a pale, transparent ghost under the barrage. He'd made it safely out underneath the shield and screen projectors and was now in the rubble that, until fifty-four hours ago, had been the city of New Egypt's Nuit Starport, five kilometers outside of town. Thank God the bombardment hadn't turned the ground surrounding the city into molten lava yet. That would come later, if the bombardment continued.

It was possible, of course, that the enemy wanted to capture the colony more or less intact, rather than scrape it off the surface of the planet. Ground troops—the hulking, vaguely humanoid giants identified as Nungiirtok—had been sighted in the blasted ruins outside the central city, and that suggested that the bad guys wanted to take and hold the planet rather than sterilize it.

A trio of tactical nukes went off against the city's shields, dazzling flares of raw, white light, followed seconds later by the sound of the detonations and the shrieks of the shock waves. Well, maybe they didn't want the city after all. . . .

Quinton lay flat in his hole and let the storm-fury rage overhead. As the noise subsided, he crawled up and over the crater's lip. Three mushroom clouds boiled into the overcast sky on the horizon now, bracketing the colony's defensive shield dome.

Osiris—70 Ophiuchi AII—had been a garden world until the Turusch and their Nungiirtok allies arrived. That had been three short, local days ago.

Osiris, along with Chiron, New Earth, and Kore, was one of the handful of worlds among the near stars enough like Earth that humans could live there without elaborate environmental protection, where they could even breathe the air without filter masks or helmets. The primary was a double star—a K0 yellow-orange sun circled by a slightly smaller, cooler K4 star. Seventy-A was mildly variable—the star was a BY Draconis type, with heavy starspot activity—and that drove the planet's often-stormy weather.

New Egypt was the colony's capital, with a few outlying cities—Luxor, Dendara, Sais, and others—on the same southern continent. There was a thriving native ecology biochemically similar to its terrestrial counterpart, and even a native species that might well prove to be sentient—the atechnic marine cuttlewyrms.

Quinton's motion detector picked up a mass fifty meters to his right, and he went to ground once more. There was something out there, probably on the other side of that tumbledown mass of wreckage that was all that was left of a spacecraft hangar. He could hear it, now . . . a *crunch-crunch-crunch* of heavy limbs moving through piles of broken ferrocrete. He brought his linac rifle up, pressed the power-up, and waited.

The Nungiirtok appeared around the corner of the collapsed hangar seconds later, a three-meter headless mecha, stooped far forward on digitigrade legs, massively armored, and carrying a plasma weapon of alien design in three-fingered gauntlets. The towering threat looked like a machine . . . but it was the Nungiirtok equivalent of Marine combat armor. At its feet, a dozen armored Kobolds thrashed forward, each on three armored tentacles. No one knew if they were robotic machines under the Nungiirtok's control or another organic species. They only appeared with the big Nungiirtok, however, apparently in the role of combat scouts.

There could be no doubt that the enemy had already spotted Quinton. It lumbered around the corner with its plasma weapon held high, loosing the first bolts as soon as the weapon was clear of the building. Quinton, flat on the ground, rolled to his left as the white-hot packets of incandescence hissed past him, missing his suit's backpack by scant centimeters and sending a shrieking hiss of static over his com link.

Quinton triggered his linac as he rolled, using his in-head display to keep the weapon's targeting cursor centered on the armored giant in front of him. The linear accelerator rifle was considered to be a sniper's weapon, but with a fully charged battery pack, it had a two-per-second fire/recovery rate that could slam off thirty-gram depleted uranium slivers almost as fast as he could press the trigger button.

At a range of just forty-five meters, Quinton put three rounds into the monster's center of mass, each magnetically accelerated to nearly 800 kps. The impacts punched through the armor as jets of white-hot molten carbon-fiber-laminate, with explosions like the detonation of thermal grenades. The three-meter giant staggered as it took two rounds in the chest area and a third close by the left shoulder. Shrapnel hurtled from the impacts as the arm tore away, spinning off into the rubble nearby. Quinton stopped his roll as the Nungiirtok dropped the plasma weapon, drawing a careful bead now on the deeply recessed sensor cluster that seemed to serve the Nungies in place of heads and loosing a fourth KK round. The giant lurched backward, then fell, trailing a stream of smoke from its smashed-open visor.

As fast as he could, Quinton began popping the swarming Kobolds as they surged toward his position. Each round was powerful enough to shatter one of the armored little horrors like a bullet-struck eggshell. He smashed five of them before the others began scattering, scuttling off into the rubble.

They would be bringing in more Nungiirtok giants, though, and quickly. Quinton didn't have much time.

Rising to his feet, but staying bent over and low to the ground, he began running, making his way toward something that looked like a concrete-walled casement with an opening the size of a large garage. The faded and shrapnel-gouged letters cms showed on one side. *Please, God, let the launch tube be open. . . .*

A round caught him in the side, slamming him hard. Spinning and dropping, he saw the Kobolds advancing once more.

His linac rifle had a twenty-round magazine, and he'd already expended nine. Coming up to one knee, he brought the heavy rifle to his shoulder and calmly began squeezing off shots. The rifle's acceleration compensators took care of most of the recoil, but enough leaked through to pound against his armored pauldron, like a hard slam from a baseball bat with each round.

One target . . . one shot . . . one kill . . . but more and more of the dog-sized horrors were boiling out of the ruins. Either there'd been more than a dozen Kobolds with that Nungie, or a *second* Nungiirtok was close by and moving in. His rifle beeped a warning over his implant at three rounds left . . . and again for two . . . and finally for one. Automatically, he palmed the rifle's slagger, turning its mechanism into molten metal as he flung it away.

He killed the last three Kobolds with his service-issue handgun as they scrabbled over the last pile of debris, just three meters away.

Hurrying ahead, pistol clenched in his glove, he jogged

the last ten meters to the packet launch tube. His side hurt. The Kobold shot had not penetrated his armor, but enough force had been transmitted through the shock-absorbing laminates to bruise him, and just possibly to fracture a rib.

Please let the damned tube be open. . . .

It was. The aboveground opening gave access to a long, ruler-straight tube descending at a slight angle into the ground beneath the starport tarmac, a tube over two hundred meters long. By the time he was halfway down, the opening—the only source of light within the tunnel—was so tiny that he was moving through almost total darkness. Switching to IR, he could see the heated elements of the launch structure ahead, and the dull glow of the HG packet resting on its cradle.

Somehow, he made it up the access ladder. Normally, the packet was reached through a personnel accessway leading from the starport tower, but that structure had been among the first vaporized by Turusch KK rounds fired from orbit. He just hoped the power systems were still intact.

On the gantry at last, he took time to strip off his armor. He wouldn't need it now, and there was no room for it inside the form-fitting cockpit. He heard a clang, followed by scrabbling noises coming down the tunnel, and the faint light here was momentarily obscured.

Shit. A Nungie was coming down after him.

Stripped to his utility skinsuit, Quinton palmed open the hatch and squeezed inside. To his immense relief, the packet began powering up around him.

He'd been maintaining radio contact once he'd left the city, but there was no need of stealth now, not with the eight-hundred-ton mail packet beginning to power up. Right now, every Trash and Nungie detector in the system must be lighting up, screaming out his intent. He had only seconds now.

"New Egypt Flight Control, I'm aboard the packet and powering up. Everything looks good on this end." Power was already at 70 percent, and climbing. He could hear the low whine spooling higher behind his cockpit as the power tap engaged.

"Copy that, Lieutenant." The voice of Colonel Sandowski came over his implant. "We're tracking a couple of Nungies near the entrance to your tube. Better light that thing and clear out."

"Aye, aye, Colonel. I . . ."

He stopped, swallowed hard. There were twelve hundred USNA Marines stationed at New Egypt, and every fiber of his being, every instinct born of training and experience, demanded that he stay, that he not *run.*

But he'd volunteered for this mission, and there was no backing out now.

"I wish I could stay. . . ." he managed to say at last.

"Stow, it Lieutenant," Sandowski replied. "They need to know what's going down out here, back home. You can come back with the relief force."

"Yes, sir." He did a fast mental calculation. Three days to Earth . . . nine days back. "See you in two weeks."

He heard the hesitation in Sandowski's voice. "Roger that, Marine. Two weeks!"

"Semper fi!" Quinton yelled, and he brought his hand down on the control contact pad. He felt movement, then gathering acceleration, pressing him back against the embrace of the seat. He overrode the safeties with a thought command already downloaded into his implant by the chief programmer at the colony. Instantly, the gravs engaged, dropping him into weightlessness as the tiny ship hurtled forward.

Engaging the gravitic drive while he was still underground was not standard practice . . . but no one was expecting to use the launch system again anytime soon. At over three hundred gravities, the mail packet flashed out of the launch tube, the tube structure collapsing in a rippling pulse of twisted space as he exited the tube mouth.

If there'd been any Nungies in the tube, he didn't feel the impact. If there'd been any there, or any close by the mouth of the launch tube, he doubted that they'd felt a thing either . . . unfortunately.

Trailing his own sonic boom, Quinton flashed through the overcast, emerging in the bright yellow-orange light of

Seventy-A, the green-tinted sky fading to ultramarine, then to black emptiness in seconds.

Sensors recorded ships in orbit, *lots* of them, but his launch time had been deliberately chosen to correspond to the time when the majority of the Turusch fleet was on Osiris's night side. The nearest ships were firing at him, but he was already outpacing everything they were throwing at him save light, and he was far enough from the nearest of the enemy vessels that they couldn't accurately track him.

The HAMP–20 Sleipnir-class mail packet was the smallest human-made vessel capable of interstellar travel, and the fastest. The boat could accelerate to over a thousand gravities, and during FTL flight, where most fleet ships had a maximum Alcubierre rate of 1.7 to 1.9 light years per day, the mail packet could manage 5.33.

Earth, sixteen light years distant, was a nine-day flight for the fleet, but only three days for the mail packet.

But it was going to be a hell of a long three days. . . .

Chapter Eleven

4 January 2405

Sarnelli's
Earth Synchorbit, Sol System
0035 hours, EST

Half an hour later, the five of them were at a bar called Sarnelli's, located in the same hab but five decks down. It didn't have the Overlook's view, but erotic dancers writhed and twisted on the elevated stage to free-form AI music, and cozy alcoves grew themselves around the patrons, creating the illusion of privacy despite the crowds.

"You risk much by intervening in this, yes-no?" Gru'mulkisch was saying. "With your fellow humans? With the human-in-authority at the place of feeding?"

"Nah," Gray replied. "That guy doesn't mean anything. I just wanted to get you two out of there before the damned Authorities showed up."

"Does that kind of prejudice bother you two?" Tucker asked. "I mean . . . being treated that way . . ."

"Treated in what way?" Dra'ethde asked.

"Being turned away like that. Being told humans didn't want to eat with you."

"As we explained," Dra'ethde said, "we do not eat in public as you do. It would be, what is the word . . . taboo? Impolite?"

"A breaking of proper etiquette," Gru'mulkisch suggested.

"We are learning Human social customs," Dra'ethde added. "For us to violate accepted taboo would be expected. Yes-no?"

Gray shook his head. The two Agletsch seemed remarkably friendly, open, and sociable. It was difficult to guess what they were really thinking or feeling, however, because no emotion came across with their translated speech. The movements of their upper-manipulator leg-arms, the way they moved and shifted their eyestalks, and even the way they held their bodies might all have been clucs to what they were actually feeling, but the humans simply couldn't read them.

Going by the translated words alone, however, they weren't at all upset by the rudeness of the Overlook's maître d', and Gray was having some trouble understanding that. He'd been refused service more than once when some officious twit had scanned his id and realized from his place of birth that he was a Prim, or that he didn't have the rights of a full citizen.

At least Sarnelli's didn't seem to be as stuffy as the Overlook. A number of people had looked at them oddly when they'd walked in with their two alien friends, but no one had said anything. Service was strictly electronic, with no human waitstaff, and if some of the patrons didn't like it, they could leave.

Two of the other Navy people who'd left the Overlook had joined them. Lieutenant Carstairs was another pilot, from VFA–31, the Impactors, and Lieutenant Ryan was a newbie, just arrived from Oceana with VFA–96, the Night Demons.

"So what *was* that jerk's problem with these two?" Ryan asked. "Just that they're nonhuman?"

"I think he must have heard how Agletsch eat," Tucker said. "It *would* upset humans nearby trying to enjoy their own food." She glanced at the two Agletsch. "Uh . . . no offense."

Neither of the beings responded. Perhaps they hadn't understood her disclaimer as having been directed at them.

Curious, Gray pulled down an encyclopedia entry on Agletsch physiology, opening the download window in his mind. The spidery beings were actually similar to houseflies in one respect: they regurgitated their upper stomach contents onto their food before ingesting it again. That could be a pretty serious business in a creature over a meter long and massing forty kilos.

He wondered if Gru'mulkisch's statement about Agletsch only eating in private had been a polite lie to reassure the humans. In the century or so that humans and Agletsch had interacted with one another, perhaps they'd learned that humans reacted strangely to them when they sat down together for a meal.

How the hell did you know when an alien was lying?

"I hate seeing *anyone* discriminated against," Ryan told Tucker. "Calling the fucking Authorities. I don't care how these two eat!"

Gray looked at Shay Ryan, intrigued. Her id said she was from Maryland, on the USNA East Coast. Her accent, though, as well as her attitude, suggested that she might be from the Periphery. She was attractive in a hard-edged way, wearing her uniform instead of civvies like the rest of them.

"Same here," he said. "I don't like to see people pushed around, even if they do have more legs than us. Where are you from, anyway?"

"Bethesda. What business is it of yours, Lieutenant?"

He shrugged. "Just wondering. I'm from—"

He felt her ping his id, and her eyes widened. "Manhattan, huh?" she said. Her attitude seemed to soften a bit. "My family is in Bethesda . . . but we started out in D.C."

"Thought I recognized the accent."

"Old home week for you two, huh?" Donovan said.

"Not exactly pleasant memories," Ryan said. She looked hard at Gray. "What's wrong with the way I talk?"

"Not a thing. But growing up peri-free, without being linked into the Nets . . . the way we say some words tends to drift a bit. And the way you said *Authorities*, like it left a bad taste in your mouth. . . ."

"Please," Dra'ethde said. "What . . . *bleep* . . . weak about old home?" She placed a small data disk on the table's ordering contact panel, transmitting a credit exchange and an order to the bar's AI.

Whatever their dining preferences, the Agletsch had no problem *drinking* with humans. After a moment, a glass filled with vinegar rose from the table's dispenser, and Dra'ethde grasped it with all four upper leg-arms and placed it carefully on the floor.

Agletsch anatomy didn't permit them to use human chairs, of course; to drink, they squatted above the glass and unfolded a kind of pouch in their lower abdomen from which a fleshy, black organ disturbingly like a tongue emerged, filling the glass and sopping up the liquid. Acetic acid, Gru'mulkisch had explained earlier, was a mild euphoric to Agletsch physiology, acting something like alcohol in humans. Gru'mulkisch had already ordered four glasses of vinegar, and Dra'ethde five. Their translators appeared to be struggling now with the language—perhaps as their belchings of words became less and less distinct. The programs were having trouble with both English syntax and grammar, and occasionally a word that simply could not be translated emerged as a sharp electronic bleep.

"A human expression," Gray explained. "Donovan meant that Lieutenant Ryan and I have some things in common."

"Then good *bleep* meeting are," Dra'ethde said. "Yes-no? *Bleep* . . . this."

"Bleep," Gru'mulkisch agreed.

"Lieutenant Gray," a voice said in his head. "This is Lieutenant Commander Hanson of ONI. We have downloaded a rider into your ICH."

ICH stood for intracerebral hardware, Gray's brain implants. A rider was a limited-scope AI that could see and hear everything Gray saw and heard, and transmit everything to another site.

"What the hell are *you* doing here?" Gray replied, subvocalizing so no one at the table would hear. By *almost* speaking out loud, the neural impulses associated with speech still traveled to his larynx; nano-grown devices in his throat picked them up there, translated them, and redirected them to Gray's Netlink.

"Your secmon alerted us to the fact that you were having an extended conversation with two aliens," Hanson told him.

"It also told us that you'd overridden the secmon's security warning. That gives us the authority to monitor the conversation, under the provisions of the Enemy Alien Act of 2375, Chapter One, Paragraph—"

"Fuck off," Gray told the voice, "and get the hell out of my head!"

"I'll remind you, Lieutenant, that you are addressing a superior officer." Hanson paused, then added, "We understand that this . . . intrusion might have caught you off guard. No charges will be filed *this* time. However, we do wish to elicit your cooperation. The two intelligence targets with you appear to have had their inhibitions somewhat relaxed under the influence of acetic acid. We would like you to casually question them about why the Sh'daar have attacked us."

"Do your own damned spying," Gray snarled, and he said it loud enough that the other humans at the table looked at him curiously. "And *get out of my head*!"

He braced himself, expecting an argument, but the voice remained silent.

"Are you okay, Trev?" Tucker asked him.

"Yeah. Sorry. Must've been a software glitch." He wondered if the rider was still there, and how much it had already seen and heard. Damn it, life in the Periphery had been brutal and it had been rough, but the one perk out there had been a distinct lack of government intrusion into people's electronic enhancements, because they'd had no enhancements in the first place. Privacy was more or less taken for granted in the wild areas outside of government control; you might not have healthcare or free transportation as a right, but you didn't have some bureaucrat looking out through your eyes and spying on you either.

Donovan drained his glass, an unlikely-looking green concoction called a Nasty Fish, then turned to the two Agletsch. "So . . . one thing I always wondered about," he said. "How come the Sh'daar are so hot to kill us?"

"Yeah," Carstairs said. "We never did anything to *them*."

"Ah . . . ah . . . ah . . ." Dra'ethde said with a curious weaving motion of her top left leg-arm. "Information *bleep-bleep-bleep* price."

"I, ah, didn't quite catch that," Donovan said.

Gray palmed a table contact and ordered another drink for himself. The damned ONI must have electronically canvassed all of the humans at the table. He wondered if any of the others had refused to help them.

"I think she's saying," Gray said carefully, "that the Agletsch *trade* information, and don't give it away. Is that right?"

He'd seen that in a download someplace. The Agletsch were, first and foremost, traders, interstellar merchants seeking new markets and outlets for their wares. There actually were very few things found in one star system that would be worth the price of shipping them to another, however—especially when applied nanotechnology could create vast supplies of *anything* from software blueprints. Every star system had vast amounts of raw material in the form of cometary and asteroidal debris—every natural element from hydrogen to uranium—and even works of art could be perfectly duplicated and nanufactured from detailed scanning specs.

Which meant that *information* was the one unique commodity that made interstellar trade feasible.

For almost forty years now, humans had tried to elicit information about the Sh'daar from Agletsch traders, but with little success. The alien traders appeared to value such information quite highly—so much so that no one had ever found any information that they were willing to accept in exchange.

Did the ONI actually think these two would reveal their most precious secrets just because they were drunk on vinegar?

"Truth," Dra'ethde said, replying to Gray's question.

"Bleep," Gru'mulkisch added. "Yes-no?"

Gray palmed the table contact and ordered himself another grav squeezer. The Agletsch, he thought, must have their own credit accounts through the ConDepXR, allowing them to buy their own vinegar.

"Look, there's no point in asking them about the Sh'daar," Gray told the others. "For one thing, most of them are within

Sh'daar space. These two got trapped behind the lines, as it were. They're not going to tell us anything that would jeopardize their homeworld, right?"

"Bleep," Dra'ethde agreed.

"Besides, it sounds like their translators are having a bit of trouble with the nuances right now."

"Well, that's gratitude for you," Donovan said. "We help these two, keep them from getting picked up by Security . . . and they won't even say why their masters want to pound us back into the Stone Age. Hell, I'd think that *anything* that helped end this damned war would be worth something to *both* sides."

"That one," Dra'ethde said, pointing at Donovan with an unsteady leg-arm, "*bleep* right about thing. Information *bleep* all species. Human. Agletsch. Sh'daar. Even Turusch. Even Nungiirtok."

"Don't like Nungiirtok," Gru'mulkisch said.

"Who does?" Dra'ethde said. "But help every being."

"Agreement," Gru'mulkisch said. "And these humans *bleep* help us."

The translation software, Gray decided, was having particular problem with Agletsch verbs. But if he was following the weaving conversation right, the Agletsch were working their way up to justifying *some* sort of revelation. The possibility outweighed his own dislike for the ONI and the Confederation's security apparatus. He *was* curious . . . and knowing what the Sh'daar were actually after might well help the Confederation finally understand its implacable enemy.

Dra'ethde reached out and grasped Donovan with putty-soft digits emerging from beneath the leathery armor of one leg-arm, holding him by his right wrist. She leaned a bit closer to the human, and Gray could hear her belching a word with exaggerated care, to make sure her translator got it right.

"Transcendence," Dra'ethde said, the translator somehow putting a great deal of emphasis into the single word.

The Agletsch let go of Donovan's arm and rocked back on its lower legs, as though satisfied at having revealed the greatest secret of the ages.

"What transcendence?" Tucker asked. "Or whose?"

"She means that with our technological growth as fast as it is," Carstairs suggested, "we'll soon pass the Sh'daar. *Transcend* them. Right?"

"Sh'daar," Gru'mulkisch said, "already transcended. That *bleep* part of problem."

"Transcendence," Ryan said. "That's like . . . turning into something else?"

"I think you're right," Gray said. His squeezer arrived on the tabletop, and he picked it up, thoughtful. "What's the next step after humanity? In terms of evolution, I mean."

"You mean 'transcendence' as in our technology helps us mutate into something more highly evolved?" Tucker said. "I've seen some speculation along those lines."

So had Gray. In various articles he'd downloaded on the subject, it appeared that most people assumed that the Sh'daar were trying to limit human technological development in order to keep them from developing unknown superweapons that might let them supplant the Sh'daar as masters of half the galaxy. The idea had always seemed narrow-minded and simplistic to him, however.

He sipped his grav squeezer, a concoction involving grape-orange hybrids, coca extract, and 90 percent alcohol by volume. The drink's name sparked a question. *Gravitics* weren't on the Sh'daar list of proscribed technologies, the GRIN technologies mentioned in their ultimatum, and there were already discussions in various military Netgroups about the possibility of gravitic bombs powerful enough to turn a star into a black hole. Why the hell ignore gravitics while outlawing genetics or nanotech?

But the GRIN technologies had long been seen as the principal drivers of modern human scientific development technologies that had already changed what was meant by the word "human," and which might well transform Humankind out of all current understanding in the very near future.

Was that what the Sh'daar most feared? Humans evolving into something else?

"So the Sh'daar are afraid of humans evolving into a higher state?" Gray asked.

Gru'mulkisch's eyestalks wove back and forth in an unsettling pattern. *"Bleep-bleep."*

"Agreement," Dra'ethde added. "We *bleep* all we *bleep*." The Agletsch then straightened up, extending its leg-arms as far as it could, inverted its upper stomach, and collapsed in a steaming pile of its own stomach contents.

Gru'mulkisch had folded its leg-arms and appeared to be unconscious.

"I think, Commander Hanson," Gray said out loud, "that you've gotten all you're going to get out of these two tonight."

CIC, TC/USNA CVS America
Sol System
1045 hours, TFT

"*America* is cleared for release, Admiral," Buchanan informed him. "Ship is at full power and ready to proceed."

"Is everybody aboard?"

"The Executive Officer reports the last liberty party came on board at zero-six-twenty, sir."

"Very well, Captain Buchanan," Koenig said formally. "Take us out."

"Take us out, aye, sir."

Over the command net, Koenig heard Buchanan giving the orders to cast off umbilicals and mooring lines, release magnetic grapples, and engage tugs. He felt a light nudge as the tugs began moving the *America* away from the naval docks. Slowly, ponderously, the star carrier began the first leg of her new deployment.

His orders had read "on or before" 5 January, or "as soon as provisioning and resupply for an extended voyage of at least seven months" was complete. Koenig had pulled some strings with the base supply depot, and the larger vessels in CBG–18 now carried consumables enough to last for a full year, while the supply vessels *Salt Lake*, *Mare Orientalis*, and *Lacus Solis* would keep the fleet's smaller ships—destroyers, frigates, and gunboats—stocked for the same period. With the battlegroup provisioned, there was no reason to stay in synchorbit any longer, though he knew the personnel due for liberty ashore would disagree with that assessment.

Minutes passed, and the naval base, together with the rest of the SupraQuito facility, receded farther and farther into blackness, until it could barely be seen against the half-phase blue-white body of Earth. Well clear of the synch-orbital structures, *America* rotated on her axis, aligning herself with an invisible point in the constellation Pisces and began accelerating.

At five hundred gravities, the Earth and moon fell away astern with startling rapidity, becoming a tiny, double point of light that was swiftly lost in the glare of a dwindling Sun. Other ships in the battlegroup, those that had not preceded the fleet already, kept pace. Even at that fearful acceleration, however, once Earth and Moon vanished, the patterns of stars sprawled across the black emptiness of the sky remained unchanging, so distant were they.

"Admiral Koenig?" Buchanan said, once ship's in-system routine had been established. He was using the private, off-record channel.

"What do have for me, Randy?"

"Administrative detail, but it's got some delicate aspects. I wondered if you wanted to take this one."

"What is it?"

"ONI alerted the Exec to a possible security breach this morning involving several of *America*'s pilots. He referred them to CAG, and CAG referred them to me."

"And now you're bumping them up to me? Okay. What security breach?"

Buchanan filled Koenig in on the incident, which had happened at a bar in SupraQuito around midnight, ship's time. Several of *America*'s flight officers had fallen in with a couple of Agletsch, who themselves had been assigned to *America*'s battlegroup for this deployment. There didn't seem to be any problem, actually, but several of *America*'s officers were reported by the ONI Security Directorate as having been "uncooperative."

As Buchanan spoke, Koenig opened the records of the officers in question—Lieutenant Gray of VFA–44, and Lieutenant Ryan of the newly arrived VFA–96. Other officers present during the incident—Lieutenants Donovan, Carstairs, and Tucker—had cooperated with the ONI by asking certain questions of a pair of vinegar-inebriated Agletsch, as ordered. Ryan and Gray had refused those orders, and had done so in direct, abrupt, and insubordinate terms. The remanding officer, a Lieutenant Commander Hanson, had indicated that he was not going to charge either officer at first . . . but that their language and attitudes both had been bad enough that he'd changed his mind.

He checked the background records of the two officers, and groaned.

"What about the two Agletsch?" he asked Buchanan.

"Their shipmates cleaned them up and carried them back on board, Admiral."

"Their shipmates—that included Gray and Ryan?"

"Yes, sir. In fact, Lieutenant Gray told the OOD that they never leave a shipmate behind. There was some concern that the Synchorbit security forces might have been looking for the two Agletsch . . . something about an incident at a restaurant earlier in the evening. No charges were filed, however, and as far as Sam Jones is concerned, they're clean."

"And what was the ONI after with two expatriate Agletsch?"

"I asked, sir. The local ONI replied that it was a classified matter."

Koenig imagined that Naval Intelligence had been trolling, had become aware that some naval officers were drinking with the two Agletsch attachés and tried to get the humans to roll the aliens for some hard intel.

Damn it, the handful of Agletsch datatraders trapped within the Confederation were the closest thing humans had to allies among the other starfaring species. ONI had probably seen an opportunity to get a couple of drunken bugs to talk about the Sh'daar and their motives for the war. The idiots were going to cost Humankind friends they couldn't afford to lose.

"Where are Ryan and Gray now?"

"In their quarters, sir."

"Okay. I'll talk to them. ViR-patch them through to me here."

"Thank you, sir."

Koenig understood why this particular disciplinary problem had been passed up the line to him. So far as he could tell, no crime, no infraction existed, save just possibly for the use of insubordinate language . . . and these two were both ex-squatties from the Periphery, which meant they didn't care much for official authority figures in the first place, especially when those authorities were bureaucratic, heavy-handed, officious twits.

A signal light came on in his head, indicating that Ryan was on-line. A moment later, a second light switched on. "Ryan? Gray? This is Admiral Koenig."

"Yes, sir."

"Yes, Admiral."

A virtual scene opened around the three of them, a shared space resembling Koenig's shipboard office. He sat behind his desk, while the two flight officers, in dress blacks, stood at attention before him.

"At ease," he said. "I understand you two crossed swords with the spooks last night."

"They wanted me to spy for them," Ryan said. "Ask some questions of a couple of friendly bugs we'd picked up. Can they *do* that?"

"Technically," Koenig replied, "yes. Yes, they can. Both Agletsch were the targets of an ongoing ONI investigation, and intelligence officers are allowed to recruit uniformed military personnel to aid them in such investigations."

"Lieutenant Ryan was in uniform, Admiral," Gray told him. "The rest of us were in civvies, and all of us were off duty. Hanson came in and told me he'd dropped a rider in my hardware after he'd already done so. No warrant, no request. That violates the right to privacy of the Confederation military charter."

Koenig gave Gray a cold look. "You striking for space lawyer, son? Think you have all the answers?"

"Sir, I know the government can't just come in and start rummaging around in our minds without our permission!"

"You'd be surprised what the government can do, Mr. Gray . . . especially given that you surrendered a number of basic rights when you volunteered to join the Navy."

"As I remember it, Admiral, I didn't have a hell of a lot of choice."

"Both of you are from Periphery areas, right?"

The two glanced at each other.

"I'm from D.C.," the woman said.

"Manhattan Ruins."

"Which means neither of you grew up with having the Confederal Social Authority looking over your shoulder or parked inside your implant hardware. The rest of human civilization has lived with it since the Islamic Wars. That's what, three and a half centuries now?"

"You're talking about the White Covenant, sir?"

"Among other things. Yes."

The White Covenant, arising from the devastation wrought by the Islamic Wars of the twenty-first century, declared that no person, no government, and no religion had the right to dictate religious beliefs to others. The Covenant was seen as a guarantee that there would never again be a nuclear Islamic jihad, but it also meant that other proselytizing religions were prohibited from trying to convert others as well, whether peacefully or by force. Telling someone that they were doomed to hell was viewed as a terroristic threat.

But how could such a law be enforced? For world communities attempting to rebuild after jihad, allowing the Authorities to eavesdrop seemed much the better option. Powerful AIs monitored telephone systems; even with personal phones switched off, certain words like "God" or "believer" could be picked up by the network, triggering AI monitors that could record conversations, track individuals, or summon the Authorities.

And if some churches or synagogues protested this invasion of privacy, most people were happy to allow the Authorities to listen in on any conversation involving religious belief. Once most people began having computer implants nanogrown within the sulci of their brains, the enforcement of the White Covenant became even simpler.

Officially, once the danger had passed, the government wasn't supposed to listen without cause, but most people assumed that the AIs were still listening for anything subversive. Some religious groups—the Islamic Rafadeen, for example—even moved off world to escape the scrutiny of a high-tech Big Brother.

And, of course, there'd been no telephone system, no cybernetic implants, and no molecular microphones planted in public areas in the ruins of the Periphery—the peri-free, as many inhabitants called it. Most of the squatties living in such places did so by choice.

"The ONI became interested in your group," Koenig told the two, "because they were already watching the two Agletsch."

"They called them intelligence targets, sir," Gray said. "I thought the bugs were on our side."

"Those two were. . . . We think. Most Agletsch living inside Confederation space are. . . . We think. But we don't *know*, because no human can really understand how a nonhuman thinks, what it feels, what it really believes. That's part of the definition of the word *alien*. The surveillance was routine. The request that you help intelligence operatives was also routine. In a case like this, you *do* have the right to refuse to be involved. What I recommend is that in future, you be more . . . politic in your refusal. Telling a superior officer to 'fuck off' is not a career-enhancing act. Am I clear?"

"Yes, sir."

"Clear, sir."

"Very well. In light of the fact that we are going on deployment, and you'll not be going ashore at SupraQuito for a rather long time . . . I think we can let this whole matter quietly drop. I'll file a report with Fleet HQ that you've both accepted nonjudicial punishment—let's say restricted to the ship for one week, except for flight operations in the normal observance of your duties. NJP does not go on your records . . . and if you keep your noses clean, stay out of trouble when you return to Earth, nothing will be said."

"Restricted to the ship, sir?" Ryan said, surprised. "We can't go anywhere anyway!"

"Exactly. Just stay out of trouble. CAG and the exec are going to be keeping an eye on both of you. Dismissed."

"Thank you, sir."

"Thank you, Admiral."

The virtual office vanished, and Koenig again was strapped to his seat in *America*'s CIC. In point of fact, he fully agreed with Gray's and Ryan's attitude. He didn't like the specter of government surveillance of the general population either.

Life in the Navy was subject to plenty of rules and regulations, but for the most part, privacy was respected.

There were times when Koenig was *very* glad to be casting off from port and deploying into the Great Abyss.

Chapter Twelve

7 January 2405

Fleet Rendezvous Percival
Pluto Orbit, Sol Kuiper Belt
1214 hours, TFT

Trevor Gray watched the surface of the ice-locked world on a bulkhead display in the squadron ready room. *America* was over the night side, now, but he could see a tiny constellation of lights gleaming in the darkness one hundred kilometers below.

The run to Fleet Rendezvous Percival took just over nineteen hours. Early in the morning on January 5, according to shipboard time, the Star Carrier *America* decelerated into orbit around the dwarf planet Pluto, some forty astronomical units out from Earth within the icy wilderness of the inner Kuiper Belt.

Pluto remained a strange and somewhat controversial object circling far out at the limit of Sol's planetary system. Described as a planet for seventy-six years after its discovery, it had been reclassified as a dwarf planet early in the twenty-first century, a status periodically challenged and reconfirmed as scientific tastes changed and astronomical conventions were upheld or overturned. The worldlet itself didn't seem to care what humans called it. A little over 2,300 kilometers in diameter, with a mass less than two tenths that of Earth's moon, it swung about a dim and distant Sol once every 248 years. Like the far larger Uranus, Pluto lay on its side; its axial tilt of 120 degrees meant that darkness lasted in much of the northern hemisphere for over a century, followed by an equally long north-polar summer where the surface temperature never rose above 55 degrees Kelvin. The surface actually was some 10 degrees colder than it should have been at that distance from the sun; when nitrogen ice sublimated to a gas with the growing heat of summer, creating a temporary and very thin atmosphere, it actually drew heat away from the frigid surface in what was called an anti-greenhouse effect.

Despite this, there *was* a human presence on Pluto. That cluster of lights sliding past beneath *America*'s keel was the PDBP Base—usually pronounced "peed-beep"—housing a few dozen lonely xenobiologists and nanodrilling experts from the Confederation's Department of Applied Xenobiology.

Radioactive decay within the dwarf planet's small, rocky core actually generated enough heat to create a salty ocean at the boundary between core and mantle, a layer of warm water some fifty kilometers thick and buried beneath two hundred kilometers of solid ice. Wherever liquid water existed, there was the distinct possibility of life. The idea that a place as cold as Pluto might actually have a native biosphere would have shocked the xenobiologists of three or four centuries earlier, but the discoveries of thriving populations of organisms beneath the ice caps of Europa, Callisto, Enceledus, Triton, deep in the permafrost layers of Mars, and beneath the antarctic ice cap on Earth had demonstrated the incredible resiliency, scope, and sheer, dogged determination of life.

The Pluto Deep Biosphere Project, an attempt to bore a sterile hole through two hundred kilometers of ice in order to explore Pluto's deep ocean, had been under way for just over thirty years now.

The lights of the Pluto facility slid off over the horizon astern and, a few moments later, the sun rose above a white-lit crescent of ice. At a distance of just over forty astronomical units, the sun was little more than a very bright star; a crescent bowed away from the sun near Pluto's horizon, its largest moon, Charon. The drilling project had been set up on an ice plain ninety degrees around Pluto from Charon, which was tidally locked with Pluto in its six-day-long rotation. The tidal pull of Charon had made the ice mantle above the Plutonian ocean thicker on the worldlet's Charon side and at the antipodes, thinner at the ninety-degree points.

The crescent grew thicker as the sun slowly rose higher. Gray could see colors now in the ice, ranging from charcoal black to reds and oranges to brilliant white, and the curl of occasional wisps of cloud. Most of the surface was nitrogen ice, with small amounts of frozen methane and frozen carbon monoxide. Up close, the world showed as much surface contrast, however, as Iapetus, the starkly black-and-white moon of Saturn.

Gray wondered what caused the rich blend of colors. A download request to *America*'s library simply mentioned eon-long accumulations of dust, and the fact that Pluto's surface features changed with each partial surface melting, when the oddball dwarf swung slightly closer to the sun than did the planet Neptune. The project had begun at the beginning of the planetary summer, when Pluto's highly eccentric orbit actually slipped it inside the orbit of Neptune, and surface temperatures actually struggled to as high as 55 degrees Kelvin. Pluto's last warm period had ended in 2395, just ten years earlier; it might be another ten years before human machines would swim those stygian waters, searching for native Plutonian life.

"Why so serious?" a voice said behind him.

He started. It was one of the new pilots, Ryan.

"Oh, hi," he said. "Didn't hear you come in."

"Obviously. What has you so transfixed? We can't go down there, you know. We're still restricted to ship!"

He chuckled. "It's not like Pluto is a decent liberty port."

"Not unless you're into freezing your ass off."

"I was just wondering if they'll find anything alive down there. It seems pretty impossible."

She shrugged. "So what if they do? Join the Navy. Travel to distant worlds. Meet exotic alien life forms. Kill them."

"I downloaded an article from the shipnet last night," he told her. "A xenobiologist named Dr. Kane is suggesting that, given what we've found so far, the most common type of life in the universe might be aphotic deep marine forms, living beneath the ice caps of places like Europa and Pluto."

"What's 'aphotic'?"

"No light. They live in oceans deeper than anything on Earth, beneath tens or hundreds of kilometers of solid ice."

"Shit."

He looked at her. "Why 'shit'?"

"They would never be able to look up at the stars."

He was surprised by the sentiment. Ryan seemed to be hard and bitter in some ways, and she often made cracks like the old join-the-Navy joke she'd just rattled off.

"Well, yeah. I guess so. Of course, mostly we're talking about bacteria or fungi, *maybe* critters as advanced as jellyfish or shrimp. But nothing that would look at the stars and *think* about them, anyway."

"But there *might* be intelligent life down there."

Gray nodded. "Possibly. Very unlikely. They would be atechnic sophonts, like whales or woolimarus."

One of the most astonishing revelations of the past few centuries had been the realization that the concept of *intelligence* had been rather too narrowly drawn. As more and more species had been discovered off world, sophontologists had been forced to reexamine their criteria for just what constituted intelligence. Whales, the larger dolphins, elephants, great apes, even surprises like gray parrots and large octopi all now qualified as thinking species. It was just too bad that so many of those species had gone extinct before their special status had been recognized.

On other worlds, meanwhile, a bewildering number of species had been cataloged that appeared to exhibit intelligent behavior, including language use and strategic thinking, but without developing anything like a recognizable technology. The hexapodal arboreal mollusks called woolimarus, on Epsilon Eridani II, were just one of thousands of such; the dividing line between *intelligence* and *animal* had turned out to be completely fallacious.

"So why such deep thoughts?" Ryan asked him.

"I don't know. Just feeling philosophical, maybe. Talking with those Agletsch the other evening got me thinking, I guess. The Sh'daar don't want us to develop high technology . . . but our technology tends to grow and evolve just by its own nature. A million years or so ago we picked up a rock and invented the hand ax . . . and there's been no turning back since. I don't think we *could* turn back, even if we wanted to. I was wondering if people could give technology up entirely, go back to being clever apes."

Ryan chuckled. "Most people think folks in the Periphery are like that already. You know—primitives. Living in shells of old buildings, no computers, no electronics, no nano. They think we're stupid. Like animals, almost."

"Most people confuse *ignorant* with stupid," Gray said with a shrug. "When we were in the Ruins, we didn't have cerebral implants, so we couldn't have downloaded educations. But the first guy who invented the hand ax . . . or the spear . . . or who figured out how to start a fire, he didn't have implants either, but he had to have been one hell of a sharp Prim."

"Do you think people will give in to the Sh'daar? Give up high tech?"

"Like I said, I don't know how we could. And I guess that's why we're out here—making sure the Sh'daar aren't going to dictate to us what we can and can't do. Right?"

Outside, two more moons—Nix and Hydra, far beyond the orbit of Charon—were rising now, minute crescents just above the sunlit horizon.

"Even with our technology," Ryan said, "we're still just clever apes. We'd find a way to get back at them. Somehow."

"Against beings who are as far ahead of us as the Sh'daar are supposed to be?"

"Maybe they're not."

"Not what?"

"Maybe the Sh'daar aren't that far ahead of us. I mean . . . if they're worried about us becoming more advanced than them, getting fast enough that we could kick their asses . . ."

"It's a thought. The Agletsch said . . . what was it that one said? That the Sh'daar had already transcended? I still don't know what she meant by that."

"Maybe the Sh'daar are . . . are kind of what was left behind."

"What do you mean?"

"They were going along like us, their technology growing and improving. Then they hit the Technological Singularity. *Whoosh!* They turned into pure energy or pure thought or pure information on their equivalent of the net. But *what if they didn't all go*?"

Gray wrestled with the concept. "Why wouldn't they? Why wouldn't . . . oh." He got it.

"Right. When we were Prims, we weren't part of the technological mainstream. We are now, of course . . . but what if the Technological Singularity had hit five or ten years back, when I was fishing for a living in the D.C. swamps, and you were doing whatever you did in the Manhattan Ruins? All of Humankind would be off on another plane or dimension or wherever transcended beings go . . ."

"And we'd be right back there on Earth wondering why we'd been left behind."

"Exactly."

"I think . . . I think I'm going to need to give that one some thought," Gray said.

Humans tended to think of the Sh'daar as some sort of monolithic empire of godlike aliens . . . but wasn't it likely that they would have their dissenters, their rebels, their neo-Luddites, their *Prims*, just like Humankind? The idea put a whole new face on the Confederation's unseen enemy.

The two of them sat in silence for a long time after that, watching the cratered, dusty, dimly lit ice of Pluto's surface drift past below.

Admiral's Office, TC/USNA CVS America
Fleet Rendezvous Percival
Pluto Orbit, Sol Kuiper Belt
1412 hours, TFT

As it happened, Admiral Koenig was also thinking about the nature of intelligence, and of transcendence. Earlier that morning, an intelligence update had been broadcast through the solar fleetnet, based, it appeared, on the information uncovered by several of *America*'s pilots in a bar at Supra-Quito.

It was possible that the mainstream Sh'daar culture had reached Technological Singularity, possibly millions of years ago, and that the Sh'daar the Confederation faced now were castoffs, rebels, or Luddites left behind for some reason.

Koenig found the theory less than compelling, but intriguing nonetheless. It might explain why the Sh'daar seemed afraid of certain technologies, but not of others—specifically why they feared the GRIN technologies that served as drivers for transforming biological species into something else.

There was no way of testing the theory, though, not when the Sh'daar were in short supply. Perhaps at Arcturus or, deeper into the galactic night, Alphekka.

Koenig was seated behind his desk in his office, the overhead and two bulkheads set to display the appalling emptiness of space outside, with Pluto in half phase below. The sun was so small, so dwindled in light and heat, that it emphasized the terrible loneliness of this remote corner of Sol's dominion. *America* and thirty-four ships . . . against so much emptiness. . . .

"Admiral Koenig?"

It was Ramirez, on the communications watch.

"Koenig here."

"Sir . . . we've intercepted an incoming emergency message. I think you should hear it."

"What's the source?"

"A Sleipnir-class mail packet, sir. Origin is 70 Ophiuchi. The packet dropped out of metaspace and started broadcasting immediately. They're flashing Priority One-Urgent. Audio only."

"Patch it through."

Koenig heard the hiss of interstellar static, overlaid by a raspy voice. ". . . large force—Turusch warships and Nungiirtok ground forces! The main colony is under bombardment both from orbit and by ground forces. We need immediate help. Repeat, we need immediate help! I am en route to Fleet Base Earth. I request emergency docking clearance, and reinforcements for the Osirian colony. Message repeats. Priority One Urgent! This is Lieutenant Quinton, 2/2 Marines on Osiris. Five days ago, the Osiris colony came under attack by a large force—"

Koenig cut off the voice, and closed his eyes for a moment. *Shit! Not now! Not* now!

"Time delay to the mail packet?"

"Thirty-five minutes, sir," Ramirez replied.

Which meant that Quinton's radio transmission wouldn't be heard yet on Earth for something like five hours.

Which put Koenig in one hell of a nasty position.

Osiris—the 70 Ophiuchi system—lay just 16.6 light years away from Earth. This represented a serious and alarming change in enemy strategy. For more than thirty years, the Sh'daar and their allies had been nibbling away at the Confederation's outer perimeter. It had started in 2368 with the disastrous Battle of Beta Pictoris, 66 light years from Sol, and since then they'd been working their way inward system by system until they'd gotten as close as Eta Boötis, just a few months ago.

Eta Boötis was still 37 light years from Sol. Now, though, the Sh'daar alliance had staged two strikes into the very heart of the Confederation—the attack on Sol in October, and now this: an invasion of a Confederation colony that was, as astronomical distances go, right next door to Earth.

The Confederation Senate, when they got this news, was going to have a collective meltdown.

Koenig had worked under the Senate's authority for long

enough to know exactly how things were going to play out. His authorization to conduct Operation Crown Arrow would be withdrawn, his current orders canceled. The star carrier battlegroup would be ordered to remain within the Sol System to protect Earth.

He doubted that Quinton's request for reinforcements would be granted. A counterstrike *might* be ordered . . . but only after 70 Ophiuchi had been reconnoitered, and the enemy forces there thoroughly scouted out. It was all too likely that any Confederation counterattack would be too little and too late, striking at 70 long after Osiris had fallen to the enemy.

The same thing had happened before, a pattern repeating again and again, at Rasalhague, at 37 Ceti, at Sturgis's World, at Everdawn.

Koenig mindclicked a control and opened a 3-D map in the space in front of his desk. The volume of space occupied by the Confederation was represented by a lopsided blue egg filled with several hundred brightly lit stars containing colonies, bases, and outposts, scattered among several *thousand* ghosted stars, within that same volume of space, that had not yet even been visited by humans. A bite had been taken out of that egg, however, in the general direction of the constellation of Boötis.

Not only had the attack at 70 Ophiuchi leapfrogged past dozens of human colonies, it had also swung a full 150 degrees around the Confederation's borders, striking from almost the exact opposite side of human space. The capture of Osiris demonstrated that the Sh'daar alliance could freely hit any point within the Confederation, striking from any direction.

There were no front lines in this war . . . no safe areas in the rear, because there *was* no rear.

Koenig thought about strategy. . . .

In warfare, there were a number of principles key to managing and winning a prolonged conflict. Basic to these was the principle known as center of gravity.

Centuries ago, in warfare conducted strictly on the surface of Earth, the concept had been called center of mass.

If a general wanted to punch through an enemy's defensive line, he needed to know where the enemy's center of mass was, the point where he had most of his troops and equipment, and he needed to maneuver his own center of mass in such a way as to catch the enemy at a disadvantage.

In the three-dimensional maneuvers of fleets in deep space, the idea was not so much center of mass as center of gravity. A small force sent deep into enemy territory could have an unexpectedly large effect on the enemy's disposition. The Sh'daar were doing that by capturing Osiris, almost at the center of Confederation space. They wanted the human defenses to pull back close to Sol . . . either so that other human colonies were left defenseless or, worse, to put the entire human fleet in one place, where it could be destroyed once and for all.

Koenig had the uneasy feeling that this last was exactly what they were planning. By striking so deep into the heart of the Confederation, they hoped the human defenders would pull back all of their battlefleets and carrier groups to protect Earth. A single battle might wipe out or scatter all of the Confederation's military assets, and leave Sol defenseless. A three-decades-long war could be ended in a single strike.

In fact, Operation Crown Arrow had been planned as a similar shift in the conflict's center of gravity . . . a strike so deep into Sh'daar-controlled space that the enemy would be forced to pull back its fleets, and perhaps abandon planned operations inside Confederation space. The risk was high, obviously, but the payoff, if it worked, would be tremendous.

The problem was to get the Confederation Senate—short-sighted, politically motivated, and contentious—to see it that way.

Koenig placed his hand on a desk contact and began pulling in data. The positions of other battlegroups and fleets appeared on the map before him. Most were within the Sol System already.

Damn it, the Confederation had been on a defensive posture since the very first battle of this war in 2368. Wars could *not* be won by assuming a strictly defensive posture and waiting for the enemy to attack. But if the Confederation waited much longer, they wouldn't have the fleet assets to even put up a defense. They needed to go onto the offensive, and they needed to do it *now.*

The strategic imperative seemed obvious to Koenig . . . but he also knew that the Senate would see the situation only in terms of protecting Earth from this new threat. The battlegroup would be ordered to stay put.

And for that reason, Koenig was determined to move before they could give him orders that he would have to disobey.

The Senate Military Directorate included military men who would see what he was doing, and Carruthers and the Joint Chiefs would probably support his decision as far as they could. Still, the decision would, in all probability, end his military career.

And if he was wrong, if he took a sizable fraction of the Confederation fleet out beyond the Confederation's borders and Earth was destroyed or conquered, he would be reviled as a traitor, or worse.

It was neither an easy nor a pleasant decision to make.

"Captain Buchanan?"

"Yes, Admiral."

"Ship's status?"

"We're at full power and ready for Alcubierre interface on your command, Admiral. All members of the battlegroup report ready for FTL."

"I take it from that that you heard the message that just came through."

"Yes, sir. Ramirez linked me in." Buchanan hesitated, then added, "If it helps, Admiral, I fully support—"

"Belay that, Randy. No sense in putting your career on the line too."

Not that it would help. If things turned out badly, the Confederation government—whatever was left of it—would be looking for scapegoats. Koenig's decision might be seen as cowardice in the face of the enemy or, at the least, an attempt to circumvent his lawful orders.

Orders. He stated that he was to wait at the fleet rendezvous at Pluto until "on or before 9 January," two more days from now, before executing the first phase of Crown Arrow. That phrase gave him a bit of leeway. He could leave early, though the assumption had been that he would stay until all possible reinforcing units could join the battlegroup.

"How many ships are we still expecting, Randy?"

"The *Jeanne d'Arc* and eighteen PE warships are still planning to rendezvous with us on the ninth, Admiral. And we're waiting to hear if the Chinese are going to send along a contingent as well."

The Chinese were always a wild card. The pan-European force would be a nice addition, but . . .

"We're not going to wait. Pass the word to all ships. We will maneuver clear of Pluto's gravity well and engage our Alcubierre drives once we reach a flat metric. Course will be toward galactic north for five hours in order to clear the solar plane, then emergence and realignment for Arcturus."

"Aye, aye, Admiral."

"Mr. Ramirez?"

"Yes, sir."

"Speed-of-light lag to Earth."

"Five hours, ten minutes, fifty-one point five seconds."

"Very well. Prepare a message for delayed transmission to Earth."

"Aye, Admiral. Recorders running."

"Message begins. For Joint Chiefs of Staff and the Senate Military Directorate, Earth, this is Rear Admiral Alexander Koenig, commanding the reinforced Confederation Star Carrier Battlegroup *America*."

He paused, thinking over what he wanted to say. Ramirez would edit out any awkward hesitations, and he needed to make his case clear. The chances were good that it would be read at his court-martial.

If any of us survive this, he thought.

"At 1435 hours Terran Fleet Time, 7 January 2405, I am initiating Operation Crown Arrow. I do this in the firm belief that striking deep into enemy-held space will force the enemy to interrupt his current military operations against

Earth and the Sol System, and alleviate some of the pressure he is currently bringing to bear on the Earth Confederation. It is my intent to do as much material damage to enemy warships, bases, and supply depots as possible, in order to shift the center of gravity of this war away from Earth and into Sh'daar territory.

"I am making this decision on my own authority, and the full responsibility is mine, and no one else's.

"I will, of course, attempt to communicate with Confederation forces from time to time by fleet packet . . . but the nature of extended interstellar campaigns, of course, is such that you will probably not hear from us for some time to come.

"Godspeed to you all. With luck, you'll know that what we're doing is working when the enemy begins pulling back from Confederation space.

"This is Rear Admiral Koenig, commanding Interstellar Carrier Battlegroup 1, ending message."

He played the message back for himself, listening critically. He'd deliberately made no mention of having heard the news from 70 Ophiuchi *before* giving his orders. The astronomically savvy among them, though, would realize that he'd heard the news and left before Earth could send him new orders. His career, clearly, would be over with this one . . . but he hoped to be able to take the fleet a very long way indeed before any new orders could catch up with him. Geneva would know he'd ordered the battlegroup out of orbit long before the ships would be able to enter metaspace . . . but he also knew how Geneva worked. They would consult, they would debate, they would consider. They would talk to the Joint Chiefs . . . and Admiral Carruthers, he knew, would do his best on Koenig's behalf.

With luck, he would be unreachably tucked away into metaspace and outward bound before orders to stay—or orders calling for his resignation—ever reached him.

"Mr. Ramirez, you may transmit the message."

"Aye, aye, Admiral."

"Captain Buchanan?"

"Yes, sir."

"Time for us to cross the Rubicon. Make to all ships in the battlegroup. Break orbit and engage gravitic drives, five hundred gravities' acceleration, galactic north, until we reach a flat metric."

"Understood, Admiral. We are breaking orbit."

His reference to the Rubicon was deliberate. When Caesar had crossed the Rubicon, the limit past which no Roman general was allowed to bring his armies without challenging Rome's authority, he'd known there was no going back. A similar boundary was being crossed now.

The frigid, white face of Pluto and its coterie of moons slid off to starboard, then dwindled rapidly into the emptiness of star-strewn space.

Chapter Thirteen

29 January 2405

Emergence
Arcturus System
0848 hours, TFT

Space exploded into being once more, as *America* dropped clear of metaspace in a nova-brilliant burst of photons. Ahead, a brilliant yellow-orange beacon blazed against the background stars—Arcturus, 36.7 light years distant from Sol.

The rough outline of the Alcubierre Drive had been worked out as long ago as the 1990s, by the Mexican physicist Miguel Alcubierre Moya. Essentially, where it was impossible for anything, mass or energy, to travel faster than light, there was no such restriction against space itself breaking the ultimate speed limit of the cosmos. Exactly that had happened, in fact, during the early life of the universe, in the so-called inflationary phase immediately after the Big Bang. Alcubierre had pointed out that a hypothetical spacecraft might enclose itself in a bubble of spacetime, motionless relative to surrounding space, while the bubble moved forward at multiples of *c*.

Of course, in the last decade of the twentieth century, no one, even Alcubierre himself, had any idea how this might actually work.

The engineering details had been worked out in the mid-twenty-second century, after the development of the gravitic drive. In order to engage the Alcubierre faster-than-light drive, two things were necessary—a flat spacetime metric, meaning no nearby planetary or stellar bodies gravitationally bending local space, and an initial velocity approaching that of light. As a ship approached *c* under normal gravitic drive, its mass approached infinity, and the Alcubierre Drive utilized this relativistic mass to form the FTL bubble, folding space around the ship and accelerating it to velocities faster than light.

Upon emerging from Alcubierre Drive, the ship's velocity remained what it had been inside the spacetime bubble—essentially zero relative to the region of space within which it had initially engaged the drive. The velocity of the spacetime bubble bled off as energy—an intense burst of EM energy from radio to gamma-ray frequencies, as well as gravitational waves, immense ripples through local spacetime.

There was no way, then, to disguise the emergence of a starship from metaspace—the term for the folded-off interior of an Alcubierre spacetime bubble. As *America* dropped into normal space, a dazzling flash of radiation flared with the momentary glare of an exploding star. Other ships in the battlegroup were emerging as well, though they tended to be scattered across a rather large volume of target space. The light from some of them would not reach *America* for some minutes yet.

"Okay, everyone," Koenig said from his seat in the CIC. "On your toes. We've just rung the front bell."

"Stellar drift at one hundred twenty-two kilometers per second," *America*'s navigation officer announced. "Two-three-three by one-zero-five by five-one-one."

The star Arcturus, with its family of planets, was an oddball in Sol's galactic neighborhood, cutting across the current of local stars instead of traveling with them. It was believed to be an outsider, a star originally belonging to a small galaxy devoured by the Milky Way some millions of years ago and now literally just passing through. As a result, its velocity was considerably higher than that of local space, and the battlegroup was going to have to accelerate hard to match velocities with the system.

America had emerged some 21 AUs from the gas giant Alchameth. In less than three hours, then, the Turusch ships gathered around the gas giant and its planet-sized moon would detect the energy surge as it crawled across 3.1 billion kilometers at the speed of light. Until then, unless the enemy had scouts or pickets lurking in the system's outskirts, the Confederation fleet was maneuvering unobserved. At one hundred gravities, a nudge from the ship's drives, it took just over two minutes to match velocities with the local system.

With *America* traveling at the same velocity and in the same direction as the star, the drives switched off. Star carriers could not launch fighters while under acceleration. The tiny vortex-singularity of intense gravitational moment projected from instant to instant ahead of the carrier's shield cap would have caught any emerging fighters in its maw and crushed them in a flash of X-rays. The gravitic projectors were off as the first two Starhawk fighters loaded into the launch tubes.

In CIC, Koenig turned to Captain Barry Wizewski, the carrier's CAG. "Commence flight operations."

"Commence flight ops, aye, aye, Admiral," Wizewski replied. "Flight decks! Commence fighter operations. Launch ready spacecraft."

VFA–44 Dragonfires
Arcturus System
0903 hours, TFT

Lieutenant Trevor Gray leaned back within the embrace of his Starhawk's cockpit, going through the downloaded mantra designed to help him relax. His in-head display counted down the seconds to launch.

America possessed two flight launch tubes running 200 meters down the carrier's spine and out through the center of the forward shield cap. Fighters were autoloaded into breech locks in the spine two by two, then magnetically accelerated along the launch rails at seven gravities, emerging through the shield cap 2.39 seconds later, traveling at 167 meters per second.

Gray was fifth in line for Tube One, his fighter wrapped in darkness as he waited in the queue. It was very much like being a bullet in a magazine, waiting to be loaded and fired.

He felt the jolt and slight sideways motion as his Starhawk advanced a step with each launch. It took about five seconds for the railgun magnetics to recycle, which meant the waiting pilots felt a *chunk*–pause–*chunk*–pause rhythm as fighter after fighter hurtled out from *America*'s forward launch tubes ahead of them. Gray then felt the sensations of his fighter slipping into Tube One's breech lock.

"Dragon Nine," a female voice said in his head, "you are go for launch in three . . . two . . . one . . . launch!"

Acceleration pressed him back into his seat, and his vision dimmed. . . .

. . . and then he was out in the empty black of space, the crushing pressure of seven gravities suddenly gone.

"Dragon Nine clear," he said.

"Dragon Ten clear," Katie Tucker added as she emerged from Tube Two.

A check aft showed the vast, dark dome of *America*'s shield cap receding in an instant to a point of light as Gray's fighter fell sunward at better than six hundred kilometers per hour. In another instant, even the star was gone, lost among clouds of real stars strewn across emptiness.

Switching to forward view, Gray saw Arcturus gleaming brilliantly directly ahead, a small, intensely bright disk. A navigation reticule marked the location of the objective, off to one side of the orange sun.

Gray let his Starhawk drift until Tucker drew up alongside, and then the two accelerated together, falling in with the other fighters that had already launched. Green-diamond icons marked the other ships, each with a string of alphanumerics giving ship number and pilot id. More and more fighters joined the tight phalanx already falling in-system, until all twelve Starhawks were in tight formation.

"Dragonstrike," Commander Marissa Allyn said over the

squadron comnet, using the codename for this op. "Configure for high-G flight."

The SG–92 Starhawk possessed transmorphic hulls that allowed them to change their outward configuration in flight. They'd launched as twenty-meter black needles, each with a central bulge housing the pilot and the control and weapons systems. At Gray's command, his Starhawk reformed itself, the complex nanolaminates of its outer structure dissolving and recombining into a blunt and mirror-smooth egg shape with a slender field-bleed tail-spike off the stern. Technically, this was boost configuration, but the pilots, with the humor typical of military personnel, routinely called it "sperm mode." His Starhawk was now only seven meters long, not counting the field-bleed spike astern, and five wide, though it still massed twenty-two tons.

"Dragonstrike Leader, Dragon Nine," he reported. "Sperm mode engaged. Ready for boost."

"*America* CIC, this is Dragonstrike," Allyn said. "Handing off from PriFly. All Dragons clear of the ship, formed up, and ready for PL boost."

"Copy, Dragonstrike Leader," a voice replied from *America*'s Combat Information Center. "Primary Flight Control confirms handoff to *America* CIC. You are clear for high-grav boost."

"Acknowledge squadron clear for boost," Allyn said. "Keep the lights on, people. We'll be back."

"Roger that, Dragonstrike. You're the sharp, pointy end of the stick, but we'll be right behind you."

"Dragonstrike," Allyn said over the squadron's tac channel. "Engage squadron taclink."

Gray focused a thought, his left hand on the palm contact. The onboard AIs of all twelve fighters were interconnected now by laser-optic comnet feeds. The squadron could move, could maneuver, could *think* as one.

"And gravitic boost at fifty K," Allyn said, "in three . . . two . . . one . . . *punch* it!"

A gravitational singularity opened up just ahead of Gray's Starhawk, a focused bending of space that inexorably dragged the starfighter forward. The singularity winked out, then switched on once more a fraction of an instant later. And again. And again.

Gray was falling now under an acceleration of fifty thousand gravities, but, since the projected gravitational field affected every atom of his gravfighter uniformly, Gray felt none of the acceleration he'd experienced during the diamagnetic launch from *America.*

He was in free fall, his speed increasing by half a million meters per second with each passing second. The stars remained unmoving despite his velocity. After one minute he was falling forward at three thousand kilometers per second, or 1 percent of the speed of light.

And in ten minutes he was swiftly approaching the speed of light itself.

CIC, TC/USNA CVS America
Arcturus System
0918 hours, TFT

America had dropped into Arcturus space at precisely 0848:16.4 TFT, and the light announcing her arrival had started spreading out in all directions. Thirty minutes later, other ships in the battlegroup up to thirty light minutes out could see her. As other ships continued to arrive, the light bearing news of their arrival began spreading out across local space in overlapping bubbles.

As each ship became aware of the position of other ships in the battlegroup, optical communications lasers flashed out, linking the fleet into an interconnected whole.

America's Combat Information Center was the heart of the battlegroup's command, control, and communications, the nexus of that vast web of precisely aimed laser-optical communications, but the web's growth was agonizingly slow. The CBG ships were emerging within a zone nearly a light hour across, and the speed of light imposed a hindering time lag to the fleet's organization.

"How are we doing?" Koenig asked, joining a knot of CIC officers floating above the main tacsit display, a tank three meters across filled with glowing, colored icons marking the CBG fleet.

"Twenty-three ships have merged and linked in, Admiral," Commander Sinclair announced. "We estimate that all of the others have arrived by now. We just can't see them yet."

Koenig nodded. Space combat was dominated by the speed-of-light time lag.

The other ships, having established communications with *America*, were beginning to close with her. One by one, the vessels aligned themselves within a few thousand kilometers of the *America* and then gradually began accelerating.

At five hundred gravities, Alchameth and its moon, Jasper, were nearly fourteen hours away. The fleet would accelerate steadily for half of that time, at which point they would be traveling at four-tenths of the speed of light. They would then begin decelerating for the second half of the journey into circum-Alchameth space.

Five fighter squadrons had been launched so far—the Nighthawks, the Impactors, the Dragonfires, the Night Demons, and the Black Lightnings; the remaining two, the Death Rattlers and the Star Tigers, would be held in reserve for combat space patrol during the CBG's close passage of Alchameth. Only the Dragonfires and the Night Demons had been fired off through the launch tubes. The rest had dropped from the centripetal launch bays and were accelerating now down the first two squadrons' wakes.

The Dragonfires, the Lightnings, and the Night Demons would decelerate into circum-Alchameth space in 178 minutes, the sharp, pointy end of the stick, as Wizewski had just told Commander Allyn. Just three hours from now, they would hit the enemy ships close to Alchameth and Jasper, arriving minutes after the photon wavefronts generated by the emerging battlegroup reached them.

Their mission would be to pin the enemy vessels near Alchameth until the rest of the battlegroup reached them, some ten hours later.

According to the oplan, the *America* battlegroup would stage a "shoot-and-scoot," a fast and furious in-and-out moving at high velocity past the gas giant and its moon, smashing every enemy ship and installation it could reach. The idea was to cause as much damage as possible and, in particular, to destroy Arcturus Station, the large orbital base above Jasper.

That, it was hoped, would get the Sh'daar's attention, and perhaps cause enemy fleets now threatening the inner core of the Confederation to break off and return to Arcturus.

By the time they did so, of course, *America* and her consorts would be long gone.

Key to the attack were the three squadrons sent in ahead of the rest of the fleet. They could cause tremendous damage to capital ships with their Krait missiles and particle beams, especially if the enemy was caught napping, and their sensors would locate every enemy ship for the fleet's targeting AIs. The problem lay in how long it would take the rest of the fleet to arrive.

For the thirty-six fighters of those three squadrons, it would be an agonizingly long ten hours before the fleet came zorching in behind them.

Arcturus Station
Jasper/Alchameth
Arcturus System
1136 hours, TFT

Vrilkmathav wondered if the Sh'daar Seed could have made a mistake.

The very thought was disturbing, of course. *Unthinkable* . . . if not for the fact that it had, indeed, thought it. It checked to see if the Seed had picked up the thought, and decided that it had not.

Vrilkmathav was a Jivad Rallam, a species that had served the Sh'daar faithfully for tens of thousands of cycles. The Jivad had witnessed the Change that had seen the Old Sh'daar disappear . . . and since the Jivad had not been able to follow them, they had continued to serve the Remnant ever since, ultimately accepting the Seeds as marks of honor, as emblems of the close bond the Jivad Rallam still maintained with the galaxy's masters.

Could the Masters have made a mistake?

Vrilkmathav rolled through the alien corridors, rippling its way toward the captives' den. The Jivad were massive tentacular decapods, with under-body tentacles held in a tight, writhing ball as they moved forward on undulating twists, tasting the ground as they moved.

It reached the hatch leading into the den, a massive nanoseal entryway flanked by two armed and heavily armored Nungiirtok guards.

"Here for another one?" the lead guard asked him in thickly accented *Drukrhu*, the Agletsch-designed *Lingua Galactica* used by most of those of the masters' servant races that relied on audible, air-generated phonemes for communication. "You *thabbik* are going to use them all up soon."

Vrilkmathav didn't know what *thabbik* were, and didn't particularly care. It suspected that the guard was attempting to be humorous, but they didn't appear to have the capacity for making jokes. In any case, the ponderously rumbling Nungiirtok were difficult to understand even with a perfect translation interface through a Seed.

These guards didn't have Seeds, however, so Vrilkmathav simply produced a memory card from its pouch and waved it above the reader beside the door. Recognizing Vrilkmathav's clearance, the device turned the black metal of the seal to cool, rigid liquid, and the Jivad rippled through.

One of the guards followed it in. "The *klippnizh ag* have been troublesome lately," he said. "You'll want me in there with you, believe me."

"Fine," Vrilkmathav replied. "Just try not to burn so many of them if there's trouble. As you say, we don't have many to spare."

A small airlock had been built beyond the first door, with a second seal. Vrilkmathav took down a Jivad respirator, fitting the two masks tightly over the breathing tubes on either side of its massive body, then waved the data card over a second reader. The doorway liquefied, and the Jivad and the Nungiirtok passed together through the black seal into misery.

The Jivad didn't believe in anything like the human concept of hell; the closest thing they had to a deity was the Sh'daar Remnant itself. The Agletsch word *ngya*, however, translated roughly within its thoughts as "misery," did come close. It was a Sh'daar Remnant term referring to the devastation and emptiness of being left behind, to being abandoned and alone. And the mob of filthy creatures beyond the black door certainly seemed to express such emotions.

Several thousand of the creatures calling themselves human had been captured within this huge, orbital base when it had fallen to Turusch forces just over two Jivad years ago. That had been a remarkably lucky break, for until then the masters' forces had known little about human physiology or psychology. The population of this captured base had provided the Turusch and Jivad researchers with numerous specimens to question, study, and dissect as they attempted to build up a coherent picture of the race of beings comprising the Earth-human Confederation.

The captive population, however, was not doing well. All of the surviving humans had been herded into a single compartment in the space base, the largest space on board—most likely a room for feeding and for group meetings. Nanoreplicators producing food and water had been left intact to keep them alive, but other replicator circuits had been disabled to prevent them from building weapons or escaping the compartment.

At first, the captives had organized themselves, with leaders who'd attempted to establish communications with the Jivad and Turusch scientists who were studying them. They'd shown considerable spirit, too, attempting to break out several times by rushing the Nungiirtok guards when a researcher went in, and trying to tear them apart with their bare manipulators. Hundreds of the creatures had been burned down in those attempts.

Over the past half dozen *matye* or so, however, the humans had . . . changed, somehow, seeming to sink gradually into a poisonous, sullen squalor. They no longer attempted to communicate, no longer exercised, no longer even kept themselves clean. The prisoners' den reeked of bodily excretions, filth, and the subtle tastes of ammoniate chemicals Vrilkmathav had come to associate with human fear and hopeless desperation.

The population of imprisoned humans still numbered almost a thousand individuals crammed into a space roughly two hundred by three hundred *vri* in floor area, but they were dying off at an increasing and alarming rate. Nungiirtok servitors moved through the compartment every diurnal period, removing the newly dead.

But they kept dying, whether from disease or from despair, Vrilkmathav could not tell.

Vrilkmathav surveyed the room, the Nungiirtok standing uneasily beside and in front of him. It was aware of the stares of human eyes; humans possessed eyes quite similar to those of the Jivad, though fewer of them. It could also sense the fear, the loathing, the horror behind those stares.

"I require only one," it told the guard. "A female, if possible."

The guard lumbered toward the mass of creatures, which struggled backward, the front ranks pressing back against those behind. A vast keening of moans and wails and shouts—meaningless words—rose from the group as the Nungiirtok picked out one creature. It struggled as the guard lifted it off the floor with its massive, armored hand. The guard then turned the specimen, extending it for Vrilkmathav's inspection.

The Jivad accepted the creature, holding the squirming thing gently but firmly with one manipulator tentacle while using others to strip away the filthy and half-shredded textiles with which these creatures ornamented themselves. Humans, unlike the Jivad, were bisexual, with numerous morphological differences between the genders to distinguish them from each other, but it was difficult for the Jivad to tell at a glance which was which.

There was one gender-related difference, however, that made sexing the creatures easy. They generally wore decorations over that difference, however, hiding it for some reason.

"No," Vrilkmathav said, tossing the squalling creature aside. "Another one."

The guard picked another struggling, screaming human and held it up for Vrilkmathav's inspection. It checked the creature's sex, then gave an assenting flick of its fourth manipulator. "This one will do," it said, pinning the creature's thrashing limbs with its first and third manipulators. It could taste the sour tang of ammoniates, the bite of sodium chloride on the thing's outer integument.

"Stop you!" one of the creatures shrieked in clumsy but intelligible *Drukrhu*. "Why you this do?"

Vrilkmathav rolled one of its eyes to regard the human, which had stepped out from the crowd and was looking up at the Jivad with outstretched manipulators. "No do! *No do!*"

Several of the humans, apparently, had already known *Drukrhu* when the base had fallen to the masters' forces, apparently through earlier trade relations with the Agletsch. The Jivad had been encouraging those few to teach the language to the rest, since it made verbal interrogations easier.

This one took another unsteady step forward, pointed at the creature Vrilkmathav held, and said something unintelligible, probably in its native language. Than it straightened up, still pointing. "No take . . ." and it lapsed into gibberish again. "Take me!"

Vrilkmathav thought the daring human was male, though it couldn't be sure. A sexual-bond pairing of some sort—a mate?

It scarcely mattered. Vrilkmathav had the specimen it needed. *"Myeh,"* it said, one of several basic *Drukrhu* terms for negation.

"No do! Why you this do? . . ."

"To understand your kind," Vrilkmathav rumbled in reply. "So that we may save you."

It turned away, rolling on its tentacles toward the door. Vrilkmathav felt an emotion similar to compassion for these imprisoned beings, and didn't like doing what had to be done. Jivad Rallam biology had three reproductive sexes, plus the maternal-neuters evolved as child rearers and protectors. Vrilkmathav was a neuter, completely sexless . . . but it possessed a powerful nurturing instinct that, it found, tended to interfere when it worked with these humans. The creatures were small and helpless and tended to squall like a clutch of Jivad young still trapped in the nursery tidal pools. They evidently were not adapting well to their long imprisonment here, and were failing. The knowledge tormented Vrilkmathav. They'd been put in Vrilkmathav's care; it wanted to *help* them.

Which led it to the central question once more. Had the masters made a mistake, ordering some thousands of human prisoners to be confined here as Turusch and Jivad Rallam researchers interrogated, experimented on, and studied them? Would it have been better, perhaps, to release them as a gesture of goodwill, in order to get the human Confederation to talk to the masters' representatives?

Was so much pain and death really necessary? Vrilkmathav didn't know how much the creatures really felt what was done to them, but they appeared to feel pain in a manner similar to Jivad. The agitation of this human male seemed to indicate that they felt emotions akin to their captors. And why not? They were a star-faring species, like the Javid Rallam, and passion, curiosity, intellect, and self-awareness all were necessary for such exploratory ventures, surely.

Vrilkmathav was approaching the doorway seal when the human male shrieked and charged. The Nungiirtok burned the creature down with the flamer built into the black armor encasing one of its manipulators. The human gave a piercing wail, sickeningly like the cry of a Jivad youngster baking in the sun . . . and then all of the humans were surging forward, screaming, gesturing, a rolling tide of unthinking fury. The guard turned the flamer on them; orange fire hissed, splashed, and clung, as several humans dropped and writhed on the floor, engulfed by burning fuel. Vrilkmathav laid a tentacle on the guard's shoulder, restraining him. "*Myeh!* Leave them!"

Reluctantly, the guard began backing toward the door. Vrilkmathav rippled through first, then waited for the guard to enter the airlock as well. Reaching up, it plucked one of the respirator masks designed for humans from the wall. The human captive struggled, trying to pull the mask off, but once it was in place, a touch of one tentacle sealed it to the creature's integument.

Humans and Jivad Rallam breathed *almost* identical oxygen-nitrogen atmospheres, but Jivad required a higher percentage of carbon dioxide—almost 2 percent by volume—than did humans, and Vrilkmathav's respirator added the missing CO_2 when it entered the human den. If the human didn't wear the mask to filter out the excess CO_2 now present throughout the rest of the base, it would swiftly lose consciousness and die. Humans didn't seem to react well to carbon monoxide, either, or to several other trace compounds in the standard Jivad Rallam atmospheric gas mix.

"What . . . what want you from us?"

Vrilkmathav swiveled all four eyes down to look at the human in its grasp. Moisture was streaming from its eyes—a biological lubricant of some sort that Vrilkmathav had noted in other humans when they were in extreme pain or psychological duress. The fluid tasted strongly of sodium chloride when it touched the Jivad's tentacle.

This one spoke *Drukrhu*, then, and fairly well, better than the dead male inside the den.

"In your case," Vrilkmathav said, "we wish to explore the artificial devices implanted within your . . . *erj* . . . *erj* . . ." It didn't have the technical word.

" 'Cerebral cortex,' " the Sh'daar Seed within its primary brain suggested.

"Ah. The devices within your cerebral cortex."

The atmosphere stabilized at Jivad norm, and the outer door liquefied. Vrilkmathav rippled through the black curtain of rigid liquid.

"We have noted," it continued, "that these devices appear to be similar to something we call 'the Sh'daar Seed,' which is a microscopic set of circuits that enable us to communicate with the masters. If that similarity, in fact, exists, it may be that we will be able to create devices enabling you to experience a direct interface with the Sh'daar. We have dissected the brains and brain implants of several of the other humans—but all were male. We now wish to see if there are morphological differences between human females and males, and if the electronic implants you carry are different as well."

Vrilkmathav wasn't sure how much of what it said was understood by the human; the creature's grasp of the artificial Agletsch language seemed less than complete. It must have understood some of what Vrilkmathav said, however, judging by the way its struggles to escape the Jivad's grasp increased.

Its shrieks sounded *so* much like those of injured Jivad Rallam young.

There were times when Vrilkmathav truly hated its assignment here.

An alarm shrilled through its Seed. "What is happening?"

Several *vrith* passed before it received an answer. The Sh'daar Seed didn't so much speak as communicate through impressions, through a kind of knowing. An enemy fleet of warships had just appeared on the outskirts of this system. The energies now being detected by Turusch, H'rulka, and Jivad ships were many *thavii* old now, and likely there were fighters inbound on the very heels of those energy wavefronts.

Vrilkmathav spun about sharply, thrusting the human at one of the armored guards. "Quickly!" it said. "Put this back with the others! Gently, idiot! Don't hurt it! Put it away and join your unit! We are under attack!"

Jivad neuters were warriors before they were scientists—a function of their nurturing and protective roles in Jivad Rallam biology. It hurried off toward the ship bays as swiftly as its roiling tentacles could carry it.

Chapter Fourteen

29 January 2405

Alchameth-Jasper Space
Arcturus System
1147 hours, TFT

From Gray's point of view, the entire flight, from launch to objective, had lasted scarcely twenty minutes.

As a ship approached the speed of light, time dilation did strange things to time on board, slowing its passage to a fraction of the normal rate. Accelerating at fifty thousand gravities, the fighters had reached 99.9 percent of the speed of light in just under ten minutes, with time passing more and more slowly as they neared *c*. For the pilots of the three squadrons of the advance strike force, the following 160 minutes in the outside universe was for them just 7 minutes, 9 seconds. By skimming across 20 AUs at just less than *c*, Gray and the others had lost over two and a half hours as the rest of the universe measured time—were two and a half hours younger than those left behind in the relatively slow-moving battlegroup.

As the three Starhawk squadrons decelerated into circum-Alchameth space, subjective and objective times began to fall back into phase. Their weirdly distorted view of the surrounding cosmos, a starbow of light ringing the blackness around each fighter thirty degrees forward of center, began to smear back into the accustomed stars of non-relativistic flight.

Gray tried to shove aside the rising fear, the memories of nightmares—tried, and failed.

He'd been in the Arcturus System before. Fourteen months earlier, the Star Carrier *Ticonderoga* and seven escorts had responded to a courier request for help. Gray, fresh from a training squadron at Oceana, had been the FNG in VF–14, the White Furies, and as the *Tike* had entered the Arcturus System, he'd been spin-deployed on Combat Space Patrol.

The Turusch had been waiting for them. Probably, they'd noted the escape of the courier and guessed that Confederation reinforcements would arrive within a few days. Several enemy task groups had been scattered across the Arcturian system, and one, by chance, had been less than thirty light minutes from the *Tike*'s emergence point.

For six hours, the *Ticonderoga* had fought off waves of enemy fighters, ship-killer missiles, and gunships. She'd limped clear of the battle at last, shield cap breached and spewing ice crystals, screens gone, most of her weapons smashed, three quarters of her crew dead or dying of radiation poisoning. It had been a miracle that she'd been able to slip into Alcubierre Drive and escape, a miracle that the Turusch had not pursued her.

Gray had been back on board rearming his ship. He was one of just two White Furies to survive the Battle of Arcturus Station.

This time, of course, it was different. A powerful carrier battlegroup was launching an alpha strike at an enemy that did not know they were coming. Three fighter squadrons were hurtling into the system just behind the wavefront announcing their arrival. This was *payback*, not a repeat of the disaster of fourteen months ago.

But Gray still felt the fear. "Pucker factor," the pilots called it, the feeling that you were gripping the acceleration seat of your fighter so tightly with your ass that you were never going to be able to let go.

He focused on the immediate, routine tasks at hand, keeping his mind busy on other things. In particular, he studied again the scans downloaded from the ISVR–120 probe that had passed through this star system a month ago, noting the ship positions and tentative identifications. Much could have changed in a month, of course, but ONI's assessment held that the strategic picture in the Arcturus system ought to be pretty much the same. If anything, there might be fewer Turusch heavies here, as they prepared to move against Sol.

Long-range sensor scans from the emergence point had definitely pinpointed the two Beta-class battleships spotted by the reconnaissance probe, still close beside Arcturus Station. There was also a scattering of smaller vessels, though how many and where, exactly, was tough to pin down from 21 AU out. Their power-plant leakages tended to be lost in the glare from the local star and in the belts of hard radiation surrounding Alchameth.

Gray gave a silent command, and battlespace monitors—finger-sized robots with high-grav drives—sprayed from his Starhawk, spreading out with monitors from other fighters to create a cloud of electronically interconnected micro-detectors monitoring optical, radio, neutrino, and gravitic wavelengths throughout circum-Alchameth space.

They would know for sure in another minute or two whether the tactical situation had changed at all.

The fighter's AI continued to slow the Starhawk with an unfelt tug of fifty thousand gravities. The starbow continued to dissipate, as space took on its normal and accustomed non-accelerated shape.

Arcturus blazed ahead and to the left, golden orange and brilliant, and Alchameth was a bright star directly ahead. As the fighters continued dropping deeper in-system, the star became a tiny orange crescent, expanding swiftly as the fighters continued to slow.

"Here we go, Dragonstrike," Allyn's voice called. "Record sensor data and transmit on auto, Channel 3294."

Everything Gray's fighter picked up either from the battlespace monitors or with its own sensor array would be streamed outward, where it would be captured by the incoming *America* and other CBG vessels and fed into their tactical displays, updating them each tenth of a second.

So far, it looked like the alpha strike had caught the enemy sleeping.

A dozen large alien ships clustered near the Earthlike moon, Jasper. Largest were the two Betas, converted asteroids massing some tens of millions of tons each—oblong, dusty-looking potato shapes pocked with numerous craters and showing constellations of star-point lights and the bristle of heavy weapons emplacements. They appeared to be hanging close to Arcturus Station, pacing its two-hundred-kilometer orbit around Jasper. Eight smaller ships, Juliet- and Kilo-class Turusch heavy cruisers, floated in the asteroids' shadows.

Two more were unidentified, their shapes not listed in the warbook residing in Gray's Starhawk fighter. They were large, however, as large as the Juliets, and had already been tagged as "Red-One" and "Red-Two" on the tactical display net.

There were lots of smaller vessels scattered across the tactical display as well. Gray's fighter had pinpointed fourteen Turusch destroyers and frigates so far, and more, almost certainly, were hidden by Alchameth's broad and color-banded bulk.

"Bravo-One and Bravo-Two are the primaries," Commander Allyn's voice said over the fighter comnet. "Hit them, then fire at will. You are not clear to engage Arcturus Station, repeat, *not* clear to engage the station until we have solid telemetry on who's inside!"

That part of the operation had been endlessly discussed and dissected in tactical simulations during the voyage out from Sol. It had been fourteen months since the first Battle of Arcturus Station, but there was still a chance, a small one, that there were humans still alive and on board. How the incoming battlegroup would engage the ships in circum-Alchameth space depended in large part on whether there were human POWs still on the station after all of this time.

"Strike Nine, Kraits armed," Gray reported. "Target lock! Fox One!"

A VG–10 Krait smart missile streaked from beneath the black folds of his Starhawk's keel, its tiny high-G grav drive radiating a dazzling star of dumped heat and light. Other smart missiles began arcing in from the other fighters, their contrail-wakes curving as they swooped toward their behemoth targets. Answering contrails punched out from the enemy ships, streaking out toward the fast approaching fighters.

"Evasive maneuvers!" Allyn commanded, and the fighters began jinking, using brief, intensely focused singularities to port and starboard, above and below, to keep their vectors from becoming predictable. As the enemy missiles closed, the Confederation fighters fired sand canisters—containers of refractive particles used as point-defense against both missiles and energy beams.

White light blossomed in the silence of hard vacuum, a Krait detonating against one of the Beta battleships. Its shields were up, twisting space to deflect the blast, but enough heat and hard radiation leaked through to boil the gray, pocked surface. A second detonation pulsed against the night, knocking out shields, sending a gout of white-hot gas spewing out into space. Other missiles fell into the Turusch fleet, some striking the asteroid battleships, others homing on the cruisers. Within seconds, local space was an intolerably brilliant cascade of expanding fireballs. "Nailed 'em!" Lieutenant Donovan cried.

"Good shooting, Dragonfires!" Allyn called. "Break and engage!"

All three fighter squadrons were scattering now, each ship continuing to jink to frustrate the enemy's defensive fire.

For many years, strategic wisdom had declared that piloted space-fighter craft were an anachronism, a holdover from the long-gone era of jet-powered fighters launching from oceangoing aircraft carriers and about as relevant to space warfare as ancient oared triremes. The physics of interstellar combat, however, made them inevitable.

Capital ships—the carriers, battleships, railgun cruisers and destroyers of the fleet—had a maximum acceleration of around five hundred gravities, a limit imposed partly by the available power from current quantum energy taps, and partly by their sheer size and mass. And because the space-warping fields of their Alcubierre FTL drives required that local space be "flat," undistorted by gravitational masses, ships had to exit their FTL bubbles far from a local star—generally twenty to fifty astronomical units out.

In high-acceleration boost mode, a Starhawk fighter massed just twenty-two tons and measured seven meters in length, not counting the long field-bleed spike astern. Low mass and small dimensions let them accelerate at rates up to a hundred times greater than capital ships, which meant they could reach 99.9 percent of the speed of light in something just under ten minutes.

A cloud of high-G fighters, then, could be in among an enemy fleet deep in-system twenty minutes after the light bloom of capital ships entering normal space on the system's outer perimeter. Highly maneuverable, they could get in close and cause crippling damage to even the largest of enemy capital ships. Even a Turusch Alpha-class battleship, a converted asteroid massing trillions of tons, could be damaged severely enough by fighters that it became an easy mark for the heavy weapons of the battlegroup when it arrived hours later.

As for why fighters still had human pilots rather than AIs . . . the principal reason had to do with the prejudices of the military and political decision makers back home. Artificial Intelligences could pilot small ships—*very* small ships, in fact—independent of human oversight, but most humans still feared what might happen if AIs were given unrestricted and unsupervised control of megatons of destructive power.

And so human pilots continued to squeeze themselves into high-G fighters and let themselves be accelerated into combat, engaging in deadly knife fights with far larger and more powerful warships. Gray adjusted his ship's current trajectory to skim past an enemy Tango-class destroyer directly ahead. His fighter's AI handled the split-second timing of the combat pass, but it was Gray who gave the engage order.

He had an instant's impression of the Turusch destroyer's hull, painted in jagged patterns of green and black as it loomed ahead, then flashed past to port. Gray's AI pivoted the Starhawk, holding its Gatling RFK–90 KK cannon on-target through the pass, loosing a stream of magnetic-ceramic jacketed slugs at a cyclic rate of twelve per second.

Each round, with a depleted uranium core massing half a kilo traveling at 175 meters per second, carried a savage kinetic-kill punch as powerful as a tactical nuke as it ripped through hull metal and defensive shields. As the destroyer fell astern, gouts of light erupted from its flank; water from its reaction-mass tanks spilled into space, freezing instantly in a swelling cloud of glittering particles of ice.

"Dragon Five, Dragon Nine, this is One," Allyn's voice called over the tactical link. "You're both on close approach to the station. Drop a couple of ears on it, okay?"

"Copy that," Gray replied.

"Roger," Lieutenant Collins added. "Stay out of my way, Prim."

Gray bit off an angry response, deciding to ignore the taunt. He palmed the programming touchpad and readied a VR–5 reconnaissance probe.

Slightly larger than a human head, the VR–5 remote-scan sensor probe was identical to a battlespace remote probe, but with different programming. A Starhawk carried a battery of four VR–5s, which could be selectively programmed for specific missions.

By chance, both Gray's and Collins' fighters would be falling past Arcturus Station in another few minutes, Gray's Starhawk passing less than fifty kilometers from the structure, Collins about seventy. Gray programmed two of his VR–5s, and directed his AI to release them at the optimum launch point for intercepting Arcturus Station.

Then a trio of tactical nuclear weapons detonated a few kilometers astern, and Gray was very busy accelerating clear of the blast fronts, high-velocity expanding shells of charged particles and hot gas that could overwhelm a fighter's defenses if they hit the ship's shields and screens at close range.

There were fighters out there, punching in through the gas shells—a pair of Turusch Toads.

Toads were heavy fighters, squat and ugly, thirty meters long, fifteen thick, and massing over fifty tons. They didn't change shape like Starhawks and other more modern Confederation fighters, but they were more powerful, could accelerate more quickly, and could survive the detonation of a tactical nuke at close range. Gray flipped his fighter end for end, bringing his PBP–2 to bear on the nearest one.

The StellarDyne Blue Lightning particle beam projector mounted on his Starhawk's spine charged, then fired. Variously called a PBP, a CPG for "charged-particle gun," and, more commonly, a "pee-beep," the weapon loosed a tenth-second gigajoule burst of tightly focused protons, a straight-line lightning stroke that could overpower enemy radiation screens and boil off tons of surface armor. Gray's first shot knocked down the lead Toad's forward screens, and he followed up with a burst from his KK Gatling, using the Turusch ship's higher relative velocity against it. The explosion flooded nearby space with the harsh glare of evaporating grav singularities, and forced the second Toad to break off its approach.

Gray fired a second proton beam . . . and then his AI took momentary control of the fighter's attitude to release both VR–5s.

"Dammit, Gray," Collins told him. "I told you to stay clear!"

Her fighter cut sharply past his, twenty kilometers ahead.

"Plenty of sky for both of us," he told her.

On the tac display, four VR–5s fell toward Arcturus Station. One flared and vanished as it hit a cloud of sand, fired by the point-defense system of one of the Turusch ships. A second, then a third probe struck sand clouds and vanished.

And then Gray's fighter fell between Arcturus Station and Jasper.

The moon had swelled huge in the past few moments, a gigantic, sharp-edged crescent filling the sky ahead. Golden clouds covered much of the visible surface, reflecting the gold-red light of Arcturus. Jasper's atmosphere was primarily nitrogen and carbon dioxide, with traces of ammonia. The Confederation colonizing team had begun terraforming the world three years earlier, raising enormous nanoconverters on the surface to break down the carbon dioxide into oxygen and carbon. Presumably, the surface converters had been destroyed by the Turusch; possibly, they intended to colonize the world themselves, since they breathed an atmosphere composed primarily of CO_2.

In any case, Jasper's atmosphere was still a deadly poison, as Gray's fighter skimmed through the uppermost layers in a piercing shriek of ionizing gasses. Gray's Starhawk was traveling at over seventy thousand kilometers per hour relative to the moon, however, far too fast for gravity to more than briefly tug at him.

And then he was clear, with Alchameth and its moons dwindling behind. He'd had only a glimpse of Arcturus Station, a bright star accompanied by the constellation of the enemy fleet. Missiles arced out from one of the Beta-class battleships; the other appeared to be leaking internal atmosphere and was in trouble.

It looked like one of his VR–5s had survived the enemy's defensive volleys and made it all the way in to the station.

Gray accelerated. . . .

Arcturus Station
Jasper Orbit
Arcturus System
1201 hours, TFT

When launched, a VR–5 recon probe was a mirrored-black cylinder half a meter long and three centimeters thick. In flight, its nanomatrix hull flowed together into a black egg twenty-five centimeters long. As the surviving probe approached Arcturus Station, however, it gave a single sharp, short burst of deceleration, then unfolded like a blossoming flower, with black petals expanding and reaching out as if to embrace the station's outer hull. The orbital base possessed radiation screens, of course, but not shields. Had the station been protected by space-twisting defensive shields, the probe's penetration attempt would have been far more difficult.

As it was, however, the probe dropped through the electromagnetic screens as four petals, longer than the others, stretched out to serve as landing legs. They touched the station's hull, merged with it as the nano-charged tips rearranged the local metal chemistry, and drew the rest of the probe down to rest.

The probe's artificial intelligence was far smaller, far more limited than a Gödel 2500 or similar AI, and, though classified as sentient and self-aware, it had nothing close to human flexibility or scope. It basically had a limited set of functions within its software parameters . . . but those functions were things it did very, very well. It detected the station's screens and merged with them effortlessly, redirecting the energy flow so that the probe's landing went undetected by the facility's sophisticated sensory and monitoring equipment.

The programmed nano of the probe's business end began melting through solid layers of metal and ceramic, and the device swiftly sank from sight, leaving behind only a hair-thin wire thread to serve as a communications antenna.

In moments, the probe's penetrating tendrils encountered fiber-optic wiring and an access to the station's electronic systems. Many had been taken off-line by the Turusch invaders, including the sentient component of the base's resident AI.

But within moments the VR–5 was reading through a complete station checklist, monitoring life support settings throughout the facility and even turning on security cameras and microphones.

There was some internal damage to the station, where control panels had been melted, and power leads cut. Overall, though, the orbital base remained intact. Most of the atmosphere had higher-than-expected levels of CO_2, but temperature and the basic gas mix were close to human-norm. Better yet, the Arcturus Station AI was still present as resident software—switched off—"sleeping" in a sense—but still residing within the base computer network.

Following its programmed instructions, the recon probe opened a relay. . . .

Alchameth-Jasper Space
Arcturus System
1204 hours, TFT

Gray brought his fighter onto a new heading, whipping the Starhawk around a projected singularity fast enough that the G-force nearly made him black out. Falling in a straight line through a gravitational field—even one measuring fifty thousand gravities—was felt by ship and pilot as free fall, but vector changes—whipping around a high-G singularity—still exerted an outward centrifugal force. Make too tight a turn, and the pilot could be smeared into jelly, his ship stretched and ripped into microscopic fragments.

Fighter AIs were designed to monitor turns closely and override pilot commands that might exceed safety limits. Even so, Gray experienced nine gravities as his ship made its turn. Blood drained from his head despite the tight embrace of his seat around his legs and torso, and he came perilously close to blacking out.

Ahead, one of the mystery ships was breaking free from Jasper orbit, accelerating toward open space.

"Strike One, Strike Nine," he called. "Red-Two is on the move. In pursuit."

"Copy, Strike Nine. Take him out."

"Copy. Arming Kraits . . . target lock . . . and . . . *Fox One*!" The first nuclear-tipped Krait slid from the Starhawk's belly into the void. "And *Fox One*!"

The enemy ship was big, as big as a Turusch Hotel-class heavy cruiser, five kilometers long and massing some millions of tons. The design was clearly different, however, suggesting that it had been built by a different, possibly unknown Sh'daar client race. It lacked the jarring hull-color schemes favored by the Turusch, and the hull itself was of an unknown design, with the look of a collision involving several dozen dark gray spheres and spheroids of different sizes, from several hundred meters across to the big leading sphere, which had a diameter of more than two kilometers. Gray's guess was that the alien ship was built along the same general lines as *America* and other Confederation capital ships, however, with that forward sphere holding reaction mass. He'd ordered both Kraits to target the cluster of small spheres just aft of the big one, reasoning that, as with *America*, that would be where the alien's command-control and habitable shipboard areas would be, safe in the RM tank's shadow.

An AI alarm was shrilling in his head, seeking his full attention.

"What?"

"We have telemetry from the VR–5," the AI told him.

"Well . . . shoot it on to the *America*." There was nothing he could do about it at the moment anyway.

"I already have. Expected transmission time is 117 minutes. However, you should see the data."

This was *not* a good time. One of the Kraits vanished, intercepted by the enemy's point-defense. He armed two more Kraits, readying a follow-up strike.

"Go on."

A window opened in Gray's awareness.

"Oh, shit! . . ."

He didn't notice when the second Krait twisted through the enemy warship's defenses and detonated just behind its two-kilometer sphere.

"Make sure the rest of the strike group gets this too," Gray said.

The data was precise and complete.

There were human survivors on board Arcturus Station.

Lots of them.

CIC, TC/USNA CVS America
Arcturus System
1356 hours, TFT

America had completed just over one third of her fourteen-hour voyage from emergence to the objective. Almost five hours after beginning acceleration, she'd traveled more than 760 million kilometers, and was now hurtling inbound at over 87,000 kps, almost 30 percent of the speed of light.

Alchameth and Jasper were still more than nine hours away.

Admiral Koenig floated above the CIC's big tactical tank, watching as the ship's navigational and combat AIs continued, moment by moment, to update the display. They were 134 light minutes out from the battle, now, so everything they saw in circum-Alchameth space was 134 minutes out of date, but that state of affairs would change as they drew closer, over the course of the next nine hours.

Each of the fighters was sending a steady stream of data out to *America* and her consorts. Just eight minutes ago, they'd seen the fighters engage the enemy fleet elements around Jasper. Many of the men and women around the tank had broken into cheering as one of the Beta-class battleships was crippled . . . then again as a Turusch cruiser and two destroyers were savaged as well. The second Beta was under way, clear of Arcturus Station and moving outward, but slowly, possibly damaged. Other enemy vessels appeared to be damaged as well.

On the downside, the enemy's defenses had knocked down five Confederation fighters. The alpha strike had suffered 13 percent casualties, and the fight was only eight minutes old.

"Sir!" the CIC communications officer called. "New message coming through. Priority urgent!"

"Put it through."

A window opened in the minds of Koenig and the other senior CIC personnel. The message had been composed in the form of a standard naval communiqué.

FROM: VR–5 RECONNAISSANCE PROBE 6587

TO: *AMERICA* CIC

TIME: 1203.38.22 TFT

SUBJ: ARCTURUS STATION

IN ACCORDANCE WITH PROGRAMMED INSTRUCTIONS, VR–5 6587 HAS PENETRATED THE OUTER HULL OF ARCTURUS STATION AND INFILTRATED BASE ELECTRONICS AND INTERNAL CONTROL SYSTEMS.

BASE AI HAS BEEN ACTIVATED, ALONG WITH LOWER-TIER SECURITY AND CONTROL SYSTEMS.

CAMERA AND IR SCANS HAVE LOCATED 975 HUMANS ON BOARD

ARCTURUS STATION, LEVEL 5, COMPARTMENT 740, MESS AND RECREATION SPACES.

NO HUMANS HAVE BEEN IDENTIFIED IN OTHER AREAS OF THE STATION. HOWEVER, 2,825 LIFE FORMS OF VARYING DESCRIPTIONS HAVE BEEN IDENTIFIED IN VARIOUS STATION COMPARTMENTS, INCLUDING SHIP BAYS AND STATION CONTROL CENTER.

I HAVE MERGED WITH THE AI DESIGNATED "GUARDIAN" AND AWAIT FURTHER ORDERS.

"Christ," Buchanan said. "*That* throws some quantum uncertainty into things."

"It does," Koenig agreed. "Looks like it'll be Plan Gamma."

Chapter Fifteen

29 January 2405

Demon Twelve
Alchameth-Jasper Space
Arcturus System
1401 hours, TFT

High-G space fighters enjoyed considerable advantages in close combat with capital ships. Their speed and maneuverability made targeting them with beam weapons extremely difficult, especially at ranges where speed-of-light time lags made predicting a target's future position more a matter of guesswork than of mathematics. At longer ranges, smart missiles were the only reliable way to kill fighters . . . and fighters possessed sandcaster rounds and other point-defense weapons specifically designed to knock out incoming missiles.

Inevitably, though, as the space battle continued, those advantages began wearing away. The sheer size and mass of enemy capital ships, the numbers of weapons they possessed, the amount of raw power they could direct to shields, screens, and beam weapons began to tell. Fighters carried sharply limited supplies of expendable munitions—thirty-two VG–10 Kraits, generally, and forty-eight anti-missile rounds, ninety-six AM decoys, and two thousand depleted uranium slugs for the RFK–90 KK cannon. After more than two hours of steady combat, the Confederation fighters were beginning to run low on missiles.

More and more of the Confederation fighters were dying.

There were nine Night Demons left in the fight. Chalmers, Ball, and McKnight were gone, picked off one by one by the increasingly accurate and deadly fire of the Turusch heavies.

Commander McKnight had been the squadron's skipper, blown out of the sky when a couple of Toads had dropped onto his ass ten minutes ago and hammered him with pee-beep fire. Lieutenant Commander Jonnet had taken command of the squadron . . . though at this point it was tough to tell if *anyone* was in control.

"Break left, Demon Twelve!" Jonnet was yelling. "Break Left!"

Lieutenant Shay Ryan rolled her Starhawk left, pulling around a projected singularity with a savage pull of G-forces as three Turusch missiles swung in from high and off her port stern quarter, then kicking in a ten-K boost. By turning in to the missiles, she had a chance of shaking them off her tail, or at least of forcing them to slow in order to match her turn.

The sky around her was filled with light—pulsing flashes of nuclear weaponry detonating silently against the night. A quarter of the sky was filled by the ringed, banded giant, Alchameth, bloated in half phase and red-gold in Arcturian light. Her new vector was carrying her toward the swollen planet at over one thousand kilometers per second. Jasper and Arcturus Station were somewhere behind her, she wasn't sure where.

White light blossomed astern as one of the missiles detonated, a desperate attempt to disable her. She punched out two decoys—hand-sized robots that moved and reflected like a Starhawk fighter—hoping to ditch the remaining two incoming warheads. One of the Turusch missiles veered off, tracking the drone . . . but the other stubbornly completed its turn and continued homing on her ass. It was less than a hundred kilometers away now, and closing at a leisurely fifteen kilometers per second.

"Impact in six seconds," her AI whispered in her head.

"I know, *I know*!" she yelled into the close embrace of the fighter's cockpit. She was out of sand . . . and the loom of the super-Jovian gas giant ahead was rapidly cutting off her tactical options.

With the seconds to impact dwindling away, Ryan flipped her Starhawk end for end, dragging the targeting cursor floating in her in-head display onto the red icon marking the fast-approaching missile. She triggered a burst of high-velocity Gatling fire, hosing the incoming warhead. The target was tiny, less than four hundred centimeters wide, impossibly small for a targeting ship even with AI-assisted aim. The warhead was jinking as it approached, and she continued to squeeze off bursts at twelve per second.

The enemy warhead exploded just four kilometers off, the wavefront of fast-expanding debris and radiation washing across her fighter like a tidal wave, knocking out screens, killing her forward drive projector, sending her Starhawk into an uncontrollable tumble. The fireball dimmed, then faded.

Ryan was falling helplessly toward Alchameth.

"This is Demon Twelve," she broadcast on the general tactical channel. She felt strangely relaxed, almost accepting.

I'm going to die, she thought. "I'm hit. Mayday, I'm hit. I'm falling in. . . ."

Dragonfire Nine
Alchameth-Jasper Space
Arcturus System
1406 hours, TFT

Gray saw the fifty-kiloton nuclear detonation close by the green icon marking Shay Ryan's ship, heard her calm announcement over the taclink. He was twelve hundred kilometers behind her and closing—pure chance in the free-wheeling chaos of a space-fighter furball, but fighter pilots relied on chance, on luck, as often as they relied on the predictions of cold, hard numbers.

Alchameth was just half a million kilometers ahead. At Ryan's current speed, she would tumble into the outer layers of the giant's atmosphere in another seven or eight minutes.

"Night Demon Twelve, this is Dragonfire Nine," he called. "I'm following you down from twelve hundred out. What's your situation?"

"Dragon Nine, Demon Twelve," she replied. He could hear the stress in her voice. "Main power out, primary drives out. I'm tumbling . . . about fourteen rotations per minute. I've got . . . shit . . . looks like seven minutes and something before I burn up."

When Ryan's fighter hit the gas giant's outer atmosphere, friction would turn it incandescent, then vaporize it in the flare of a brief-lived shooting star.

He was closing with her fast. "Twelve, Nine. Can you control your tumble?"

There was a long pause. "Negative, Dragon Twelve. Maneuvering thrusters are dead."

He accelerated harder, until the green icon drifting in his view ahead gave way to a black delta shape—an SG–92 Starhawk in combat mode, crescent-shaped, with forward-arcing wings, tumbling slowly.

Gently, Gray edged his Starhawk closer, maneuvering with brief, precisely controlled bursts from his thrusters. Using his fighter's AI, he projected vectors in his in-head display, lines and angles of light accompanied by flickering blocks of alpha-numerics, showing direction, spin, and momentum.

Starhawks weren't designed for this kind of work. It was going to be a bit on the hairy side.

"Hang on, Ryan," he said. "I'm going to connect in three . . . two . . . one . . ."

In combat mode, a Starhawk's wing-arcs curved forward and down, creating a sheltered area beneath the fighter's belly. Gray was trying to use those wings as arms to capture Ryan's tumbling ship, to bleed off momentum and stop its end-over-end roll.

His fighter bumped against Ryan's ship, hard enough to jolt him and knock his fighter up and back. The transfer of momentum had robbed her tumble of some of its speed. She was still tumbling, but more slowly now.

Ahead, Alchameth filled the sky, its rings a brilliant slash across heaven. The fighters were falling toward the planet's night side, toward a point just below the dark curve of the horizon.

"You okay in there?" Gray asked Ryan.

"Yeah. A little shook up, is all."

"I'm coming in again."

"Damn it, Gray, you're not a freaking tug."

"Well, SAR tugs are in kind of short supply right now. Brace yourself."

He approached the other fighter again, once more nudging it with the body of his own ship. The impact this time was a heavy, dull thud, and the vector lines on his internal display vanished save for the big one showing Ryan's downward plummet.

"Still okay?"

"Uh. What are you doing, slamming my cockpit with a hammer?"

"Worse. I'm using my 'Hawk. I think I've about got that spin neutralized, though."

"So I'll auger in nose first, nice and neat. You can't pull my ship out of this fall. I just ran the numbers. You *can't*."

Gray was looking at the same numbers, as his AI fed them through his IHD. A Starhawk massed twenty-two tons unloaded. The projected artificial singularities used for acceleration and for turns were precisely balanced in both virtual mass and in distance. If a fighter was too close to a singularity by even a matter of meters, tidal forces could stretch it and its pilot in the so-called "spaghetti effect," resulting in both being ripped into their component atoms. Gray was asking his AI if it could handle the changes necessary on the fly to project a turning singularity that could accommodate both fighters together, a combined mass of over forty-four tons.

The results coming back were not encouraging.

He'd gone into this thinking that he might be able to lock the two fighters together with mooring lines, his ship above, hers below, then project a turning singularity forward and above, causing both fighters to go nose-high, turning away from the planet looming ahead. The hull structure of an

AG–92 simply wasn't up to that much stress. If the mooring lines broke as the fighters went into the turn, hers would be flung "down" and into the gas giant, while his fighter had a good chance of being nudged the other way, and into its own singularity.

He ran the numbers for simply holding onto Ryan's fighter with mooring cables and throwing a deceleration vortex astern, slowing the two of them. Again, the forces involved were far too great for the mooring lines Gray had available. Ryan's fighter would continue to fall—a bit more slowly, perhaps, but still with more than enough speed to slam into the planet's atmosphere within a matter of minutes.

He couldn't project a singularity through the other fighter in order to draw both onto a new vector.

Damn it, there had to be *something*. . . .

Alchameth had grown noticeably larger in the past minute, sliding off to one side. The two fighters were dropping beneath the sharp-edged plane of the outer rings now, Ryan's Starhawk nestled in spoon-fashion beneath Gray's fighter and between its drooping wings. They would plunge into significant atmosphere, Gray saw, in six more minutes. Damn it, the infalling vector was close. With only a small boost applied in the right direction, they could change vector enough to skim above Alchameth's horizon, rather than plunge beneath it.

He looked at firing his maneuvering thrusters in such a way that he could nudge both fighters higher on their descent path. The amount of reaction mass he still carried for his plasma-jet maneuvering thrusters, however, was limited. He looked at combining his reaction mass with what was left in Ryan's tanks. *Still* not enough. The numbers were close, tantalizingly close . . . but just not close enough.

Just a *little* nudge . . .

"Got it!" Gray said. He had the AI run through the numbers again, checking the new configuration. There *was* a way . . . hairy, but it gave them a chance.

"There's no way, Trevor!"

"Trust me." Reaching out to the touch pad, he fired a mooring line from his fighter's belly into the dorsal surface of Ryan's Starhawk. The tip imbedded itself in her hull's nanomatrix, anchoring the two together.

With his AI's constant help and finely calculated assistance, Gray used his maneuvering thrusters to reorient the two falling Starhawks, then start them tumbling nose over tail once more.

"*Trev!* What are you doing?"

"Trust me! This is going to work!"

He hoped.

He ran the calculations past the AI a third time. Human reactions would *not* be fast enough to pull this off, and it was entirely possible that the stresses he was setting up would render both humans unconscious. But his AI would remain aware. . . .

The tumble increased. Centrifugal force was tugging hard at Gray now, a steadily increasing sensation of out-is-down weight, of fast-growing pressure threatening to force the blood out of his legs and torso and up into his head. His vision blurred, becoming red.

The AI was in control now as Gray slipped across the ragged edge of consciousness.

And at a precisely calculated instant, Gray's fighter released the mooring cable, and the two ships, their connection broken, hurtled apart. Both were still falling toward Alchameth at seventy thousand kilometers each second, of course, but the spin-and-cut maneuver had imparted new vectors to both craft, which were now flying apart from each other.

Of course, the maneuver had added energy to Ryan's fighter, and that energy had been taken from Gray's. His new trajectory was plunging him deeper and deeper into Alchameth's gravity well.

Gray was unconscious . . . but his AI recognized the danger and engaged the fighter's gravitational singularity drive.

A fiercely powerful knot of compressed spacetime appeared ahead and to one side of his Starhawk's prow, and the fighter, under AI control, whipped around it in a ten-G turn.

CIC, TC/USNA CVS America
Arcturus System
1409 hours, TFT

This is always the hardest part, Koenig thought, staring into the tactical display tank. *Waiting while other people are out there dying. . . .*

America was now traveling at 53 percent of the speed of light, with another two hours before they began deceleration, nine hours to go until they reached Alchameth and Jasper. In the tank, both red and green icons had drifted apart from one another, filling the display with flecks of colored light. For some reason, he found himself thinking about the Solstice celebration weeks before, at the eudaimonium.

Of the thirty-six fighters sent in with the first assault, thirteen had been destroyed. Many more had been disabled, were on straight-line trajectories out of battlespace, maneuvering and grav drives out, unable to get back into the fight.

By now, many, too, would be out of expendable weaponry.

On the plus side of the tally sheet, both Beta-class battleships and both of the red-flagged mystery cruisers had been destroyed or badly damaged, and half of the smaller ships had been knocked out as well. There were still a lot of Turusch fighters hunting down individual Confederation Starhawks, but overall, the enemy fleet had been badly bloodied. One small group of five Turusch cruisers and destroyers had fallen into a tight formation and was accelerating outsystem, well away from the incoming battlegroup. They would be light hours away by the time *America* reached circum-Alchameth space, and well out of the fight. The rest, many of them damaged and adrift after the fighter swarm's assault, had been left behind.

And now it was up to the battlegroup.

The original battle plan had called for the carrier battlegroup to accelerate for nine hours before beginning to decelerate . . . but at thirteen hours after they'd left the emergence point, they would have come booming through the Alchameth-Jasper system at ninety thousand kilometers per second. With the Turusch fleet shot up by the fighter assault, the fleet's heavies would have no problem mopping up. Many of the ships in the battlefleet were already positioning themselves to launch high-velocity kinetic-kill weaponry that would sweep through the battlespace before their arrival, targeting the drifting survivors.

The discovery by an AI probe that there were human survivors—prisoners of war, presumably—on board Arcturus Station changed everything.

Under the original plan, the CBG would have swept through the Alchameth-Jasper system at high speed, destroying everything they could reach, then would have slowed, performed a difficult turning maneuver, and returned at more sedate velocities to pick up the fighters . . . or have the fighters rendezvous or dock while the carrier was still under way. Disabled fighters, the ones drifting helplessly now without drives or maneuvering thrusters, would have to be tracked down and rescued by SAR tugs.

Success in battle often required a certain bloody-minded tenacity. You created the best plan you could, practiced it, and stuck with it, no matter what . . . because to change plans in the middle of a fleet action was absolutely guaranteed to screw everything to hell and gone.

But even more often, success in battle went to the fleet best able to adapt to changing circumstances, the most flexible fleet, the fleet with the greatest number of viable options.

"Okay," Koenig said after a long moment's thought. "Oplan Gamma. Here's how we're going to play it through."

The strategic overview in the display tank vanished, replaced by schematics of the thirty-five ships of the *America* battlegroup, each model-sized and to scale, arrayed in orderly ranks. Koenig waved his hand, and the two largest ships moved off to opposite sides of the display. "The battlegroup will be divided into two squadrons," he continued. "*America* and *Kinkaid*. MSU–17 and the supply ships will stay with us. *Kinkaid* will lead a group of eight cruisers and ten destroyers.

"The *America* squadron will stick with the original plan, beginning decelerating at the halfway point, which will have us entering Alchameth space after fourteen hours.

The *Kinkaid*'s squadron will accelerate for nine hours total, passing through Alchameth space at boost-plus-thirteen hours, and with a relative velocity of ninety K kilometers per second."

Koenig had worked through the details while they'd been waiting at Point Percival weeks before. Plan Alpha had assumed the enemy was at least as strong as the reconnaissance probe had indicated, allowing the entire CBG to pass through battlespace at high speed, slow, and return to pick up the fighters. Plan Bravo had assumed that enemy numbers in the Arcturus system were significantly greater than expected, so much greater that the battlegroup would have to withdraw from out-system without even making the attempt.

Oplan Gamma gave a third option, allowing the transports and carriers to decelerate to a rendezvous in Alchameth-Jasper space after fourteen hours, and one hour after the battlegroup's big guns had passed through.

"No battle plan ever survives contact with the enemy," a voice whispered in his mind.

It took him a moment to realize that the voice was Karyn Mendelson's, his personal assistant. God, he missed her. . . .

The words, of course, were five and a half centuries out of the past, the famous aphorism of *Generalfelldmarschall* Helmuth von Moltke the Elder.

"The key," Koenig added, "is for both squadrons to stay flexible, for both to keep their options open in order to be able to adapt to anything the enemy might still be able to spring on us."

And yet, each decision he made, each change in the original battle plan, threw more variables into the mix, and made a decisive blunder more likely. Koenig's order would divide the fleet, never a good idea in the face of a situationally aware opponent.

"The *Kinkaid*'s squadron will take time to decelerate and rejoin the CBG, of course," he continued. "The Marine fighters off the *Nassau* and *Vera Cruz* will help cover the *America*'s squadron while we're at Arcturus Station."

"Almost a thousand POWs," Lieutenant Commander Charles Hargrave said. "Where are we going to put them all?" Hargrave was with *America*'s tactical department, which meant he was already juggling ships, supplies, and personnel in his mind. "I think we'll have to use the *Mars*."

As he spoke her name, one of the ship images on the *America* side of the tank glowed with its own bright halo. She was a combat stores ship, an AFS, a clumsy-looking vessel half as long as *America* and massing nearly seventy thousand tons unloaded. Her pressurized cargo decks would be uncomfortable, chilly, and in zero-G for the three-week flight back to Earth, but the nanoreplicators on board would keep a thousand rescued prisoners supplied with air, food, and water for as long as necessary.

"Offload her supplies," Koenig continued, "distribute what you can through the rest of the fleet, and load the POWs on board her for the trip back to Earth."

"Mars," Commander Morgan said. He was the CBG's logistics officer. "That's Captain Conyer. I'll talk to her and her AI about setting up a transfer schedule."

"Good. Do it."

"We may not be able to save all of the supplies, though. It could leave us short."

"The most critical stores," Koenig said, "are expendable munitions. We can find plenty of iceteroids and carbonaceous chondrites along the way for food, air, and water." He looked up. "General Mathers?"

"Sir." Joshua Mathers was the CO of the battlegroup's Marine contingent, some twelve thousand men and women assigned to MSU–17. He and his command staff were present electronically, since they were at the moment on board the *Nassau*, the command vessel for the Marine assault force. Their images above the display tank were virtual avatars projected by *America*'s CIC AI.

"I leave it to you to put together an assault plan for Arcturus Station. You'll need to burn your way on board, rescue the prisoners, and get them off onto the *Mars* as quickly as possible. Your two major headaches, not counting enemy forces on the station, will be the time it's going to take to transfer supplies off of the *Mars*, and the fact that the prisoners are going to need breathing apparatus. According to our intel from the recon probe, only the mess hall-rec space has a breathable atmosphere. The rest of the station has an excess of CO_2."

"Yes, sir," Mathers said. "We can set the replicators to cranking out breather masks, with simple filters to screen out the carbon dioxide. If we can set up a ship-to-station through-hull, we should be good to go."

"Coordinate that with Captain Conyers, please."

"Aye, aye, Admiral."

"Okay . . . the rest of you, be looking at the tacsit and tell me what I've missed."

"There is one thing, Admiral," the CIC operations officer, Commander Katryn Craig, said. She sounded reluctant to bring it up.

Koenig gave a wry smile. "You're about to mention that H'rulka warship."

"Yes, sir. The recon probe last month spotted it inside the gas giant's atmosphere. It followed the probe back to Sol, and we beat it off. Did it come back to Arcturus? Or are there more of them down in Alchameth's deep atmosphere?"

"That," Koenig said, nodding, "is a great question and I wish to hell we knew the answer."

He had a feeling, though, that they would be finding out quite soon.

"All we can do is keep an eye out, and hope the H'rulka didn't come back here," he said. He shrugged. "If she did, we take her out. Any way we can."

Dragonfire Nine
Alchameth-Jasper Space
Arcturus System
1413 hours, TFT

Prodded by his AI working through his cerebral link, Gray struggled back to consciousness. His body ached. Despite the padding provided as his acceleration couch had flowed over his body, he felt like someone, a very *large* someone, had worked him over with a length of plasteel pipe.

But a quick look at his instruments showed that his Starhawk was under power and under drive, hurtling across the face of Alchameth. His fighter had plunged into atmosphere and slowed sharply; he could feel the steady shudder as the craft plunged through roiling atmosphere. His AI had slowed him to prevent the incineration of his Starhawk, and he was now traveling at a mere few tens of kilometers per second. His fighter's broad, forward-curving wings were generating lift.

The cloud tops were still far below him. Gas giant atmospheres—mostly cold hydrogen—tended to extend some thousands of kilometers above the highest of the colored cloud bands, which were rolling past far beneath him. He was over the night side of the planet, but a ghostly luminescence—and reflected light from bright Jasper—made the clouds eerily visible below. He could see the maws of vast, swirling storms, the sheer cliffs carved from clouds falling into dark depths thousands of kilometers deep. Lightning pulsed in those depths, flickers and flashes softly diffused, masked by the night-shrouded clouds.

And ahead and below he saw . . . lights.

At first, Gray thought he was seeing lightning, but these lights remained stubbornly steady, a rigid and tightly spaced constellation, like city lights on Earth, but spread out across a far vaster background. They appeared to delineate a structure of some kind; he had to remind himself that gas giants like Alchameth had no true surface, that the atmosphere itself kept going down deeper and deeper and deeper, becoming hotter and hotter, and under increasingly crushing pressures. Somewhere down there, deep inside the planet, gaseous hydrogen turned to a kind of semi-solid hydrogen slush at fierce pressures and temperatures. Those lights, whatever they were, had to be floating near the cloud tops.

And something large was rising from the lights.

Gray and the other pilots had been briefed on the data brought back by the recon probe a month before, and they'd watched tactical feeds of the H'rulka vessel during its incursion into the solar system. Gray didn't know if this was the same or a different H'rulka vessel, but it was definitely of the same sort—bulbous, a flattened sphere in shape some twenty-two kilometers across.

The sheer scale of the thing was daunting, but so, too, was the scale of the planet from which it was rising. That titanic city or base, or whatever it was, lit by hundreds of starlike lights, must be more than two hundred kilometers across, but it was all but lost against the enormity of the world above which it drifted.

Gray had three Krait missiles left. Swiftly, he programmed them, targeting the rising H'rulka warship.

And as his Starhawk dipped ever deeper into the giant's atmosphere, the thin hydrogen wind shrieking outside his ship, he locked onto the target and fired.

Chapter Sixteen

29 January 2405

H'rulka Warship 434
Alchameth
Arcturus System
1416 hours, TFT

Ordered Ascent took the H'rulka ship up, punching through the upper layers of thin haze above the Gathering. Warship 434 had been reassembled after the battle in the alien star system, with the missing ship-section and crew members replaced by volunteers here at the Wall of Golden Clouds.

They—the composite being called Ordered Ascent—were worried.

The Golden Clouds Gathering was in effect a nomadic city, a temporary meeting place for some thirty thousand H'rulka colonizing this world. It was a delicate structure spun from metals and hydrocarbons brought down from the gas giant's rings and smaller, innermost satellites. Suspended on anti-gravity generators, it rode with the planet's storms and currents of wind, providing the "solid ground" the sky-borne H'rulka required for manufacturing and technology.

Ordered Ascent and their crew had been scattered about the Golden Clouds Gathering and riding the winds nearby when the alert had come through from the Sh'daar Seeds. The Turusch, orbiting among the debris-worlds above the planet, were under attack.

The creatures calling themselves human had shown unexpected strength and resilience in their technology. The incoming ships were so tiny they might easily be overlooked, but they channeled significant energies, energies sufficient to destroy even a H'rulka warship.

And if their warships were vulnerable, so, too, would be the Gathering below. Ordered Ascent wanted to get Warship 434 clear of the planet's atmosphere, up where it could maneuver freely and deploy the full effect of its weaponry.

One . . . no, *two* of the alien vermin were passing through the gas giant's upper atmosphere as Warship 434 rose. One was already leaving the gas giant's atmosphere. The other was approaching, dipping deep into the planet's gaseous envelope. Ordered Ascent felt, through the ship's senses, the release of three minute knots of gravitational energy.

"Maneuver clear!" Ordered Ascent broadcast to the others. "Fusion warheads descending!"

The enormous H'rulka composite vessel began shifting out of the path of the incoming missiles, but too slowly . . . too slowly. Capable of enormous acceleration in free space, the massive warship was hobbled this deep within an atmosphere and, worse, within the gravitational field of the gas giant.

"Close defense!" they boomed . . . but the incoming missiles were already too close as proton beams snapped and flared from the huge vessel's flanks.

Aiming charged particle beams within an atmosphere and this deep within a gas giant's magnetic field was a problem in any case. Shrill lightning crackled and thundered . . . and missed.

The first missile struck high and to one side, a minute and intolerably brilliant spark of light, ballooning in an instant against Warship 434's screens and shields. The detonation rocked the H'rulka vessel, slamming several of the colony-beings inside the ship against one another.

An instant later, the second and third warheads detonated against the expanding shock wave of the first blast. The electromagnetic pulse released by three twenty-kiloton fusion reactions overpowered the vessel's screens and smashed down its shields a fraction of a second later. In the hard vacuum of space, a near miss by a nuclear weapon could scour a ship's hull with an expanding bubble of plasma from the vaporized mass of the missile itself and with high-velocity clouds of charged particles generated by the blast, but there could be no shock wave as such—not when there was no air through which a shock wave could be transmitted.

Here in the high atmosphere of the gas giant, though, the ragged trio of detonations compressed hydrogen gas to create a hypersonic pressure wave that slammed into and through the H'rulka vessel. Debris spilled out, then vaporized—or folded in a blink into the nest of black holes at the ship's lower core that provided the vessel with energy tapped from the zero-point field.

Far worse, the three expanding bubbles of compressed hydrogen collided within temperatures and pressures typically found within the cores of suns, and the detonation grew, fusion fury running wild. . . .

Dragonfire Nine
Alchameth-Jasper Space
Arcturus System
1417 hours, TFT

Gray's fighter streaked through Alchameth's upper atmosphere at hypersonic velocity, leaving a meteor trail of ionized gas across ten thousand kilometers of sky. He saw the trio of flashes as his Krait missiles detonated ahead and below, the intensity of the unfolding glare damped down by his ship's AI to save his eyes.

He wasn't certain at first exactly what had happened. The explosions had appeared to merge, and then a small and swiftly growing sun had burned in Alchameth's sky. In another instant, his hurtling fighter had flashed past the short-lived sun and the enigmatic pattern of lights bathed in its glow below. As the Starhawk continued its straight-line high-speed pass, it punched through and out of the envelope of Alchameth's hydrogen atmosphere. The flare from his missile strike formed an intolerably bright spark still fiercely radiating on the giant's limb astern.

For several minutes afterward, a large, circular portion of Alchameth's night side was bathed in the light of full day.

"What the hell was *that*?" Gray asked.

"Sensory data is consistent with a fusion reaction of some hundreds of millions of megatons," the fighter's AI replied. "The alien structure beneath the H'rulka ship may have contributed to the release of energy . . . or the planet's hydrogen atmosphere may have compounded the effects of the initial detonations."

"My God . . ." As the Starhawk continued to recede into space, it looked as though a small but brilliant white star was rising behind the planet.

"Okay," he said after a long and shaky moment. "Where's Shay's fighter?"

A green icon flashed in his in-head display, and the fighter's AI began shaping possible vectors for an intercept.

"Match course and speed," he told the AI. "It's time to pull our heads in and ride this out."

Kinkaid *Squadron*
Alchameth-Jasper Space
Arcturus System
2218 hours, TFT

Thirteen hours after the carrier battlegroup had begun accelerating in toward Arcturus, the squadron of eighteen Confederation warships led by the heavy railgun cruiser *Kinkaid* arrived in circum-Alchameth space.

Over the past hour, as the range to Alchameth closed, the Confederation ships had been refining their target picture of the enemy ships around the gas giant, updating their speeds and course information constantly. Thirty seconds before passing the orbit of Jasper, the cruisers had begun firing both kinetic-kill and thermonuclear weaponry, aiming the rounds at the precise spots where their weapons AIs predicted that each target would be thirty seconds hence.

At roughly the same time, the defending vessels fired a volley of their own, hoping to claw some of the swift-moving attackers from the sky. Their most effective weapon was a series of shotgun blasts firing clouds of pellets and sand; the high speed of this accelerated debris combined with the inbound velocity of the Confederation vessels—some ninety thousand kilometers per second—added up to a devastating kinetic-kill volley.

The Confederation ships had been jinking for some minutes, now, adjusting their vectors left or right, up or down, in order to avoid aimed fire from the waiting defenders. The clouds of high-speed debris, however, expanded as they flashed toward the incoming ships. The Confederation vessels' shields flared white-hot as pellets and sand vaporized against them.

The destroyer *Emmons* fell through a particularly dense cloud of sand, her shields failed, and her blunt prow flashed into vapor. Her store of reaction mass, some tens of thousands of liters of water, exploded into space. A second destroyer, the *Austin*, suffered shield failure, and her forward sensors were scoured away by what amounted to a handful of sand, sand traveling with a relative velocity close to a third of the speed of light.

At about the same moment, the squadron's long-range salvo swept into Alchameth space seconds ahead of the Confederation ships. Many rounds missed, some by thousands of kilometers; AI targeting from almost three million kilometers away was art as much as science, and a miscalculation of a target's course and speed, even by some hundredths of 1 percent, could result in a warhead missing by many kilometers.

But many of the warheads and projectiles struck home . . . and the incoming squadron had dedicated numerous warheads to each target. Both Beta-class battleships were consumed in flares of white-hot fury, hammered time after time after time by kinetic-kill warheads traveling at tens of thousands of kilometers per second, and by tactical nuclear warheads, each with a destructive power ranging anywhere from ten kilotons to ten megatons of high explosive.

The Turusch fleet, scattered across much of circum-Alchameth space, crumpled, flared, and burned.

Two Juliet-class cruisers, jinking to avoid incoming warheads, remained untouched, and two more were unharmed save for damage inflicted by Starhawk fighters ten hours before. Three destroyers were accelerating at high speed, attempting to escape the Arcturus system. And several hundred Toad fighters remained to put up a desperate defense.

And then the *Kinkaid* squadron arrived, hurtling in just behind their long-range salvo.

Decelerating, they were still traveling so fast that they crossed the 1.8-million-kilometer gap between Alchameth and Jasper in just twenty seconds. During that time, automated weapon systems tracked, locked on, and fired, crisscrossing battlespace with bolts of artificial lightning, with gigajoule pulses of laser energy, with kinetic-kill slugs, with detonating nuclear warheads.

The defending ships returned fire.

Emmons, disabled, her shields and screens down, was hit multiple times, engulfed by a tiny, brief sun. The cruiser *Decatur*, by chance falling through a cloud of Toad fighters, began taking heavy fire, slammed again and again by particle beams and KK projectiles. The *Decatur* lashed out in reply with high-energy lasers and bolts of charged particles, knocking out Toad fighters one after another in searing flashes of hard radiation.

Austin, blinded by the defensive volley, her tactical link with the other Confederation ships cut off, had continued jinking to make herself as tough a target as possible. As it happened, she came just a little too close to the looming bulk of Alchameth, passing through the outermost parts of the gas giant's ring system. Slamming into those orbiting bits of ice and rock at ninety thousand kilometers per second, the cruiser disintegrated in a blast of raw energy. Her drive singularity continued on its original course, flaring as bright as a tiny star as it plowed through ice and rubble, leaving a shooting-star trail of brilliant light.

Both sides were taking heavy losses.

Dragonfire Nine
Alchameth-Jasper Space
Arcturus System
2249 hours, TFT

Gray had matched velocities with Ryan's fighter some hours before. Connecting with her ship once more, embracing it between his combat-mode wings, he'd applied brief and gentle bursts from his grav drive—gentle enough to avoid tearing the two linked fighters apart, gentle enough that his AI could keep the rapidly pulsed singularities balanced against the mass of two fighters. Very, very slowly, they'd decelerated together.

Astern, Alchameth was a brilliant star, accompanied by a scattering of dimmer pinpoints of light, the giant's system of moons. One of those, the brightest, was Jasper.

Between those two stars, silent detonations flickered, flashed, and pulsed, the titanic energies unleashed as the Confederation squadron zorched through the gas giant system.

"It looks . . . beautiful," Ryan said. "At least from out here."

"I'm glad we're out here," Gray replied. Fighters wouldn't last long in that firestorm."

He wondered how many of the other fighters in the three advance strike squadrons had survived, and where they were. All IFF transponders were shut down now, to keep the Turusch from hunting the Starhawks down one by one with RF-homing missiles. His AI had found Ryan's ship solely by calculating trajectories and velocities once she'd been flung clear of Alchameth.

"What's Alchameth mean, anyway?" she asked him.

They both were cut off from the fleet's datanet, of course, but as it happened he'd downloaded that bit of information some days ago. "It's actually an alternate name for the star Arcturus," he told her. "Back in the Middle Ages, in the occult traditions, there were fifteen special stars that were used in ceremonial magic. The Behenian fixed stars, they called them. *Alchameth* was what the magicians called Arcturus. Each star was associated with a different gemstone. Alchameth's was jasper. Hence the name."

"Magicians, huh? Sounds kind of far-fetched."

He shrugged. "Blame Cornelius Agrippa," he said.

"Who's that?"

"A medieval magician and astrologer."

"Dark ages stuff."

"Not really," Gray told her. "The dark ages is a kind of vague term referring to the time right after the fall of the Roman Empire. No science. The Church had the last word on everything. But what we call the Middle Ages was different. People were starting to experiment with new ideas. Astrology started to become astronomy. Alchemy flowed into chemistry and physics. Magic became science. Magicians like Cornelius Agrippa were trying to jump-start observation and hypothesis into something we'd recognize today as science, and they were doing so in defiance of the Church. It took a few centuries to get from Agrippa to Newton, and then again from Newton to Einstein . . . but eventually the new way of thinking took hold. Ah. Looks like the excitement is settling down. No more flashes. No more shooting."

"The battlegroup must have passed the planet and moved out of range," Ryan said.

"Right. They were supposed to zorch through, hitting everything they could."

"So what do we do now?"

"Now? Just what we've been doing. We drift, and we wait."

Alone, they drifted through a vast and empty night.

CIC, TC/USNA CVS America
Arcturus System
2318 hours, TFT

Alchameth showed a huge golden crescent on the CIC's forward viewer, the rings a bright white slash across its center, Jasper a gold-red sphere in half phase off to the right. *America* and the ships remaining with her, still decelerating, drifted into circum-Alchameth space. Drifting above the tactical display tank, Koenig gripped an overhead handhold and rotated to face Wizewski. "CAG, you may launch your fighters."

"Aye, aye, Admiral."

The situation was better than Koenig could have hoped, a near perfect attack that had left few of the defending forces intact in near Alchameth space. A few dozen Toad fighters were still under power, but they were scattered, many were damaged, and they posed little threat to the carriers. Within the next few moments, the carriers began spilling clouds of fighters—Starhawks, the older War Eagles, and rugged Marine Hornets from the Marine carriers *Vera Cruz* and *Nassau*—which dispersed throughout the battlespace, hunting down and destroying surviving enemy ships.

The enemy's capital ships had fled or were out of commission—destroyed or crippled. Two—one of the huge Turusch Betas and the unknown Juliet-sized vessel designated "Red-One"—still had a few weapons in service and were adrift, all but helpless, but the fighters would make short work of those.

Koenig was pleased, but the price had been steep. Three Confederation ships—*Emmons*, *Austin*, and *Decatur*—had been destroyed in the flyby, along with an estimated fifteen fighters. The surviving fighters were scattered all over the inner system. One of the first orders of business as *America* drew close to Jasper was the release of a dozen SAR tugs, search-and-rescue vessels with muscle enough to match velocities with outbound derelicts, dock with them, and drag them to a halt, hauling them back to the immediate vicinity of the fleet.

"All remaining fighters are deployed, Admiral," Wizewski told him. "The Rattlers have begun engaging a flock of Toads near Jasper."

"Very well. Get the SAR tugs away. We need to start rounding up our people out there."

"Aye, aye, sir."

The surviving fighter pilots had been locked up in their ships for fourteen hours now. It was time to bring them home.

As *America* slid into orbit around Jasper, Nassau released six Marine Crocodiles, combat boarding craft each carrying forty Marines and their equipment. They were ugly, slow brutes, heavily armored, like space-going tanks, sporting a pair of turret-mounted particle cannon and a nano-docking collar at their prows. Arcturus Station was eight thousand kilometers ahead, around the curve of the cloud-smeared moon.

"Admiral?" Commander Sinclair, *America*'s tactical officer, looked puzzled.

"What is it, Tacs?"

"We may want to send a team down to that target Lieutenant Gray waxed in the gas giant's atmosphere.

"The H'rulka ship?"

"As near as we can tell, there's nothing left of the warship. But according to Gray's telemetry, there was some sort of a brightly lit structure down deep in the atmosphere, a base, possibly, or a city. Sir, we're getting signals from them in Agletsch."

"What are they saying?"

" '*Duresnye n'drath,*' sir." He hesitated, then added the translation. " 'Help us.' "

"Get some probes where we can see in there."

"I've already dispatched battlespace drones, Admiral. We should be getting images in a few minutes."

"Good." He thought for a moment. "The spooks were working on the H'rulka language after that last fight back home. They might want in on this."

"I'll patch a call through to Commander Morrissey and Dr. Wilkerson, sir."

"Very well."

He was glad that Wilkerson had transferred back on board *America* after his brief deployment on the *Kinkaid*. The man had an excellent working knowledge of Turusch thought processes—the odd layering of two individuals' thoughts. He had a gift for being able to drop human bias and opinion from the equation when dealing with the genuinely alien.

"Images coming through from Alchameth now, sir," a CIC sensor technician reported.

A bulkhead screen lit up, showing the broad curve of the giant's limb. The city, or whatever it was, still lay in darkness, but the dawn terminator was fast approaching over the horizon a few thousand kilometers ahead. Though dark, the tops of the cloud bands were visible by moonlight—light scattering off of Jasper, especially—and also from the underside of the rings sweeping overhead. The canyon depths between the cloud bands were in deep darkness, though pulses and flickers of silent lightning flared against the night, each flash briefly illuminating the nearest clouds.

And there was the city. . . .

The structure, Koenig thought, might not be a city, as such. That was a distinctly human concept, and the H'rulka did not think like humans. The ranks and clusters of lights, however, gave the impression of a city seen from the air at night. One side, however, was dark, and appeared to have crumpled.

"We're still not sure exactly what happened," Sinclair said. "Telemetry from Gray's fighter was spotty—interference from the planet's magnetosphere. We'll know more when we can interrogate his fighter directly. But we think that two or more nuclear explosions—Gray's Kraits—triggered a runaway fusion reaction in Alchameth's hydrogen atmosphere. The blast obliterated the H'rulka ship . . . and the shock wave may have damaged the city."

"It looks like something punched through the platform," Koenig said. He pointed. "Just there . . . and there. Those look like god-awful holes."

"Yes, sir. The H'rulka apparently use artificial singularities to extract zero-point energy from the quantum field, just like us. When the containment fields collapsed . . ."

"Right. At least two fair-sized black holes heading for the nearest major gravitational mass . . . in this case, Alchameth."

"Right. And that gas-bag city happened to be in the way."

"Admiral?" a familiar voice said, speaking in Koenig's head. "Wilkerson here. I'm in communication with a H'rulka group-organism that calls itself Abyssal Wind. They claim to speak for the Golden Clouds Gathering. That's the name of that brightly lit structure adrift in Alchameth's upper atmosphere."

"What do they have to say?"

"Admiral, they need our help to evacuate the planet."

It sounded at first like an offer of surrender. On the other side of the large CIC compartment, dozens of viewscreens were showing a confusion of images coming in from the Marine assault on Arcturus Station. Moments before, the Crocodiles had nudged into the huge, orbiting complex, their docking collars molding themselves into and through the station's bulkheads, disgorging their combat-armored Marines. There'd been some resistance, but so far it sounded like the Marines were making good progress, and had already reached the compartment where the human prisoners were being kept.

The battlegroup had *won*, a singular victory in a thirty-seven-year war that had seen precious few victories.

"I don't think we can look at it as a surrender," Wilkerson told him. "They're asking for . . . for cooperation, I think."

For the past hour, Wilkerson, down in *America*'s intelligence department, had continued to talk with the surviving H'rulka. A round-trip distance of 3.6 million kilometers meant a time-delay of twelve seconds on all radio traffic, but that was an annoyance at worst. The H'rulka were eager, even frantic, to communicate.

The Gathering had indeed been damaged by the shock wave when Gray's missiles had triggered a runaway fusion reaction, and things had been made much worse when a pair of rogue black holes had plunged through the city's main deck. Perhaps a third of the platform had broken away and vanished into the black depths of the abyss below. Power was failing, and the surviving H'rulka feared that the anti-gravity lift pods that supported the massive construct would die. If that happened, the rest of the platform would fall as well.

At first, Koenig thought that the H'rulka wanted to be rescued, and for the life of him he'd not known how he could pull that off. Individual H'rulka were *huge*, hot-air balloons each a couple of kilometers across. Koenig's battlegroup didn't have any ship with an internal compartment large enough to carry even one of the group-organisms . . . and there were over twenty-five thousand survivors down there. There was no way the Confederation fleet could evacuate the platform.

As the conversation continued, however, it became clear that even if the floating city collapsed, the remaining H'rulka were not in immediate danger. They were floaters, after all, at home in the open atmosphere of gas giants like Alchameth. The Golden Cloud Gathering, Koenig was given to understand, was less city than manufacturing center . . . and apparently it was also the resting place of a small H'rulka starship.

And they wanted to use that ship to send a message home.

"They *are* the enemy, Admiral," Captain Buchanan pointed out. "We generally try to *block* enemy communications, don't we? At least, that was the fashion in vogue when I went through the Academy."

"They are distressed civilians," Koenig replied.

"Actually, Admiral," Wilkerson's voice put in, "we may not be able to make that distinction. Human society tends to assign distinct roles to individuals—doctors, politicians, technicians, soldiers. We haven't found anything yet in the H'rulka social system that represents a professional military. They may be citizen-soldiers."

"Meaning everyone in society can double as a soldier?" Buchanan asked.

"Something like that. They don't seem to differentiate. Makes sense, if you think about it. There's no such thing as an individual H'rulka. They're colony organisms, with something like a hundred different life forms working together—gas bag, tentacles, brain, digestive system. Everything works together to create the whole."

"Wouldn't it be just as likely that they'd think in terms of different parts of the whole, each with its own function?" Koenig asked. "That would lead to class specialization, I'd think, like in a beehive. Workers, drones, soldiers . . ."

"Human thinking, Admiral. Because we're familiar with beehives and anthills, and we still think in terms of the class and caste structures humans have used throughout history. For the H'rulka, it's not every*one*, it's every*they*. It's as if humans thought about being a city, instead of being just one person living in a city. Warfare—deploying soldiers—is just one thing a city might do. It also raises food, communicates with other cities . . ."

"I'm not entirely sure I'm following that," Koenig said. "But if I do understand you, it's vitally important that we help them."

"How so?" Buchanan asked.

"What is it that defines humans?" Koenig asked.

Buchanan shrugged. "That's one of the all-time great imponderables, isn't it? Communication, building societies, adapting the environment, technology . . ."

"All of which other beings do as well, both sentient and nonsentient. But for the H'rulka, I wonder if their definition of H'rulka-hood isn't *cooperation*, working together to sustain life and civilization in a hostile environment."

"A distinct probability, Admiral," Wilkerson said. "You know . . . the H'rulka term for us translates into something like 'vermin.' And for them, vermin are insignificantly tiny organisms that attack the whole."

Buchanan chuckled. "Mean little critters that feed on the body, eh?"

"Something like that. Parasites that interfere with the sound functioning and internal cooperation of the body."

"Then maybe we can prove to them that we're not vermin," Koenig said. "I've been running numbers. A Marine carrier can function deep enough in Alchameth's gravitational field that they could lower tethers to the platform."

"Anchor it from space, you mean," Buchanan said. "That could be damned tricky. That platform is moving with the local winds."

"The carrier's AI could balance the forces involved easily enough, I think," Koenig replied. "Damn it, we have to *try*."

"How long would we have to hold the thing up?"

"We're still working on understanding H'rulka concepts of time," Wilkerson said. "But it may just be a matter of hours . . . no more than a day or so. They need to complete repairs on their ship, which they'll dispatch to one of their systems, another H'rulka colony. And they'll either send back rescue ships to pick up the colonists on Alchameth, or they'll send the ships necessary for building a new platform."

"Can we allow that?" Buchanan asked. He sounded shocked. "What if they return with reinforcements?"

"By that time, I think," Koenig said, "we'll be long gone. And just maybe we'll have given the H'rulka something to think about." He hesitated, then nodded. "We're going to do this."

From the other end of CIC, a ragged cheer broke out. The Marines had just reported that Arcturus Station was secure.

Chapter Seventeen

1 February 2405

CIC, TC/USNA CVS America
Arcturus System
0745 hours, TFT

Two days later, the Star Carrier *America* prepared to depart from the Arcturus System.

"*Nassau* and *Vera Cruise* both report they have cast off from Gathering, Admiral. The H'rulka platform is stable and holding its own. Our engineers and . . . uh . . . shore parties are on their way out."

"Very well. Have the carriers return to Jasper orbit as soon as they've retrieved their fighters."

The Marine fighters had been swarming around the two light assault carriers for the entire time, even dipping down into Alchameth's atmosphere in order to circle Golden Cloud Gathering at visual ranges. The Marines of MSU–17 were not trusting souls, at least not when it came to their assault carriers. The constant fighter patrols had been a guarantee against an ambush or a double-cross.

But there'd been no double-cross. The *Vera Cruz* and the *Nassau* had parked themselves in the planet's atmosphere above the gathering and generated ten-thousand-kilometer Bucky-weave cables, growing them from carbon brought into their machine bays by scavenger shuttles. Drones had carried the ends of the cables down to the platform, where they'd been used to secure the torn and twisted part of the structure.

After that, shuttles had gone down and landed on the platform, disgorging a small army of combat engineers and agrav techs. Dr. Wilkerson and his staff had gone down as well, in order to talk with the H'rulka directly. They'd used an array of spare War Eagle singularity projectors, mounting them on the damaged portion of the platform. With power from a couple of portable generators tuning the grav drives to a low, carefully balanced purr, they'd managed to stabilize the H'rulka platform.

Throughout the operation, Wilkerson had said, the H'rulka came and went, drifting above the platform like huge, errant balloons. It was clear that they didn't need the platform, not when they could drift above it, or out across the dizzying drop into the cloud-walled abyss below with no concern for having someplace to stand. Manufacturing, however, required solid ground.

"So . . . how did they bootstrap themselves out of their homeworld's atmosphere in the first place?" Koenig asked Wilkerson. "They would have needed something like this platform to build their first ships . . . and it's hard to imagine them being able to get the raw materials from a planet's atmosphere."

"Right," Wilkerson said. "They *are* superb chemists, and apparently they could extract carbon from atmospheric methane, carbon tetrachloride, and the free-floating organic compounds they use for food. But they had no real reason to leave their world at all until somebody called the Starborn showed up."

" 'Starborn.' Is that the Sh'daar?"

"We don't know. Not enough to go on yet. If they weren't the Sh'daar, though, they were another Sh'daar client race. But these Starborn apparently helped them expand their carbon-mining from their atmosphere . . . and apparently they taught them how to build antigravity thrusters. After a while, they were making jaunts out to their homeworld's moon system to mine heavy metals. You were right, by the way, Admiral."

"I'm glad to hear it. About what?"

"About cooperation being how these folks define *people*. The Starborn helped them achieve spaceflight and large-structure fabrication. And now we've demonstrated the same willingness to help. Abyssal Wind isn't sure what to make of that."

"You told him that there was no need for humans and H'rulka to fight? That this war is something the Sh'daar started?"

"I tried. Some of the concepts are . . . difficult. But they—Abyssal Wind is a *they*, remember—promised to talk about it with other H'rulka when they get back in touch with them."

"Good. How long before they launch their ship?"

"I don't know, Admiral. We're also having some trouble translating basic concepts of time. But Abyssal Wind seemed confident that they would be able to complete preparations and launch soon."

Koenig wondered if they should stand by until the H'rulka ship was away. There seemed little point in that, however, unless the CBG planned to stay put until the H'rulka rescue fleet arrived . . . and Koenig was not willing to trust the alien floaters *that* far, not yet.

Trust had to be earned.

By any set of expectations, the Second Battle of Arcturus had been a spectacular victory for the Confederation. The defending fleet had been destroyed and the survivors scattered, Arcturus Station had been taken back and the human prisoners held there freed. But it was possible that the most important aspect of that victory would turn out to be direct contact with the H'rulka. If the events of the past couple of days led to diplomatic contact with them, so much the better.

So little was known about the Sh'daar, and about the alliance humans referred to carelessly as the "Sh'daar Empire."

A true galactic empire in the classical sense, with emperor and central ruling world, was ludicrous in Koenig's opinion. The galaxy was so large, composed of so many suns and worlds and so many unfathomably diverse forms of life and mind. No emperor, no one ruling race could possibly keep track of everything taking place within such a realm. No conquering army could hold billions of worlds in thrall. No imperial decree could have the same meaning for hundreds of millions of different sentient species. Human xenosophontologists couldn't even yet agree on what the word *intelligence* meant, much less figure out how to relate to them all.

Whatever form or philosophy of rule the near mythical Sh'daar had imposed on a large portion of the galaxy, it must be fairly loosely structured in order to encompass beings as mutually alien as H'rulka, Turusch, Jivad Rallam, and Agletsch. And that meant that, just possibly, some of those species could be pried away from their alliance.

For his part, Koenig was not completely convinced that there were such beings as Sh'daar. The Turusch and the Agletsch certainly thought there were, but no member of either species had ever admitted to actually seeing one. In Koenig's opinion, it seemed likely that the term "Sh'daar" referred to an *idea* rather than a physical group of beings. Maybe "Sh'daar" was a word for "union" or "alliance" that had taken on a life of its own uncounted generations ago.

But then again, humans had only just begun venturing out into the interstellar sea. First Contact with the Agletsch had occurred less than a century ago. The Agletsch claimed to have been starfaring for millennia—even they didn't seem to be sure just how long.

It might be, though, that the *America* CBG had discovered the first small crack in the monolithic façade of whatever the Sh'daar Empire actually might be.

And now was the time to exploit that.

"Admiral Koenig?" Lieutenant Ramirez said. "The Sleipnir reports she's ready for boost."

Koenig nodded. "Very well. Tell her Godspeed."

On one of the CIC bulkhead display screens, a black, egg-shaped ship turned slowly, orange sun-glint sliding across its curved and mirrored surface. The ships of the CBG carried a number of HAMP–20 Sleipnir-class packets, the only way the fleet would be able to stay in even tenuous contact with Earth. They were piloted by AIs copied from *America*'s CIC artificial intelligence; they could carry human pilots, of course, but Koenig was concerned about what might happen to them when they reported to Fleet HQ. They couldn't toss an AI into the brig.

"You're being paranoid again, dear," the voice of Karyn Mendelson whispered in his mind. "If they throw anyone in the brig, it will be you."

"True," he thought back. "But if they can't get me for a court-martial, they might take it out on whoever is handy. I'm not going to risk someone else's career."

"Admiral Carruthers will cover you."

"Until he gets fired. Or quits."

Koenig had examined the distress message from Osiris for long hours. By now, three weeks after the news of the enemy capture of 70 Ophiuchi II reached Sol, the Confederation Senate must be frantic, expecting another enemy attack on Sol at any moment. He'd half expected to find a Sleipnir here at Arcturus waiting for him, with orders for him to return with his fleet immediately to protect Earth. He suspected Admiral Carruthers' hand in that. Carruthers knew how important Crown Arrow was . . . and he pulled a lot of mass with the Senate and with Regis DuPont. Koenig hadn't disobeyed orders yet, since he hadn't yet received orders to return the CBG to Sol.

But he knew those orders were coming, and by boosting out of the Sol System before they could have reached him, he was violating the spirit of the law, if not the letter.

Sooner or later, those orders would catch up with the CBG, and then he would face a truly difficult decision. . . .

"Why so gloomy?" his personal assistant asked.

"You're dead," he told her in his mind. "You're dead and I'm talking to an electronic ghost. It's not the same as having . . . as having you here."

God, but he missed her.

On the bulkhead display, the Sleipnir packet had rotated to face a relatively empty patch of sky—the unremarkable constellation Cetus. Even this far from the Sol, the constellations still held their familiar shapes, with a few minor distortions.

From Arcturus, Sol appeared in Cetus, a seventh-magnitude star invisible to the naked eye.

Aligned with that unseen star, the packet began accelerating, vanishing within a handful of seconds into star-strewn emptiness. She carried a complete record of the battle. That, at least, would be welcome news to the Senate and to the Confederation at large. She also carried a list of the personnel rescued from Arcturus Station, and the news that they would be arriving on the AFS *Mars* after a three-week voyage.

The packet should reach Sol in one week.

Mess Hall 2, TC/USNA CVS America
Arcturus System
0812 hours, TFT

America had no fewer than three separate mess halls, one in each arm of the rotating hab-module cluster behind the carrier's forward shield. With more than five thousand people on board, the mess halls still had to work in shifts.

Gray had come in to grab a late third-shift breakfast. Shay Ryan was already there, seated at one of the tables. "Morning."

She looked up. "Good morning. Here to take in the view?"

Like other common areas on board *America*, the mess hall bulkheads and overheads could project live hemispherical panoramas. During the visually dull weeks when the ship was under Alcubierre Drive, wrapped up in its own, tight little bubble of spacetime, those images were generally from an extensive library of land- and seascapes, both from Earth and from other worlds Humankind had visited.

When in planetary orbit, however, the views usually were from external camera feeds, showing surrounding space with a resolution high enough that it was easy to forget that there were walls. Although the mess halls were in the rotating outer hab modules, with a half G of artificial gravity, the panorama was from a non-rotating perspective. Having the sky swing around the ship for a complete turn every thirty seconds had turned out to be a bad idea where people were eating.

Much of the panorama at the moment was dominated by Jasper, swirls and flecks of orange-gold clouds above red oceans and ocher continents. On the opposite bulkhead, Alchameth was a slender crescent pierced by the thread-slender silver streak of its rings. Arcturus shone brilliant beyond the crescent's bow, the orange-hued daylight casting shadows across tables and deck.

But Gray grinned and winked at Ryan. "You *do* look lovely this morning."

"*That* view," she said, pointing up. "Not me!"

"You take in your view," Gray said with a shrug, "and I'll take in mine. How are you feeling?"

"Clean bill of health," she said. She'd been suffering from hypothermia by the time the SAR tug had reached them. Her fighter's power systems had been down, and her life support throttled back to a battery-powered minimum. She'd also picked up a few rads from the thermonuclear blast that had disabled her ship and from Alchameth's radiation belts, so Ryan had spent all of yesterday in *America*'s sick bay.

"Good to hear it."

"I . . . didn't get the chance to thank you, Trevor," she said.

He picked up a plastic cup of fruit juice—grapefruit juice, it was supposed to be—and took a cautious sip. All food on the ships of the fleet was nanoconstituted from the CHON lockers—supplies of carbon, hydrogen, oxygen, and nitrogen, the basic compounds of life, with the necessary trace elements added in. The food assemblers were pretty good, but the output tended to be a bit on the bland side . . . and sometimes it was tough to distinguish what a given item of food or drink was supposed to be.

Definitely grapefruit juice.

"No thanks necessary," he replied, putting the cup down. "All part of our friendly Prim service."

"Don't joke about that, please," she said.

"About what? Prims?"

"I've worked hard to get away from that . . . that part of my past," she told him. "My family worked hard. But the only thing open to us was shitwork." She gave a bitter laugh. "How do people show off their affluence, the fact that they have money, when every home has an assembler to nanufacture everything you could possibly need? You hire servants. *Human* servants. People you can dress in ridiculous livery and train to bow and scrape and say 'yes, sir' and 'yes, ma'am' and 'yes, master' and . . . and . . ."

She broke off the increasingly shrill tirade. Gray shrugged. "Sorry. For me . . . it's just something I've lived with."

"Being a second-class citizen? Being a non-citizen, a non-*person*?" She was trying to control her anger. "We finally get out of the D.C. swamp, and we end up being servants for the Chevys. Cleaning their bathrooms. Serving their meals. Sleeping in their fucking beds."

"Chevys?"

"What D.C. swamptsers call the rich people up north of Georgetown. From the Chevy Chase Arcology. That's a tower community where a lot of the local elite live. The *citizens*." She said the word as if it had a foul taste.

"A lot of the people on Manhattan went north too," he said.

She shrugged. "You go where the work is. Growing crops on top of half-flooded buildings gets old after a while."

"Well, well. The two Prim sweeties having breakfast together by Jasperlight. How romantic." Lieutenant Collins had just walked up and was standing beside them with an unfriendly grin. Evidently, she'd just finished breakfast and was on her way out.

"Good morning, Lieutenant," Gray said, his voice held neutral. He knew Collins was trying to bait him, trying to get him to lose control. She and her cronies had been riding him since he'd joined the battlegroup. It had started off as a kind of vicious hazing. Gray had tried to ignore it . . . then managed to get himself in trouble when he decked Collins' wing and bed partner, Howie Spaas, a few months ago.

But then at Eta Boötis, Spaas had ridden a damaged 'Hawk into one of *America*'s landing bays for a very bad trap and died. After that, the hazing by others in the squadron had continued, more or less . . . but Collins had turned downright bitter, as though she personally blamed *him* for Spaas' death.

"Where the hell were you during the furball out there the other day?" Collins said. "They *say* you scorched the gas-bag city, Gray . . . and wiped out a few thousand civilians. Then you hightailed it and sat out the rest of the fight with your girlfriend, here."

"So, when does your buddy Kirkpatrick go back to duty?" Gray asked, ignoring her comments. Kirkpatrick had been confined to quarters for a month after bypassing his deet and getting spaced on novasuns at the eudaimonium solstice gig. Collins had pulled a couple of weeks of extra duty for trying to cover for him, and for showing up late to the scramble recall from *America*. "I missed him out there."

She laughed, a harsh noise. "You should talk! Is that how squatties do it? Running out on their squadron? Or couldn't you figure out how to work the interface on your Starhawk?"

"Fuck you, Collins."

"I'm serious, Prim. You think you can pull out of a fire-fight and play the hero by floating out beyond the battlespace, you're wrong."

"I used up the last of my Kraits on the H'rulka ship," he told her. "My Gatling was almost dry." He shrugged. "*Everybody* was pulling a drift-off, okay?"

"Drift-off" was the term employed by fighter pilots referring to the battle's endgame, when combat damage and dry expendables lockers forced them to break off contact and get clear of the enemy.

"Not everybody, Prim. Some of us were fighting for our lives in there. If you couldn't kill the enemy, you could have *distracted* him."

"Ryan's fighter was disabled. The enemy had toads out in hunter-killer packs. I was covering her."

"She's not your fucking wing, Prim. Tucker is, last I heard, and she was in there turning and burning with the rest of us! Seems just a bit too convenient, you two squatties going off by yourself! You know what I think?"

"I don't particularly care what you think, Collins."

"I think you're a damned coward, and you ought to be hauled up in front of a court-martial board."

Gray looked at the woman for a moment, thoughtful. Then

he stood up, picked up his cup of grapefruit juice, and emptied it in her face.

"Oops," he said.

CIC, TC/USNA CVS America
Arcturus System
0845 hours, TFT

"Admiral?" Ramirez said. "The transport *Mars* reports readiness for boost."

"Very well. She's clear to leave the battlegroup at her skipper's discretion. Signal good luck."

"Very well, Admiral."

The *Mars* was currently invisibly distant, half a million kilometers away, but she would soon begin her transit back to Sol as well, arriving two weeks after the packet.

"Admiral?" Commander Sinclair said. "General Mathers reports that his people are standing ready to dust the station."

The facility was visible now on another of the CIC screens, a few kilometers off *America*'s port bow. Koenig nodded. "Do it."

Arcturus Station itself had posed something of a problem, now that it was back in Confederation hands. The battlegroup would be leaving the system momentarily, leaving no ships and no personnel behind to hold the Arcturus system; there would be nothing to stop the Jivad or Turusch from reoccupying the orbital base.

And so Koenig had ordered Marine combat engineers to disassemble it.

The Marine assault force had encountered only twelve Jivad Rallam and fifteen of the smaller creatures called Kobolds when they'd stormed aboard the station. Eight Jivad had been killed in the firefight. The four survivors, all of them wounded, plus the Kobolds, had been packed into a cylindrical hab container set to maintain their CO_2-rich atmospheric preference, along with a supply of water and CHON for the life support nanoassembler inside. The pod had been transferred to the *Mars*; with luck, the prisoners would survive the claustrophobic three-week voyage to Earth. Little was known about the Jivad, other than their ferocity on the battlefield. Perhaps the ONI xeno department could uncover more about them and how they related to the Sh'daar back at the Mare Crisium.

The orbital facility appeared to be growing fuzzy, the edges softening, then blurring into a growing haze.

Rather than detonating a nuclear warhead inside the empty station, Koenig had suggested using a nano-D device, releasing a cloud of programmed nanodisassemblers that could be dispersed throughout the station by way of the air circulation ducts. "Dusting," the process was called, because by the time the molecule-sized nanodisassemblers reached the end of their carefully programmed life span and switched themselves off, the target would be reduced to a cloud of debris, sand-grain-sized and smaller. The cloud would remain in orbit around Jasper, where the H'rulka would find it once their ships returned to Arcturus. Perhaps they would use the cloud as a source of raw materials for their airborne platform.

A peace offering, of sorts.

"Captain Buchanan," Koenig said. "Prepare the battlegroup for acceleration."

"Aye, aye, Admiral."

He palmed a contact, ordering a fleet-wide link.

"Officers and enlisted personnel of the fleet," he said. "At Arcturus two days ago, you won an important victory. Together with the victory won in the Sol system last October, the Second Battle of Arcturus marks the turning point in the long war against the Sh'daar Empire. Until now, victories over the Sh'daar's client races have been few and far between. Until now, Humankind was on the run, desperately trying to hold on against a numerically and a technically superior enemy. Until now, Humankind was losing this war.

"But no more. Two days ago we took back the Arcturus system. And now, today, we take the war to the enemy.

"There is, in modern space warfare, a military axiom which describes the ability to put your forces deep inside the enemy's lines, to take the fight to him, to put him on the defensive and force him to react to you. The axiom is called *center of gravity*, and suggests the idea of keeping the war out of our backyard, and inside his. This morning, we are going to shift this conflict's center of gravity deep into Sh'daar space. Our objective is the Alphekka star system, 41.5 light years from Arcturus . . . and 72 light years from Sol. I don't need to tell you that we will be going farther out into the galaxy than humans have ever been before."

The farthest extent of human explorations so far had been the nascent system of Beta Pictoris, 63 light years from Earth.

"Intelligence has identified the Alphekka system as a possible Sh'daar base and staging area, quite possibly for their operations at Arcturus and Eta Boötis and, ultimately, against Sol. We are going to hit whatever is at Alphekka, and we are going to hit it hard. We're going to take it down before the enemy fully realizes what we've done here at Arcturus. We hope that this will make them, at the very least, reconsider their operations against Sol and the Confederation's inner colonies, and force them to pull back to regroup. This will, at the very least, buy time for the Confederation, allowing them to build up their own defenses.

"The Confederation is counting on us. And I am counting on all of you. It's twenty-four days to Alphekka." He paused for a moment before adding the Confederation's motto. *"Ad astra!"*

As a speech, he thought, it was probably a bit overblown . . . but the crews of the battlefleet's ships needed something impressive to mark this moment. Once they dropped into the metaspace bubbles of their Alcubierre Drives, they would be putting themselves beyond reinforcements or resupply from Earth. The fleet would be utterly on its own, unless and until Koenig decided to reestablish contact.

Someone in the CIC, one of the techs, had begun clapping his hands. Commander Sinclair joined in, followed by more and more men and women, until the compartment was ringing with sustained applause. The applause, the wild cheering, Koenig learned later, had spread throughout the fleet, accompanied by crew members chanting, over and over, *"Ad astra! Ad astra! Ad astra! . . ."*

"Captain Buchanan?" Koenig said, as the noise began to dwindle. "Set course for Alphekka."

"Aye, aye, sir."

If they hadn't been committed before, they were now.

Slowly, *America* began gathering speed, sliding past the growing gray cloud of the disintegrating orbital station, picking up speed, and breaking orbit.

He wondered if the H'rulka on their jury-rigged platform were watching the battlegroup leave, and what they might be thinking.

Alien Visitors' Quarters, TC/USNA CVS America
Arcturus System
0849 hours, TFT

The Sh'daar Seed was listening to Koenig's inspirational speech.

A portion of a supply locker on the Number Three Hangar Deck had been sealed off for the use of the nonhumans currently on board *America*, a place where temperature and humidity could be maintained at comfortable levels, and where private eating booths gave the two Agletsch the civilized amenities.

Dra'ethde and Gru'mulkisch were still attached to the Confederation Department of Extraterrestrial Relations, but had been "seconded," as the humans called it, to *America*'s intelligence department. "Native guides," one human had called them. In the coming weeks and months, *America* and the ships with her would be traveling deep into space no human had ever visited, and their knowledge of Sh'daar client species and worlds would be invaluable.

Gru'mulkisch was carrying a Sh'daar Seed.

She wasn't aware of it, of course. The Seed was a tiny complex of artificially grown and interconnected molecules embracing a quantum computer smaller than a typical bacterium. It had been ingested by one of her males and transferred to her circulatory system when he had attached himself to her face. Eventually, it had lodged within her brain and attached itself to certain ganglia associated with her auditory system; the Seed could not see, but it could hear quite well . . . and it could use Gru'mulkisch's own memory to translate languages—including English.

By itself, the Seed was not intelligent or self-aware, and had neither volition nor judgment of its own. It was simply a listening device programmed to store conversations overheard by its host, to analyze what it heard based on certain fairly narrow criteria, and to upload data deemed important by that criteria to network nodes when the opportunity presented itself. Sh'daar Seeds could, at times, serve as hosts for more intelligent subsets of the Sh'daar Remnant's metamind, but that was not the case with the artificial virus currently inhabiting Gru'mulkisch's auditory center.

When it analyzed Koenig's speech, it noted several data of interest.

"Our objective is the Alphekka star system, 41.5 light years from Arcturus . . . and 72 light years from Sol."

"It's twenty-four days to Alphekka."

"Intelligence has identified the Alphekka system as a possible Sh'daar base and staging area, quite possibly for their operations at Arcturus and Eta Boötis and, ultimately, against Sol. We are going to hit whatever is at Alphekka, and we are going to hit it hard. . . ."

With no direct link to the portions of Gru'mulkisch's brain containing navigational data, the Sh'daar Seed had no way of knowing what was meant by the word "Alphekka." It was a human star system name, obviously . . . but *which* star, of some hundreds of billions in the galaxy? The Seed did not know what was meant by "light years," either, or by the word "days."

But none of that mattered, because the Sh'daar Seed inhabiting Gru'mulkisch was still sensing the local H'rulka radio net and, within it, the echoes of other Seeds inhabiting other beings . . . the H'rulka of the gas giant the humans called Alchameth.

Drawing energy from its host's metabolism, the Seed accessed the local net and uploaded Koenig's speech.

By the time *America* and her consorts got up to speed and had folded space around themselves, the data was being shared by the Sh'daar Seeds inhabiting some hundreds of H'rulka on Alchameth, including those readying the starship for boost.

Other Sh'daar agents, higher up in the hierarchy of Sh'daar sentience, would know just what to do with it.

Chapter Eighteen

25 February 2405

Admiral's Office, TC/USNA CVS America
Approaching Alphekka System
0915 hours, TFT

Admiral Koenig had been studying the data for so long he had it memorized.

STAR: Alpha Coronae Borealis

COORDINATES: RA: 15^{H} 34^{M} 41.2681^{S} DEC: +26° 42'52.895" D 22P

ALTERNATE NAMES: Alphekka or Alphecca, Gemma, Gnosia Stella Coronae or Gnosia, Asteroth or Ashtaroth, 5 CrB.

TYPE: A0V/G5V; **PERIOD:** 17.3599^{D}; **SEMIMAJOR AXIS:** 2.781×10^{7KM};

ORBITAL ECCENTRICITY: 0.37

MASS: 2.58/0.92 SOL; **RADIUS:** 2.89/0.9 SOL; **LUMINOSITY:** 74/0.81 SOL

SURFACE TEMPERATURE: ~9,700°/5,800°K

AGE: 314 million years

APPARENT MAGNITUDE (SOL): 2.21 (2.24 / 7.1);

ABSOLUTE MAGNITUDE: +0.16/+5.05

DISTANCE FROM SOL: 72 LY

PLANETARY SYSTEM: Probably none. IR evidence suggests the presence of a large protoplanetary disk of dust, gas, and cometary debris.

He'd pulled the data up once again on the large projected display in his office. After three weeks in a metaspace bubble, *America* was preparing to re-enter normal space, and the question occupying the mind of every CIC officer and fleet tactician was what they would find waiting for them when they emerged. In particular . . . why did the Sh'daar or their clients have any interest whatsoever in a star like Alphekka?

Obviously it wasn't for the ambiance. Alphekka was a double star—an A0 star two to three times bigger and 74 times brighter than Sol orbited by a G5 sun a bit smaller and a bit dimmer than Sol. The semimajor axis of that orbit was less than thirty million kilometers, the two swinging around one another with a period of seventeen days, so the two stars were close. The two stars would have a single habitable zone, extending from about seven to twelve AUs from their common center of gravity.

The problem was that there wouldn't be planets there, at least not *mature* ones. Alphekka was an extremely young star system, just 314 million years old. IR satellite readings going as far back as the late twentieth century showed an excess of infrared energy at wavelengths of twenty-four and seventy micrometers, suggesting the presence of a thick and very broad disk of dust and gas circling the two stars, the raw material out of which planets might one day form. If there were any planetary bodies in the system now, they would be small and molten protoplanets, subject to ferocious meteoric bombardment as planetesimals continued to come together within Alphekka's stellar womb. A number of stars possessed protoplanetary clouds; Beta Pictoris was one, Vega another, Fomalhaut a third. Stars so young could not possibly be host to native civilizations; life would not be able to evolve for some hundreds of millions of years, yet; on Earth, it had taken 800 million years before the first single-celled organisms had appeared within the planet's newborn oceans, and another 2.8 *billion* years before the appearance of multicellular life. Alphekka didn't yet have any real estate worth colonizing.

So why had the Sh'daar chosen the place? What could they be doing here?

Evidence of a Sh'daar presence at the system had come from WHISPERS, the weak heterodyned interstellar signal passband-emission radio search. Ten-kilometer-wide radio telescope antennae orbiting Pluto, Eris, Orca, and Sedna formed a very wide baseline for interferometric studies of other radio signals coming in from other stars. Although radio signals tended to fade out and become lost in the hash of background noise from the galaxy, large antennas and interferometric baselines several hundred AUs across let AI listeners sift the noise for heterodyned signals. Hundreds of thousands of heterodyned signal sources were known today; Alphekka had been identified not long after WHISPERS had come on-line in the twenty-second century. *Someone* had been out there for over two hundred years at least, and while ONI couldn't read what those signals were saying, they seemed to match frequency patterns and modulations favored by the Turusch, the Jivad, and other Sh'daar species.

There was a very good chance that those signals were military.

The ONI's best guess was that Alphekka was a supply depot and military staging area for Turusch fleet elements, possibly for operations directed at Arcturus and Eta Boötis, though it was important to remember that the signals WHISPERS was picking up today were seventy-two years old. Had the Turusch been planning their attack on Arcturus Station that long ago? Or were enemy activities at Alphekka simply directed at reconnaissance of star systems along the periphery of human-explored space?

A sneak-and-peek reconnaissance probe to Alphekka might have answered some of those questions. Koenig had suggested sending one when he'd originally written up the proposal for Operation Crown Arrow a year ago. The idea had been down-checked by the Senate Military Directorate, however, for fear that a probe *might* be detected . . . and if it was, that would call the enemy's attention to the Confederation's interest in the system, and even, possibly, result in the Turusch laying some sort of a trap in advance of the CBG's arrival.

Given that the enemy had spotted the ISVR–120 probe passing through the Arcturus system last December and followed it back to Sol, Koenig had to admit that the concern was valid. Once the battlegroup had reached Arcturus, the question was moot; the fleet could not afford to wait seven weeks for a probe to make the voyage out to Alphekka, record what it found, then travel all the way back to Arcturus to report. Having hit Arcturus, they needed to move on to Alphekka *now*, with an absolute minimum of delay, before the enemy figured out that Alphekka might be the battlegroup's next target.

They would know soon enough, now. *America* was scheduled to break out of metaspace in just two more hours.

"And what will you do then?" Karyn's voice asked him.

"Depends on what happens at Alphekka, doesn't it?" he replied.

"Operation Crown Arrow ends there," the PA avatar said. "But you've been thinking about other operations, deeper into Sh'daar space."

"Of course. Every good senior military officer is always thinking about the next step, even while he's carrying out the last one. I do know we, the Confederation, can't fall back on the defensive. If we carry the war's center of gravity to the enemy, we have to keep it there."

"But for how long, Alex? The Confederation is still an insignificant fraction of the entire galaxy . . . a few hundred star systems against four hundred billion stars, untold billions of worlds, hundreds of thousands of civilizations."

He gave a wry grin. "It's worse than that, Karyn. The Confederation would make peace with the Sh'daar if they could. And they may yet. We have thirty-one ships in the battlegroup. Thirty-one ships against a galactic empire."

"But you don't believe in a Sh'daar Empire."

"No, but the concept will do until something more descriptive comes along. Whatever the Sh'daar are, they seem to have won the hearts and minds of a lot of sentient beings—the Turusch and the Jivad, especially. And the H'rulka, unless what we did at Arcturus makes a difference there."

"So . . . my question still stands. How long will you keep fighting? How far into enemy space do you intend to take your thirty-one ships?"

"As far as I have to," he replied. "We still have a good chance, so long as we can stay at least one jump ahead of the enemy. A series of lightning-quick raids, taking out their supply depots and advance bases . . . We may end up with half the galaxy chasing us, but as long as we don't let ourselves get cornered somewhere, we can pull this off. I wouldn't be gambling with the lives of my people if there were no chance of survival at all."

"And Earth? The Confederation Senate?"

"We show them that we can win. We bloody the Sh'daar Empire badly enough that they back off and leave us alone, at least for a few more centuries."

"You're gambling on the Vinge Singularity, aren't you?"

"It's kind of tough to gamble on a theoretical concept when you don't have the faintest idea what that concept means," Koenig said carefully. "Especially when the stakes are forty-two thousand men and women under your command . . . and, ultimately, your entire civilization. But . . . yeah. The Confederation needs time to develop new technologies and to let some old ones mature. We know the Sh'daar don't want us going further with GRIN tech. They *fear* us, or they fear what we may become. That gives us an advantage."

"Humankind has been on the verge of the Technological Singularity at least since the early twenty-first century," Karyn pointed out. "There were a number of writers, philosophers, and scientists then who expected that advances in nanotech, computers, and robotics, especially, would bring about a new age where life would essentially be unrecognizable to earlier generations within twenty years or so. But what happens to us if it's *another* five centuries in coming?"

"You're unusually cheerful this morning, Karyn."

"I'm concerned that you've not thought this through. It's possible that you're putting your career, your life, and the lives of those under your command at risk with little or no justification."

"It's called 'taking a chance,' Karyn. Something AIs like you have trouble with."

His PA avatar withdrew then, leaving Koenig with his own dark thoughts.

CAG's Office, TC/USNA CVS America
Approaching Alphekka System
0945 hours, TFT

"So, Gray. Have you learned anything?"

"If you mean, sir, that I shouldn't throw grapefruit juice into the face of another flight officer . . . yes." *Even if the little troll deserves it,* he added . . . but kept the thought to himself.

Although he physically was in a ViR lounger in the Dragonfire ready room, Gray was, in his mind, standing at attention in front of the desk of Captain Barry Wizewski, *America*'s CAG. Wizewski was a lean, leathery-looking man with a heavily creased face. He looked fit but *old.* Scuttlebutt within the squadrons suggested that he consistently refused anagathic treatments for religious reasons, that he was sixty years old and actually *looked* it. White Covenant protocol made it impossible to ask him about his personal religious beliefs . . . but it was hard to imagine another reason. Even Gray, now that he was a full citizen, received nananagathic treatments every time he went to the sickbay for his once-yearly checkup. Prims were notorious neo-Luddites.

"Last September, Lieutenant," Wizewski continued, "you got into a brawl with a brother officer, Howie Spaas. Your Fitness Reports over the last five years show a predilection for getting into fights—verbal altercations at the very least—with other officers. You do realize that your naval career depends on your fitreps, right?"

"I'm very much aware, sir."

"And do you realize that your counseling session will ride with you in your records throughout your naval career."

"I know, sir."

Four days after the juice incident in *America*'s Number 2 Mess Hall, Gray had been called on the carpet in front of Wizewski. Collins had been there as well, as the aggrieved party. Wizewski had listened to them both—Gray's side, that Collins had called him a coward, and Collins' side, that he'd made himself scarce during the battle off Alchameth. Collins had been dismissed, then, with a warning that she'd better learn to get along with her fellow officers no matter what their social or economic background. Gray had remained for a remarkably thorough out-chewing . . . followed by an order to report to the neuropsytherapy department for a therapy update.

The year before, Gray had been diagnosed with PTED—Post Traumatic Embitterment Disorder, a potentially serious emotional sickness brought on in his case by the loss of his wife, his former life and home, and his enforced commissioning in the Navy. He'd undergone a therapy set already and been declared fit for duty.

PTED was particularly insidious, however: a mixture of depression, helplessness, and hopelessness mixed with thoughts of revenge or of having been wronged that could drag on for many years after the triggering event. Therapy had included a number of virtual reality revisitations of his PTED triggers—playing parts of his life back with memory resolution enough to have him feel like he was reliving the events of five years ago. Combined with cognitive-behavioral therapy, getting him to recognize inappropriate thoughts or distortions in his view of reality and actively changing them, the sessions had taken a lot of the burn out of his memories.

But not all. He would *always* have to live with the memory of having lost Angela. He suspected it would always hurt. The therapy had been aimed at teaching him not to immediately assume that authority-types were persecuting him . . . or that the gossip, innuendo, and outright viciousness of a few twisted zeroes like Collins mattered.

Wizewski's order had taken Gray off active duty for almost three weeks, while the neuropsych people had, once again, taken him back into memories that he really wished could be forgotten. Angela had once again suffered a stroke, and once again he'd made his desperate flight north to the Columbia Arcology medical center in Morningside Heights. Once again he'd watched the change in her behavior toward him, her loss of affection, of love.

Once again, the voice of the neuropsytherapist riding with him through his memories pointed out how what had happened to Angela had not been his fault, nor had it been the fault of the Columbia Authorities. There was no *fault*. No blame. Only . . . events. Happenstance. *Life*.

He'd thought he'd been done with all of that.

He realized that Wizewski had just spoken to him, and he didn't have a clue what he'd said. "I beg your pardon, sir?"

"I said, do you want a transfer?"

"What . . . to a deck division?"

"To another squadron. You seem to have a number of enemies in the Dragonfires."

Gray thought about this. He'd put in for a transfer twice before last year, but Commander Allyn had shot it down. She'd talked to him about needing to fix what was wrong, rather than running from it. And now, the new CAG was offering him a chance to start over with another squadron.

"That's . . . tempting, sir. Thank you. But I don't think it would be a good idea."

"Why not?"

"Do you mean . . . other than the fact that I'm going to be launching in another hour and a half?" He let his avatar grin. "Pretty bad timing for *that*, sir."

"No, I can't pull you from VFA–44 now. But I could . . . afterward."

Assuming we're still alive, Gray thought. Again, he didn't voice the comment within the shared virtual reality of the meeting.

"The way I see it, sir, is that I'm pretty well stuck where I am. If I transferred to another squadron, I'd just be starting all over with a different bunch of pilots. And they'd all be assuming I screwed up with the Dragonfires, wondering why I couldn't get along, or figuring I had some kind of Prim chip on my shoulder."

"And do you?"

"Do I think I'm as good as the other pilots in VFA–44? Yes, sir. Absolutely. Do I think I'm better?" He shrugged. "I don't know. Maybe I do. But I don't let that influence me off duty. *All* Navy pilots assume they're the best, right sir?"

"They do if they're any good."

"I know I have a couple of transfer requests in my folder, sir. But Commander Allyn talked me out of that last year. I have a good handle on the PTED. I do have a problem with people who make certain . . . assumptions about me because of my past. But I'm learning to cope."

"Are you?"

"Look at it this way, sir. Five months ago I hauled off and slugged the risty clown who called me a squattie. This last time, I threw a glass of juice instead of a punch. I'd say that qualifies as an improvement in attitude, wouldn't you?"

"Yes, Lieutenant. I would. The problem is that I need a one hundred percent improvement from you. Not eighty. Not ninety-nine point nine. *One hundred percent.* Am I chasing *c* here?"

The reference was to the fact that no physical artifact, no ship, however powerful, could *ever* reach *c*, the speed of light. It might reach 99 percent, and then tack on an almost inexhaustible string of nines after the decimal point, a ship could never reach *c*, not without pulling local space up around itself into an Alcubierre metaspace bubble.

"No, sir. One hundred percent."

"If I have to separate you and Lieutenant Collins like a

couple of children in first-year download, I will. I'll do it to preserve the morale of my squadrons. But as it happens, I think you're right. If you a have a problem with Collins, you need to settle it yourself, and not have me acting like your daddy."

"Yes, sir. I'll handle it, sir."

Wizewski appeared to withdraw for a moment, as though he was thinking something over. "Corders off," he said.

That startled Gray, but he disengaged his implant recorders. Normally, records were made of *all* ViR conferences, if only because people's memories were faulty unless their implant ROMs were active.

"Corder is off, sir."

"I assume you've heard the scuttlebutt about my religion."

Ah. Wizewski had ordered the recorders off for *that* reason. Technically, it wasn't against the law to discuss religion, but the terms of the White Covenant, the Covenant of Human Dignity, made it illegal to attempt converting someone else. People who didn't agree with the declaration of non-interference with another's religious beliefs, or who used religion as an excuse to kill, physically mutilate, or emotionally harm another human being, were denied Confederation citizenship. The Muslim *Rafadeen* were a case in point. So were the Refusers of some Baptist, Pentecostal, and Alien Rapturist churches. While Gray sincerely doubted that Wizewski was about to try to convert him or tell him that he was going to hell, he could understand the CAG's reluctance to have *any* discussion of religion put into an official record.

"Nothing specific, sir," Gray replied. "I guess some of us wondered why you weren't using nananagathics."

"I'm not a *complete* neo-Ludd," he said. "I wouldn't be in the Navy if I were. But I *am* a Purist."

"Ah . . ."

That made a certain amount of sense. *Neo-Ludd* referred to that tiny and generally marginalized portion of the human spectrum that rejected, for one reason or another, any technological enhancements or infrastructure. There were degrees within such belief, of course. Usually, it meant a rejection of nanotech and other invasive technologies—cerebral implants, cosmetic transmogrification, or Netlinks, but stopped short of banning fire, textiles, or water purification. There were peoples still living in isolated corners of the Americas, Australia, South Asia, and Africa where local cultures rejected *all* technology more advanced than subsistence agriculture, but those were rarities. Life in the modern world demanded a certain amount of interaction with information technology, if nothing more. When he'd been living in the Manhattan Ruins, Gray had lacked a basic neural implant because he'd not been a full citizen at the time . . . but that had been for social and economic reasons, not a matter of personal faith or belief. He'd liked the fact that the government couldn't look over his mental shoulder, as it were, but he'd envied a lot of the risty high-tech advantages like global communication access, net downloads, and full healthcare that citizens took for granted.

Purists, though, were a branch of the Rapturist Church of Humankind, an offshoot of the old Pentecostals that believed that it was important for believers to be *fully human* if Christ was one day to return for them. While most modern RCH members accepted nano-grown implants that enabled them to communicate, interact with computers and implant-linked machinery, and engage in basic economics, they tended to reject more serious modifications to the basic human somatype. No cosmetic nano or physical enhancements. No genetic prostheses or modification, either *in utero* or later. No cyborg blendings of human and machine.

And no anti-aging nano.

The Purists seemed to pick and choose among which bits of technology were forbidden, and which were allowed. Many would accept basic medical care, for example, for emergency first aid or for disease prevention, though quite a few rejected any nanotechnic or genetic tinkering with what they saw as God's creation. Gray found the idea ridiculous; there'd been Christian sects a few centuries before that prohibited blood transfusion or, in extreme cases, any medical treatment at all, and the Purist philosophy struck him as just as irrational as those.

But, of course, it was their basic and unalienable right to believe anything they chose, so long as they didn't try to harm others with their antiscientific nonsense.

"The church I grew up in," Wizewski continued, "believed that you shouldn't mess with the human body, shouldn't *change* it, because we were all created in God's image."

"Including nanogrown implants?" Gray asked. He tried not to smile. "Or gene-therapy inoculation?"

"That was . . . a matter of personal belief," he said. "There were a few, including our pastor, who paid the fine."

To be a citizen of the Union of North America, you *had* to have at least a basic Class One cerebral implant. Otherwise you would have trouble paying for goods or opening locked doors. The law mandated heavy fines and compulsory neurpsytherapy for people who refused; the government authorities could do so under the terms of the White Covenant by assuming that any who refused the basic advantages of the technological infrastructure were harming their ability to interact with society and, therefore, were harming themselves.

"We were *not* idiots," Wizewski went on. "If we were sick, we accepted treatment, even if it was gene-therapy or nanomeds. But injecting ourselves full of nano in order to change into an animal or change our skin color or to add a pair of arms or make ourselves super-strong or to turn our bodies into movie screens . . . no. If a fetus had a genetic predisposition to heart disease or depression, we would treat that. But try to make ourselves live for five hundred years . . . or make ourselves look like we were twenty for the rest of our lives? Uh-uh."

"That seems a little . . . selective, sir." Gray honestly wasn't sure how far he could go with being critical of the man's religious beliefs. There was a fuzzy area here between freedom of speech and freedom of belief, and he was glad Wizewski had asked for the corders to be turned off. "How is giving yourself a life span of more than a few decades against God's will if preventing a life-threatening illness is not?"

Wizewski smiled. "I often wondered that. Maybe a short life isn't so bad if it's not a short *miserable* life."

"And maybe God doesn't care if we use our intelligence to make our lives better. Healthier and happier."

"Maybe. I won't argue the point. It's up to me to draw the lines, right?"

"Of course it is, sir."

"But I told you all of this so that you would know. I do understand your position."

"Sir?"

"You're a Primitive . . . or, rather, you *were*. You grew up without all of this hardware"—he tapped the side of his head with a forefinger—"inside your brain. And every person you meet, damned near, assumes you hate technology and can barely make a credit transfer, much less strap on a Starhawk and fly the thing. It's a common prejudice, and one that you and I are going to be facing for the rest of our lives. However long they might be. Understand?"

"Yes, sir."

"If you need to talk to someone, I'm always here. That goes for Ryan too, if she needs it. Having a set of social and personal beliefs outside of the mainstream can be crippling, especially in the military, where you're forced to fit in, to assimilate. Sometimes the need to keep a low profile can make you feel like you're absolutely the only person in the universe who feels the way you do. But that's not true. Understand?"

"Yes, sir, I do. Thank you, sir."

"Don't thank me. Just assimilate, damn it, because the next time you assault another man or woman in this battlegroup, I'm going to skin you alive and nail the bloody hide on *that* bulkhead in my office as a warning to the others. Clear?"

"Clear, sir."

"Then get the hell out of here. Preflight in thirty minutes. Launch in forty-five."

"Aye, aye, sir!"

The virtual reality link was broken, and Gray was again in the lounge chair in his squadron's ready room. A number of the other flight officers were there, including both Collins and Kirkpatrick, but both of them were on the other side of the compartment and none were paying attention to him.

Which was good. He needed a little time alone with his thoughts.

Enforcer Shining Silence
Alphekka System
0945 hours, TFT

Tactician Diligent Effort at Reconciliation considered its preparations yet again, and was satisfied. Every preparation was complete, every ship and weapons system at full readiness.

It was impossible to gauge precisely when the Human fleet would arrive in-system. The intelligence received from the H'rulka Seedcarriers had noted when the enemy had begun acceleration, but human FTL systems were less efficient than were those of the Turusch and other allied species. Based on Turusch understanding of human technologies, the enemy fleet *could* have been here fifty *g'nyuu'm* ago. Or they might not arrive for another hundred to come.

"Threat," the Turusch's Mind Above cried, shrill and writhing. *"Anxious waiting! Impatience! Act!"*

But Diligent Effort at Reconciliation had long experience and considerable training in shunting the narrowly focused demands of the Mind Above aside, allowing rationality and forethought to rule. To the Turusch, the inner voice they called Mind Above represented a more primitive, more atavistic part of themselves that had been the whole of Turusch sentience millions of *g'nyi* ago. The Mind Here was the modern, more rational complex of thought, memory, and planning, while the Mind Below was the melding of separate minds . . . and, for those gifted with the Seed, the link with the Sh'daar masters.

"Patience," the Mind Below counseled. *"The enemy will be here soon. There is nothing more to be done that has not been done."* Part of that thought had originated with Dili-

gent Effort's twin, the other Turusch, which shared its name, with which it was life-paired. But part, too, had come from Diligent Effort's Seed.

It was good to know the masters were here, that they would be watching and guiding the Turusch Fleet's effort soon.

"Very soon, now," the Seed said, reading the thought. *"And victory will belong to us."*

"Kill!" cried the Mind Above.

Chapter Nineteen

25 February 2405

CIC, TC/USNA CVS America
Outer Reaches, Alphekka System
1112 hours, TFT

At a precisely calculated instant, *America*'s metaspace bubble collapsed and the star carrier dropped into normal space, excess velocity bleeding off in the intense pulse of photons characteristic of FTL deceleration. She'd emerged at the fringes of the Alphekka system, some fifty astronomical units from the two close-spaced suns.

The carrier was drifting above an immense, red wall of light.

Alphekka's protoplanetary disk was enormous, a flattened ring of dust, gas, and debris with a sharp, inner edge thirty astronomical units from the star, trailing off to a fuzzy outer rim well over a hundred AUs out. Invisible to the naked eye, the disk glowed an eerie, sullen red at IR wavelengths; *America*'s AI was superimposing the infrared data on the optical, making it visible as a broad and somewhat grainy-looking ring. Such disks, Koenig remembered, had first been detected from Earth using IR telescopes. The dust grains picked up radiation from the central stars, then re-emitted it at long, infrared wavelengths.

In toward the double sun burning at the ring's center, thousands of comets gleamed with an icy, blue-white light, their tails streaming away from the brilliant stellar pair. Many of the larger specks of debris along the inner stretch of the ring also showed comet tails, as volatile gasses were heated and blasted out-system by radiant sunlight.

Several planets glowed brightly under infrared, including a large one, perhaps three times the mass of Earth, circling at the sharp inner edge of the ring. Under magnification, its surface showed as a partially molten, ember-glowing sphere.

A planetary system in the making. . . .

The scene stretched across the CIC bulkheads and overhead, spectacularly and indescribably beautiful, held the personnel in *America*'s CIC spellbound for a moment. "My God in heaven," one voice said against the silence.

"Duty stations, people!" Commander Craig snapped, all business. "There'll be plenty of time for rubbernecking later!"

In the tactical tank, a dozen green icons showed those members of the battlegroup that had emerged within a few light seconds of *America*. One by one, farther and farther out, other Confederation ships began dropping into view.

Koenig continued studying the big overhead display. *America* appeared to be skimming above the surface of the disk, which was perhaps five astronomical units below. A number of glowing red knots were visible to the naked eye, protoplanets forming as debris and planetesimals clumped together.

One point of light was highlighted by a targeting reticule, however, and carried the identifying alphanumerics Al–01.

"*America,*" Koenig said, addressing the ship's AI. "What is target Al–01?"

"Unknown," the ship replied in his head. "Sensory data so far suggests an artificial structure one hundred twelve kilometers across and massing at least two point eight times ten to the sixteen tons."

"That's gotta be a mistake," Sinclair said, shaking his head. "No ship . . ."

"Enhance and magnify," Koenig demanded.

An inset window opened up on the bulkhead display. The object remained fuzzy and quite grainy, at the very limits of optical resolution. Oblong in shape, it glowed with intense infrared heat, and appeared to be skimming just along the upper fringe of the main body of the ring. A readout in the window gave the estimated range: 12 AUs.

"What makes you think it's artificial?" Koenig asked. To his eye, the object appeared to be an irregularly shaped planetesimal, the first stage in the creation of a planet.

"The object is radiating more heat than it would receive from the suns at that range," the ship's AI replied. "It is also the source of numerous radio transmissions of intelligent origin, as well as gravity wave signatures characteristic of paired artificial singularities used for quantum power generation."

"It might be a Turusch base built on an asteroid," Craig suggested.

"Or a converted asteroid vessel," Sinclair added. "Like their Alpha- and Beta-class ships. Just . . . bigger."

"*Much* bigger," Koenig agreed. "It's got to be a base of some kind, not a ship."

"We are also detecting numerous point sources of RF transmissions," the ship added, "in the immediate vicinity of the object. These transmissions are consistent with Turusch fighters, operating in large numbers."

"*How* large?" Koenig asked.

"I have so far identified four hundred ninety-five discrete RF sources in close proximity to AI–01," the ship's AI said. "I am also picking up other clusters of small ships scattered about the system, including three separate concentrations of gravitic, IR, RF, and coherent EM radiation that are almost certainly large numbers of enemy warships. I estimate a total of more than five hundred capital ships, and perhaps one thousand fighters."

"Distance to the nearest concentration."

"Eight point two astronomical units."

Koenig checked the time. The battlegroup had begun emerging from FTL at 1112 hours; the light announcing their arrival would reach those ships at something just over sixty-five minutes . . . call it 1217 hours. *America* had that long before the enemy became aware of their presence.

The sheer number of enemy ships facing them in the Alphekka system was daunting, as daunting as the size of that base ninety-six light minutes away. Koenig had been expecting some sort of supply depot in the Alphekkan system, and possibly a number of Turusch warships as well . . . but the capital ships alone outnumbered the entire Confederation fleet, and on a strictly fighter-to-fighter basis, the enemy outnumbered the Confederation fighters by more than six to one.

Koenig's first thought was to order an immediate withdrawal. The Confederation battlegroup couldn't face a fleet that large, not with any hope at all of survival.

But not all of the battlegroup's ships had emerged yet from metaspace. Stragglers might take as long as another ten minutes to arrive, and they would be scattered all over a sphere as large as thirty light minutes across. It would take a half hour or more to contact them all and give them new orders.

Ships arriving late would die.

Was there a chance?

In modern space combat, there is a blunt aphorism that dictates the shape of all fleet maneuvers: Speed is life. The battlegroup had to begin accelerating—it didn't matter much in which direction—to build up the highest possible velocity. If they weren't moving when the first flock of Toads reached them, they were in for a beating.

Essentially, two choices presented themselves. They could order the battlegroup to accelerate out-system, hoping to build up enough velocity to switch over to Alcubierre Drive before the full weight of the enemy fleets caught up with them. . . .

Or they could plunge into the system's heart, toward that enigmatic monster object skimming above the Alphekkan protoplanetary disk, and seek to cause as much damage as possible.

If they turned outward, all but that one closest body of ships would be behind them, chasing them with higher accelerations than Confederation capital ships could manage. If they headed in-system, the situation became . . . more flexible.

"How many of our ships have checked in?"

"Twenty-eight so far, sir. Three are still missing . . . *Crucis*, *Diablo* . . . and *Remington*."

Koenig thought about this. Two frigates and an AKE . . . the replenishment ship by far the most important of the three.

But he couldn't hold the rest of the battlegroup for them.

"Make to all commands," Koenig said. "Target Al–01 and go to maximum acceleration. CAG?"

"Yes, Admiral."

"We will be launching for CSP only."

"All combat squadrons are ready for launch, Admiral."

"You may commence launching the first three. We'll hold on the rest until we need them." *And we will. . .*

CSP—Combat Space Patrol, the modern analogue to flying CAP over the fleets of old-time oceanic navies—required that fighters fly in fairly close formation with the carrier and other vessels of the battlegroup, rather than accelerating to near-*c* for a long-range strike hours in advance of the capital ships. At five hundred gravities, the alien objective was just over ten hours away. If he ordered a long-range high-G fighter strike, the fighters would reach the objective in sixty-five minutes. He would keep that open as an option, but Koenig wasn't going to exercise it until and unless he needed to. Fighters operating on their own for more than six hours before the rest of the CBG arrived faced annihilation.

He stared up at the overhead display, wondering what that bracketed point of light against the disk might be. Fortress? Warship? Asteroid base? Supply depot on an unimaginable scale?

The tactics he decided upon—and the chances of survival for the next few hours, both for the fighter wing and the battlegroup, depended upon the answer.

"CAG? I want a flyby of Al–01. Bring Commander Peak into this, will you?"

"Aye, sir."

They needed to know what they were facing in there.

Drop Bay 2, TC/USNA CVS America
Outer Reaches, Alphekka System
1114 hours, TFT

"Pilots. Man your fighters!"

Gray stepped down into the deck hatch, put his arms up high, and slid, the narrow boarding tube dropping him three meters into darkness. He dropped into the soft and narrow embrace of his fighter, feeling the acceleration couch mold itself around his legs and torso. His palm came down on a touch panel, and the cockpit lit up. Data flowed through his awareness, letting him know that the ship was powered up, checked green, and ready for launch. The fleet's objective came up within a mental window.

"What the hell *is* that?" Lieutenant Canby asked.

"A baby planet," Collins suggested.

"A big rock," was Lieutenant Ben Donovan's guess.

"Cut the chatter, people," Commander Allyn said. "And listen up. The squadron is on indefinite hold."

Several of the pilots groaned in chorus. *Indefinite hold* meant they wouldn't be launching immediately, that they would be stuck inside the bowels of *America* until someone up in CIC decided to set them free. The wait wasn't entirely uncomfortable. Starhawk cockpits, after all, were designed to accommodate pilots for missions lasting for many hours, even days. Gray's jackies and the seat beneath him took care of his biological output needs, and a small food assembler provided him with meals and fresh water when he needed them. But it was boring, waiting for hours, possibly, before PriFly decided to dump him into the Void.

Gray and the other pilots of VFA–44 would be launching from the drop bays this time, rather than being fired out of *America*'s twin spinal rails. Located aft of the rotating hab modules, they connected directly with the hangar decks above them. When it came time to launch, Gray's Starhawk would pivot ninety degrees, pointing out-and-down relative to the bay, the magnetic clamps would release, and the hab module's rotation would drop him into space with a half G of acceleration—about five meters per second.

A speed of 5 mps was insignificant compared with the 167 mps velocity of fighters fired from *America*'s 200-meter spinal launch rails, and the vector was out from the carrier, rather than straightforward, toward a distant objective. Both velocities, however, were insignificant compared with near-light, a speed the fighters could approach after just ten minutes of acceleration at fifty thousand gravities. The magnetic launch tubes were holdovers from an earlier day, when space fighters had been limited to eight to ten Gs because their acceleration was felt by their pilots. Periodically, critics of the Navy's star carrier program wondered—often vociferously—why carriers had the launch tubes at all . . . or why they weren't converted into kinetic-kill cannon like those carried by the *Kinkaid* and other rail-gun cruisers.

Of course, so far as the hotshots in the squadron were concerned, there was simply no contest. Where was the coolness factor . . . getting dumped from a rotating hab like garbage, or being fired off the carrier's bow at seven Gs? A fighter pilot had his or her *image* to consider, after all.

Gray tried to approach the issue as a professional. It didn't matter how you launched, so long as you had the delta-V to engage the enemy.

He wondered what was waiting for them out there.

Combat space patrol, though, meant they would be sticking close to the carrier battlegroup, deploying in a cloud just beyond the Confederation fleet's perimeter. The idea was to keep the enemy far enough off that the capital ships could get through.

"Hey, Prim!" Collins called, breaking his thoughts. "You'd better be in the fight this time!"

"Lay off the kid, Coll," Lieutenant Tomlinson said. "He was right where we needed him last time."

"Keep it down, people," Allyn repeated. "Zen out and wait for it."

Gray waited.

Shadow Probe 1
Drop Bay 1, TC/USNA CVS America
Outer Reaches, Alphekka System
1232 hours, TFT

"Shadow Probe One ready for launch." Lieutenant Christopher Schiere added an electronic acknowledgement over his palm pad.

"Copy that. You are clear for launch, One." That was the voice of Commander Avery, *America*'s primary flight controller, better known by the term "space boss." "Good luck, good hunting!"

"Thanks, Boss."

"And launch in three . . . two . . . one . . . *drop*!"

The CP–240 Shadowstar pivoted and dropped, plunging into space beyond the deeply shadowed bulk of the *America*. Within seconds, it emerged from the shadow of *America*'s forward shield, already turning to orient itself on the enigmatic object designated Al–01.

"*America* CIC, this is Shadow Probe One, handing off from PriFly and ready for acceleration. Morphing to sperm mode."

"Copy that," a different voice said in his head. "Shadow One, CIC, you are cleared for boost at your discretion."

"Thank you. I'll see you guys on the other side."

The CP–240 was a slightly larger version of the SG–92 Starhawk, massing twenty-nine tons instead of twenty-two, and including provisions for a second pilot-passenger in its highly adaptive cockpit. Its AI was a Gödel 2500 artificial intelligence, a self-aware system far more powerful and flexible than the 900 models incorporated aboard Starhawk fighters. The spacecraft mounted no weapons, however, and its shields were considerably weaker. What made the CP–240 special was its effective invisibility.

Experimental invisibility had been around since the early twenty-first century, but the science had matured from those first, single-wavelength laboratory demonstrations. Radiation passing through the Shadowstar's shields fell onto an outer sheath of programmed nanoconduits that directed it around the recon craft's hull and re-emitted it at a precisely calculated angle on the far side, making it seem as though light or radar signals had passed *through* the shielded space, rather than around.

The technology wasn't perfect. It worked best in open space, where most of the surroundings were black emptiness; if the ship passed between an observer and a complex background object such as a planetary disk or another vessel, there was distortion and a wavering halo effect around the Shadowstar's edges. The invisibility wasn't as good at higher wavelengths, either. Short ultraviolet tended to scatter rather than redirect. Perhaps most limiting, though, was the need to bleed off excess energy at high velocities. Like its SG–92 sister, when the Shadowstar was accelerating, it had to shed hard radiation from its quantum power tap along the slender aft spike that gave the high-velocity incarnation the name "sperm mode." If it didn't, the ship would incinerate, but the high-e photon tail when it was boosting was a dead giveaway. So was the gravitational warping of nearby space as the ship fell toward its own projected singularity.

But within certain parameters, the CP–240 was *very* good at what it was designed for, which was stealthy long-range reconnaissance.

"The objective is at a range of ten point seven AUs, Lieutenant," his ship informed him. "That is one hundred sixty-seven minutes at fifty thousand gravities."

Like all self-aware AIs, the artificial intelligence had a name—in this case *Roger*, after the twentieth-century mathematical physicist Roger Penrose. That choice of name amused Schiere, whose hobbies included the philosophies of physics. Penrose was still somewhat notorious for his strongly stated beliefs that computers could *never* become conscious or self-aware.

That had been true, certainly, in the earliest years of AI research, when computers were algorithmically deterministic, and when, as Penrose had insisted, the known laws of physics could not explain human consciousness. All of that changed with the advent of quantum computers, of course, with software that was far more powerful than human intelligence, at least within certain narrow boundaries.

"Allowing for a one-hour drift," Schiere replied.

"That has been included in the calculations, Lieutenant. Do you wish to see the precise mathematical evaluation?"

"No, Roger," Schiere replied with a laugh. "I trust you. Initiate boost."

"Accelerating at fifty thousand gravities."

The Shadowstar's drives switched on, projecting an artificial singularity ahead of the ship for a tiny instant, switching off . . . then on . . . then off . . . creating a gravitational strobe forever flickering just ahead of the CP–240's bluntly rounded nose. In that first second, the Shadowstar traveled five hundred kilometers. The vast, dark bulk of the star carrier alongside vanished, whipped away into the distance astern.

And within moments, the universe itself began to reshape into the warped strangeness of relativistic flight.

CIC, TC/USNA CVS America
Outer Reaches, Alphekka System
1516 hours, TFT

Almost four hours into the boost, and *America* was now 1.2 million kilometers from Al–01, traveling at 73,200 kilometers per second . . . about 24 percent of the speed of light. The view ahead, as displayed by *America*'s AI across the low, domed overhead of the CIC, was just beginning to show the visual distortions invoked by the carrier's high velocity, the stars beginning to bunch together toward the ship's direction of travel.

The three remaining ships of the inbound battlegroup, *Crucis*, *Diablo*, and *Remington*, had dropped in and formed up, though the bulky *Remington* was still lagging slightly behind the main body of the fleet.

And by now, Lieutenant Schiere and his AI ought to be nearing the objective, whatever the hell it was.

"America," he said in his head, connecting with the car-

rier's AI. "Update on the enemy fighter packs."

"All enemy fighters have begun accelerating, and are vectoring toward the fleet. They appear to have been caught somewhat by surprise, however, as most of them had outbound vectors. It will take many hours for most of them to intersect with our flight path. One fighter swarm, however, the nearest and designated 'Fox-Sierra One,' is decelerating now to match velocities with us. Fox-Sierra One will intersect the fleet in another thirty-one minutes."

"Understood. Thank you."

The enemy fighters, a swarm of at least sixty of them, were visible in the tactical display now, a cluster of red arrowheads astern and to one side of the fleet, playing catch-up.

"The fighters near the objective don't seem to be boosting at all," Commander Sinclair pointed out. The CIC weapons officer had been linked in with the AI conference. "They're sitting tight."

"That's to be expected," Koenig replied. "If they accelerate toward us, they would have to pass us, decelerate behind us, then accelerate again to catch up. They could do that, of course, and they probably will . . . but they'll wait until we're closer."

Matching velocities with another ship to the point that you could engage it in combat was always a tricky proposition. Fighters had enough of a delta-V advantage over capital ships that they could manage it, but it took time and finesse, and the target fleet could make things tough by jinking, changing acceleration, and throwing up clouds of antifighter munitions—sand clouds and high-G KK projectiles. The fighter swarm designated Fox-Sierra One had been the only fighters more or less astern of the main body of the carrier battlegroup, the only ones that could match vectors with relative ease.

And that, in fact, had been a part of Koenig's strategy. Had he given the order to turn tail and run, nearly every fighter in the system would have been astern and burning hard to catch up. Moving at close to *c*, they would have caught up long before *America* could slip into the metaspace safety of Alcubierre Drive. Plunging directly into the heart of the system—toward Al–01—gave the fleet a chance . . . at least until they'd passed the objective and began heading *away* from the objective, through the debris plane of the protoplanetary disk and into the depths of space beyond.

"Let me see a long-range on the tac display," Koenig said, looking into the tank. The image flickered and jumped. The twin stars glowed as tiny, side-by-side spheres at the center, surrounded by the broad red ring of the protoplanetary disk.

He still couldn't see the outer edge of the disk, however. "Take it back another notch," Koenig said.

The view jumped again. This time, the double star showed as a single point. The outer edge of the ring shaded off into ragged nothingness. Koenig pointed at a red icon out beyond the edge of the disk, and a third of the way around from Al–01's position. "I thought I saw another fleet element out on the periphery," he said. "What is that?"

"We have designated that 'Fleet Red Two,'" *America*'s AI replied. "It is the primary body of enemy capital ships in this system."

"What's the range?"

"Currently one hundred forty-two point five AUs."

A long way . . . nineteen light hours.

"Still no grav signatures?"

"No, Admiral."

Which was reasonable, since, at nineteen light hours' distance, the light from the battlegroup's emergence hadn't reached them yet. What was puzzling, however, was the fact that—at least as of nineteen hours ago, since what *America* was picking up from CS–1 was nineteen hours out of date—the enemy fleet, composed of an estimated 315 capital ships and perhaps twice that many fighters, was so far completely inert. *America*'s long-range sensors had only just been able to pick them up as dim reflectors of starlight, and then only because a flashing radio beacon had announced their presence.

It seemed strange to post so many warships together out beyond Alphekka's debris disk, power them down, and simply let them drift in slow orbit. Koenig was beginning to think that they might be a mothballed fleet, ships unscrewed and unpowered. That would support the idea of Alphekka being some sort of a Turusch fleet depot, however. And so long as those ships hadn't switched on their quantum power plants and started accelerating, they wouldn't be a threat to *America*'s battlegroup.

Which was good. There were 71 capital ships in the general area of Al–01, spread through a volume of space nearly 4 AUs across, plus 112 fighters. The odds against the Confederation fleet were quite long even without those silently drifting vessels.

Perhaps they would know more when Schiere completed his recon flyby.

Shadow Probe 1
Inner Protoplanetary Disk, Alphekka System
1517 hours, TFT

"That thing," Lieutenant Schiere said, "gives me the fricking willies."

"Which?" Roger replied. "Al–01? Or what's behind it?"

"Both, I guess," Schiere replied. "But I was talking about the disk."

The protoplanetary disk showed on the Shadowstar's screens and within Schiere's own in-head display as a seemingly infinite plane composed of a kind of red graininess, like a low-res image of a red surface. His AI was continuing to superimpose infrared data on the optical image; even this close, at visible wavelengths the protoplanetary disk was a rather thin haze of dust and gas, and the larger chunks of rock were invisibly distant. The recon Shadowstar was coming in toward the plane of the disk at a fairly flat angle. Schiere's velocity was now twelve kilometers per second, down from the near-*c* zorch of the majority of his 10.7 AU passage. He was, his instruments told him, already passing through the outer fringes of the disk.

The protoplanetary disk was relatively thin even this far out from its star: 50 AUs from the two Alphekkan suns, it was less than seventy thousand kilometers thick. The objective, Al–01, was just skimming the outer fringe above the face of the disk, which had no clear-cut or definite boundaries. The Shadowstar's sensors were actually detecting a wake behind the alien artifact as it plowed ahead through the thin haze of dust and gas. Nearby asteroids and comets—at 50 AUs from the double star, of course, none of the comets possessed tails—appeared as faint but gleaming stars compressed into a flat arc extending into the distance and curving around the suns.

Schiere checked his instrumentation again. When he'd cut his drive an hour ago, he'd been more than 70,000 kilometers away from Al–01. Since then, he'd drifted 43,200 kilometers toward the object, while the object, orbiting the suns at 7.5 kilometers per second, had traveled 27,000 kilometers toward him. Their combined velocities had closed the remaining distance rapidly. It also meant that he would be flashing past the object at 20 kps, and most of the mission objectives would be carried out through Roger's superhuman senses.

Another three hundred kilometers. The objective was visible now as a tiny gray-white point of light ahead.

Simply *seeing* the object, to say nothing of the protoplanetary disk and the nearest asteroids, was a major technological feat, one requiring Roger to sample small amounts of incoming radiation from the Shadowstar's shields and use them to build up an image of the universe outside, even though most of that radiation was bypassing the invisible fighter entirely. With his drives off and his quantum power plant down—the Shadowstar's remaining systems were operating on battery power alone—he was still effectively invisible to the universe outside.

Which, he decided, was a very good thing. Roger was pinpointing and highlighting more and more ships as they drew closer. The objective swam through the protoplanetary disk within its own small cloud of capital ships and accompanying fighters.

To make matters worse, the enemy would know that he was coming. At high-G accelerations, his Shadowstar gave off gravitational waves that could be detected across millions of kilometers, and they'd scanned him repeatedly on the way in with radar and laser-ranging sensors. They couldn't see him *now*, but they would have a pretty good idea of where he was.

Throughout the past thirty minutes, they'd taken repeated shots at him. He'd jinked enough during the final phase of deceleration that they couldn't be certain of where he was, exactly. But they were throwing up a hell of a lot of kinetic-kill projectiles, along with clouds of anti-missile sand. Individual grains had been pecking at his shields for ten minutes now, some from the protoplanetary disk, some from sand canisters fired hopefully in his direction.

So far, nothing had come in heavy enough to do him any damage.

But the enemy ships were starting to move, accelerating out from their huge consort, shifting into a defensive phalanx to attempt to block him. Roger was already using some of the fighter's limited stores of reaction mass to slightly change vectors in unpredictable directions, just so they couldn't guess exactly where he was by extrapolating earlier data on his incoming course and velocity.

How close could he get before the shit really hit the fan?

One hundred kilometers. Objective Al–01 swelled huge ahead, five seconds away and growing larger. Roger had calculated the final inbound path to carry them within ten kilometers of the huge object, which now filled the sky.

And Lieutenant Schiere studied the object now, his eyes growing wider.

So *that* was what the thing was!

It was astonishing. Awe-inspiring.

And terrifying . . .

Chapter Twenty

25 February 2405

CIC, TC/USNA CVS America
Alphekka System
1628 hours, TFT

"Admiral! We're getting a signal from Shadow Probe One! Priority urgent!"

The probe had been 69 light minutes ahead, the signal that far out of date. *America* was still 6 AU from the objective.

"Let's hear it."

Lieutenant Schiere's voice came through, faint behind blasts of static. He was passing through the protoplanetary disk now, and the debris field was causing considerable interference.

He was also under fire, and the discharge of particle-beam bolts tended to drown radio signals in waves of static.

" . . . Huge, bigger than any man-made structure. It looks . . . factory! Incredible scale . . . data . . ."

The voice faded out for a moment. Then:

" . . . Scrambling fighters to catch . . . going into stealth mode . . . blackout . . ."

"The signal from Shadow Probe One has cut off, Admiral," Ramirez said.

Almost a billion kilometers ahead, Lieutenant Schiere was fighting—no, had *been* fighting—for his life. With no weapons, the Shadowstar's only viable tactic was to shut down almost completely, going into full stealth mode, which was why the radio signal had been cut off.

By now, Schiere was either dead or fifty thousand kilometers past the objective, drifting through the plane of the protoplanetary disk.

"Did we get a data stream from his AI?"

"Yes, sir. It's going through the cleaner now. We'll have something useful in a few seconds . . . here. Coming through now, Admiral."

Within Koenig's in-head display, a new window opened up, and for the first time he could see the enigmatic Turusch object in close-up detail. Range and vector data appearing in the corner of the visual field showed that the object was currently seventy kilometers away, moving toward the cameras at a velocity of almost twenty kilometers per second. The video had been slowed by a factor of ten, however, so that the target drifted slowly through the field of view.

The leading hemisphere of the object looked like an enormous gray-silver doughnut, with a central opening half as wide as the entire structure . . . more than fifty kilometers. The surface appeared to be a solid, curved sheet of metal, with a shimmer that suggested there were defensive shields up. As the Shadowstar drifted past, however, the opposite hemisphere came into view, an uneven, almost ragged structure of struts, beams, spheres and cylinders, conduits, and radiator panels. It was those heat-shedding panels that were the source of most of the infrared from the object; whatever was going on inside was creating a *lot* of waste heat.

A factory, Schiere had said. A titanic space-going factory 112 kilometers across and massing almost 30 quadrillion tons . . .

"I think I understand," Koenig told the others. "That thing's designed to orbit through the Alphekkan protoplanetary disk, probably with a slight tilt to swing it a little above and below the ecliptic. That opening, that . . . *mouth*, sucks in debris, gas, and dust and rocks small enough to digest, and uses them as raw material."

"Yeah," Craig said, her voice low, almost solemn as she watched the transmission in her head. "Raw material for *what*?"

"Look in there."

Using his implant controls, he zoomed in on the image, until their viewpoint plunged past the outer forest of struts and girders, centering on a cluster of objects just inside. It was difficult to make out the shapes through the beams and surrounding structure, but the magnified image appeared to be of a group of Turusch warships. Koenig could see at least four of them—round-snouted, awkwardly bulked cigar shapes that looked like Juliet-class cruisers. If so, each was three quarters of a kilometer long and massed something like 300,000 tons.

Curiously, those bundled cruisers were plain, dark gray metal. Turusch warships generally were painted in jagged patterns of either black and red or black and green; these, apparently, were unpainted.

There were other ships drifting outside the huge structure's shell, trailing just behind the monster in its wake. Papa-, Romeo-, and Sierra-class cruisers, Tango-, Uniform-, and Victor-class destroyers, dozens of Toad fighters . . . and all appeared to be inert. The warships gathered outside the structure had been painted in the typical Turusch duotones, red and black, green and black, and other combinations. One destroyer was even fitted out in bright pink-and-black livery.

"It's a shipyard," Koenig said. "An orbital shipyard designed to scoop up raw materials by the gigaton and transform them into starships."

"One industrial facility to mine, smelt, tool, and build that many ships?" Buchanan said from the bridge. "It's not possible!"

"Why not?" Koenig replied. "We use Scroungers to pick up raw elements from asteroids, comets, and small moons, and nanoassemblers use those materials to turn out whatever the fleet needs. Food, water, and air, mostly, but spare parts and replacements too . . . even entire fighters. Why not capital ships as well?"

"Yeah, and we use synchorbital nanufactories to build them," Buchanan said. "We haul raw materials in from different places throughout the solar system and assemble our ships in orbit, either at Earth Synchorbit or at Mars."

"Seems to me the Turusch have just streamlined the process a bit," Koenig said. "That protoplanetary disk contains *everything* that will go into a planetary system someday. Volatiles, in the form of various ices. Carbon. Metals. Even radioactives."

"Yeah," Commander Craig put in. "All they have to do is sift out what they need, and nanotech would certainly give them that capability. We do as much on Earth when we nanogrow an arcology tower from dirt and ancient landfills. But . . . they're doing it on such a huge scale!"

"If you have the raw material to do it, why not big?" Koenig said.

"This might explain Fleet Red Two," Lieutenant Commander Hargrave suggested. He was one of *America*'s tactical officers. "New ships, waiting for delivery."

"Which begs the question," Buchanan replied. "Where are the crews?"

"There'd be no point in keeping thousands of Turusch personnel here waiting for their ships to grow," Koenig said. "They probably bring them in on transports or troop ships periodically." He pointed. Several Turusch fighters were accelerating past the silent, waiting fleet, closing with Schiere's recon probe. "There are some crews based here, at least."

"That monster is big enough," Craig observed, "to base the entire Confederation fleet, and then some."

"America," Koenig said. "We need revised estimates on the number of *active* warships in this system."

"This is necessarily a rough estimate, Admiral," the AI's voice replied. "But long-range scans coupled with data received from Shadow Probe One have so far identified forty-three capital ships that appear to be powered up and crewed, all within ten light minutes of Objective Al–01. We are tracking fighters in the vicinity of Al–01 as well. Several of the active warships, however, are types known to carry Toad fighters, and so more crewed fighters could be forthcoming."

Koenig felt a surge of excitement at that. The Confederation battlegroup was composed of twenty-six ships, not counting the five transports and supply vessels attached to the fleet. They were *only* facing forty-three enemy ships near Al–01, not the hundreds they'd first assumed to be combatants. *And* the CBG possessed the initial advantage of velocity.

Speed is life.

"Admiral," Sinclair said, interrupting. "Excuse me, sir, but Fox-Sierra One has increased its acceleration and is closing. Time to intercept . . . twelve minutes."

"Very well," Koenig said. "Captain Buchanan?"

"Yes, sir."

"We are commencing launch ops. Please cut ship acceleration. Mr. Ramirez? Pass that on to the other ships of the fleet."

"Aye, aye, sir."

America and the other ships of the fleet were currently traveling at 94,749 kilometers per second, and continuing to accelerate by 5 kilometers per second per second. If *America* was going to launch her fighter contingent, she had to be moving at a constant velocity, and without the powerful space-warping effects of her drive singularity bending space in her immediate vicinity. A fighter passing through that encapsulating zone of bent space could be torn apart.

And the entire fleet had to decelerate together, coordinating the maneuver over the fleet tactical link; otherwise, one second after *America* cut her drive, every other ship in the fleet would have left her behind.

"All commands report acceleration has ceased, Admiral."

"Very well. CAG? You may begin launching your fighters."

"Aye, aye, Admiral. Some of my pilots are probably ready to tear their way out into hard vacuum with their bare hands by now."

"*Close* CSP, CAG. I don't want them scattered."

"Aye, aye, sir."

"Mr. Ramirez?"

"Yes, sir!"

"Make to all ships of the battlegroup. Prepare to commence deceleration, maximum gravs, on my command."

"Sir . . . *de*celeration?"

"You heard me."

"Aye, aye, sir."

Speed was life . . . but sometimes it had to be *controlled* rather than flat-out.

VFA–44
Alphekka System
1630 hours, TFT

"Dragonfires, this is PriFly. Carrier acceleration has ceased. You are now cleared for drop. Tactical updates are coming through on your primary feeds now."

"About damned time!" Kirkpatrick said.

"It's time to do some turning and burning!" Lieutenant Walsh added.

"Okay, Dragons," Allyn said. "Drop on my mark in three . . . two . . . one . . . *drop*!"

Twelve drop bays accommodated one squadron of fighters on the outboard aft section of each rotating hab module. The ships of VFA–44 pivoted, facing down, then dropped as one, falling out into the night.

America was traveling now at 94,749 kilometers per second, over 31 percent of the speed of light, but with her drive powered down, both *America* and the fighters now emerging from her launch bays shared that same forward velocity. From the fighters' points of view, however, the huge carrier hung motionless in space as they fell outward in all directions, a ring of fighters expanding at five meters per second.

"Engage drives," Allyn commanded. "One hundred gravities for one second in three . . . two . . . one . . . and *boost*."

Accelerating to one kilometer per second—a hair over, actually, since they were already moving at 5 mps—the fighters raced out into a much larger circle, clearing the five-hundred-meter curve of the flattened dome of the carrier's forward shield.

"CIC, Dragonfires, handing over from PriFly." Primary Flight Control handled only the launches and recoveries of fighters. Everything else was CIC's responsibility.

"We've got you, Dragonfires."

"Roger that. We are clear of the ship."

"Copy that, Dragonfires. Stay well clear. We're about to decelerate at five hundred Gs."

"Copy."

And suddenly, the star carrier was no longer there. With singularities projected aft, *America* began decelerating at five hundred gravities, which meant that, from the fighters' viewpoints, she suddenly receded into the distance, five kilometers away after one second, fifteen after three, falling farther and farther astern with each passing second.

Commander Allyn gave a sharp command, and the twelve Starhawks of Dragonfire Squadron rotated 180 degrees and began accelerating after the huge ship, catching up within moments, then matching accelerations in order to maintain their relative distance from her.

The maneuvers were routine, easily handled by the fighters' AIs. Gray monitored the process, while continuing to skim through the tactical downloads.

An enemy fighter swarm was closing fast, would intercept *America* in just a few minutes. The most problematic aspect of the tacsit was *Remington*, currently two light minutes behind *America* and off to one side. VFA–44 was being assigned to protect the *Remington*, to keep the Turusch hunter-killer packs from cutting her out from the rest of the herd and pulling her down.

"Combat check, everyone!" Allyn called. "Dragon One, set!"

"Dragon Two, set."

"Dragon Three, go!"

"Dragon Four, good to go!"

The roll call continued, ship by ship. Gray was Dragon Nine, his wingman, Lieutenant Katie Tucker, Dragon Ten.

"Dragon Nine, ready for boost," Gray called.

"Dragon Ten, go!

"Eleven, good to go!

"Twelve, ready."

"Target the nearest fighters," Allyn ordered. "It'll be tight, so have your AIs check your KK streams and beam fire. We don't want any own goals, okay? Pass through, hard reverse, and then hit them from behind. Three thousand gravities on my command. And three . . . two . . . one . . . *boost*!"

And this time it was the Star Carrier *America* that was left behind.

CIC, TC/USNA CVS America
Alphekka System
1635 hours, TFT

"Toad fighters are closing with the *Remington*," Sinclair reported. "Dragonfires are accelerating to intercept, with Death Rattlers moving in behind as an active reserve."

"Very well."

It was situations like this one that kept fleet-op tactics from becoming a by-the-numbers exercise for the big fleet AIs. When *Remington* and two frigates arrived later than the rest of the Confederation ships, Koenig had been forced to begin acceleration without them. The frigates had joined up, but the AKE *Remington* was still straggling, gamely pushing to keep up with the rest of the fleet but falling farther and farther astern over the past few hours.

A single pack of Toad fighters had been out-system from the battlegroup, had been following them in from 8 AUs astern.

And the *Remington* now lay directly in the path of the oncoming Toads.

"Toad fighters have launched on *Remington*," Craig said.

Koenig watched the battle unfold in the tactical tank. The CBG's abrupt deceleration had thrown the enemy attack off.

Many of the fighters had held their original courses too long, and were now on trajectories that would carry them in front of the fleet, well out of range. They would have to decelerate in order to engage.

Which they would. Toads were less maneuverable than Starhawks, bulkier, more massive . . . but they could pull plenty of gravities and would easily be able to match course and speed with *America* and the other Confederation warships.

"Toad fighters have now launched on us," Craig announced. "CSP is diverting to block incoming fire."

Decelerating at 500 Gs, it would be another four and a half hours to the fleet's flyby of Al–01, at which point they would still be traveling at over ten thousand kilometers per second.

"Tactical! We need a fire-control working group."

Koenig was less concerned at the moment with the incoming Turusch fighters—there was nothing left to be done about them—than he was about the objective.

Rewriting combat orders on the fly, while in the middle of an op, was always risky.

They needed to trust the fighter combat space patrol, and start planning for the intercept of that space-going factory now.

VFA–44
Alphekka System
1637 hours, TFT

"I've got a group of twelve missiles inbound!" Gray yelled over the squadron channel. "Targeting, locking on with proximity fuse . . . and *Fox One*!"

A VG–10 Krait with a warhead tuned to a twenty-kiloton yield slipped from the belly of his Starhawk, its grav drive visible as a fiercely hot point of light flickering into the darkness. The enemy missiles were locked on to the *America*, but they were tightly clustered. A single nuclear detonation directly in front of them should vaporize them all, or so badly mangle their circuitry that they became inert, tumbling lumps of fused metal.

"I've got another missile swarm at three-three-seven by two one," Lieutenant Tucker called. "Locking . . . *Fox One*."

A dazzling, silent fireball blossomed ahead of Gray's fighter, followed seconds later by another. His AI scanned space ahead and reported a clean field. The two missile swarms had been wiped from the sky.

But more missiles were coming.

Gray's AI, linked in now with the capital ships of the battlegroup as well as the other fighters, was coordinating targets. In essence, all of the fleet tactical AIs were joined together into a single mind, noting threats, determining strategies, assigning assets. Because many of the threats were still light seconds, even light minutes away, the "mind" worked slowly. A major reason that human pilots still strapped on fighters was the need for creativity and intuition to overcome the tactical limitations imposed by the speed of light.

Gray's IHD showed fields of fire and tracking locks as transparent lines and cones of light. A massive collection of cylinders and struts behind the characteristic mushroom cap of a forward shield appeared ahead—the AKE *Remington*. The AKE prefix designated her as an underway replenishment ship, and she was, arguably, one of the more important vessels in the battlegroup. The planners of Operation Crown Arrow expected that the *America* battlegroup would be away from Sol for a long time, operating far behind enemy lines. The two AKEs in the battlegroup, *Remington* and *Lewis*, carried the SKR–7 Scrounger spacecraft that could extract necessary metals, hydrocarbons, and volatiles from asteroids and comet nuclei, while nanufactory facilities on board the AKEs allowed them to grow almost anything the fleet might need while on deep-space deployment, up to and including new fighters.

If the Turusch managed to disable or destroy the *Remington*, the fleet's operational range and flexibility would be sharply limited.

Gray's fighter hurtled past the dark, shadowed bulk of the

Remington, which was still accelerating in an attempt to catch up with the main body of the battlegroup. The nearest Toads were just 220,000 kilometers beyond, already decelerating hard in order to engage the Confederation fighters. There were twenty Toad fighters in that pack.

"*Remington*, Dragonfires," Commander Allyn called over the tactical channel. "Watch your fire. We've got your back."

"Copy that, Dragonfires," a worried-sounding voice replied. "Glad to have you with us."

An AKE like the *Remington* mounted twelve turret-mounted point-defense weapons, a mix of high-velocity KK Gatlings and StellarDyne pee-beeps, both essentially identical to the RFK–90s and PBP–2s mounted on the Starhawks. Enemy tactics would involve trying to overwhelm the *Remington*'s defenses with missile and beam fire, seeking to burn out shields and knock out active weapons.

The Dragonfires added some flexibility to the AKE's defense. The battlespace astern of the AKE, however, would have to be very carefully managed, or the good guys would be scoring some own goals.

"One volley of Kraits," Allyn ordered, "then blow through and return. Target front to center of the pack . . . and fire!"

VG–10 Krait missiles, nuclear-tipped and deadly, rippled out from the oncoming Starhawks, streaking across intervening space. Five were disabled by the Turusch defenses, beam weapons and sand clouds, and then nuclear fireballs were pulsing and strobing through the enemy fighter group. One hit scored . . . two . . .

And then the first Turusch missiles began exploding among the Starhawks as well. A dazzling wall of light unfolded directly ahead of Gray. His fighter punched through the debris cloud an instant later, his sensors shrieking, warning of particle impacts and hard radiation searing across his forward shields. . . .

. . . And then he punched through into open space, one of his shields flickering on the verge of failure but still holding. Lieutenant Dulaney's Starhawk was tumbling, shields down, power failing, but the other eleven fighters closed with the enemy fighter swarm. Other fighters, like Gray's, had taken minor damage.

But now the real slugging match began.

Gray targeted a Toad coming in directly ahead. The differences in vectors—the two fighter swarms had a combined difference in velocity of nearly forty thousand kilometers per second—meant there was no time for fancy maneuvers. Gray's AI jinked left to avoid a head-on collision, pivoting right at the same instant to train a stream of high-velocity kinetic-kill slugs on the enemy as it passed less than fifty kilometers to starboard.

His targeting sensors indicated a hit, but he was too far away now to check the damage personally. Flying tail first now, facing back the way he'd come, Gray locked on to the Toad with his particle beam and fired. In general, if you couldn't burn them down with nuclear weapons, it was best to fight enemy fighters with kinetic-kill projectile streams. The Toads, with heavier shields and power plants than Confederation fighters, could generally use those shields to deflect incoming particle beams and laser fire. But KK rounds depended on kinetic energy to make a kill, and when the enemy was receding at high speed, those rounds lacked the solid punch necessary to do any real damage. If his first volley had damaged the enemy's shields at all, however, a particle beam traveling at close to *c* might be able to burn through.

He fired and, an instant later, saw a bright flash in the distance.

"Dragon Nine," he reported. "Score one!"

"Dragon Five," Collins said. "Kill!"

"Dragon Four!" That was Will Canby. "Got one! I got one!"

But the battle now became a twisting confusion of mass and movement, "turning and burning" as the slang term from ancient aerial fighter combat so succinctly termed it. The Turusch swarm had numbered twenty fighters coming in. Gray's AI was only tracking ten now, which suggested that the initial salvo had killed seven, and three more had been burned down as VFA–44 passed through the enemy formation. The odds now were almost even as the fighters slowed and reversed course, and now the true ship-to-ship capabilities of human and Turusch fighters would be tested.

Tactical studies carried out by various Confederation military research groups gave Turusch fighters the advantage overall. Toads were bigger, could accelerate faster, had more powerful shields and screens, appeared to carry heavier and more powerful weaponry, and could absorb more damage than the lighter Starhawks. Perhaps even more important, the enemy deployed Toads in much greater numbers—typically in fighter swarms of anywhere from fifteen to thirty, compared to human squadrons of nine or twelve. Those advantages, especially the numerical advantage, had been brutally telling at a number of space battles over the past thirty-some years—Beta Pic, Rasalhague, Everdawn, and First Arcturus Station.

And yet, the human Starhawks had demonstrated a clear advantage at more recent battles—Eta Boötis, Sol, and now Second Arcturus. They were much quicker on the uptake, quicker in their response and counter-response than the heavier Toads . . . and the pilots who survived one ship-to-ship encounter with the enemy, both human and cybernetic, were proving that they could skew the statistics. One study suggested that humans learned faster than their Turusch counterparts.

Toads, it was now known, carried two pilots apiece; the Turusch appeared to be closely paired biologically, with two beings actually thinking of themselves as one—a bit of alien neurobiology that humans were still struggling to understand. Possibly, a single human pilot in tandem with his AI simply made decisions more quickly, was better able to intuitively respond to a threat.

Whatever the reason, Turusch fighter losses tended to be a lot higher than those of the human squadrons, especially when the humans were able to take the fight in close—"knife-fighting range," as the Confederation pilots called it. Toads preferred to stand off and pound the enemy with long-range nukes; human tactics preferred high-speed point-blank encounters one-on-one.

And VFA–44 was now making the best of that one slim advantage they possessed.

The fighter swarms merged, as nuclear fireballs flared throughout the battlespace.

Chapter Twenty-One

25 February 2405

CIC, TC/USNA CVS America
Alphekka System
1655 hours, TFT

"We've completed correlating all of the targets," Commander Sinclair told Koenig. "The sooner we release the KK volley, of course, the more velocity they'll have at the target."

Long-range kinetic-kill weapons were typically fired when the ship was moving as fast on approach as possible, before beginning deceleration. The more velocity they had when they hit the target, the bigger the release of energy.

"Of course," Koenig said. He used a cursor to indicate the leading, heavily shielded end of the ship factory, freeze-framed for the moment in the tactical tank. "But I'd like to avoid targeting this section here. It looks like it's massively shielded. It would have to be, since it's plowing through clouds of dust and meteoric debris at a fairly high velocity. Any hits here will be a lot less effective than elsewhere."

The working group consisted of Sinclair and several of *America*'s fleet weapons and tactical officers, plus their counterparts from the other combat ships of the fleet. Their task was to work out the best times and angles for both an initial volley from several AUs out and for targeting the enemy during the flyby. They would be passing the ship factory at over ten thousand kilometers per second. They'd been running various possibilities through simulators, to give them the best possible chance of success.

"It'll be tough to hit anything behind that shield," Commander Horton, of the weapons department on board the *Kinkaid*, pointed out. He pointed to the image of the factory. "The shield is mostly facing us, with only this thin crescent here visible from this angle."

"The good news," Sinclair said, "is that the thing appears to be a satellite, not a ship. It's in a two-hundred-sixty-eight-year orbit around Alphekka at a slight inclination to the debris field. We can be confident that we'll know its *precise* position four hours from now."

The worst issue in planning space combat was the realization that what you were seeing in your tactical display was out of date by however many light minutes separated you from the objective. You had to cover vast distances in a naval battle, and you could never assume the enemy was going to do what you thought he was going to do. But a space station that massive was going to keep moving along in its orbit; this one was moving at a relatively sedate 7.5 kilometers per second.

Koenig studied the screen for a moment. "It appears that the factory is traveling just a little faster than the debris. Its orbit is somewhat eccentric, so it's cutting across the debris field slightly, coming from behind and catching up with the rocks. That suggests that the intake there might be a weak point."

"Can't be *too* weak," Craig said. "Otherwise it would have chunks of rock smashing into whatever's inside and gumming up the works."

"No. But it isn't designed to have KK slugs slamming into it at 10 percent *c*, either. Maybe we can 'gum up the works'—as Commander Craig put it—ourselves. Even if the leading hemisphere of that thing is heavily shielded, a direct high-v bombardment ought to do a hell of a lot of damage."

"Yes, sir," Sinclair said. "Then, as we scoot past, we have our AIs rotate our ships so we can drop fire into the thing's ass end, where there's nothing but struts, exposed hardware, and newly minted starships."

"I'd be surprised if there wasn't some shielding aft as well," Koenig replied, "but it sounds like a plan. Everyone start feeding this to your AIs." He checked his implant's time sense. "We have two hundred fifty-four minutes to passage. I want to get off our long-range volley as soon as possible—five minutes if we can swing it. Questions?"

There were none.

"Let's do it, then."

"Admiral?" Craig said.

"Yes?"

"You should probably check the dogfight aft. Things are getting pretty nasty."

Koenig shifted his IHD to a battlespace channel, one showing a graphic presentation of the firefight unfolding astern. The incoming Turusch fighters appeared to have broken off their run on *America* and the nearby ships of the battlegroup, and were concentrating instead on the *Remington.*

As he watched, a pair of Toads dropped onto the tail of a Starhawk, slashing at the Confederation fighter with a barrage of particle beams until it flared bright and vanished.

VFA–44 was fighting for its life.

Dragonfire Nine
VFA–44
Alphekka System
1656 hours, TFT

"This is Dragon Four! Dragon Four! Two on my tail! I'm—"

Lieutenant Will Canby's Starhawk vanished in a blossoming cloud of fragments and hard radiation as his shields fell and the Toads' CP beams tore his power plant apart. Gray and Tucker, in close formation, had been pulling around to drop onto the two Toads' tails, but they pulled out of the high-grav turn too late to help him. "Target lock!" Gray yelled, and then he mindclicked the trigger. *"Fox One!"*

A VG–10 Krait streaked from beneath his fighter, arrow-ing toward the two Toads. The Turusch fighters broke left and right; the missile followed the one to the right, passing the Toad by a scant few meters before detonating just ahead of it, a 20-kiloton flash engulfing both of the enemy spacecraft in a silently unfolding blossom of light.

The Toad to port emerged from the fireball tumbling and scorched; the one to starboard didn't emerge at all. Tucker snapped her fighter past the out-of-control Toad, pivoting as she overtook it to rip it apart with a KK burst from her RFK–90.

"Ten, Nine," Gray called to Tucker. "Let's close in to the *Remington*."

"Copy that, Nine. Looks like it's getting a little intense back there."

Together, their Starhawk AIs in close synch, they threw their drive singularities off to the side and whipped around them in a five-G turn. The *Remington* was now some 300,000 kilometers ahead. Since the AKE had continued to accelerate while the main battlegroup decelerated, the rest of the fleet was growing close, now, just over half a million kilometers away and closing fast.

Collins' accusation that he'd left his wing at the fight over Alchameth still burned a bit. In fact, given the realities of space-fighter combat, sticking close to your wingman was more of a suggestion than a rule. There were times when piling two on one provided a significant tactical advantage, and it helped to have someone close to brush a bad guy off your tail if you couldn't shake him; but the fact that fighters could flip end-for-end to directly confront an enemy fighter coming in from behind weakened the argument that you needed someone on your wing to provide cover.

Instead, winning a fighter action meant dominating the local battlespace, and that was easier to do with twelve separate but coordinated fighters than with six fighter pairs. In most dogfights out here in the night, you stayed linked with the tacnet and didn't wander too far off, but you only rarely found yourself relying on—or being relied upon by—your wing.

Nonetheless, Gray was sticking close to Tucker.

Along with Ben Donovan, Lieutenant Katerine Tucker—"Katie" or "Tuck" to others in the squadron—was as close to a friend as Gray had in the Dragonfires. She wasn't a Prim—she'd been born and raised just outside of the Toronto Arcologies, deep in the heart of the USNA.

Still, citizens of the former Canadian Commonwealth suffered their share of prejudice at the tongues of so-called *real* citizens, career discrimination, and jokes about Canucks and "eh?" Katie seemed to understand what Gray had been going through in attempting to integrate with the squadron, and sympathized.

Sometimes it was awfully good to know that you weren't alone.

So he was sticking close.

The Turusch fighters were beginning to hammer at the *Remington* close enough now to savage the AKE with particle beams. Gray and Tucker were coming in behind a couple of Toads that appeared to be focused completely on the all-but-helpless replenishment ship ahead.

"I got the left, Tuck," Gray called.

"I'm on the right. Target lock . . . *Fox One*!"

The term "Fox One," an ancient holdover from the days of oceangoing naval aviation, referred to the launch of any self-guiding or AI-controlled missile—usually a Krait with a variable-yield warhead, but occasionally other forms of intelligent ordnance as well.

Gray called "Fox One" as well as he loosed another VG–10 Krait. It was a long shot—at a range of nearly 100,000 kilometers—but both missiles settled onto the Toads' gravitic signature and relentlessly streaked after them at one thousand gravities. Just over 130 seconds later, Tucker's Krait, traveling now at over 1,200 kilometers per second, reached the target and proximity-detonated, followed an instant later by Gray's strike. Other nukes were strobing throughout the volume of space encompassing the *Remington*. The Starhawks of the Death Rattlers had moved in close to the AKE, catching the Toads between the two squadrons. For a brief moment, a handful of Toads stood sharply silhouetted against Rattler fire. Then the fighter swarms interpenetrated, passing through one another in a swirling confusion of velocity, fire, and death.

Gray speared a Toad with a particle beam. The bolt didn't penetrate the enemy's shields, but the Turusch fighter twisted away . . . and moved directly into the path of a heavier bolt from one of the *Remington*'s point-defense particle cannon. A kilometer away, Tucker turned hard as a Toad pursued her. Gray tried to match the turn, but had to break off as the *Remington* grew huge just ahead. For an instant, the replenishment ship's hull blurred past Gray's awareness. He caught a glimpse of one of the big SKR–7 Scrounger auxiliaries mounted on her aft spine above her drive containment spheres, like an enormous insect; the mobile disassembler had been savaged by Turusch fire, was gaping open and leaking a glittering spray of frozen water and volatiles. *Remington*'s forward shield had taken damage as well, but his fleeting glimpse showed no damage to the turning hab modules, and *Remington*'s point-defense weapons were much in evidence, lashing out at the closest Toad fighters and burning them down.

The enemy fighters pulled back then, apparently breaking off.

"We got them!" Collins yelled. "We've got them on the run!"

"I'm dry on KK!" Kirkpatrick yelled. "Permission to go to Krait-knife!"

"Negative, Eleven," Allyn called. "Negative on Krait-knife!"

"Krait-knife" was slang for using the nuclear-tipped VG–10 missiles at ranges of less than fifty kilometers—virtually point-blank range. Commander Allyn had forbidden the maneuver either because Kirkpatrick was too close to his target and a shot at that range might damage him or, more likely, he was too close to the injured *Remington*, and might score own-goal damage.

But the Turusch appeared to be wavering . . . then scattering. There were five Toads left, now . . . then four . . .

. . . And then the survivors were accelerating in toward Al–01, fleeing at fifty thousand gravities.

"Let them go!" Allyn called. "Repeat! Let them go! Don't get drawn out by them."

Gray's heart was pounding, his hands slick with sweat. They'd lost seven fighters in exchange for sixteen . . . a decent enough kill ratio of better than two to one, certainly, but not one that they could maintain for long.

The enemy had a *lot* more fighters in reserve. . . .

CIC, TC/USNA CVS America
Alphekka System
1705 hours, TFT

"All capital ships in the battlegroup possessing long-range offensive armament report that they're ready to fire, Admiral," Commander Craig told him. "Fields of fire are clear, and the target is locked in. All personnel report they are ready for firing."

"Very well," Koenig said. "Make to all commands. Commence fire."

Across the battlegroup, railguns accelerated kinetic-kill slugs at up to five hundred gravities. Koenig, sitting now in his CIC acceleration couch, felt the heavy lurch as *America* kicked two projectiles down her spinal launch tubes.

Every action has an opposite and equal reaction; a pair of kilogram masses hurtling from *America*'s launch tubes gave a substantial nudge to the far more massive *America*, enough, at any rate, to be felt. Any time capital ships began slinging metal around like this, their crews had to strap in. Less massive ships with longer launch rails, like the railgun cruiser *Kinkaid*, could accelerate rounds to much higher velocities and, as a result, suffered significantly harder recoils.

The different lengths of launch rails throughout the fleet meant different velocities for the projectiles, which, in turn, meant a long temporal footprint for the impacts. Incoming rounds would begin striking Al–01 and nearby targets within another two hours, and would continue striking them for another half hour after that.

For that reason, the higher-velocity rounds, like those from *Kinkaid*, were targeted against enemy warships, since the fastest rounds would arrive first. Slower-moving rounds, like those from *America*—which had launch rails only two hundred meters long—would arrive long after the Turusch vessels had begun to move out of the way.

Instead, they were aimed at Al–01, the massive space factory in orbit around the Alphekkan double star, which couldn't change course or speed and which would, therefore, be precisely at the point *America*'s targeting AIs predicted it would be 138 minutes after firing.

The barrage caused two logistical difficulties, but had been timed and tuned to keep those to a minimum. Each KK launch had the effect of slightly slowing each firing ship, in accord with Newton's Third Law. Since each ship type had launch rails of different lengths—*America*'s, designed for launching manned fighters at low accelerations, were only two hundred meters long, while *Kinkaid*'s were half a kilometer—each ship was decelerated at a different rate, less for massive, short-railed ships like *America*, more for less massive, longer-railed ships like *Kinkaid*.

The result was that the battlegroup was scattering again . . . not by much, but enough that the different fleet elements were forced to maneuver in order to regain a semblance of their original flight formation.

The second problem was that *America* needed to bring some of the CSP fighters back on board—specifically the Starhawks of VFA–36 and VFA–44. Both squadrons had expended a considerable percentage of their Krait missiles and KK Gatling ammunition in the short, sharp firefight around the *Remington*, and they needed to re-arm.

America had answered the second problem by matching it with the first. The carrier had cut all acceleration, so that she could take the Dragonfires and the Death Rattlers back on board. The other squadrons flying close CSP around the main fleet had not been in the fight, and would continue holding position around the battlegroup's defensive sphere. The other capital ships would use *America* as a steady-velocity marker, and would form on her.

Remington, Koenig noted, had taken some damage in the fight—a couple of near misses by thermonuclear warheads and Turusch particle beams. Several of her shields were down, she was leaking reaction mass from her shield cap, and one of her SKR–7s, mounted on her hull, had been badly damaged. The shield cap leak was the most serious problem; *Remington*'s CO had deployed nanorepair robots to fix the leak. Other damage could be repaired later, though the SKR might well be a total loss.

That wasn't an insurmountable problem so far as the battlegroup went, however. The fleet still had seven operational Scroungers, more than enough to meet battlegroup needs for the foreseeable future.

And *Remington* had now rejoined the CBG and was under the umbrella of *America*'s CSP. There didn't appear to be any further threats out there in the making, not until the battlegroup made its close passage of the Turusch factory some three and a half hours from now.

"Admiral Koenig?" the space boss's voice said over the shipboard link. "The first fighter is coming in now, sir."

"Thanks, Randy," Koenig replied. "Let me know when the last one is on board."

"Right."

Commander Avery, right now, had the tough job on board the carrier—sorting out the survivors from twenty-four space fighters, some of them damaged and limping, and bringing them all in for a safe trap on board the carrier. He did not envy the man his job.

Koenig checked the tactical records. The cost of the fighter action had been heavy. Four fighters from VFA–44 had been lost—Canby, Walsh, Tomlinson, and Dulaney. Three had been lost from VFA–36—Burke, Mayall, and Zebrowski—plus one streaker.

Fighters could be replaced; that was the purpose of the CBG's lone manufactory ship, the AVM *Richard Arkwright*. Experienced pilots could not. Basic pilot training could be downloaded through a recruit's implants, but it still required experience and the relentless accumulation of flight-time hours to become proficient. The combat losses, both at

Arcturus and here at Alphekka, would be damned tough to make up.

And what Koenig had in mind after Operation Crown Arrow would require *lots* of experienced pilots.

The single streaker—thank God there hadn't been more of them—was a particularly vexing problem.

"Commander Craig?" he asked.

"Yessir."

"That one streaker . . . from VFA–36."

"Lieutenant Rafferty, Admiral."

It was tougher when they had a name.

"Is he alive?"

" 'She,' Admiral. Alma Rafferty. Telemetry from Rattler Five has ceased. We don't know if she's alive or not. Commander Corbin reports he's ready to launch a capture mission."

Corbin was the CO of the DinoSARs, one of *America*'s SAR squadrons.

Koenig thought for a moment.

Streaker was fighter slang for a ship that had been damaged but not destroyed, and which was traveling on a high-speed vector away from battlespace, unable to decelerate or to change course. That sort of thing happened in fighter combat a lot. Grav-singularity projectors were particularly prone to crippling damage if a fighter was badly smashed about, and a fighter simply couldn't carry enough reaction mass to use conventional thrusters to slow or change course.

Carriers carried SAR tugs for this purpose, search-and-rescue craft with powerful projectors, able to match outbound vectors with damaged fighters, latch on, and drag them home. *America* possessed two SAR squadrons, the DinoSARs and the Jolly Blacks, each with six tugs; and the two Marine assault carriers, *Nassau* and *Vera Cruz*, each carried one more SAR squadron.

That was a total of twenty-four tugs. In another few hours, the fighter squadrons of all three carriers were going to be locked in an epic furball, and losses—including streakers—might be high. Koenig had to decide whether to dispatch one of *America*'s SAR tugs after Rafferty's damaged fighter. The longer he waited, the farther Rafferty would be from the fleet, the tougher it would be to catch her, and the longer it would take to bring her back, *if* she could be found in all that emptiness at all.

If he dispatched a SAR tug, though, that tug might not rejoin the fleet for many hours, possibly days. Worse, since the CBG was committed to a high-speed pass of Al–01, it was possible that tactical necessity would force them to keep going and jump into Alcubierre Drive after completing that pass. That would doom both Rafferty and the five-man crew of a tug when the vessels were left behind.

The conservative play was to preserve his assets this early in the game. Losing one pilot—who might well be dead already—was better than losing a pilot *and* a tug with five experienced crewmen. There were no guarantees that the CBG would survive the close passage of Al–01.

And yet . . .

Rear Admiral Alexander Koenig was fifty-four years old, and had been in the Navy for thirty-two of them. He'd joined as a midshipman cadet in 2372. Two years later, he'd been a very junior lieutenant j.g. on his first deployment, flying one of the old SG–12 Assassins off the star carrier *Constellation*. After two years of download-training at the academy, he'd been posted aboard the *"Connie"* just in time for the Battle of Rasalhague.

Rasalhague—also known as Ras Alhague or Alpha Ophiuchi—was a type A5III giant forty-seven light years from Earth. The star had a companion star, Rasalhague B, 7 AUs away and with an orbital period of 8.7 years.

There hadn't been much there—an astronomical research station on an airless rock called Rasalhague B II. Rasalhague A was at the point of evolving off the Main Sequence, turning into a giant some twenty-five times brighter than Sol. The research station, supporting a couple of hundred astronomers and cosmologists, was there to watch the contraction of the helium core that would mark the beginning of the star's death.

Unknown ships had arrived suddenly and obliterated the

colony. Confederation Intelligence wouldn't learn the identity of the attackers for several years yet, but the bicolored spacecraft would turn out eventually to be those of the Turusch—that species' first confrontation with Humankind.

Connie and seven escorts had been at a deep-space naval base twelve light years from Rasalhague when a badly shot-up scout-courier had come in with news of the attack. Admiral Benedix had ordered the squadron in for a closer look.

The Battle of Rasalhague had been a nasty defeat for Confederation forces. All six escorts, two cruisers and four frigates, plus a stores ship, had been destroyed before they could slip back into their Alcubierre FTL bubbles. The *Constellation* had escaped—barely—but she'd lost two of her three hab modules in the process, and nearly two thousand members of her crew; another five hundred had suffered severe radiation burns and died before the ship could get to a safe port.

Benedix had been court-martialed upon his return to Fleet Base Mars. He'd delayed the jump to metaspace in order to recover a dozen tugs hauling in disabled fighters. Because of that delay, a quartet of thermonuclear warheads had gotten through the point-defense fire, and the cruisers *Milwaukee* and *Vancouver*, which had closed with the *Connie* to provide covering fire against the oncoming waves of Toads, had been destroyed.

Benedix was acquitted by the court-martial board. After beating off that first wave of fighters, there'd been no way of knowing that there were so many more coming in behind the first. Benedix had ordered the radars shut down to avoid giving away their position. The board decided he'd done everything possible, given the bad hand he'd been forced to play.

But he never commanded a fleet again.

The Battle of Rasalhague was just one of the long string of defeats suffered by Confederation forces early in the war, and a relatively minor one at that. But it held special significance for Koenig.

Lieutenant j.g. Koenig had been one of the pilots rescued by Benedix's delay. Those old Assassins were no match for

Turusch Toads. During the first encounter, every SG–12 in two fighter squadrons had been destroyed or sent tumbling helplessly into the void. The young Koenig spent a *very* cold and lonely couple of hours with no power and a dying life support system, until the tug pulled him into *Connie*'s single remaining landing bay.

Benedix had gambled that there were no more nearby enemy fighters tracking the fleet, and he'd lost. Twelve pilots had been saved . . . but 4,500 people had died, counting the crews on board those cruisers. "Benedix Exchange" became a catchphrase throughout the Navy and the Confederation Marines, meaning to save a little by losing a lot.

And ever since, Koenig had wondered what he would have done in that nightmare situation.

This situation was different, of course, but he was facing the distinct possibility of having to employ a Benedix Exchange of his own.

But the deciding factor was Koenig's own experience. He'd been in the position of Alma Rafferty—alone in a crippled hulk, tumbling helplessly through the night, alone in a way that very few people could begin to imagine.

"Tell Commander Corbin to dispatch a SAR. Make sure the crew is volunteer-only . . . and make sure they know we might not be able to wait for them."

"Yes, sir. I was told volunteers are already standing by."

Koenig nodded. He had a good crew, devoted to one another.

And that, he believed, was the most powerful asset he possessed in the fleet.

Chapter Twenty-Two

25 February 2405

Squadron Common Area, TC/USNA CVS America
Alphekka System
1722 hours, TFT

"Are you okay?" Gray asked her.

Shay Ryan turned away from the viewall, her arms still crossed, hands tightly clutching opposite elbows. Ryan was trembling inside and she couldn't stop it. She despised showing weakness, any weakness at all. . . .

"I'm fine," she said. "I'm . . . fine."

Gray nodded at the viewall. "The Admiral takes good care of his people."

The screen currently showed a view of the *America* from a camera mounted on the outer rim of the shield cap, looking aft. One of the Brandt space tugs, a clumsy-looking assembly of spheres and canisters and folded grappling legs that gave it the look of an enormous mechanical insect, was emerging from Auxiliary Docking Bay One. *America* had, once again, cut her deceleration, in order to launch the SAR recovery vehicle.

"Who is it going after?" Ryan asked.

"Not sure," Gray replied. "Scuttlebutt says it's a streaker from the Rattlers. Lafferty? Rafferty? Something like that. Anyway, it wasn't someone from the Dragonfires, and the

Death Rattlers was the only other squadron turning and burning with us out there."

"You don't *know*?"

"Hey!" Gray said, grinning. "We have, what? Something like two hundred fighter pilots on board *America*, counting the reserves? I can't know *all* of them."

"Fewer than that," Ryan replied slowly, "after that last fight. But . . . I know what you mean. I don't play well with others either."

"There is that," Gray said, the smile vanishing. "Not what I meant, but . . . yeah."

On the screen, the SAR tug was accelerating under thrusters. The ugly little craft had singularity projectors far stronger than those mounted on fighters, drives powerful enough to stop a fighter in mid-tumble, bring it to a halt, and boost it back to the star carrier. Those faceted globes at the bow that looked so eerily like the compound eyes of an ungainly insect were particularly powerful field compensators, which extended the free-fall zone far enough that tug and fighter together wouldn't be torn apart by tidal effects. SAR tugs, though, had to be *very* careful about switching those projectors on in the vicinity of a larger ship to avoid twisting *part* of another vessel into unrecognizable wreckage. The usual safety radius was two kilometers, twice the length of the *America*.

"Do you think they'll find the pilot?"

"I imagine so. They wouldn't launch a SAR tug if they didn't have a good idea where the streaker was. Especially while we're still in the middle of a combat op."

"All that emptiness . . ." She felt cold. *Terrified* . . .

"Well, they found us okay when we streaked at Alchameth. Right?" He looked concerned, and reached out to touch her arm. "You sure you're okay, Shay?"

"I'm *fine*!" She pulled away from his touch.

"If you say so."

"I'm just . . ." She stopped, and tried again. "Trevor, I don't know if I can still do this."

"What? Strap on a fighter?"

"That. And, and *everything*. Blend in with these people,

be a part of them. Sometimes they seem as . . . as alien as those bugs at the Overlook."

"The Agletsch? I thought you liked them."

"I did. I do." She shrugged. "Hell, I stick up for anyone who's getting stepped on. Those two were getting a raw deal."

"Just like a couple of Prims from the Periphery, eh?"

"That's just it. We're fucking *Prims.* How do you do it, Trev? How do you keep from killing Kirkpatrick and Collins and the rest of those zeroes?"

"I dunno. Take it a day at a time."

"When I was falling into Alchameth, you came for me. I'm grateful."

"All in a day's work."

"And then you took a load of shit because you *did* help me."

"Take nothing. I tossed a cup of grapefruit juice in the troll-bitch's face."

"And got in trouble for it."

"Not so much. Three weeks off duty and a stretch with the neuropsytherapy people? That was *nothing.*"

"Well, the point is that you came and got me. But . . . but despite that, I feel so damned *alone.* And when I was out there off Alchameth, drifting into nothingness in a junked fighter . . ."

"Yeah?"

"I've felt alone most of my life. Even when I was still . . . home. In the D.C. swamps. But I never felt the way I felt at Alchameth. No other human for a million kilometers. No one but *you.*"

"Like I said, all in a day's work. Us Prims need to stick together."

"Bullshit. You won't always be there to rescue my ass. You *can't.*"

On the viewall, the tug was now clear of *America*'s shield cap. A moment later, the carrier's deceleration resumed and the tug vanished off the screen in an eye's blink, flashing past the shield cap and into the emptiness ahead of the larger ship.

"Shay . . . you're not alone. And you won't be. Some of these pilots, the risty zeroes, especially, are hard to live with, yeah. But they're all part of the family and we all look out for one another." He nodded at the viewall. "Koenig's sent a tug out after our lost Rattler. He'll send one out after you, too."

She nodded, but not because she believed him. At the moment, paradoxically, what she wanted more than anything else was to be alone, to be *left* alone. And at the same time, she was terrified of dying alone. . . .

Shay Ryan often wondered why they'd steered her into naval aviation, back when she'd joined the military and left the risty enclaves of Bethesda and Chevy Chase forever. They'd claimed the battery of aptitude tests and simulations they'd given her at Oceana had shown she was perfect as a fighter pilot . . . but why? What the hell had they been looking for?

For some reason, she remembered the chase. . . .

At last, that was how she thought of it. She'd been fifteen, that day, not long before her family had decided to leave the swamps and head north. She'd been trapping out on the Mall, which meant running her twelve-foot skiff from buoy to buoy, checking the fish traps that had been set beneath each colored, tethered balloon floating on the dark and oily water. The Rebs had ambushed her among the huge mangrove trees that now filled what once had been the Washington Mall—had almost caught her.

The Rebs—the Virginia Rebels—were a Prim gang that came over from Arlington once in a while to raid the Community's fish traps or moored barge farms. Usually they weren't more than a nuisance . . . but if you were an attractive young woman living in the D.C. swamps you did *not* want to get caught by them. Some girls from the Community had vanished when the Rebs came raiding, and had never come back. The adults told dark stories. . . .

They'd come at her in boats from two directions, but she'd switched on her skiff's little hydrogen-cell powered electric motor and rammed one of them, banging hard against the bigger boat's side and bumping along its hull, scraping mid-ship to stern, as leering faces yelled at her and outstretched hands tried to grab her. She fended one of them off, slashing at his face with her trap hook, the long-handled tool she used to fish up the traps, and as she slid past the other boat's stern, she'd used the hook to rip the jury-rigged fuel line from the gasoline-powered outboard motor and then opened her own throttle wide.

The other boat had chased her . . . and it was a bigger, faster speedboat with a more powerful engine that should have caught her easily, but she knew the mangroves crowding the Mall and she knew the tangled architecture of the ancient and half-fallen public buildings beyond. Weaving in and out, she'd led the second Reb boat on a desperate chase through forest and ruins, never emerging into the open where her pursuers could catch her in a flat-out run.

That nightmare game of hide-and-seek had continued for fifteen minutes, until an arrow had sprouted from the chest of one of the Rebs, knocking him overboard into the shallow water. A Community Watch boat had roared in then, with Jeb Fullerton in the bow, drawing his bow and loosing arrow after arrow at the raiders. The rebs hadn't stayed to fight, fortunately, but had put about and roared off toward the south, back to the Virginia side of the swamp.

Her interviewer at Oceana, she remembered, had been very interested in the details of that chase, had talked a lot about hand-eye coordination and a good sense of distance and vector over the water.

Had they figured that she would be good at piloting a fighter because she could zigzag among the mangrove roots without crashing into one of the massive, looming trees?

Maybe. But what they hadn't questioned her about was her problems with fitting in, either with her own family, or among the damned risties of Chevy Chase.

Being alone . . . being cut off from anyone who cared . . .

The thought still terrified her.

Enforcer Shining Silence
Alphekka System
1915 hours, TFT

Tactician Diligent Effort at Reconciliation was, in fact, a single three-part mind with two bodies. And it had a problem.

Eons ago, geological ages before the rise of Mind Below, the Gweh—slow and patient armored gastropods dwelling within the mountaintop biomes of the storm-wracked homeworld they called *Xchee'ga'gwah*, the Place of Coming Forth in Light—had begun making foraging expeditions into the depths they called the Abyss. Food and certain necessary metallic supplements were scarce in the Heights Above, abundant in the Abyss Below.

There was another sophont species on the homeworld. They were called Ma'agh, and they lived down there among the storms and lava flows of the Abyss, breathing the thick and poison-laden air. The small, exoskeletal creatures were primitive and violent, but willing to trade with the Gweh. They gave the foragers food and metals in exchange for the mildly narcotic circulatory fluid harvested from *grolludh*, the immense hydrogen-floater filter-feeders adrift among the mountaintop plateaus. The Ma'agh could leave their steaming pools only briefly, and would have suffocated in the cold, pure, thin air of the Heights.

Individual Gweh attempting to make the journey into the Abyss, however, rarely returned to the bright, clear safety of the Heights. The Ma'agh were capable of ambushing and killing lone Gweh if they thought they could get away with it, and there were countless other dangers within the Depths. Would-be traders faced abyssal whirlwinds, searing lava flows, poisonous gasses, and the *d'dhuthchweh*, a diminutive relative of the *grolludh*. The name meant "emphatic blossom," and it could kill with an electric charge anything that brushed against the sweep of its dangling tentacles.

But *pairs* of Gweh, generally, had returned.

So vital to the species' survival was the trade with the Abyss-dwellers that over twelves upon twelves upon twelves of *g'nyi*, close pairings of Gweh had become, first, a cultural imperative, and eventually, a biological one. Exquisitely sensitive to sound, they read one another's droning hum of subvocalized thoughts in a way that seemed to be telepathic to aliens, their thought processes intermingled to the point where the two spoke simultaneously, the sounds blending to carry three meanings: those of the two individuals, and a third, expressed by the two heterodyned frequencies. So powerful a survival mechanism had been this pairing that within 12^5 *g'nyi*, the individual members of a Gweh pairing no longer thought of themselves as separate beings. They were *one*, in a sense that non-Gweh observers found it difficult to understand.

And yet, despite this essential oneness, each Gweh was divided. Their earliest, most primitive mind, what they called the "Mind Above," was impulsive, direct, and savage—a necessary tool in dealing with a world as inherently hostile as *Xchee'ga'gwah*. The Mind Here had evolved later, while the Mind Below, a synthesis of the Mind Here of two or more individual Gweh, was the most recent, the most *civilized* development in the species' psychology.

Eventually, the Gweh had developed technic civilization and gone to the stars. They'd gone as traders, but also as warriors; the Mind Above made them superb soldiers—fearless, ruthless, and unstoppable. As interstellar traders, then, and as mercenaries, they'd met the alien Agletsch, who'd given them the strange and unpronounceable name "Turusch."

And through the Agletsch they'd met the Sh'daar, received the Gift of the Sh'daar Sced, and becoming, in time, one of the Sh'daar's principal warrior species.

And this was a part of Diligent Effort's problem. It was senior tactician—the commanding officer, though it didn't think of the position in those terms—both of the Gweh warship *Shining Silence* and of twelve twelves of warships protecting the manufactory in this infant star system. Its Mind Below was tracking the incoming enemy warships, preparing the fleet to engage them. Its Mind Above was shrieking battle cries, eager to engage the enemy and destroy it . . . and

Diligent Effort's Mind Here felt that an *offensive* operation would best interpret its orders.

But Diligent Effort also carried a Sh'daar Seed, that tiny implant running a bit of programmed Sh'daar awareness that intertwined with the Mind Below and guided each decision he made.

And the Seed was requiring, was *demanding*, that the fleet stay in place, guarding the immense star-orbiting factory.

As a result, Diligent Effort's consciousness was fragmenting, and that could be deadly in combat. Mind Here was being torn between Mind Above and Mind Below; normally, Mind Here and Mind Below could agree to tune out Mind Above's shrill fight-or-flight cacophony of hate, fear, and action, but the discordance caused by the Seed was actually causing the Mind Here of the two *physical* components of Diligent Effort's being to diverge. The harmonics of its two voices were dissolving into chaos, and that threatened its communications link with others of the *Shining Silence* crew, and with the rest of the fleet.

Normally, the Seed simply suggested and the joint Mind went along . . . but with the divergence, Diligent Effort was momentarily paralyzed by uncertainty. The Gweh—the Turusch—worked through internal consensus, not by blindly obeying orders. The dissonance was . . . crippling.

The Seed had warned the system's defenders that the humans would be coming here, had directed the disposition of the fleet. Now, though, the Seed appeared confused, even conflicted. It had expected the enemy to see the numbers of Turusch, Jival, and Soru waiting here and flee, Diligent Effort thought. That the enemy fleet had been accelerating toward the manufactory for several *g'nyuu'm*, now, was unexpected, worrisome, and internally divisive. As the Seed hesitated, the link within Mind Below trembled and threatened to fail.

An enemy long-range bombardment might already be on the way. At such long range, it was difficult to determine if or when they'd loosed a volley, but Diligent Effort would have fired one some time ago, had he been the tactician commanding the enemy fleet.

"We *must* move the ships, at least," Diligent Effort told the Seed. "If the enemy has already begun a bombardment, they will have targeted them first, knowing that they can be moved once we know we are under fire."

As always, the Seed's reply was more emotion and a sense of knowing, as if from a memory, rather than an inner voice or coherent thought.

The memory seemed to be one of dismissal . . . and an awareness that the enemy could not decelerate as quickly as Turusch vessels. When the human ships arrived, they would be traveling far too quickly to pose a serious danger to the fleet.

"But they may have already released a volley. They will target our ships. . . ."

Again, an unspoken memory. What was important was the manufactory, nothing else. The Fleet would stay tucked in close to protect it from enemy fighters. Those *could* pose a threat to the huge structure, like *d'cha* swarming in for the kill on a huge, drifting *grolludh* on far distant *Xchee'ga'gwah*.

Diligent Effort did not understand the Sh'daar. No, it decided. That wasn't quite true. Rather, it didn't understand the intelligence encapsulated within the Seed. It had never met a physical Sh'daar, and knew no Gweh that had. It wondered if they were as abrupt, as hard, as seemingly unconcerned with the survival and well-being of individual Gweh pairs as were their electronic avatars.

The tactician understood, it thought, why the Sh'daar Seed was holding back. If the Turusch vessels had begun accelerating toward the oncoming enemy fleet, they would have to pass through that fleet, decelerate, then turn and accelerate again . . . and at this point they would not be able to accelerate long enough to catch up with them. Sound tactical thinking demanded that they stay put near the manufactory, and try to engage the enemy ships when they passed through this volume of space.

But surely that didn't require that individual ships stay where they were, as helpless targets.

"All ships will begin low-order acceleration," it said. "We

will shift position by a few *lurm'm* only, just enough to avoid incoming kinetic-kill missiles."

The Seed disagreed . . . and Diligent Effort felt its Mind Below ripping apart. Its twin, the other physical part of Diligent Effort, felt that it was necessary to obey the Seed precisely, to the letter; the Seed seemed to have difficulty grasping distances in the real world, as opposed to its own virtual universe, and thought that movement meant more than a slight change of position. Diligent Effort's communications link with the rest of the fleet wavered, the harmonics of the Mind Below momentarily broken.

The tactician's full name, Diligent Effort at Reconciliation, was derived from its talent in finding compromise and unity among disparate points of view. Partly, this grew from its rather keen sense of rationality, its experience at seeing how things were, even through a haze of conflicting emotions. Partly, too, it grew out of its native talent, its ability to use its voices—all three of them—to *impose* unity of purpose and thought within a dissenting Gweh community. Essentially, its heterodyned Mind Below voice could sing louder than the voices of others around it, forcing acquiescence, then agreement, then harmony.

For a moment, for a horrible moment, it could not find that third voice.

He could not give the necessary command.

"Turusch!" a harsh voice rasped over the fleet communications link. "Give the order to maneuver!"

That was the commander of one of the three Soru vessels in the fleet. Unable to pronounce the twittering, singsong chirps of the Gweh, it used the Agletsch *lingua franca*, and so referred to the Gweh by the alien version of the species' name.

"Y'vasch!" Diligent Effort managed to say in the same language. *"Go!"*

The Soru ships were smaller than most Gweh vessels, curved like slashing claws and brightly painted in ultraviolet. They began to move. . . .

And then one of the Turusch ships nearby, a converted

asteroid enforcer called *Bright Lightning in the Fog*, staggered as a piece of metal traveling at a fair percentage of the speed of light slammed into it, releasing a dazzling flash of liberated kinetic energy with the collision. Sensors detected several other high-velocity impactors passing through the space between the ships.

The enemy bombardment had begun, unguided but precisely targeted rounds flickering in from the night.

"Move! Move! Move!" That voice was almost wholly from Mind Above, a frantic screaming that overrode the momentary paralysis of the Mind Below. It felt the hard nudge as *Shining Silence* fired its thrusters and slowly began to accelerate. There might still be time. . . .

A Brilliance in the Night took a direct hit, the entire forward third of the vessel vanishing in a flash that left the rest tumbling wildly end over end, trailing debris and a glittering spray of freezing atmosphere. Moments later, the remnants began to crumple and vanish as they were inexorably drawn into the singularities of the warship's power plant.

The Soru ships were already far ahead, still accelerating.

Bring them back, a memory whispered within Diligent Effort's thoughts. *Return them to their place!*

"I cannot. They have released themselves from the fleet's control."

The tactician's control over the alien Soru had been tenuous at best. It didn't know if they possessed—or were possessed by—the Seed.

Working with aliens was always difficult. The tactician felt a certain kindred understanding of the H'rulka. Perhaps that was because both species knew an Abyss, and both feared the storms that could arise there, but even the H'rulka gas bags didn't think properly or in a rational way.

For that matter, neither did the Sh'daar.

It wished the five Jival ships with the fleet would request a release as well. If the tactician could let its Mind Above issue that order, it would be eight ships attacking the humans far out in space, well away from the precious manufactory.

But the Jival tended to stick close to military protocol and refused to stretch the orders given them. They were unimaginative, by Gweh standards, strictly, as a human would say, "by the book." Their ships, in any case, mingled the jobs of troop transport and fighting vessel, and were not as efficient as single-purpose warships like those of the Soru or the Turusch.

The Soru were fierce and implacable warriors, evolved from chlorine-breathing plains-runners that could bring down fast-galloping prey animals many times larger than they. Perhaps they would be able to deal the approaching enemy a crippling blow.

Another incoming round slashed past a Turusch ship, the *Abyssal Wind*, but it was only a glancing blow, enough to vaporize a few *m'ni* of rock on the converted asteroid but not to cause any serious damage. The fleet was moving, as Diligent Effort had commanded. Other Seeds, within other vessel tacticians, had failed to block the order.

Good. . . .

CIC, TC/USNA CVS America
Alphekka System
1940 hours, TFT

America continued to slow, backing down toward the enigmatic artificial moon dubbed Al–01. They were traveling now at 40,149 kilometers per second. The actual passage would take place so quickly that merely human observers would not even be aware when it happened. There would be time for a single focused volley from every ship in the battlegroup, but both the targeting and the firing would be handled by the fleet's AIs, with reaction times that made human reactions seem glacial by comparison.

"Make to all ships," Koenig ordered. "On my mark, cut drives. CAG, prepare to bring the CSP back on board."

"Aye, aye, sir."

There would be no opportunity for dogfighting during that nearly instantaneous passage; Koenig had deployed them against the possibility of the Turusch launching a fighter assault during the long flight in . . . and the tactic had paid off when the enemy had tried to pick off the *Remington.*

In another sixty-eight minutes, however, the battlegroup would sweep past A1–01; a few heartbeats later, it would pass through the debris field beyond, the vast, flat disk of protoplanetary dust, meteoric rubble, gas, and ice circling the Alphekkan suns. The fighters wouldn't be able to engage the enemy ships, and with lighter shields than capital ships they'd be at risk trying to pass through the debris field. They would ride out the passage on board the carriers, and redeploy once the battlegroup had slowed and reversed course.

"CSP is now forming up for trap, Admiral," *America*'s CAG told him.

"Very well."

The squadrons currently on patrol were the Nighthawks and the Lightnings. Two more, the Night Demons and the Dragonfires, were on ready status, meaning they were loaded up and ready for launch. As soon as *America* had slowed on the far side of the protoplanetary disk, those two squadrons would be launched and, in short order, so would the rest of the fighters on board the carrier. The idea was to hit the enemy as hard as possible with the capital ship volley in a few minutes, then come back with everything they had and mop up what was left.

Of course, it wouldn't be *that* simple. It never was.

"Admiral!" Commander Craig called. "Trouble!"

"What is it?"

"We're tracking three enemy warships leaving the fleet, approaching head-on at high acceleration. They'll be here in . . . three point one minutes!"

"What kind of warships?"

"Undetermined, sir. They appear to be a new design . . . possibly a new species we've not encountered before." As she spoke, a window opened in Koenig's mind and a computer-generated schematic came up, showing an oddly designed ship consisting of three intersecting crescents, like claws. The image rotated, giving a sense of a third dimension. "Mass . . . about the same as one of our destroyers, sir. Power plant emissions suggest a similar energy curve."

Destroyers. Assuming they filled the same role as Confederation destroyers, they would be fast, and they would be armed with lethal ship-killers of some sort.

"Shall I order the trapping squadrons to abort, sir?" the CAG asked.

"Do it," Koenig said after a moment's thought. "And launch the ready squadrons."

He would take no chances with enemy warships of unknown capabilities.

Chapter Twenty-Three

25 February 2405

VFA–44, TC/USNA CVS America
Alphekka System
1945 hours, TFT

"Dragonfires!" Allyn's voice snapped across the squadron's communications link. "New orders coming through! Stand by for drop!"

Gray watched the tactical feed downloading into his in-head display. Three alien ships of unknown design were racing toward the carrier battlegroup almost head-on.

America had been drifting for several long minutes, her drives switched off, but that had been to allow VFA–31 and VFA–51 to come back on board the carrier. He'd not been expecting a drop order for another seventy-five minutes, after the CBG passed Al–01 and engaged the enemy fleet. The appearance of those three ships, with their wickedly curved hulls, had changed the equation.

"Dragonfires, PriFly. You are cleared for drop."

"Copy, PriFly. VFA–44 dropping in five . . . four . . . three . . . two . . . one . . . *drop*!"

Gray's fighter swung to face the out-is-down emptiness of the drop tube, and then he was falling, accelerated at half a gravity by the rotation of the carrier's hab and docking bay modules. In an instant, he was out in space, drifting away from the apparently motionless *America* at five meters per second.

The other Starhawks drifted with him, to either side. The squadron had lost four ships and their pilots, defending the *Remington*. There were only eight of them now.

He applied a burst of acceleration with his maneuvering thrusters, increasing his velocity. Out here, everything appeared to be stationary. *America* was traveling at better than forty thousand kilometers per second right now . . . but so were the Starhawk fighters now drifting out from the carrier behind the massive bulk of her shield cap. At first, the fighters were in deep shadow, but then the two Alphekkan suns emerged above the shield cap's rim in an artificial sunrise, a brilliant duo, one blindingly bright, the other much dimmer. As Gray's Starhawk emerged from behind *America*'s shield cap, he could see the vast, flat, red plane of the protoplanetary disk—invisible at optical wavelengths, but given form and substance by his fighter's sensors and AI.

A tiny, tight trio of red stars, bracketed by his targeting display system, marked the location of the enemy ships rising toward them from the disk.

"*America* CIC, Dragonfires. Handing off from PriFly."

"Dragonfires, CIC. Acknowledge hand-off from PriFly. Carrier will decelerate in another twenty seconds. Good hunting, people."

"Thank you, CIC."

The fighters continued to drift clear of *America*, the only movement against the staggeringly vast scale of that panorama. They could hear the voice of Commander Craig in CIC counting down the seconds to deceleration: " . . . three . . . two . . . one . . . and *now*!"

And the star carrier vanished, wiped from the sky as it again began decelerating at five hundred gravities, while the fighters continued hurtling forward at 40,149 kilometers per second.

"Okay, Dragons," Commander Allyn ordered. "Form up on me. We're on lead. The Night Demons will follow us in. Calculate for minimum-time intercept."

"Where the hell are the Lightnings and the Nighthawks?" Collins, Dragon Five, called.

"Already deploying ahead of us, Five," Allyn replied. "You just worry about where *you* are. Gray, Tucker, you two take point."

Gray urged his Starhawk into the lead, letting his AI calculate the intercept. Paradoxically, the Dragonfires would be turning about to present their tails to the oncoming enemy ships. If they tried to meet them bow-on, they would have such an enormous relative difference in velocities there would be no time for an engagement. Instead, they would accelerate at 25,000 gravities along the same vector the enemy ships were on . . . first canceling out the 40,000 kps of residual velocity from the carrier, then boosting to match the enemy's outbound acceleration.

He saw the green blips representing the other two fighter squadrons, now some five thousand kilometers distant, decelerating for intercept. And the space between the battlegroup and the enemy vessels was beginning to fill now, with initial, long-range shots.

There was little chance of hitting anything on either side, of course. The two groups were still a light minute apart, and both the enemy and the Confederation vessels were now beginning to jink randomly, so that the other aside couldn't predict where á given target would be when a KK round or proton beam reached its vicinity. AI-directed smart missiles were also beginning to crisscross through the void. Point defense lasers and canisters loosing high-velocity sand clouds began reaching out toward the missiles, strike and counter-strike, weapon and anti-weapon, all in absolute silence.

The trio of enemy ships passed the fighters at a distance of some twelve thousand kilometers, racing toward the *America*. The Dragonfires continued accelerating, dropping now onto their wakes of rippled spacetime and closing the range rapidly.

"It's beginning," Tucker told Gray.

The Black Lightnings and the Nighthawks had reached the enemy destroyers, merging with their formation. White flares of nuclear detonations flashed and strobed against the night.

"Hey, Skipper?" Gray called. He was studying his long-range sensor readouts.

"What is it, Nine?"

"I'm getting hard gamma from up ahead."

"Nuclear detonations, Gray. They give off gamma."

"No, ma'am. This is more like backscatter, and there's too much for nukes. I think . . ."

"The spectrum is consistent," Gray's AI put in, "with the discharge of grazer beams."

Grazers—gamma-ray lasers.

The numbers of the Black Lightnings and the Nighthawks were dwindling fast. The enemy destroyers were picking them off almost as swiftly as they approached.

"Shit," Kirkpatrick said. "The squatty's right. Those things are *hot*!"

The Confederation had never deployed coherent gamma-ray weapons, though the concept had been around, certainly, for hundreds of years. The principle was simple enough, and single-shot prototypes using nuclear explosions to generate the requisite energy had been designed as far back as the twenty-first century. Theoretically extremely powerful, they would suck down enormous quantities of energy and be extremely difficult to cool or to direct. They would also be dangerous to their own crews on manned vessels, requiring massive shielding to protect the gunners. Confederation military technology hadn't yet worked out the details of how such weapons could be deployed practically or safely on crewed warships.

In his in-head, Gray watched battlespace close-ups of one of the craft as power levels grew within it, then were discharged in a single, fierce half-second pulse, the optically invisible bolt rendered a dazzling, electric blue by his display graphics. That beam, he noted, was being directed by the forward-sweeping points of those claw-wings; the enemy ships appeared to have a field of fire across a full one hundred degrees of sky forward.

A good piece of intelligence, that, something good to

keep in mind. A single gamma beam slashed across one of the Black Lightnings at a range of over a million kilometers. Shields and screens fell in an instant, and the Starhawk flared and vanished, a moth caught in the glare of an electric-arc torch. Three Confederation fighters had already been burned down . . . now four . . . now five. . . .

The aliens were also burning down incoming Krait missiles. Sometimes the missiles would be triggered, detonating far short of their intended targets, but usually the missiles would simply vanish in those intense blue flashes of radiation.

"Heads up, people," Commander Allyn warned. "Stay clear of their bows!"

But even as she gave the warning, one of the aliens spun swiftly to face a Nighthawk coming in low and off its stern quarter. The movement was incredibly swift, the big ship as nimble as a fighter. The incoming Starhawk never had a chance. . . .

"Spread out, Dragonfires," Allyn ordered. "Our missiles aren't getting through. Use your pee-beeps at long range."

Gray and Tucker, ahead of the main body of the squadron, were sliding into PBP range now. "I've got a target lock," Gray said, centering his cursor on the nearest of the vessels. It was, an analytical portion of his brain noted, about five hundred meters from wingtip to curving wingtip, but the central hull at the intersection of the wing-crescents was just over two hundred meters, prow to stern, close to a Confederation destroyer in length. The surface was a rippling, glossy black with scarlet markings. There was nothing in the Starhawk's warbook about any vessel like this. It appeared to be a complete and genuine unknown.

The three alien destroyers were working in perfect harmony with one another, spinning, flipping, and rotating to face and destroy each and every incoming threat—Krait missiles, KK rounds, and fighters—as swiftly as it approached. They continued accelerating until they'd passed the carrier battlegroup. Then they began decelerating, killing their forward momentum. In another few minutes, they would be accelerating again, coming down the battlegroup's wake. If those monsters got in among the CBG ships with those gamma-ray weapons, the battlegroup would be obliterated.

The eight Dragonfires swept in, closing with the three destroyers.

CIC, TC/USNA CVS America
Alphekka System
1949 hours, TFT

Koenig studied the image in the tank for a moment, as it was relayed in from the fighters. He made a decision.

"Dr. Wilkerson?" he said, opening a new channel.

"Yes, Admiral."

"I need a secure link with one of the Agletsch."

"A *secure* link?"

"Yes."

The fact of the matter was, Koenig did not trust the bugs.

He'd known there was a risk when he'd decided to bring the pair on board. Since most of their kind resided somewhere out in Sh'daar-controlled space, it was possible, at least, that some of the Agletsch within Confederation space were working for the enemy.

Espionage and counter-espionage were difficult enough when you were dealing with humans. When the subject was nonhuman, when she didn't even think like humans or have the same consideration for human values or concepts like *loyalty* or *gratitude* or *reward* or even *sex*, intelligence work became all but impossible.

The two Agletsch, Dra'ethde and Gru'mulkisch, held Level Five-green security clearances, and had been cleared both by the ONI and by the Confederation Department of Extraterrestrial Relations. But how could you be *sure* of an alien being, how could you trust it when you couldn't even read the expression on whatever passed for its face? What Koenig did know was that Alphekka had been intended as a trap.

The clue came from the positioning of the various groups

of enemy vessels around the system, small, hunter-killer groups like Fox-Sierra One, pursuing their slow orbits around the distant Alphekkan suns, spaced out to cover the likeliest approach paths from the direction of Sol and far enough out that an emerging Confederation battlegroup would have been unable to turn and flee without finding itself boxed in. The placement had been perfect . . . but it meant that the enemy had kept those hunter-killer squadrons out there for extended periods of time, replacing them occasionally perhaps, but still maintaining those formations as if waiting for the battlegroup to arrive.

Perhaps the Turusch were simply cautious. The Confederation kept High Guard squadrons on patrol throughout Sol's outer system, though they had other things to watch for besides emerging alien fleets. Koenig thought it possible that the defenders at Alphekka had been warned that the *America* battlegroup was coming, and assumed the best possible defensive stature as a result.

Had the battlegroup's two Agletsch guests and guides leaked word to the enemy ahead of time? They would have had the opportunity when the CBG accelerated out of Arcturian space, communicating, possibly, with the H'rulka city in the skies of Alchameth. The various species associated with the Sh'daar all had somewhat better starflight capabilities than did humans; a warning could easily have been dispatched from Alchameth to Alphekka, arriving well before the human fleet.

Koenig had discussed his concerns with the ONI officers on board *America*. They'd listened, shrugged, and pointed out that Dra'ethde and Gru'mulkisch had been cleared. Besides . . . how could they have talked with the H'rulka? Both possessed small translators of alien design cemented to their thoracic areas, but those had been carefully examined and simply did not have the power to have sent a radio signal from *America* to the H'rulka city, not without detection.

By demanding a secure channel, Koenig wasn't simply guarding against others eavesdropping on the conversation. He was also making certain that *America*'s two alien guests did not have access, through the ship's Net, to other parts of the ship's electronic anatomy. If they'd sent a covert message at Alchameth, they could do it here, with the nearest enemy ships less than a light minute distant.

"Admiral?" Wilkerson said. "They're here, and I have them online. Secure, as you requested."

"Thank you. Please stay on the link, would you? In case I need help with them."

"Of course, Admiral."

"Gru'mulkisch? Dra'ethde? This is Admiral Koenig."

"We greet you, Admiral," one of them said.

"How may we be of service?" the other added. Although the translated voices were slightly different in tone and timbre, Koenig had trouble telling the two apart.

"We have encountered warships of an unknown design," he told them, uplinking to the tactical tank and pulling in the telemetry images of the alien vessels. "I'd like you to look at it, and tell me what you know."

"Ah," one of the Agletsch said. Had there been something like dismay in that mental voice? Surprise? Or something else? "That would appear to be a Soru claw."

"Soru. What's that?"

"An alien sophont species," one of the Agletsch said. "From very deep within Sh'daar space."

"We think they may have an empire—subservient to the Sh'daar masters, of course—in toward the galactic core, within what you humans call the Sagittarius star clouds."

"Agreed. If the Sh'daar have brought in Soru and their vessels, they must consider you of the Confederation to be a serious threat, yes-no?"

"Why do you say that?"

"The Sh'daar have . . . let us say, serious concerns about species with advanced technology. Weapons technology in particular. When the Soru were absorbed into the masters' empire, they were already at quite a high level of technological development. The Sh'daar gave careful thought to the possibility of exterminating them, in fact, but ultimately decided to bring them under their direct rule."

"We know little about the Soru directly, Admiral—only that they are extremely dangerous."

"They are . . . what would the human term be? Arrogant. They see every other sophont race as inferior, except, just possibly, the Sh'daar."

"So if they're so powerful, how do the Sh'daar control them?"

"The Sh'daar are by far the oldest species remaining in this galaxy, Admiral, and have the most advanced technology. *Anything* is possible to beings of that scope and power."

"I see." Koenig thought for a moment. He was tempted to ask the Agletsch straight out whether they'd passed a message to the enemy at Alchameth, but decided against it. At the moment, the aliens wouldn't know that he suspected that such a communication had taken place, and Koenig knew enough about intelligence work to realize that such ignorance could be useful.

"What can you tell us about Soru military tactics?" he asked instead.

"We are not trained in military matters, Admiral. We know that they make extensive use of extremely powerful lasers, operating at extremely short electromagnetic wavelengths . . . what you call gamma radiation. So far as we know, they do not use unguided kinetic munitions."

"Missiles?"

Bleep.

"I don't think Gru'mulkisch understood the question," Wilkerson's voice put in.

"Do the Soru use missiles? Small, guided craft carrying explosive warheads?"

"We don't know, Admiral."

"What are the Soru like physically?" Koenig asked. He was looking for insight, *any* insight, into how they thought, what they were like.

"I fear we do not have the . . . *bleep* . . . to answer."

"Do you know anything about their homeworld?"

"They are likely from the world of an extremely bright, hot star, Admiral."

"Why do you say that?"

"Notice the images you have shown us. There are markings here . . ."

Koenig looked at the image of the Soru ship in his in-head window. He saw a cursor dance along one of the ship's curving wings, but saw no markings.

"I'm sorry. I don't see what you mean."

"Ah. Perhaps if you use false-color enhancement, yes-no?"

"Yes," the other voice added. "Look for ultraviolet."

Koenig gave a command, and an AI shifted the image colors. The scarlet panels faded until they were a reddish gray hue . . . and along the wing a series of loops and slashes appeared, glowing bright purple. Apparently the Soru saw further into the ultraviolet end of the spectrum than did humans. Since brighter stars were richer in UV radiation, it might mean the Soru hailed from a world bathed in the stuff.

Or . . . it might not. Terrestrial honeybees and numerous other insects saw in UV light. All the discovery really did was rule out a red dwarf as the Soru home sun, since they gave off very little UV compared with longer wavelengths.

"Okay. Thank you both. I'd appreciate it if you would stay linked with Dr. Wilkerson, in case I need to ask another question in a hurry."

"It would be our honor to do so, Admiral."

And what would an Agletsch mean by the word *honor*?

Still, they'd seemed willing enough to help. The information about Soru vision had no immediate application that Koenig could think of, but it had been something, information they'd not needed to give. Were they trying to ingratiate themselves for reasons of their own, or were they genuinely committed to helping the Confederation battlegroup?

"Ah . . . one more thing, please?"

"Yes, Admiral?"

"I intend to apply a *great* deal of deceleration within another few minutes," Koenig said. "I intend to bring this battlegroup to a complete stop relative to that orbital factory up ahead, get in close, and pound it to pieces. Do you think those three Soru vessels will be able to stop us from doing so?"

"I . . . am sorry, Admiral. I don't know how to answer that. The Soru claws are extremely powerful, but your fleet outnumbers them by a considerable margin. Your plan may work, but if the Soru get close, you will suffer severe casualties."

"Thank you, both of you," Koenig said. "I'm done, Dr. Wilkerson."

Sinclair was watching him from across the tactical tank. He'd been following the conversation, patched in through the secure CIC net. "Some kind of ruse, Admiral? We *can't* decelerate at more than five hundred Gs. We're going flat-out max now, and no matter what we do we're going to zorch past that factory in something quicker than the blink of an eye."

"Of course. The Agletsch may not know our capabilities exactly. Even if they do, the Turusch are likely to play it safe, just in case we've developed something new."

"And if the Agletsch *are* in communication with them? What do you expect them to do?"

"If they think we're going to pull up alongside of the factory, they're going to go for the Holy Grail."

"'Holy Grail,' sir?"

"Englobement."

Sinclair's eyes widened and he nodded. "*Very* slick. . . ."

So far, the majority of the Turusch defensive fleet at Al–01 had been tucked in close and tight next to the deep-space factory, providing a quite literal close escort. It was a static defense, which would be a weakness in combat, but it was the best defense possible if they wanted to use their point-defense and anti-missile weapons to best effect, parrying the Confederation battlegroup's strike as they flashed past.

It would also be a deathtrap if the Confederation ships *could* halt relative to the station. They would have trouble maneuvering without fouling one another, and would be easy targets for concentrated fire from the human warships, *especially* the fighters.

No. If they thought *America* and the rest of the CBG was going to match speed and course with Al–01, they would pull back, possibly by thousands of kilometers, spreading out in a cloud with Al–01 at the center. When the human fleet slowed, they would close again, with the human fleet trapped at the center.

Englobement was an old, old concept in space-fleet tactics, but it was a chimera, a tactic that quite simply could never be pulled off. Space combat, generally, was a matter of speed, the faster the better, and you could never count on an enemy to stay put or go where you expected him to go. It was impossible to englobe an enemy when they were moving at a high relative velocity to the englobing fleet, and jinking all over the sky to boot.

Of course, if the Agletsch passed on this tidbit to the Turusch, it was unlikely that the enemy would move immediately. They would wait until the last possible moment so that they would not tip whatever it was they used for their hand.

"Comm," Koenig ordered. "Make to all ships. The enemy may reposition himself at the last moment. Watch out for it, and keep a lock on your targets. Be certain that AI targeting interlocks are on. It's going to be a confused mess in there, and I don't want anyone scoring an own goal."

"Message transmitted, sir."

"Good." He checked the navigational readouts: 50 million kilometers to go. A third of an AU . . . about twenty minutes more.

He turned his attention to the fighter squadrons closing with the enemy ships, now accelerating from astern and less than five minutes from intercept.

These Soru could still wreck everything.

VFA–44
TC/USNA CVS America
Alphekka System
1954 hours, TFT

"All Dragons," Allyn called. "Go to combat mode. Spread out and keep jinking. We need to get *closer*!"

The fighters had been launched in sperm mode, jet-black teardrops with long energy-bleed spikes stretching out astern. At Allyn's command, however, their variable-geometry nanoform hulls began reshaping themselves, flattening out, and extending the Starhawks' characteristic drooping, crescent-shaped wings, a configuration reminiscent, Gray thought, of the multiple crescent-wing shapes of the enemy. He wondered if there was a chance in hell that the enemy would be confused by the change . . . then decided that was a bit too much to hope for. The enemy would have been tracking them ever since their release from *America*.

Still accelerating, the Dragonfires hurtled toward the enemy ships. Gamma-ray bolts snapped out toward them, but they were still far enough out—almost one light second—that the enemy was having trouble locking on.

But the closer they got, the more accurate the enemy's deadly fire.

"Jink, people!" Allyn was screaming over the tactical channel. *"Jink!"*

Then a Starhawk took a direct hit, flaring into a dazzling, unfolding fireball as the fighter was transformed into plasma at star-core temperatures. Dragon Two—Commander Allyn's wingman Thom Evans.

He hadn't even known the man, Gray realized with a start. Just another one of the strangers within the squadron.

Gray fired his Starhawk's particle beam, saw the beam discharge across an alien's oily black hull. Those crescent-winged ships were still too distant to be seen directly, but battlespace drones relayed images of circumambient space, and his AI used those to present a targeting picture within Gray's in-head display. He could see the beam crackle as a violent electrical discharge across the alien's screens, but it seemed to do little in the way of damage. At this range, the proton beams were too attenuated to do much. PBPs were intended as medium to close-range weapons. They weakened with distance, could be deflected by magnetic fields, were scattered and defocused by atmosphere.

How the hell were you supposed to kill those things?

And then Gray thought he just might see a way. . . .

Chapter Twenty-Four

25 February 2405

VFA–44
Alphekka System
1959 hours, TFT

"Dragon One, Dragon Nine!" Gray called. "Sandcasters! A Fox Two volley might disrupt those beams!"

In space-fighter combat, a call of "Fox One" signaled the launch of a Krait or other all-aspect homing missile, usually with a variable-yield nuclear warhead. A "Fox Two," however, was an AS–78 AMSO, or anti-missile shield ordnance. Accelerating at two thousand gravities, its detonation released a cloud of compressed lead spherules, each roughly the size of a grain of sand. Spreading out like the blast of a shotgun, the cloud from a sandcaster round could be deadly to any ship or missile traveling at a high relative velocity. Usually, the intended target was an incoming enemy missile, since impact and ablation through the sand cloud would vaporize, or at least cripple, any but the very largest missiles.

But a sand cloud would also absorb light . . . and it ought to absorb or scatter even high-energy radiation beams, like gamma-ray lasers. The beams would vaporize the sand, of course, but enough would block a half-second pulse. And the resultant plasma cloud, if Gray was right, would also serve to scatter and diminish additional shots.

"You're suggesting we use sand clouds like a shield?" Allyn asked.

"It might let us get close enough that our weapons can do some good."

"If it doesn't work . . ."

"I volunteer," Gray said. "Let me give it a try!"

There was the slightest of hesitations from the other end. "Okay. Go."

"I'm going in with him," Tucker added.

"Copy. Good luck . . . and we'll be coming in behind you."

"Pull this off," Kirkpatrick's voice added, "and we're gonna have to change your handle from 'Prim' to 'Sandman.' "

Months earlier, in the desperate fleet action in Sol's Outer System, Gray had suggested using sandcaster rounds released at near-*c* as an anti-ship weapon. The idea had worked well, well enough to get him a commendation in his personnel jacket from Admiral Koenig himself.

And now he was using sandcaster rounds in a different way. But . . . why not? They were relatively low-tech weapons that could be extremely versatile—when you factored in the laws of physics—cheap, and almost impossible to counter.

Gray opened up his drive and accelerated. "I'm on target," he said. The nearest of the alien destroyers was rotating now to face him, and he had the targeting cursor lined up with the ship's bow, smack between the reach of those curving and outstretched wings. *"Fox Two!"*

The first of his AMSO missiles streaked from the belly of his Starhawk, its drive burning brilliantly as it boosted to fifty thousand kilometers per second. An instant later, the simple-minded AI on board triggered the warhead.

At almost the same instant, the Soru destroyer fired—possibly aiming at Gray, possibly at the incoming missile, which appeared to be the most immediate threat. The beam struck the cloud of tiny compressed-lead spheres when it was still less than three meters across and burned straight through it in a searingly brilliant flash of blue-white light.

The beam missed Gray's fighter by almost a kilometer; perhaps it *had* been aimed at the missile, rather than at him.

It didn't look like the sand cloud had dampened that beam in the least, but his sensors noted otherwise. A lot of the gamma-beam's energy had been absorbed by the cloud. A few seconds later, Gray's AMSO cloud hit the alien ship, partly as high-velocity grains, partly as hit plasma, returning a bit of the alien's energy to the sender.

He couldn't tell at this range if the cloud had damaged the Soru ship. Using his fighter's AI, he programmed a string of five AMSOs to detonate in rapid succession, throwing up a chain of sand clouds moving toward the target. *"Fox Two!"* he called. "Multiple *Fox Two*!"

"And multiple *Fox Two*," Tucker added. The two Starhawks loosed a barrage of ten sandcaster rounds; then they accelerated, slipping in behind the barrage and closing rapidly with the enemy.

Gamma-ray bolts snapped toward them . . . and the space between Soru and humans lit up with repeating, strobing flashes of brilliant energy. Gray's own energy screens flared and nearly fell as leakage from the Soru fire slipped through and clawed at his fighter, but the energy had been sharply attenuated, the beams refracted enough that they lacked the focus to burn through Gray's defenses. Ahead, a glowing cloud of plasma swept between the Soru destroyer's forward-curving wings. Another Soru shot was absorbed and re-radiated as heat and dazzling light. Gray opened up with everything that he had, slamming Krait missiles, particle beams, and KK rounds straight down the Soru ship's throat.

As the universe appeared to explode with fireball brilliance immediately ahead, Gray's energy screens failed . . . along with his forward shields. Something hit his fighter hard, a chunk of whirling, white-hot metal, he thought, and then his Starhawk was tumbling through darkness.

His external sensors were dead, fried by the surge of energy.

"Damage control!" he screamed at his AI. "Damn it, *damage control*!"

His fighter's tumble slowed, then stabilized, and a moment later his sensors came back on-line. Starhawks had a considerable degree of regenerative control, using their nano systems to absorb and regrow damage. His power and drive systems appeared unharmed. He began to decelerate, searching the sky for Tucker.

There she was.

And there was the Soru destroyer, or what was left of it . . . jagged chunks of hull and curving wing section spinning out from an expanding cloud of hot gas.

"This is Dragon Nine!" he called. "I'm okay! Scratch one DD!"

Briefly, Gray wondered what type of beings had crewed that vessel . . . and why they'd come so far out among the stars to die. An update was coming through on his link with the CBG Net. *Soru*, the new race was called, according to the Agletsch liaisons.

What were they?

"Copy that, Nine," Allyn replied. "Ten! Are you okay?"

"I'm . . . okay," Tucker replied. "Got a little singed going through the—"

Tucker's Starhawk exploded in a blue-white flash, cutting off her words. A second Soru destroyer had rotated to face her fighter, had speared her with a gamma-ray bolt.

"Shit!" Gray screamed. "Shit! *Shit!* . . ."

The second destroyer lined up with him, and the shot, at longer range, missed by meters, nearly overloading Gray's already shaky energy screens.

"Dragon Ten," Allyn called. "Do you copy?"

"She's dead!" Gray replied. "Katie's *dead*!"

"Okay, Gray. Stay clear of those DDs. We're coming in."

Sandcaster rounds, dozens of them, were already slamming into the two remaining Soru ships, coming in from half of the sky as the widely dispersed fighters bore in from numerous directions. For a confused moment, the sky filled with blue-white flares of energy, tightly clustered around the destroyers . . . and the nuclear fireballs blossomed.

Lieutenant Jacosta, Dragon Twelve, died in the final seconds of the attack.

Right behind the survivors of the Dragonfires, the Night Demons came in tight and hot, adding their barrage of sand and fire. "Trevor!" Ryan's voice called. "Trev, are you okay?"

"I'm okay, Shay," he told her. "I'm not sure how."

And so many *weren't* okay. Gray found himself shaking at the realization. The Dragonfires numbered just five fighters, now: Allyn, Collins, Kirkpatrick, Donovan, and Gray.

But all three Soru warships were gone, now, reduced to drifting, ruined hulks and far-flung clouds of gas and droplets of molten metal swiftly freezing into expanding cascades of glitter.

"*America* CIC, this is Dragon One," Allyn called. "Three Soru destroyers down."

"Shit," Donovan said. "Where are the others? Where are the Nighthawks and the Lightnings?"

Gray checked his scanners. The two squadrons had merged with the enemy at high speed, and would have passed through the formation swiftly. He was picking up distant targets, now, several million kilometers out . . . six . . . seven . . .

"I've got eight on my screens," Allyn said. "No . . . nine."

Nine left, out of twenty-four in the two squadrons.

At this rate, there wouldn't be many fighters left for the endgame at Al–01.

"*America* CIC, Dragon One," Allyn called. "Target destroyed. What are your orders?"

There was no immediate reply.

CIC, TC/USNA CVS America
Alphekka System
2004 hours, TFT

"Admiral Koenig?" *America*'s space boss asked. "Do you want to retrieve our fighters?"

Koenig stared into the tank display. Four fighter squadrons had just hurled themselves at the three Soru ships, a display of stunning bravery. The cost had been far too high. . . .

"Sir?"

"Eh?" Koenig blinked and looked up. Other faces were watching him around the display tank. "No. No, tell them to take up close formation with the fleet."

"They'll be low on expendables after that little scrap, sir," Craig pointed out. "They need to re-arm."

"I know. But it will take time—time running at zero deceleration—to take them back on board, and more time to re-arm." He shook his head. "We don't have a choice. They'll have to ride through the close passage with us."

"And through the protoplanetary disk," Sinclair added. "Some of them . . . their shields and screens are pretty badly damaged. They might not survive it."

"Then they can break off and get clear before the passage!" Koenig shouted. The startled expressions on the CIC crew's faces stopped him, and he gentled his voice. "Tell them they're authorized to use their own discretion."

"Aye, aye, sir."

If *America* stopped her deceleration now, she might not be done taking the fighters on board when they passed Al–01. By allowing those able to make the disk fly-through to go in with the capital ships, he would add a small amount of additional firepower to the fleet's split-instant volley, and the far faster, more maneuverable fighters would be useful in keeping Turusch Toads from dogging the more cumbersome fleet.

But Gods, the *price*.

As a military commander, Koenig was wrestling with two distinct problems. It tore him apart to order his men and women into tactical situations that, most likely, would end with them being killed or tumbling off into the emptiness of space. That was the worst, always—sending young men and women off to die.

But from a strictly logistical perspective, he also needed to husband his resources; while new fighters could be nanufactured on board the *Remington* and the *Lewis*, he had a sharply limited supply of experienced pilots. It would be possible to accept volunteers from throughout the fleet and give them the download training for basic space fighter combat and piloting skills, but it would take a lot of time in simulators and in non-simulated cockpits before they could take on a Turusch Toad head to head and survive.

Worse, recruits were thoroughly screened for aptitude when they first entered the military, and those candidates with unusual talent and inborn skill for piloting, for three-dimensional navigation and orientation, for being able to judge vector and angle and lines of fire on the fly were invariably siphoned off for naval aviation. That suggested that there would be few *good* candidates throughout the fleet. It took a special set of mental twists to make a good pilot, and those skill sets were all too rare.

But Koenig would make do with what he had.

There were few damned alternatives.

Ryan
VFA–96
Alphekka System
2006 hours, TFT

"Stick close to me, Twelve," Lieutenant Charles Forrester called over the tactical link. "Don't wander off and get lost!"

"Copy," Shay Ryan replied. She considered adding something nasty—she didn't like Forrester's patronizing, risty attitude—but thought better of it. *This isn't the time or place. . . .*

Ryan found she was shaking inside, and bit off a sharp curse. She would *not* show weakness, not on board the *America*, and for fricking sure not out here.

But the last time she'd strapped on a Starhawk and tried to turn and burn with the bad guys, she'd ended up falling in toward that gas giant, helpless, her ship dying, and no way out . . . no way, at least, until Trevor had slipped in astern of her and nudged her into a new vector.

Forrester was her wingman, and she would do what she'd been told. But she didn't have to *like* it.

Slowly, a fighter swarm began materializing around the perimeter of the carrier battlegroup, as more and more of the surviving fighters from VFA–42 and VFA–51 caught up with the fleet and fell into formation. Five Starhawks left out of the Dragonfires, and ten from the Night Demons, plus six from the Nighthawks and just two from the Black Lightnings. Twenty-three in all.

Fifty percent casualties for the four squadrons taken together. The realization of that statistic hit Ryan like a hammer blow in the pit of her stomach. They were getting slaughtered out here, and the gold braid back on board the carrier didn't seem to give a starsailor's damn.

"Right, people," the voice of Commander Allyn said over the tactical net. "As senior officer, I'm taking command of the CSP element."

Both Dodgson and Klinginsmith, the COs of the Nighthawks and the Lightnings, were dead. Commander Taylor, of the Night Demons, was still alive, but Allyn held seniority, and the Night Demons were newly arrived on the *America*, with damned little experience before Arcturus.

"CIC has given each of us discretion to break off. If your fighter is too badly shot up, pull out and get clear. You can reform with the fleet later. Any takers?"

There were no replies.

"Gray?" Allyn said. "Your telemetry shows your forward shields are out. If you follow the fleet through the protoplanetary disk you're going to slam into a rock and vaporize . . . or fry, zorching through a dust cloud. Break off."

"Thank you, Commander," Gray's voice came back. "I think I'll stay."

"*Mister* Gray . . ." Allyn began. But then she broke off.

"I need to be here, Skipper."

"Very well," she said after a slight pause. "But don't try to make it through the disk. Set your AI to loose your weapons when the fleet does, then decelerate at fifty K gravs and change vector. Do not enter the disk. That's an order."

"Aye, aye, Skipper."

Ryan wondered what made Gray tick. He was a squattie, like her, and squatties grew up looking for the main chance, *running* from trouble, not seeking it out. Like her, when those Rebs had tried to catch her in mangrove swamp.

On the Periphery, you kept a low profile, kept your head down, and you were ready to cut and run in an instant if you wanted to survive.

Why was he following the rest of the surviving fighters in?

Well, for that matter, why was *she* going in? Her shields weren't damaged, but flying through the tangled mess of that protoplanetary disk ahead was all but a death sentence for a fighter. CIC had said the passage was discretionary . . . which meant volunteers only. Allyn had interpreted that to mean that fighters with damaged shields could opt out, but she'd seen the order come through. *Any* fighter could break off, could avoid the firestorm of this final close passage.

So why didn't she take advantage of the offer?

She wasn't sure. Gray had a lot to do with it. What was it he'd said to her? *Us Prims need to stick together.*

If he was going into the crucible, then by God she was, too.

Gray
VFA–44
Alphekka System
2009 hours, TFT

Gray was wondering why he'd decided to stick with the squadron. It wasn't as though he felt compelled to do so. Of the four other survivors of VFA–44, one—Donovan—was a friend, while the skipper was a decent-enough sort. Collins and Kirkpatrick? He certainly felt no band-of-brothers connection with *those* two, nothing that justified risking his life. If they died in the next few moments, they were zeroes, risty assholes who'd made it quite clear what they thought about him and his kind.

The hell with them.

And yet, he'd refused an order to break off, choosing to stick with the fleet on its close passage of Al–01, a choice that was very likely to get him killed. His own decision had left him bemused. Maybe he was starting to buy all of that Navy bullshit propaganda about honor, duty, and glory.

Besides, Ben *was* a friend . . . and so was Shay, in the Night Demons. Friends were a damned precious commodity, one growing scarcer by the moment, and Gray believed in being loyal to them. He wouldn't be able to live with himself if he flew clear of the coming fracas and then watched both of them get chewed up in the Turusch grinder.

He would stay, no matter what the cost.

CIC, TC/USNA CVS America
Alphekka System
2011 hours, TFT

"The fighter CSP is in position around the CBG, Admiral," Commander Craig told him. Eight more minutes to intercept."

"Very well."

His eyes never left the tactical tank. He was watching the red icons clustered about the larger symbol representing Al–01. Would they move? If he were the enemy commander, and had received intelligence like that which he'd just passed on to the Agletsch, he would wait until the last possible second before deploying.

And there was the speed-of-light time delay to consider as well. They were still a couple of light minutes out. The enemy could have redeployed that long before, and the incoming battlegroup still wouldn't have seen—

There!

The red icons were drifting apart, moving out and away from Al–01, taking up positions across the surface of a flattened sphere two light seconds—over half a million kilometers—across. They were setting the trap, gambling on the all-but-impossible chance of pulling off an englobement of the Confederation battlegroup.

He opened a channel. "Dr. Wilkerson?"

"Yes, Admiral?"

"Our . . . guests."

Koenig could feel Wilkerson's sigh over the communications link. "I've been watching over the repeater down here. Damn."

"The Turusch moved. Drop the hammer on them."

Koenig had discussed the situation with Wilkerson days ago, before they'd even emerged from metaspace. Koenig had been thinking about his decision to help the H'rulka city, knowing that the ship on the floating platform might well warn the enemy of the battlegroup's destination. Of course, the CBG's actual destination, Alphekka, could only have been transmitted to the H'rulka by *America*'s two Agletsch liaisons.

And Koenig had been weighing all of the possibilities, even before the battlegroup had emerged at Alphekka.

Wilkerson was of the opinion that the two Agletsch, if they were passing information on to the enemy, were doing so innocently. "I know they're alien," he'd said, "but, damn it, they feel sincere to me. I think they're telling the truth."

In fact, Koenig was inclined to believe that they were. The two aliens had been under constant surveillance since they'd come aboard, through sensors in their quarters, security guards walking with them, and certain areas of the ship, like the communications center, the bridge, and CIC, being simply off-limits to all but authorized personnel. Most particularly, the ship's AI had been monitoring their access to the ship's Net and, through that, to the fleet's Net. Never had they shown any interest in accessing secure or militarily sensitive information.

The danger was that one or both Agletsch carried microelectronics, perhaps even nanolectronics so small that they existed on a molecular level. Such devices could be implanted easily enough without the victim knowing it—through food or drink, for instance—and it was all but impossible to detect them. Or an ultra-small communicator could be hidden within the translators they wore, or even within the curlicues of silver body paint decorating their carapaces.

"So what are you going to do?" Wilkerson asked him. "Throw them in the brig? Their Net access is already restricted."

"The Faraday Cage around their quarters ought to be

sufficient," Koenig replied. "At least for now. They'll be restricted to quarters for the time being. See to it, please."

A Faraday Cage was an electrified mesh enclosing a space—a room, for example—which blocked the passage of all electromagnetic signals. Personnel from *America*'s engineering department had grown such a mesh around the Agletsch quarters inside the bulkheads several days ago, just in case, and the normal physical access infrastructure—water, raw materials for nanufacture, Net access, electricity—could all be individually screened to block EM transmissions.

"Yes, sir," Wilkerson said. "Under protest, sir."

"Protest all you want, Phil. It's that or chuck them out an airlock."

Koenig was a little angry with himself, since it had been his decision to bring the two on board. And it wasn't as though it was just aliens that could be passing information to the enemy. The Sh'daar had human supporters as well, some of them within the Confederation Senate, who felt Humankind's best course of action was to accommodate the Sh'daar, to give them what they wanted. It was just possible that Sh'daar agents back on Earth had passed specifics about Operation Crown Arrow on to the enemy as long ago as the end of December.

It was an unpleasant thought, but all too plausible.

"Look," Koenig added. "Confinement to quarters—house arrest—is our best option for right now. We can discuss the situation with them later on, see what they have to say about it. We might be able to arrange dropping them off somewhere where their fellows can find them and pick them up."

He didn't add that yet another option would be to continue feeding the two false information, "disinformation," in the lexicon of the ONI.

"I understand the need for security, Admiral. I guess I'm just . . . disappointed."

"Me too. Now excuse me. I have a battlegroup to manage."

"Yes, sir." There was a pause. "The Faraday Cage is on, Admiral. They're cut off now, except for what we decide to allow through."

They should, Koenig thought, have done that from the beginning. But the two Agletsch *did* have security clearances. Such measures should not have been necessary.

He reminded himself that, out here, so far from the rest of Humankind, they needed to make their own rules. Earth's rules, Earth's bureaucratic intrigues, Earth's official clearances and approvals—none of that mattered here.

"Open a channel for me to all ships," Koenig said.

"You're on-line, Admiral," Ramirez replied.

"All ships, this is Admiral Koenig. As you can see on your tac displays, the enemy formation is moving. I want you to stay with your assigned targets. Have your AIs track your target's movement and adjust your firing solutions to match. If your target no longer has a viable firing solution—it's hiding on the other side of the factory, for instance—reprogram for a secondary target. Secondary targets include Al–01 itself, plus the larger Turusch warships, the Alphas and Betas. Be very sure that a change in attitude doesn't put a friendly ship into your line of fire.

"Good luck, everyone. Koenig out."

He listened for a moment to the chatter of telemetry between the ships, watching the tank as individual members of the battlegroup began reorienting themselves. During the close passage of Al–01, there would be no time to point your ship at a target, no time to take aim. The entire setup had to be performed by the super-human intellect of the CBG's interlinked AIs, with each ship positioned so that it would be pointed at a target as it zorched through the enemy position. As the number of light seconds between CBG and objective dwindled away, the AIs kept watch, continually tweaking each warship's attitude in order to take advantage of the constantly updating tactical picture.

How long, Koenig wondered, before artificial intelligences ran all parts of the distinctly human game called war? In situations such as this one, there was simply no way human eyes or brains or reflexes could contribute.

For the next several minutes, it would all be in the electronic hands of the Fleet's AIs, which could think thousands of times faster than humans.

Koenig was counting on this in the coming close-passage of the enemy factory complex.

"Three minutes," he said. "All systems on automatic. Hand it over to the AIs. Tell the fighters to choose targets of opportunity, and to fire at their discretion."

The enemy's defensive fire was already reaching toward the battlegroup.

Chapter Twenty-Five

25 February 2405

CBG–18
Alphekka System
2018 hours, TFT

Although there was no good way to directly compare the human brain with a computer, the raw computational power of the human brain was generally estimated to be around 10^{15} operations per second, and good implant software could effectively increase this to 10^{17}. Modern AI hardware typically ran in the range of 10^{21} operations per second, some ten thousand times faster.

Among other things, that meant that AIs could think *extremely* quickly, by human standards. They could, in essence, speed up their processing of incoming data in such a way that time, for them, seemed to run slowly. What passed for a human in less than the blink of an eye could stretch on for seconds or minutes or even hours for a fast computer.

CBG–18, the individual ships already positioned and aimed in different directions, passed through the sphere of Turusch warships. A few seconds before reaching Al–01, they passed through the outer shell of waiting enemy ships.

The frigate *Knowles* was hit going in by an enemy proton beam that chewed through its shields and punctured its shield cap, spreading a cascade of water droplets across the sky. The hit was off center, the impact enough to put the *Knowles* into a tumble. Before the ship's AI could get the ship back under control, the *Knowles* slammed into one of the Turusch ships, a Tango-class cruiser, and the fireball momentarily illuminated the scattering of disk debris below.

Turusch ships opened up then with everything they had. At some point, the enemy commanders realized that the Confederation ships were *not* slowing to engage the factory, but that they were passing through at high velocity. Missiles and KK projectiles were too slow at this point; proton and electron bolts and high-energy laser beams snapped silently across emptiness, seeking targets.

CBG–18 passed the outer defensive layer of Turusch ships, one light second from the factory. And three seconds later . . .

Close passage.

Gray
VFA–44
Alphekka System
2018 hours, TFT

Gray had found a way to protect his weakened fighter during the passage. He'd slipped his fighter in tight behind the black curve of *America*'s huge shield cap.

The star carrier had rotated so that it was traveling backward along its line of flight, so that the twin launch tubes, their tiny, open ports visible at the center of the shield cap dome, would be aimed at the vulnerable rear half of the orbital space factory once it had hurtled past. Gray was hugging the surface that normally would have been the leading side, designed to protect the carrier from micro-impacts at high velocities.

America's current velocity was less than three tenths the speed of light. Gray was following the shield surface, maintaining a distance of less than one hundred meters. The carrier had ceased deceleration for the passage of Al–01; once it started decelerating again, Gray risked slamming into that surface at a relative acceleration of five hundred gravities. From his perspective, when her drives switched on again, *America* would leap toward him at five kilometers per second squared.

For the moment, though, this slot offered safety from the bits and pieces of debris that filled this area of space—the hurtling wreckage and debris from enemy ships hit by the fleet's initial bombardment, and the first sharp-ticking dust motes of the protoplanetary disk beyond. *America*'s kilometer-long bulk swept along through space, leaving an empty, swept-out zone in her wake.

For now, both Gray and *America* were in free fall. Some of the other fighters tucked in with Gray as well. The others were spread through the fleet. Beams from enemy ships stabbed and probed, invisible to the naked eye but drawn by AI graphics on Gray's tactical screens and in-head display; *America* was hit three times, but her screens absorbed the strikes, which were attenuated by distance.

The frigate *Reasoner* took a direct hit that burned through her shield cap, crippling her.

They passed the outer shell of the Turusch defenses, just over one light second from the factory. Almost at the last possible instant, the fighters loosed a Fox-Two volley of AS–78 AMSO missiles, sending expanding, high-velocity clouds of sand sleeting through battlespace.

But across a fire-laced sky, Confederation fighters were dying. The heart of a general fleet action was a deadly environment for small and relatively lightly protected fighters. As the CBG approached the factory, large numbers of Turusch fighters began accelerating to match velocities with the fleet, merging with it to attack individual ships. The Confederation fighters, fulfilling their space combat patrol function, engaged the Toads. Point-defense fire from the Turusch capital ships hammered at the human fighters, smashing down shields, overloading energy screens, and ripping the Starhawks to pieces.

The Starhawk piloted by Lieutenant Georg Kirkpatrick slammed into a fast-accelerating Toad and disintegrated in a glare of expanding hot gas. By the time the CBG passed the factory, nine Starhawks had been destroyed, and there were only fifteen left.

Three more seconds . . .

CBG–18
Alphekka System
2019 hours, TFT

Close passage.

The roughly spherical deep-space factory was 112 kilometers across. The incoming fleet was traveling at 37,000 kilometers per second, which meant the human ships flashed past the factory in twelve one-thousandths of a second, far too swiftly for human reflexes to act. At a precisely calculated instant, every human ship carrying weapons fired, with beams and missiles and KK projectiles lancing out in all directions.

A very great many things happened, all at once. From the points of view of the fleet's AIs, however, each action, each event, unfolded with crystal clarity and slow deliberation, as an avalanche of fire erupted around them.

Most of the battlegroup's fire was concentrated on the Turusch factory, especially at the vulnerable rear open section hidden behind the gaping, armored maw forward. Beams, traveling at *c* or near-*c* had distances of only a few hundred or, at most, a few thousand kilometers to cross, and struck almost instantaneously. Missiles and KK rounds took longer; by the time they reached their targets, the battlegroup would be gone.

The railgun cruiser *Kinkaid* was aimed almost in the opposite direction of its line of flight. Its target was the unprotected back side of the factory, and as soon as the massive magnetic spinal gun was lined up, it fired, and then continued to fire, cycling off a round every two and a half seconds.

America, too, had been rotated to face almost directly

back along its incoming path, positioned so that it could use its twin launch rails as KK cannon. They weren't capable of the same acceleration as the *Kinkaid*'s main armament, which ran along over half the length of her spine, but the two projectiles carried a considerable punch in raw kinetic energy. *America* was farther from the target than the *Kinkaid*, and its projectiles were slower. The factory shuddered as the railgun cruiser's rounds struck first. Seconds later, *America*'s volley ripped through the target's struts and structural supports and slammed into the collection of Turusch ships moored inside.

The heavy missile carrier *Maat Mons* was also targeting the factory, loosing swarms of multi-megaton nuclear warheads as she penetrated the Turusch defensive sphere. Designed as a bombardment ship, the *Maat* concentrated half of her missiles against the Al–01 factory, but had programmed the rest to seek out Turusch ships by their characteristic energy emissions and home on them. Only a few of those missiles made it through the defensive fire of enemy ships, but the fact that they were knocking down *Maat*'s missiles meant, for the most part, that they couldn't lock on to the Confederation capital ships as they flashed through.

Nuclear violence erupted through the defensive sphere. Several Confederation ships took damage simply from overloaded radiation screens as the sky around them flared with a brilliance rivaling a swarm of nearby suns.

Maat expended about half of her large store of nuclear missiles within the few seconds of passage.

The heavy cruiser *John Paul Jones* had as its target a Turusch Alpha-class battleship, and at the firing point it loosed every weapon that would bear, a swarm of nuclear missiles, lasers and PBP fire, and magnetically accelerated kinetic rounds, all slamming into the converted planetoid as the *John Paul Jones* hurtled past at a range of less than twenty kilometers.

Close behind the *John Paul Jones* was a second cruiser, the *Isaac Hull*. Working in close concert with the *John Paul Jones*' AI, the *Hull* targeted those portions of the enemy's artificial structure, the domes and turrets visible above the solid rock, that were taking hits from the first cruiser's salvo. Shields failed, turrets blasted open in the nuclear inferno, and the incoming volley of missiles slashed deep into the Alpha's heart.

The Mexican destroyer *Tehuantepec* had been set to fire into a Turusch Gamma-class warship, a vessel that Confederation ONI had equated with a heavy battlecruiser, but the target had moved within the past several moments, and was now masked by the enemy factory. The *Tehuantepec*, then, had retargeted, adding her fire to the salvos being loosed at the factory. Sweeping toward the factory, while still 100,000 kilometers out, she loosed Krait missiles from every available tube, twenty of them. One second later, as she passed the target at a range of just under 12,000 kilometers, she opened up with lasers and PBP fire.

The energy weapons struck the target immediately behind the UV laser salvo fired by the Canadian frigate *Huron*, burning deep into the disintegrating structure. Eight thousandths of a second later, *Tehuantepec* slammed at 30,000 kilometers per second into an oncoming tumbling fragment of a Turusch Romeo-class cruiser massing nearly nine thousand tons.

Half-molten debris sprayed out along *Tehuantepec*'s forward vector like the blast of a shotgun, causing damage to two other Turusch craft.

Her missiles slammed into the factory nearly twenty seconds later, each nuclear detonation building upon the last in a cascade of searing fireballs burning ever deeper into the structure.

The destroyer *Drummond* loosed its volley at a Turusch Sierra-class cruiser, then took two direct hits from a Tango 80 kilometers away. The enemy beams sliced into the *Drummond*'s power plant, freeing the artificial singularity trapped inside. In a flash, *Drummond* whipped end over end, then crumpled into nothingness, its ten thousand tons of non-singularity mass crushed into the event horizon of a small but voracious black hole.

The Tango died in almost the same instant, as three Krait

missiles fired by a Black Demon Starhawk during the approach moments before detonated alongside.

Within the space of a couple of heartbeats, three human capital ships and nine fighters had died, along with some fifteen hundred human naval personnel.

Enemy losses were unknown.

Gray
VFA–44
Alphekka System
2019 hours, TFT

Two Toad fighters vectored in toward the *America* in the final seconds of her approach. Alerted by his AI, Gray passed control of his fighter's attitude and weapons system over to the computer. The fighter rotated sharply, the suddenness of the maneuver threatening to slam Gray into unconsciousness. His PBP beam fired twice, and then two Krait missiles streaked from his ship, erupting in intense and death-silent flowers of light; an instant later, *America* and Gray's trailing Starhawk zorched past the enemy factory.

His fighter's sensors noted the firing of *America*'s two railguns. A powerful surge of magnetic fields grabbed at the ferrous components of Gray's Starhawk and threatened to put him into a helpless tumble. His AI, still in control, recovered. Through his palm implant, Gray ordered the AI to begin increasing the distance from *America*. The carrier would begin decelerating again very soon, and it would be best to put some distance between his fighter and that vast black wall in front of him.

More Toads were coming in fast. Gray accelerated to meet them, leaving the shelter of the carrier's wake. He opened up with his KK cannon, rolling as he hurtled past, and the Toad came apart in fragmenting pieces.

"Dragon Nine!" he screamed over the tactical channel! *"Kill! . . ."*

Ryan
VFA–96
Alphekka System
2019 hours, TFT

Ryan flinched as Lieutenant Forrester's fighter flared to port like a tiny sun gone nova and vanished, speared by a gigajoule bolt of laser fire that burned through his energy screens and hull shielding and turned the arrogant, risty fighter into a brief-burning cloud of expanding plasma and debris. Pieces of hull metal struck Ryan's Starhawk with a sound like a fistful of rocks hurled against sheet metal, clattering through the tiny ship's interior. Her Starhawk lurched and trembled, but remained intact. A quick check of her damage-control panel showed that she was still in one piece.

She left the overall control of her fighter under her AI. Her sky was filled with incoming targets—Toad fighters and missiles and hurtling bits of debris. Things were happening far too swiftly for her to determine which potential targets posed the greatest threat, or to direct the SG–92 to aim, track, or fire. She *was* able to single out one Toad that had slipped through *America*'s inner point defenses and tell her AI to take it down. Her Starhawk dropped onto the enemy ship's tail as it hurtled scant meters above *America*'s aft hull, headed for the turning hab modules forward. A precisely targeted proton beam devoured the Toad from behind, sending a spray of hot fragments cascading more or less harmlessly into the aft side of the carrier's shield cap.

Seconds later, the Confederation fleet emerged from the far side of the Turusch defensive sphere, still firing with devastating, computer-guided precision at every target within range. The Turusch continued to lash back, following the intruders out of the sphere, but the sheer savagery of the human strike had rattled Turusch gunners and swept away a large percentage of their targeting sensors.

By the time the CBG passed the factory, nine Starhawks had been destroyed, and there were only fourteen left out of all four squadrons.

CIC, TC/USNA CVS America
Alphekka System
2021 hours, TFT

Admiral Koenig was watching the CIC's viewalls during close passage. There'd been little to see during the Al–01 close engagement, an instant's blip of light, followed by darkness and unmoving stars.

"We're bringing the ship back around on a normal heading, Admiral," Captain Buchanan said over the com link with the bridge.

"Very well."

He took a moment to study the after-combat telemetry, as the ship AIs correlated and compiled combat statistics. It could have been worse . . . a *lot* worse. Casualties were high among the fighters that had been outside, but he'd expected that. Three capital ships—*Tehuantepec*, *Drummond*, and *Reasoner*—had been destroyed, though there were still personnel alive on board the *Reasoner.* The *Lewis* would be attempting to grapple with the hulk and get them off.

The tallies coming through on the enemy fleet were a lot more vague. There'd been forty-three enemy capital ships in that battlespace. The savage human attack had destroyed or damaged perhaps half of them. How many were destroyed and how many were damaged but still in the fight was unknown.

"Commander Craig. What's the range to the nearest group of enemy ships other than the ones at Al–01?"

"Fifty-one light minutes, sir. And an hour twenty to the next nearest beyond that."

"No movement from either of them?"

"No, sir."

There likely would not be, either, until the EM wavefront bearing the outcome of the close passage crawled out to meet them, and the images of their response crawled back. They were probably waiting to see what CBG–18 would do next before committing themselves.

Fleet combat tended to be a drawn-out affair.

By any standards, the close passage of Al–01 had been

a victory, with the human forces scoring hits at a seven-to-one ratio over the enemy. Koenig's ruse, letting the Agletsch pass on disinformation to pull the enemy ships out of position, had worked better than he'd dared hope. CBG–18 was still badly outnumbered, however, if you counted all of the other Sh'daar ships remaining in the Alphekka system. And Koenig needed to decide *now* what he was going to do about it.

A shudder ran through *America*'s deck.

And then another . . . and then yet another.

It took him a moment to realize what was happening. Chunks of debris, probably meteoric bits of rock, had struck *America*'s shield cap. Her gravitic shields had diverted most of the impact, but enough had leaked through to cause a slight change in velocity. Field dampers had absorbed the excess force—if they hadn't, any personnel not strapped down would have been slammed into the ship's forward bulkheads at a velocity equal to that by which *America* had just been slowed—but the impacts had still sent ripples through the ship's structure.

They were entering the main body of the protoplanetary disk.

"Shields to maximum!" Buchanan yelled. "All personnel, strap down! This is going to get rough!"

Koenig needed to make a crucial decision within the next several hours.

Where fighters could throw out artificial singularities to one side or the other to pull the fighter into a tight, free-fall turn, capital ships were far more restricted in their maneuverability. Like fighters, they could project maneuvering singularities to their sides. Most of them, the larger vessels like *America* and the two Marine carriers, could not make a turn without risking serious damage from tidal forces. Their sheer lengths required that they make turns only at relatively low velocities . . . no more than a few tens of kilometers per second. The smallest of them, the frigates, each some two hundred meters in length, had more leeway, and could turn at higher velocities, but they could rarely exercise their maneuverability in combat. Frigates would not last long against larger enemy combatants, and generally stayed with the main fleet in a scouting or anti-fighter role.

The only way the battlegroup could reverse course—the only way they could return to the space factory and resume the battle—was to resume deceleration at five hundred gravities, slow to zero relative velocity, then begin accelerating back once more.

At five hundred gravities, it would take another 106 minutes to slow, then reverse course, by which time they would have traveled almost an AU beyond the Al–01 factory. The return trip, accelerating half of the way, then decelerating to match Al–01's orbital velocity around its suns, would take another two and a half hours.

It would take almost four and a half hours, total, to return to the factory and resume the battle, so demanded the cold and unyielding dictates of the laws of physics.

On the other hand, he could order the CBG to begin accelerating instead. In a bit under fifteen hours they would reach 99.9 percent of the speed of light, at which point they could drop into Alcubierre Drive and slip into the safety of metaspace.

Close passage of Al–01 had expended a lot of the battlegroup's available munitions. *That* would be an issue as well.

Five hours in or fifteen hours out. Either way, the other enemy ships in the system would wait to ascertain what CBG–18 was doing—attacking or retreating—and then begin closing in from every direction. Koenig saw no way to avoid another major battle, and expendables were already running tight.

One thing was clear. If he elected to get out of Dodge, he would lose some more pilots. Telemetry from the remnants of the four squadrons showed several of the ships were damaged. They might not be able to catch up with the fleet, might not be able to weather a passage of the protoplanetary disk in pursuit.

Besides, there was still that one streaker lost in the *Remington* scrap earlier, Rafferty, and the crew of the SAR tug sent to get her. *And* Lieutenant Schiere, who might still be alive somewhere out there in the emptiness.

If they retreated, they would lose everything won so far. If they returned to finish it, they might still lose . . . but at least there would be a chance of retrieving the MIA pilots.

"CAG?" he said, deciding.

"Yes, Admiral!"

"Commence immediate launch of all remaining fighter squadrons, please. Pass the word to the Marine carriers to launch as well. We're going back, and the fighters will lead the way."

"Aye, aye, Admiral."

"How long to get all of *America*'s fighters spaceborne?"

"Ten minutes, Captain. We only have four squadrons remaining, and three of them are loaded, set and ready for drop in bays one, two, and three."

Was there a hint of recrimination there?

Koenig chose not to notice if there was. "Once the fresh squadrons are away, bring in the fighters that are out there now." *Those that are still alive . . .*

"*Yes*, sir."

"Captain Buchanan?"

"Sir."

"As soon as we have those fighters back on board, you may resume deceleration. Plan for turnover in two hours, and a return to Al–01."

"*Yes*, sir!"

There was no cheering in the CIC, but he sensed a change, a lightening of spirits. Tensions had run high before and during the close passage. Now, though, they simply wanted to finish what they'd begun.

And to do that, they would have to return.

Another faint shudder rippled through *America*'s hull.

Gray
VFA–44
Alphekka System
2022 hours, TFT

"Orders coming through, people," Allyn said. "We're going back. They're getting set to launch the Rattlers, the

Tigers, and the Reapers now, and the Impactors will follow as soon as they're loaded into the bays."

Gray had expected as much. There were only the four fighters left in VFA–44—himself, Commander Allyn, Ben Donovan, and Collins. All the rest were dead, and the realization had left Gray feeling lost, a little stunned. Perhaps Koenig would order the handful of surviving fighters back on board.

"Heads up! We have incoming!"

Gray pulled his Starhawk into a tight turn, slipping once again out from behind the comforting shadow of *America*'s shield cap. Koenig might be about to bring them back on board, but until he gave that order, Gray and the others were still on CSP. The enemy had finally pulled himself together and dispatched a flight of Toad fighters to pursue the CBG. The remnants of the four CSP squadrons would have to hold them off until fresh fighters could be launched.

He accelerated with the others to thirty thousand gravities, pushing hard enough to wipe out his shared vector with the fleet through the protoplanetary disk and begin piling on velocity in the opposite direction, back toward Al–01.

It was fourteen fighters against fifty, impossible odds.

But the Toads would know they'd been in a fight.

"Hey, Prim?" The voice coming over his com link was familiar. The transmitter was identified on his display as Impact Seven. "That was a brilliant maneuver you pulled back there with the Remington. I, ah, just wanted to let you know."

"Thanks." He didn't think he knew anyone in the Impactors. "Who is this?"

"Frank Carstairs. We spent a fun evening ashore last month, at a joint called Sarnelli's. With the bugs, remember?"

He did. He'd forgotten that Carstairs was one of the Impactors. VFA–31, he saw, was down to just five ships.

"I remember. I'm glad you're still here."

"Well, *that* might not be the case for much longer . . ."

"Bottle it, people. You two can buy each other a drink when we get back to Earth."

Allyn was right. It wasn't good to talk about what might be about to happen. Focus on the positive. . . .

"Deal," Gray said. "See you at Sarnelli's, Carstairs, and the drinks are on me."

Missiles were reaching in from the oncoming Toads, bright points of light accelerating toward the battlegroup.

"Let's give the big boys some cover," Allyn called. *"Fox Two!"*

"Copy, Dragon leader. *Fox Two!*"

Sandcaster rounds lanced out across the fast-dwindling space between the two groups, detonating in rapid succession and hurling high-velocity clouds of sand into the enemy missile's paths. Flashes of nuclear fire illuminated the dark ships of both squadrons.

Gray lined up his targeting cursor on the icon representing a Toad ten thousand kilometers ahead. "Target lock!" he cried. "And . . . *Fox One!*"

And then the two groups of fighters interpenetrated, passing through each other. Gray pivoted his fighter to track a Toad coming down his starboard side, firing his PBP, sending to rapid-pulse bolts into the enemy. The first shot overloaded the Toad's screens and shields; the second, close behind, burned through blue and black hull metal and slagged down the drive system buried within. The molecule-sized black hole running the Toad's quantum power tap broke free, tunneling through the fighter in a searing burst of X-ray and gamma radiation.

And the final battle for Alphekka was joined.

Chapter Twenty-Six

25 February 2405

Gray
VFA–44
Alphekka System
2024 hours, TFT

Human Starhawk fighters had the clear advantage over Turusch Toads when it came to maneuverability, but the Toads, massing more than twice as much, were tougher and they had more punch behind their particle beams. There was no way that fourteen Starhawks were going to stop fifty Toads in a head-to-head fight.

Fortunately for the Starhawks, the Toads weren't interested in them. If the capital ships of CBG–18 were destroyed, the fighters would be helpless, cut off and trapped. The Toads ignored the battlegroup's fighter screen and kept closing on the capital ships, continuing to launch volleys of long-range missiles as they advanced.

The battlegroup, however, had its own heavy defenses up. The heavy cruiser *Valley Forge*, the missile ship *Maat Mons*, and the frigates *Schofield* and *Miller* had dropped back to the rear of the battlegroup formation, positioning themselves in order to give as many of their weapons turrets and missile bays as possible a clear field of fire aft. As the enemy fighters bore in, the four ships, operating in their anti-fighter mode, threw up a withering fire of nuclear-tipped missiles, charged particle beams, and point-defense weapons. The Toads had lost eight of their number as they briefly interpenetrated with the Starhawk formation; now, more Toads erupted in stark flashes of plasma and radiation, or crumpled into their own onboard singularities, or simply vanished in the megaton-blossoms of nuclear fire as the barrage from the *Maat Mons* reached them.

The Confederation fighters were coming in behind the Toads, and suddenly surrounding space was more than usually deadly for the thin-skinned Starhawks, this time as they entered a volume of space swept and crisscrossed by fire from their own side. Krait missiles and the *Maat*'s heavier Vulcan missiles wouldn't deliberately lock on to Confederation ships—they were *smart* missiles, after all, possessing low-level AIs at their controls—but expanding clouds of plasma at star-core temperatures, sleeting storms of radiation, and hurtling chunks of high-velocity debris did not possess the same sensibilities or care.

Commander Allyn's Starhawk hurtled through the fringe of an expanding nuclear fireball, emerging an instant later in a helpless tumble.

"The Skipper's gone streaker!" Donovan yelled. "Log her vector before we lose her!"

"I've got her!" Collins replied. "Watch out for that Toad at your low twelve!"

"Got him! Got him!"

Gray pulled up and back, clearing the kill zone astern of the fleet. Without forward shields, he wouldn't have survived for three seconds in that soup of energy and debris. Out here, there was still a threat from random bits of dust and meteoric particles as the battlegroup continued to plow through the protoplanetary disk, but the actual disk density was relatively low. It was only from a few astronomical units off that it appeared to merge into a single, solid ring.

One Krait missile left. *Just* one.

Make it count!. . .

His AI pointed out a lone Toad, moving at high acceleration out and around the CBG's flank. The pilot—no, *pilots*, since the Turusch always worked in pairs—were trying to avoid the death trap at the battlegroup's rear and come in from around the fleet's side.

Gray gave a silent command, and his Starhawk stooped after the enemy ship, accelerating hard. It was a long way off . . . forty thousand kilometers or a little more, but he was able to get a target lock, then fire.

His last missile streaked toward the enemy at two thousand gravities.

Collins
VFA–44
Alphekka System
2037 hours, TFT

The Toads, what was left of them, were fleeing, turning away from the Confederation battlegroup and accelerating back toward Al–01 and the Turusch ships remaining there. Pulling around in a hard, tight turn, Collins struggled to close with one of the retreating Toads, dropping onto its tail and opening up with a volley of KK fire.

"I'm on him! I'm on his six!" she yelled over the tac channel. "Target locked . . . *kill*!"

Less than ten kilometers ahead, the Toad exploded, coming apart in tumbling, jagged pieces. Collins was traveling too quickly for merely human reflexes to act. Her AI took control and pulled her onto a new course to avoid the hurtling debris. . . .

She hit . . . *something*. . . .

Gray
VFA–44
Alphekka System
2038 hours, TFT

Sixty-three seconds after he fired his last missile, it swept in behind the lone Toad fighter and detonated, wiping the threat from the sky.

The other Starhawks, he saw, were breaking off from the engagement. There were eight of them left now, and little more they could do to protect the fleet. The fire from the four screening capital ships had killed or disabled all but ten of the remaining Toads, which were scattering now, fleeing the battlespace.

For the moment at least, the CBG was in the clear. More and more fresh fighters were streaming in from the *America*, the *Nassau*, and the *Vera Cruz*.

In the clear . . .

"Dragon Five is hit," Ben Donovan called. "She's gone streaker."

Gray swiveled his head, searching the crowded and fire-laced sky displayed on his cockpit screens. He linked in with his in-head displays, throwing up brackets and id alphanumerics, trying to make sense out of disordered chaos.

There she was . . . leaving the battlespace at a high rate of speed. She wasn't headed toward him, but her path wasn't headed away, either.

"Got her," Gray said, recording her vector for transmission back to *America*. "How the hell did she get that kind of speed?"

"I think she hit a Toad dust ball," Carstairs replied.

Damn . . .

Ships, from the smallest fighters and couriers up to *America* herself, used projected artificial singularities to achieve high accelerations. Each projection cycle lasted only a tiny fraction of a second, *just* long enough to shape local space into a gravity well that pulled the projecting ship forward in free fall. The projection winked off, then winked on once more, but a little farther along as the projecting ship continued to accelerate. The trick was known as *bootstrapping* among gravitational-drive physicists, and was the high-tech trick that allowed a ship, even one as long and as massive as *America*, to accelerate at high speed, to warp space around it in an Alcubierre bubble, and even to twist space at the ship's outer surface enough to serve as a strong defensive shield. Tricks you could play with gravity . . .

Drive singularities were the equivalent of *very* massive

stars compressed into a tiny pocket of space. Created by directly warping the fabric of space through intense and tightly focused energy drawn from the quantum foam, they had no material existence. Usually, when the power from the quantum taps died, the singularity vanished. It was, after all, just empty space.

Once in a while, however, a drive failure resulted in a longer-lived and self-sustaining singularity. Often, as a ship traveled at high-grav acceleration, dust, gas, and debris became trapped in a kind of bent-space eddy immediately behind the singularity's event horizon, unable to fall as that horizon continued inexorably to move away. If not cleared periodically by switching off the drives for more than their fractional-second cycle, the debris could fall into the singularity as power was switched off, and the grav field would take on a life of its own, hurtling off through space with the same velocity the fighter had possessed when the projectors failed. Called "dust balls," they were a nuisance more than anything else, but rarely, in combat, they became a part of the debris from a dying ship, tiny vortices of intense gravitational energy, invisible, fast-moving, and deadly.

If another ship struck a large dust ball head-on, it usually meant that ship's destruction. If a ship missed the dust ball, but by a fairly small margin, the intense gravitational slope of local space acted like a maneuvering field, whipping the incoming vessel around in a tight turn. A capital ship, generally, would be ripped apart by tidal stresses. Fighters, designed to ride curves of warped space, might survive as they slingshot around the singularity, but the pilot might not survive the centrifugal force of the turn, or the tidal stresses if his fighter passed too close to the event horizon.

Collins, evidently, had slingshot around a dust ball released by a Toad she'd killed an instant before, picking up a tremendous amount of speed in the passage. She was receding from the CBG now at a velocity of some eighty thousand kilometers per second.

"Dragon Five, this is Dragon Nine," he called. "Do you copy?"

There was no reply. Collins might be dead or unconscious,

or her fighter's communications system might not have survived the encounter.

He couldn't reach her AI either.

At that speed, she would be lost within the cluttered abyss of the protoplanetary disk in short order. Her fighter wasn't giving off any signals, including IFF.

He wondered if she was still alive.

Damn, damn, *damn* . . .

"*America*, this is Dragon Nine," he called. "I'm dry on missiles, almost dry on KK rounds. "I have Dragon Five on my display, but she won't be there for long. I'm going to try to get her."

There was a long pause before the voice of *America*'s CIC came back.

"We copy, Dragon Nine. You understand that we might not be able to come get you."

"Copy that, *America*. But I've got a good chance to catch her."

He was already accelerating after the tiny, fast-receding spacecraft.

Enforcer Shining Silence
Alphekka System
2040 hours, TFT

Tactician Diligent Effort at Reconciliation trembled with uncontrollable grief. The other part of itself, its literal other half, was dead, as the asteroid enforcer slowly crumpled from within. A portion of the cell from which it commanded both ship and fleet had been partially crushed, the wall smashing in and mangling Diligent Effort's twin.

"No! No! No!" Its Mind Above was shrilling an endless mental cacophony of denial. It was becoming harder to think, harder to even consider what to do.

The *Shining Silence* had been crippled by multiple hits, its weapons down, its power systems failing. Diligent Effort wasn't sure of the extent of the damage. It could no longer communicate with other Turusch on board. Too many communications links with other parts of the asteroid ship had been cut; besides, it could no longer speak, not in harmony with itself.

The Sh'daar Seed, however, remained within its Mind Below, speaking wordlessly within its thoughts.

The information from our agents within the human fleet was false. We must alert others against the possibility of deceit.

"Communications are out," it replied aloud, struggling to focus its thoughts as a single voice, rather that blending with its twin to create a third layer of speech within the harmonics. The shrilling of its atavistic Mind Above made speech more difficult still. "You must communicate with your fellows on your own."

The rock walls of this fortress are too thick. . . .

"Not," Diligent Effort replied, "for very much longer." It felt a telltale rumbling deep within the rock and metal surrounding it, a steady pounding that appeared to be getting louder moment by moment. The vibrations, it knew, were caused by the black hole used to extract energy from the vacuum, sealed deep within the heart of the ship. That singularity had broken free, was moving now slowly out from the center of the ship.

Or, to be more precise, the massive singularity was continuing on its original course in orbit around the two distant stars of this system; the asteroid ship around it, nudged by a succession of nuclear detonations, was drifting now to one side, with a difference in vector of several degrees and several *d'lurm'n* per *g'nya.* And as it moved, the singularity continued devouring rock and steel and Turusch bodies and everything else that it touched, growing as it moved and spilling a steady blaze of X-rays as it relentlessly fed.

The *Shining Silence*, Diligent Effort knew, was finished.

"Your guidance in this battle was flawed," it said aloud. *There!* It had spoken at last the thought, the *unthinkable* thought, that had been growing within the Mind Here for *g'nya* upon *g'nya*. "We should have been free to meet the enemy fleet sooner, and farther from the factory."

It felt something that was the equivalent of a shrug within, felt meaning form, as if in a rising memory. *The defenses were dictated by the situation. More enemy ships might have been coming in behind the first wave. That initial assault might have been designed to draw you out of position.*

"Our instincts said otherwise," Diligent Effort replied.

Your instincts are flawed. They require . . . guidance.

Tactician Diligent Effort bristled at the implied insult, but couldn't reply. The steady shriek of denial from its Mind Above was growing louder and more shrill as the loose singularity grew closer.

If *Shining Silence* was finished, the rest of the fleet was not. The Turusch squadron had taken terrible damage from the human high-velocity strike, but the enemy was still badly outnumbered. Command now devolved upon the enforcer warship *Intrusive Storm*, positioned nearly twelve-twelves of light-*g'nya* out-system. Before losing contact with the rest of the fleet, Diligent Effort had noted that the enemy appeared to have begun slowing once again. They intended to stay and fight.

Intrusive Storm would react, and the enemy would die.

But so, too, would *Shining Silence* and so many other vessels of the Turusch fleet.

Diligent Effort at Reconciliation, however, was feeling its own and personal loss too keenly to mourn the loss of others.

Gray
VFA–44
Alphekka System
2045 hours, TFT

What, Gray thought to himself, *are my chances?*

Not good, he decided. *Not good at all.* Koenig was returning the CBG to Al–01, and when he got there, the Turusch would be waiting.

Maybe Koenig had some devious trick up his sleeve.

Maybe he was counting on the sheer audacity of turning back to face the surviving enemy ships.

And maybe he'd just run out of options, had decided to stay and fight if only to give people like Collins a ghost of a fighting chance.

Maybe there were no answers, no strategy, no meaning, no hope.

Maybe . . .

Gray refused to think about that. The fleet was still there, decelerating down from its hell-bent charge at nearly a third of *c*. There was no indication that the other Turusch ships in the system had reacted yet. They were spread out so far from one another and from Al–01 that they wouldn't even know the result of the battle so far for an hour or more to come.

His particle cannon fired, triggered by the AI with superhuman reflexes. Radar had detected a bit of rock on a collision course, and the AI used the proton beam to vaporize and it. Individual atoms of hit gas were less damaging to the fighter than lumps of rock.

Collins was eight thousand kilometers ahead now. He was gaining on her, very slowly.

Gray couldn't accelerate at his Starhawk's full potential. He could fry particles larger than thumb-size to avoid hitting them, but even his AI couldn't identify dust motes, and without forward shields even a dust mote might cause serious damage at these speeds. In fact, at this point he was relying on his own projected singularity to sweep most of the gas and dust clear from his path, creating a dustball of his own.

He stayed on Collins' tail and pushed as hard as he dared, slowly, slowly closing the range between them. Collins' path had taken her in-system, almost directly through the plane of the protoplanetary cloud. The two stars of Alphekka, one brilliant, one smaller and dimmer, shone almost directly ahead, just over thirty astronomical units distant. They should, he thought, be emerging from the inner edge of the debris-field ring any moment now. His AI had marked a nascent planet just ahead and to one side; that planet, he recalled, was just inside the inner edge of the ring, having swept its orbital path clear over the course of some millions of years as it grew.

"Dragon Five, this is Dragon Nine," he called. "Do you copy?"

No answer. He wondered if the bitch was dead.

Why, he wondered, was he even trying this? It wasn't as though he *liked* Collins. Since he'd joined the Dragonfires a year ago, she'd given him more than the usual allotment of grief. She was a "risty," a hypocrite, a bitter and angry zero with a special prejudice against Prims like Gray. He hated the creature; a part of him was still telling him he should let her go.

He would have come after Ben Donovan, if it had been him. He would have gone after Commander Allyn had he noted her trajectory before she'd been swallowed up by emptiness. He *did* go after Shay Ryan at Alchameth.

Why try to save Collins?

And he honestly didn't know the answer. She was a fellow naval officer and pilot, a fellow Dragonfire, a fellow member of *America*'s officers and crew. Perhaps he owed her that much. She might have the vector data on the skipper. Maybe saving Collins would save Marissa Allyn.

And maybe he was doing it just because he would have wanted someone else, *anyone* else, to do it for him had he been in her situation.

You stood up for your fellow warriors, pulled for them, helped them, and by God went after them and *saved* them even if you hated their guts.

His fighter emerged from the debris field with startling suddenness. With the CGI overlay of red behind him, he could see more clearly ahead. Comets blazed in every direction; the newborn planet shone as a brilliant spark to port. Collins' hurtling fighter was seven hundred kilometers ahead.

Five hundred.

One hundred.

Decelerating now, Gray crept up behind her. He could see her ship, now, black against the glow of the two Alphekkan suns thirty AUs ahead.

They were traveling at a bit over two astronomical units per hour, with fifteen hours to go before they fell into the vicinity of those stars. *Plenty* of time.

If nothing went wrong.

Gently, he moved toward Collins' Starhawk. She wasn't tumbling, thank God.

And Gray had practiced this maneuver before.

He knew exactly what to do. . . .

CIC, TC/USNA CVS America
Alphekka System
2350 hours, TFT

Three hours had passed since the fiery flyby of Al–01. *America* and the other battlegroup ships had finally killed their forward momentum, and had been accelerating again back toward the factory for an hour now.

"Admiral!" Commander Craig called. "We're getting movement from the enemy fleet!"

Here it comes, Koenig thought. He was in his CIC command chair, leaning back, eyes closed, his in-head displays switched off. He'd been trying to catch some sleep at his station. "Tell me."

"Two groups of ships . . . the ones still at Al–01 . . . and group Fox-Sierra Seven. They've begun accelerating."

"How long until intercept?" Koenig asked, his eyes still closed.

"Sir . . . no, you don't understand! They're accelerating *out*bound! *Away* from us!"

Koenig's eyes snapped open and he released his chair's harness, floating over to the display tank. "*Away?* You're sure?"

Commander Craig pointed into the display tank, which showed a large portion of this side of the Alphekkan system—translucent red protoplanetary disk, a tight cluster of green stars marking CBG–18, and several widely scattered clumps of red icons marking Turusch vessels under drive. As he watched, a third group, even farther out, began accelerating as well.

All were headed in the same direction, roughly toward the galactic center. None were on a course that would bring them anywhere near the battlegroup.

"That doesn't make sense," Koenig said. "Reduce scale."

The display dropped to a lower scale, showing even more of the star system, all the way out to the thin and ragged red edge of the debris ring.

"There," Sinclair said, pointing, and a new cluster of icons was highlighted by the display. "We have new incoming!"

Turusch reinforcements, was Koenig's first thought.

And then the id tags for the newcomers began appearing in the depths of the tank.

They were scattered across a full light hour or more, ships emerging one by one from Alcubierre Drive. They were above the plane of the ring, the nearest nearly twenty-five AUs out.

"Sir!" Sinclair said. "That's the *Jeanne d'Arc*!"

"And, by God!" Craig added. "The *Abraham Lincoln*! And the *United States of North America*!"

"De Gaul," Sinclair continued. *"Frederich der Grosse. Illustrious. Haiping. Cheng Hua. . . ."*

"They're *ours*!" Craig yelled. "They're fucking *ours*!"

It was . . . a miracle. Twenty-one ships had already materialized, emerging from Alcubierre metaspace twenty-five AUs out from the *America*, a distance of some three and a half light hours. More were emerging every moment.

Koenig thought rapidly. At that distance, they must have dropped out of metaspace at just about the same time as CBG–18 had made its close passage of Al–01, and were just now catching the wavefront bearing the images of that brief and terrible battle. In the same three and a half hours, the images of the emerging ships reached *America*'s sensors.

"Admiral!" Ramirez said. "Incoming transmission! Sir . . . it's Grand Admiral Giraurd, of the *Jeanne d'Arc*!"

"Put it on speaker! Let them *all* hear this! . . ."

". . . have emerged from Alcubierre Drive, and see the battle taking place in-system three point five light hours from here. We are deploying to assist. Message repeats. Attention Star Carrier *America*. This is Grand Admiral

Giraurd of the Pan-European Star Carrier *Jean d'Arc*, in command of a Confederation naval task force, operating in concert with the Chinese Hegemony Eastern Dawn Expeditionary Force, a total of forty-one combatants. We have emerged from Alcubierre Drive, and see the battle taking place in-system three point five light hours from here. We are deploying to assist. Message repeats. . . ."

Pandemonium ensued within the CIC, cheers and shouts and even a few somersaults in zero-G.

Koenig let them cheer.

Forty-one ships, some Pan-European, some Chinese. They must have been the vessels that were supposed to have reinforced CBG–18 at Pluto. No . . . forty-one ships? He'd not been expecting that many. He detected the hand of Admiral Carruthers and the Confederation Joint Chiefs here.

Captain Buchanan emerged from the ship's bridge, grinning from ear to ear. "You *did* it, Admiral! You damn well *did* it!"

"Hardly, Randy. We didn't know they were coming!"

"Yeah, and neither did the Tushies! Look at 'em run!"

Across the Alphekkan system, group by group, the Turusch battlegroups were beginning to accelerate, clearly moving to leave the system, clearly not attempting to intercept and engage the newly arrived Confederation forces. It would take time for the wavefront bearing news of the human fleet's arrival to reach every Turusch ship . . . but none of them were staying to contest ownership of the system.

Well, they couldn't know how many more Confederation and Hegemony ships were coming in. The Sh'daar's minions tended, it seemed, to play a somewhat conservative game.

And the humans could use that as a weapon against them.

Victory . . .

"Commander Craig?"

"Yes, Admiral!"

"Pass the word to all ships of CBG–18. We will cease acceleration in order to bring fighters on board, and to dispatch SAR units."

"Yes, sir!"

"CAG?"

"Yes, Admiral!"

"Put out the word to our pilots. We're bringing them in."

"Aye, aye, Admiral!"

America's children, those who remained, would be coming home.

Epilogue

28 February 2405

VFA–44 Ready Room, TC/USNA CVS America
Alphekka System
1437 hours, TFT

Trevor Gray stood on the Dragonfires' ready-room deck, facing the viewall that covered an entire bulkhead, deck to overhead and fifteen meters wide. It showed local space, but from the perspective of a nonrotating camera mounted somewhere on *America*'s shield cap. Comets gleamed icy and cold across blackness. A planet drifted in the distance, its surface a black and tortured disk with cracks and craters exposing its hot-glowing interior.

The world had been named Elpheia, the ancient magicians' name for Alphekka within the list of Behenian fixed stars. If you looked closely, you could occasionally see the twinkling flash of an impact as it continued to draw in meteoric debris and asteroids. *America*'s astrophysics department estimated that Elpheia was a rocky planet already twice Earth's mass, that one day it would be a "super-Earth," with three to four times Earth's mass, and—this far from its suns—a deep and frigid, dense atmosphere. Rocky planet? Gas giant? The experts didn't know yet. A lot of things out here didn't fall neatly into established categorical boxes.

A brand-new world.

In the foreground, between *America*'s camera and Elpheia, several of the new ships from Earth drifted in orbit with the carrier.

"Hey, Trev," Shay Ryan said at his back. "You okay?"

He turned, gave her a thin smile. "Yeah. I'm not sure why." He noticed her mood, bright and positive. *Perky*. It wasn't like her. "Why are *you* so happy?"

"Why not? We made it! Not bad for a couple of damned misplaced Prims!"

"Not all of us made it. . . ."

At the moment, VFA–44 consisted of just three people—Gray, Ben Donovan, and Collins, though Collins was in the sick bay with a dozen broken bones, a punctured lung, and numerous other internal injuries. She'd been all but crushed when she whipped around that Turusch dust ball, and hadn't yet regained consciousness.

But Gray had brought her back. It had taken hours of maneuvering, slipping in close to her spacecraft, connecting to it with his nano-tipped grapples, pulling her in tight, then *gently* putting out a maneuvering singularity to alter course by a few degrees. Eventually, he'd altered her course enough that she was no longer dropping toward the suns. A SAR tug rendezvoused with them a dozen hours later.

The tugs had been busy for the past two days. They'd brought back the streaker Rattler pilot, Alma Rafferty. They'd even recovered Lieutenant Schiere, alive and well, adrift a billion kilometers from the wrecked alien factory.

They hadn't yet found the skipper, though. Commander Allyn was still out there somewhere. The SAR tugs were tracking her. Maybe . . .

The fleet, meanwhile, had taken up orbit around Elpheia, avoiding the bombed-out mess of Al–01 which was now highly radioactive. The Turusch fleet-building complex in the Alphekkan system had been rendered utterly useless. Perhaps over the course of the next few million years, it would begin accreting rock, dust, and gas from the protoplanetary belt and become the core of another new, infant world.

"They say they're going to rebuild all four squadrons," Ryan told him. "We'll be the old hands, y'know? Maybe we can start over, you and me, trying to fit in."

"Maybe. I'm more interested in knowing what happens now with the battlegroup. Operation Crown Arrow is complete . . . a success."

"Scuttlebutt says we're going to wait a month or two and find out if the pressure's been taken off of Earth," Ryan said.

Gray managed a grin. "Do you really think Koenig is going to sit on his ass that long?"

"No, I guess not. But . . . he's not in command anymore, is he? That Pan-Europe admiral . . ."

"Giraurd."

"Yeah, Giraurd. He outranks Koenig. Grand admiral trumps rear admiral, y'know? I heard he's going to take over the fleet."

And *that*, Gray decided, helped define his own sense of loss . . . and empty letdown. So many people had died, and for what? To drive the enemy out of a system that had very little in the way of advantages for Earth—no habitable worlds, no new allies. They said that crushing and scattering the enemy fleet here would keep the enemy from attacking Sol again . . . but would it? At worst, the Turusch and their Sh'daar masters had been dealt a setback.

And if the Confederation government decided now to bring the fleet back to Earth, to abandon what had been won here and at Arcturus . . . then what the hell was the point?

Gray was unhappy with what seemed to be very limited options, and he knew that a number of other pilots in the fleet felt the same way.

A pair of ships drifted into the panorama . . . the hulk of the *Reasoner* within the oddly insectlike embrace of an SKR–7 Scrounger off the *Lewis*. Several hundred crewmen had been rescued from the frigate, and the Scrounger was now devouring the frigate's corpse, breaking down hull and control systems and structure, creating stocks of materials that would be used to build new ships, fighters, missiles, and parts for fabrication and repair on board the ships of the fleet. The rebuilding would not be on the same scale, perhaps, as with the destroyed Al–01 factory, but repairs and reconstruction would take place.

If they could train the pilots, the wrecked fighter squadrons might be replaced as well.

"You know," Gray said slowly, "Koenig's got to have something else up his sleeve. I can't imagine him handing over command to Giraurd and meekly going home."

"They say the Senate wants him to be president."

"Yeah, they wanted that before and he turned them down cold. I wonder what the son of a bitch has in mind?"

Alexander Koenig, Gray knew, thought in layers upon hidden layers. Since his return to the carrier, Gray had heard dozens of rumors, some of it wild scuttlebutt, but some things . . .

Yeah, he'd heard the rumors about Giraurd taking over, of course, and that the fleet would be going home. There were rumors that a peace deal was in the works with the Sh'daar, rumors that the Turusch had surrendered, rumors that the enemy was massing near Earth, preparing to invade.

Gray didn't believe any of that.

But he'd also heard from Donovan and Carstairs that Marines had boarded the radioactive hulk of Al–01 and discovered working Turusch computers and data cells, with information about Turusch bases and facilities across this entire stretch of the Milky Way galaxy.

Might that be true?

Something quickened inside.

Gray felt little allegiance to Earth, less to the Confederation. With a start, he realized that his loyalty lay with the battlegroup, with the *America*, and with CBG–18's commander, Alexander Koenig.

He didn't think the old man would be turning around and heading back to Earth anytime soon.

He would be headed outbound, deeper into a hostile galaxy, seeking to end the threat to Earth and Humankind's way of life once and for all.

And Gray felt a rising surge of excitement, knowing that when the Star Carrier *America* boosted for deep and enemy-held space, *he* would be with her too, headed outbound.

Admiral's Office, TC/USNA CVS America
Alphekka System
1450 hours, TFT

Admiral Koenig was not quite alone in his office. The electronic ghost of Karyn Mendelson was there as well. As always . . .

"It's very pretty," she said.

"It may be the single most important piece of intelligence we've gathered in this damned war," Koenig replied. "We've been fighting blind until now."

The projection glowed in the holo-display field above Koenig's desk. It didn't show the *entire* galaxy, but enough was there to show gleaming stardust from the ragged outer fringe of one spiral arm in to the densely packed core. A mental interface allowed him to single out stars and star groups and have them identified, to bring up regional and district capitals, to show the individual zones controlled by myriad alien star-faring species, to reveal their routes for trade and exploration.

It even showed the Sh'daar capital, a name shaped by Agletsch phonemes as Daar Sha'ng'lamyd.

It showed the Galactic Empire, or a part of it—a third, perhaps. The data had been recovered from the Turusch equivalent of a computer network on Al–01, converted to a format intelligible to human systems, and translated. The two Agletsch had earned their keep with that one; he still didn't know if they were *knowingly* passing data on to the enemy, but they'd made up for it, big-time, by helping with the electronic conversion to something *America*'s AIs could work with.

"They're calling it the *Encyclopedia Galactica*," Koenig said. "After something in an old work of fiction about a galactic empire."

"And how is this going to help us win a war?" Karyn asked. "For that matter, how is it going to keep Giraurd and the Senate off your back?"

"Knowledge is always power, Karyn."

"Granted. And what this knowledge shows is just how many races and fleets and trillions of enemy soldiers there are out there, getting ready to bring us down. Alex . . . *how are you going to take them on? . . .*"

"It shows us, Karyn, where we're going next."

And the milky glow of the galaxy map illuminated his smile.